WASHINGTON, D.C.

"A SERIOUS NOVEL, WRITTEN BY A MAN WHO UNDERSTANDS WHAT POLITICS IS ABOUT . . . If Mr. Vidal had only nerve one might dismiss him. But when nerve is combined with talent and intellect, one must take notice. One must applaud —with vigor."

—*Chicago Daily News*

"Vidal picks an assortment of on-target political themes, adds several pinches of off-beat sex, and cooks it all over a good melodramatically licking flame . . . a 'page-turner.'"

—*The New York Times Book Review*

"Exciting stuff . . . Gore Vidal's Washington is . . . a Sodom of political corruption and diseased ambitions wherein the life expectancy of a good intention is about that of a snowball in hell."

—*Boston Globe*

Also by Gore Vidal
available from Ballantine Books:

MYRON

1876

GORE VIDAL

WASHINGTON, D.C.

A Novel

BALLANTINE BOOKS • NEW YORK

Library of Congress Catalog Card Number: 75-42768

ISBN 0-345-27463-6

This edition published by arrangement with
Random House, Inc., New York

Manufactured in the United States of America

First Ballantine Books Edition: November 1976
Second Printing: October 1977

For

Barbara and Frederick W. Dupee

One

1

THE STORM BROKE over the house. Rain fell in dark diagonals across the summer lawn. An abrupt wind bent willow trees, tore sumac, shook elms. The storm's center was now so near that the flash of lightning and the sound of thunder almost coincided, ending darkness, shattering stillness. At rapid intervals, spears and tridents and serpents' tongues of blue fire showed trees bending, rain falling, and the black rush of the river at the foot of the hill on which the house stood.

Peter Sanford took cover beneath an elm, and wondered what the odds were of being hit by lightning. Excellent, he decided, as three snakes of fire intertwined, vanished among the trees at the far end of the lawn, and a heartbeat later thunder sounded. Too late he clapped hands to ears; his head rang painfully from the sound.

Then the wind shifted. Rain splattered his face. He pressed hard against the bole of the tree and through narrowed eyes watched the mock-Georgian façade of the house appear and disappear in rapid flashes like an old movie print, jerky and overexposed. Within the house, the party continued, unaware of the beautiful chaos outside.

"Go on!" he shouted to the sky. "Go on!" The storm went on. Excited by this obedience, he stepped out of the shelter of the tree and, opening wide his arms, threw back his head and let the rain fill his face. At last he was nature, and a thing to be feared in the night.

Suddenly with a sound like an ax splintering wood, blue lightning shattered the sky, setting his teeth on edge, enveloping flesh in a vast tingling web. Then he smelled sulphur. A tree had been struck nearby.

"Come on!" he roared into the next roll of thunder. "I dare you! Here I am! *Strike!*" But this time there was only darkness for answer, and a dropping of the wind.

The circuit of power broken, he ceased to be a god and so, like Lucifer before the dreaded hordes of Light, he ran across the lawn. But shoes filled with water slowed his progress, like the dream in which he knew that he could never outdistance pursuers. Breathing hard, he galloped slowly past a marble Venus and a plaster Pan; then down a flight of shallow steps to the swimming pool, where he stopped and took off his shoes.

Barefoot, he crossed to the poolhouse. The door to the men's changing room was open and in the darkness music sounded: someone had left the radio on. As he started to go inside, lightning revealed a man and a woman making love on a rubber mattress. The man wore nothing except shoes and socks and garters that hung half on and half off as he went about his single-minded work between long legs which circled him like those of a wrestler in the terminal bout. No faces were visible, only the necessary bodies. Then lightning ceased, and the revelation ended.

He stood in the rain, unable to move, not knowing if the lovers were real or simply creations of the lightning and when it stopped, they stopped; unless of course he was dreaming one of those dreams from which he would awaken in that pain which is also sharpest pleasure, having loved in sleep. But the cold rain was real; and so was the sudden soft moan from the poolhouse. He fled.

He entered the big house through the back door. At the far end of a dim corridor that smelled of beef stock, he could see the kitchen, a square white room full of light and heat and the sound of the French cook raging at his Swedish helper. Unobserved, Peter climbed the back stairs to the second floor where, like a thief, he opened the soundproofed door which separated the servants' quarters from the main house and darted across the landing to his own room at the head of the staircase. Then he paused, perversely hoping that someone might see him: *Where have you been? You're soaked!* But there was no one in sight and so, unchallenged, he stepped into the bedroom, shut the door, and turned the key; safe at last.

Pulling off wet clothes, he rubbed himself with a towel, in front of the mirrored bathroom door. There was no getting around the fact that he was sixteen and not yet old enough to begin a grownup life. He had been a child forever, an intolerable state of affairs that could not last much longer. Rough towel on skin together with the memory of what he had seen excited him. Should he or should he not? Deciding not, he did pushups until the moment passed. Martyred daily by the flesh, he knew that if he did not soon hold another body in his arms, he would explode, like one of those white novae whose final starry burst destroys a thousand worlds, just as he in his solitary state would like to do. Sometimes at night he would strike the pillow again and again with the force that kills, all the while knowing that there was as yet no one anywhere on earth for him to love, or to murder.

Glaring at himself in the mirror, he let loose a long harsh Tarzan roar that hurt the throat but soothed the spirit. And as he did, with a stranger's detachment, he watched the veins knot at the temples, while neck and cheeks turned scarlet. For an instant he and the thunder sounded together. Then he stopped; the thunder went on.

Relieved, he dressed in a white suit identical with the one he had worn earlier at dinner. No one must know that he had been out of doors, least of all the lovers, who had been, he was convinced, if not at dinner, among those who had come in after. In any case, he must now track them down ruthlessly, like the inspector in *Les Misérables*. And when at last he found them . . . He paused in his reverie, wondering just what he would do. But of course he did not have to *do* anything. It was enough that two new images could be added to his gallery of phantom lovers, substitutes for what surely must soon materialize as solid flesh.

Peter Sanford entered the drawing room, just as his father was about to propose a toast.

"All right now. Quiet everybody! This is a victory

3

toast." Blaise Delacroix (pronounced "Della Crow") Sanford was swarthy and fierce with a harsh New England accent dissonant not only to Southern ears but to those of his own son Peter who spoke the soft speech of Washington, D.C., with its slow long vowels and quick slurred consonants. But Blaise Sanford could have spoken Latin and been listened to respectfully, for he was uniquely rich. His grandfather had clothed the women of the West in gingham, making it possible for him to leave a fortune to Blaise's father, an indolent and melancholic man who had doubled his inheritance by accidentally investing in the right railroad. Unnerved by this coup, he forsook America for France, settling at Saint Cloud where he did his best to enjoy the Bell Epoque; with his second wife Emma, Princess d'Agrigente, only daughter of the American historian Charles Schermerhorn Schuyler, himself the illegitimate son of Aaron Burr, a connection that delighted Blaise who liked to claim, inaccurately, descent from the saturnine Vice President: Blaise's mother was not Emma but a Southern lady who had died while giving birth to Blaise. Nevertheless, a portrait of Aaron Burr hung in the library; and a bundle of papers belonging to Charles Schermerhorn Schuyler was locked in Blaise's desk. The papers were said to be scandalous. Although they were often discussed in the family, no one had ever actually read them.

In due course Blaise's father was again a widower (oddly, the beautiful Emma died much as his first wife had died, giving birth; but then, Emma had not been young). Sanford went into a deep depression that did not end until one day while riding, he was thrown from his horse onto a railroad track just as the Blue Train hurtled past, giving, wits said, added significance to the stylized locomotive he had incorporated into the Sanford coat of arms. As soon as Blaise inherited the fortune, he returned to the United States with every intention of dominating that easygoing if somewhat out-of-the-way Republic (the First War had not yet happened and Americans abroad were still a novelty and source of amusement). But as a family friend had once observed to Peter, though his father had the ambition of Caesar his political style was unfortunately that of Coriolanus. Too fierce and proud to show his wounds in the marketplace, he was forced to seek the same world elsewhere.

Blaise bought a moribund newspaper, the *Washington Tribune,* and made it a success, largely because he was fearless where those of less income tend to be timid. He became a power in politics. On the Virginia side of the Potomac he built a mansion in the Georgian style, and named it Laurel House. Here he received Senators and Cabinet members, Justices and diplomats; the great and the rich, the quick and, had he the power, he would have summoned the dead as well. Even the powerful backwoods politicians, proudly uncouth (red suspenders, collarless shirts, cowboy boots: each had his folksy trademark), gladly discarded demotic trappings in order to go to Laurel House and become, if briefly, a part of that magic circle which was true center. If Paris was worth a mass, Laurel House was worth a dinner jacket.

Peter admired his father without liking him, just as he liked his mother without admiring her. But then, ever since June when school let out, he had been playing god, studying those about him as if through the wrong end of a telescope. But though they were properly diminished by his scrutiny, he still found the adult world puzzling; he was particularly confused by those who gathered in his father's drawing room. They seemed to be engaged in some sort of charade, known to them but not to him, and though there were times when he thought he knew what they were up to, something odd would happen and the mystery would resume. Yet he was confident that one day it would all be plain to him. When it was, he would call out across the room to the players, "All right! I've got it. I know the game. I win! You can all go home!" But for now he was back at "Go," and the game would obviously be a long time playing before yielding him its secret.

At the room's center, Blaise stood short and straight beneath the chandelier with its three crystal feathers, emblem of the Prince Regent, Mrs. Sanford always remarked to those visitors who admired it.

Peter joined the group that had gathered about his

father like wolves circling a sheep. No, he decided, like sheep circling a wolf, eager to serve the carnivore. That was the one aspect of the game Peter had always understood. Blaise was rich, others were not. Yet money in itself did not impress Peter as much as what he had seen at the poolhouse. Unbidden, the vision returned and he was forced to put a hand in his trousers pocket. As he did, he looked about the room, wondering whether or not the lovers had returned. If not, who was missing?

There had been a dinner for twenty; afterwards another dozen couples had arrived. It was the usual Laurel House mingling of politicians and diplomats and visitors from the distant world of New York. The mood was high and some of the most dignified of the men and the most glittering of the women were talking and laughing much too loudly; his father, however, made silence.

"Everybody got a glass? You, Burden? No? Damn it! Give Senator Day a glass. He's why we're celebrating!" The butler poured Senator Day a glass of champagne.

Of all the Senators, James Burden Day most resembled Peter's ideal of the classic Roman Senator. White-haired and stately, Burden Day moved with a conscious dignity that beguiled rather than appalled. With a flourish, the Senator held his glass high. But though he smiled a politician's smile, his eyes were those of a man who had just seen the hour and date of his death written upon a wall, a somberness of expression Peter found most attractive for he too was something of a melodramatist, having read Poe the previous winter.

"I won't give Burden all the credit . . ." began Blaise.

"Naturally," said his wife. Frederika Sanford's fair hair and gentle expression put new acquaintances so much at their ease that they were quite overwhelmed when they discovered that not only did Frederika have a sharp tongue but that she was also quite unable to permit a silence or even a pause in someone else's speech to go unfilled. She was a mistress of the sudden interjection; the small hard word, delivered like a stone from a slingshot. As a result, those who lived with her had become powerful conversationalists, never pausing for a word in terror that she might give them the wrong one.

Blaise spoke through his wife's "naturally." "The distinguished Senator from the American heartland, helped by the *Washington Tribune!*" Mock applause and hooting as Blaise indicated himself.

Peter looked about the room to see who was missing. On a sofa sat Diana Day, the Senator's daughter, whose legs he had for one moment thought he recognized in the lightning's flash. But it was unthinkable. Diana was far too shy to give herself to a man with falling garters in a strange house, during a party. Besides, she was plain, with no makeup, and her hair was like the feathers of a brown hen. But though she dressed in clothes too old for her, Peter was aware of a good body beneath dull cloth.

"But Burden and I and a few other men of principle . . ."

"Hear! Hear!" from the room.

"We managed to stop our distinguished President, the *dis*-Honorable Franklin Delano Roosevelt!" Boos and cheers from the room. Most of those present were enemies of the Administration, although, as usual, there were a few New Dealers in attendance, eager to show Blaise Sanford that their horns were detachable, their hooves hearsay, and their need for publicity as poignant as any man's

"This is a big day for us. For the country. For our kind of government. We must all remember it. July twenty-third, 1937." Having blundered, Blaise was forced to contend with his wife's uncanny memory for dates and numbers.

"July twenty-second, dear." Frederika came in hard on "1937," abandoning her usual policy of waiting for the natural pause.

For an instant Blaise scowled; then he laughed. As always, others laughed, too. "And here I was about to inscribe the wrong date on everyone's heart. All right, July twenty-second, 1937, in the Senate of the United States the President's bill to pack the Supreme Court and subvert the Constitution was buried for all time.

Which means that the dictatorship Mr. Roosevelt dreams of has been at least delayed. And for this respite, we have to thank Burden Day and his Judiciary subcommittee. Ladies and gentlemen, Senator Day!"

The toast was drunk seriously because politics was taken seriously at Laurel House. Peter knew that his father believed everything that he said for the simple reason that he himself believed the same things. Not once had Peter even questioned the wickedness of the President or the virtue of his enemies, of whom James Burden Day was now the most conspicuous.

Senator Day responded to the toast, affecting a diffidence which did not strike Peter as altogether satisfactory in one who only this morning had humiliated a President in full view of the world. "Blaise, friends . . . I won't say 'my friends.' " He mimicked the President with startling exactness and everyone laughed. "We have done good work today. According to the papers, I was out to 'get' the President because I don't like him. Well, I don't like him. But that wasn't what was at stake. And even though I'm a good Democrat . . ."

The Senator paused and got his reward. "No such thing," said Mrs. Sanford. The guests laughed again. The Senator smiled tolerantly. Then, unexpectedly, he spoke of the recent death of his friend Joe Robinson, the majority leader of the Senate. He described how he had helped Joe on the floor of the Senate when he had felt the beginning of the heart attack which was to kill him later that night. He described sitting beside Joe in the cloakroom, and as his friend rocked back and forth, struggling for breath, they spoke of the Court bill which Robinson had sworn to deliver to the President. He believed he had a majority. Burden Day knew for certain that he had not; but suspecting that Joe was dying, he assured him that the bill's passage was certain because "I loved Joe Robinson. We all did."

"I loved Joe Robinson. We all did." Peter repeated this to himself in his own inner voice. Some words sounded in his head; others turned to script; many translated to pictures. But whenever he tried to decide exactly how it was that his mind worked, he lost

8

all sense of himself, the way he did on those clear nights when, staring at the sky, he was overwhelmed by the thought of an infinitude of suns and nonhuman worlds. Sky. Night. Stars. Mars. Tars Tarkas of Thark, the green giant, was beside him, as they crossed the red desert of ancient Mars to the place where cowered the beautiful Princess Thuvia. Red dust appeared on the horizon. "Here they come," he muttered grimly to his green comrade-in-arms. "We're ready for them, O Peter," said Tars Tarkas, and with his four arms he removed four swords from their scabbards.

"We buried Joe last week in Little Rock. I don't think I give away any secrets when I say that on the train back to Washington, the Vice President turned to me and said, 'Well, that's the end of Franklin. And I hope you boys find some decent way of layin' this bill to rest.' We did. Today. And I have a hunch that the President may have learned a lesson he won't soon forget. That not even he can upset the system of checks and balances which our forefathers . . ." But Burden Day, obviously aware that his voice had gone from that of drawing room guest to politician, abruptly finished with a few muttered words that without the *Washington Tribune* and Blaise Sanford there might be at this very moment thirteen rather than nine Justices of the Supreme Court. After a round of applause, the talk became general.

Alone beside the fireplace, Peter drank sarsaparilla and ate potato chips while killing the last of the white-wigged Martian Priests. Then he turned to Thuvia, who lay among the red dunes of Mars, waiting for him with parted lips and silver legs spread wide . . . He knew whose legs those were.

In a jonquil yellow dress his sister Enid materialized in the room, pale face flushed, eyes huge from pleasure, hair still full of rain despite a recent combing. Her return had gone unnoticed, a fact unusual in itself since the whole point to Enid was that she was always noticed, with no effort on her part. She glided to the bar and poured herself whisky, again unusual: Enid seldom drank. Peter looked toward the hall to see who it was she had been with. But the man with the garters had either gone home or would reappear later, to avoid suspicion. Fiercely, Peter tried to recall who had been at dinner. He shut his eyes, the better to concentrate.

Enid twirled his hair against the central cowlick, causing sudden tears of pain.

"Stop it!" He struck away the hand. Each was experienced in the torturing of the other. Although she had the advantage of being older than he by three years, his biological age had now made him physically stronger than she but to no purpose, since in the process he was now no more able to touch her physically then he could hold fire in his hand. It was too dangerous, as they both knew well.

"Where have *you* been?"

"At the poolhouse." He was startled by her candor, and then by the swift serenity with which she lied. "I took a walk after dinner and got caught in the storm. My hair's still wet. Listen to that thunder." But Peter could hear nothing but the dull rapid thud of his own pulse beat.

"Who'd you go with?"

"My lover, who else?"

Against his will, Peter found her unexpectedly impressive. "You have a lover? Here?"

Enid laughed and twisted the cowlick right way round, a not unpleasant sensation. But he could not bear to have her touch him. He leaped from the chair. "Which one is he?"

But Enid merely smiled and stretched languorously before the fire and Peter, confronted by the fact of her body, was furious. "Who?" He could barely get the word out.

Enid looked at him hard, no longer smiling, more puzzled than suspicious. "Who do you think I was with, you idiot? I was alone."

"Were you?" His tone was so inquisitorial that Enid laughed at him. "All right. I wasn't alone. I was with Harold Griffiths. We made love on a rubber mattress in the poolhouse, in the men's dressing room, while listening to the radio. I forget which station. Are you satisfied?"

Peter looked past her at Harold Griffiths who was short and barrel-chested with a great lion's head and pale agate eyes. He was a poet from New York who worked as critic for the *Tribune*. He almost never stopped talking and Peter thought him the most brilliant man in Washington. But he was certain that Harold had not left the house. In any case, those short bowed legs were not the ones he had seen in the poolhouse.

Peter shook his head. "It wasn't Harold."

"But it was. And I'm going to marry him, too. He's got to make an honest woman of me, after what we did."

Peter turned from her. "Go to hell," he murmured, suddenly neutral. He selected and ate the largest of the potato chips. After all, it was no business of his.

He was about to leave the room when his mother motioned for him to join her and Senator Day and Diana. All three were lined up side by side on a sofa, like rifle targets at Glen Echo Amusement Park. Peter wished suddenly that he had a gun. Bang bang bang, down they would go. One two three, and he would win a stuffed bear. But then they would pop right up again, ready for the next customer.

He sat down opposite them, and looked attentive. He knew that whenever his mother summoned him to join the grownups it was because Important Things Were Being Said.

The Senator was speaking of the President. Peter had seldom heard him speak on any other subject. The President was the Senator's white whale, to be pursued to the death and after. "It's too simple to say that he wants to be a dictator. Actually, I don't think he knows what he wants. He has no master plan, thank God. But all his improvisations, all his gestures are those of a man who wants to center in himself all power."

"But why?" Diana Day, who seldom spoke, blushed; obviously she had startled herself, while delighting her father, who beamed at her as Mrs. Sanford said, "Because he's that sort of man!"

"What I meant was," and Peter noticed that Diana spoke with a slight stammer, "perhaps he thinks it right, what he's doing, the way it was in 1933 when he had to create jobs."

11

"Conceited!" exclaimed Mrs. Sanford, linking her new interjection with the last as if Diana had not spoken at all. "The way he throws his head back, and that horrible grin! It's all because he's a cripple," she added with finality. *The brain was affected.* Everyone knows."

"That's too easy." Senator Day twirled his highball glass first clockwise then counterclockwise. Peter's cowlick hurt. "Diana," and the Senator gave his daughter a curious smile, "I suspect you of being a secret New Dealer."

The girl turned a deeper red; tears came to her eyes. Though Peter had known her all his life, he had seldom heard her say more than a conventional phrase or two. He had always thought her dull as well as plain. But now that she was grown up he decided that she was not really plain, only shy, and grimly turned out. Under one arm he saw the fastener of a zipper, and mentally he gave it a tug. The cloth parted, to reveal . . . With an effort he recalled himself. It was plain that he was going mad. He could think of nothing but rape.

The Senator said, "I don't see Roosevelt himself as bad . . ."

"Bad!" One of Mrs. Sanford's best effects was the repetition, in a different key—and often meaning—of a single word.

But the Senator knew his competition. He continued. "Good and bad are relative, of course. But I do see him as more helpless than most people think. I see him riding the whirlwind." Peter thought of lightning; thought he heard thunder beyond heavy curtains and rose-red brick; thought of the poolhouse. . . . Desperately he concentrated on the Senator's words. "Since then the Executive has grown stronger, while the Legislature and the Judiciary grow weaker."

"Which is their own fault, isn't it, Father?" Diana stammered on the first syllable of "Father."

The Senator nodded. "To a degree. We don't have the leaders we used to have when I first came to the Senate. And though in some ways, I'm glad the Aldriches are gone . . ."

"I love Senator Borah." Mrs. Sanford looked absently about the room to see if the guests were mingling, laughing, gossiping, as they ought.

"Now there are those who think this process is inevitable in our form of government. I don't." Peter was aware that since his mother's attention had strayed to the room, the Senator was speaking directly to him and he was embarrassed to find himself the sole recipient of so much wisdom and courtesy.

"You see, I think our kind of government is the best ever devised. At least originally. So whenever a President draws too much power to himself, the Congress must stop him by restoring the balance. Let him reach too far and . . ." The long white hand moved abruptly toward Peter who gave a start as though the hand were indeed a tyrant's, grasping power. "We shall . . ." The Senator's other hand, rigid as a knife, made as if to chop the tyrant's hand from its wrist. *That* was power, thought Peter, chilled. Fortunately the Senator was far too skillful a performer to end on too high a note. He broke the tension with a laugh. "On the other hand, no pun intended, F.D.R. has a lot more tricks up that sleeve of his. I just hope we can always manage him as well as we did today."

Across the room someone struck a chord on the grand piano. The room was silent. As in most Washington drawing rooms, the piano's essential function was to serve as an altar on which to display in silver frames the household gods: photographs of famous people known to the family. The Sanford deities were suitably impressive, consisting mostly of royalties whose signatures slanted in bold letters from lower left to ascending right, unlike those of presidents and other democratic figures who favored long inscriptions suggesting intimacy.

But now the Washington correspondent of a London newspaper had seated himself at the altar, and others gathered around him. In honor of the day's victory, "The Battle Hymn of the Republic" was played, though none but the Englishman was certain of the words. This was followed by a powerful rendering of "Old Man River," the Englishman's party piece, in which even the lowest notes were accurate. Half the group was now gathered about the piano, proposing songs and singing. The rest accompanied Blaise to the adjoining cardroom.

Then Harold Griffiths, exuberantly drunk, usurped the Englishman's place as song leader. To everyone's delight, because Harold was fun, as Mrs. Sanford often said, even if he was probably a Communist. Harold knew theatre people; he wrote a lively column; and once he had been a poet, though no one that Peter knew had ever read Harold's poems, or those of anyone else except Ogden Nash.

Mrs. Sanford joined the singers, leaving the Senator and Diana to Peter. The Senator finally looked at him, as opposed to facing him.

"What," began the Senator, and Peter knew already the ritual question, "do you plan to do when you're . . ." With that charming hesitance which had won him so much favor, he paused and exchanged the traditional "grown up" for the more flattering "finished with school?"

"I wish I knew." Peter looked at Diana, as though for guidance; she nodded encouragingly. "Politics . . ."

"Don't!" Feigning horror, the Senator sat back in the sofa; the white hands clapped together with a sharp retort.

"But I like it."

"Like it but don't practice it. Of all the lives I can think of, politics is the most . . . the most . . ." This time the hesitation was not for effect. The Senator was actually searching for a word. "The most *humiliating.*" The smile faded. Peter believed him. "You must be accessible to every fool who wants to see you, since the only person who can never escape a bore is the man who needs his vote. Woodrow Wilson used to say that the worst thing about being President was continually being told things you already knew. Well, it is the same for all of us. And then, at the end, your place is taken by someone else and you're forgotten, and nothing you ever wanted to get done at the beginning seems anywhere near fulfillment. The lucky man is the one who dies during a victory, like Lincoln, though even he had that dream—what was it? Something about a ship in a dark sea, far from shore, lost."

"But the ship was moving," said Diana.

"Yes, it was moving." The Senator recalled himself, with a laugh. "Was there ever such a gloomy old politician as me? Pay no attention. I'm just offering a nervous hostage to fortune. You see, today is an extraordinary day for me. I've actually managed to do something I thought important. I proved a point." He stopped, recalling how the conversation had begun. "If you like politics, publishing the *Washington Tribune* is a good way of being political, without pain."

Peter grinned. "I don't think my father wants me to run the paper just yet."

"You should study journalism." Diana took the conversation seriously in a way neither Peter nor the Senator did.

"If I ever graduate, I will." Though Peter was entered at Harvard, he could not bear the thought of New England, cold weather, hard work. Since he was Southern and lazy, he preferred a college closer to home. Unexpectedly his mother agreed with him. Frederika wanted only for her children to fit with ease into a society she thought exactly right the way it was: the world of the estates that ringed the city of Washington, of the Italianate palaces on Massachusetts Avenue, of the small restored houses in the Georgetown slums which had lately become fashionable. For all Frederika's seeming vagueness, she had a precise sense of what the world was, and she had made it plain to both Peter and Enid that she was prepared to put up with any sort of behavior as long as it was not openly eccentric or disruptive of what the newspapers called Society, a word never used by those so designated. In her way, she was a splendid social tactician. Not idly had she married for money. It was an old Washington joke that Blaise Sanford had paused once too often and that Frederika had filled the silence with a swift "I do." Peter smiled, recalling this story. He was used to hearing gossip about the family, though he realized that the worst of it would not be said in his presence.

"Well, you look happy, Pete!" It was Clay Overbury, Burden Day's administrative assistant. "The Senator been telling you one of his stories?"

"Nothing so good," said the Senator. "I was boring him with the news that power is bitter and dominion terrible."

"It certainly is for the President tonight." Clay sat beside Diana on the sofa. Although he was only a senatorial assistant, Clay was often invited to great houses, largely because of the way he looked: tight blond curls, violet eyes, and a short nose somewhat thickened as a result of a recent fall during a Warrenton hunt. An excellent athlete and a good listener, he was expected to go far, if only as the future husband of Diana Day. No one had ever been able to think of anything to say against him except Frederika, who once remarked that Clay was too good-looking, as though to be too good-looking were somehow wrong for a man, like wearing brown shoes with a blue suit or using a cigarette holder like the President. But Peter was well-disposed toward Clay who treated him as a fellow adult.

"I understand the President's gone off on his yacht." Clay smiled at Diana who smiled back.

"One wonders, will it sink?" said the Senator with a sigh.

"We can always hope." Clay mopped his brow though the room was no longer warm. Someone had opened the French windows and cool rain-smelling air had begun to circulate. Peter strained to hear thunder, but there was none. The storm was over and a nightbird sang, its harsh voice audible despite Harold Griffiths's loud rendering of "Once There Were Four Marys." Harold knew by heart a thousand songs, and was willing to sing them all in his dramatic if somewhat nasal tenor.

"But just before he left, he opened a television studio in Washington. *Television!* He's wonderful. He says that in a year or two we'll be able to see the news as well as hear it."

"He can hardly wait, I'm sure." The Senator shook his head sadly. "Imagine having to *watch* him day after day! It's enough just to hear him, that terrible patronizing voice. Why do I find him so unbearable?"

16

"Because he's the President." Diana was unexpectedly direct.

The Senator looked at her with respect. "I hope you're wrong, but you may be right. I have never liked the President, no matter who he was. Familiarity, I suppose. And then we are natural antagonists, Senate and White House."

Clay nodded briskly at what was obviously a familiar argument. "Another thing I just heard on the radio . . ."

"Heard *where?*" Peter was suddenly alert.

"On the radio. The President plans to appoint . . ."

"What radio?"

Clay's violet eyes went wide with annoyance. "The radio in your father's library." Then he told the Senator what he had heard, and Peter was fascinated by the boldness of the lie. There was no radio in the library. There was no radio downstairs. But there was one in the poolhouse. As Peter stared at Clay, a single drop of rainwater detached itself from the golden curls and streaked toward the chin, as close to the ear as though it were indeed perspiration; even random nature contrived to shield Clay who suddenly crossed his legs; Peter wondered if the garters were now properly adjusted.

Then Clay and the Senator spoke of the next day's business, and Peter, triumphant, joined Enid at the piano. Harold Griffiths's huge repertory had at last overwhelmed the company. Having come together as performers, only to find themselves used as audience, they had all drifted away except Enid who seemed really to enjoy Harold's singing. She leaned now against the piano, the yellow of her dress bright against dark wood. "Having a good time?" she mocked Peter gently. "Been spiking your Coke?"

"Sure, I'm high as a kite." He chose a soft friendly voice. "But you know what I don't understand?"

"Why, just about everything. Now be still. Harold, sing that song in French, the fisherman song. What's it called?"

Harold told her and then he began to sing a medieval song in a minor key. *"Mais sont-ils morts?"* was the refrain.

"What I don't understand is . . ." But Peter's delib-

17

erately soft and friendly voice could not compete with Harold's singing. The words were lost.

"Peter, shut up and *listen!*" Enid's frown was almost as awesome as their father's scowl. She would resemble the old man one day.

"I said," Peter made his voice both hard and audible, "that what I don't understand is why when Clay laid you, he didn't take off his shoes." Enid turned and stared at him, without expression, until he could bear it no longer. With *"Mais sont-ils morts?"* sounding in his ears, he hurried from the drawing room.

Safe in his own room, he locked the door, and for a moment stood dumbly, holding his head with both hands as though to prevent the blood from breaking through distended arteries. Yet even in his anguish he knew enough to ask himself with a cold curiosity why it was that he felt betrayed.

2

From the bathroom window, James Burden Day observed the green of Rock Creek Park, already hazy in the morning heat. Fortunately the house was cool. Built of solid gray stone, it was exactly the sort of house he had always wanted. Walls that would last for centuries, high-ceilinged rooms, long windows with a view of gardens. He was hardly a rich man but he had never once regretted building the house, which had, in any case, saved him from being wiped out by the Depression. For no reason other than a desire to build a great house, he had taken his money out of the stock market and put it into stone, mortar, wood, slate, glass, and made something beautiful which would last forever, despite a recently increased mortgage. Thought of money made him frown; his hand shook, the razor nicked his chin and blood stained the white of the lather. "Damn!" he said as scarlet mingled with white, like a strawberry shortcake.

Briskly Burden washed his face and stuck toilet paper onto the cut. Then he pulled off his nightshirt and stood for a moment, revolving his arms idly in the air, eyes shut in order not to see the old body which he never ceased to recall as it had been in his fair and vigorous youth before the muscled arms had gone slack and the legs become blue-veined and spindly and the once flat belly thrust forward into a heavy ellipse of flesh which now overhung contracted genitals. But of course none of this was permanent, he told himself, beginning to dress. Whenever he chose, time could be reversed. Diet, exercise and the implantation of a goat's glands would make the loose skin taut, the muscles firm, the sex responsive. It was just a mattter of deciding when to take off a month or two for the metamorphosis to occur. It was unthinkable that he would not ever be young again.

Meanwhile, Burden knew that it was quite enough to live in a present suddenly grown marvelous. Never had a President so soon after a huge electoral victory been so thoroughly repudiated by his own party in Congress. "I will bring him down," he said to the mirror, knotting the polka-dot bow tie, his trademark, beloved of caricaturists. Happily he went down to breakfast.

In the dining room, tall windows revealed a shaggy green garden. A warm breeze stirred heavy curtains. On the window sill, a cardinal sat, waiting for Burden's wife to feed it. Wild birds came to her. People, alas, did not.

Burden sat down at the long empty table while the servant Henry, black and dour and pretentious, served him breakfast. Henry worshiped the United States Senate. He read everything pertaining to it ("pertaining" was a Henry word), and he was even more suspicious than Burden of the White House, regarding the Executive as a continual threat to the majesty (and natural primacy) of the Upper House.

It was not in Henry's nature to smile or betray excitement but Burden thought that he noticed a slight tremor of the hand as Henry placed the morning newspapers beside his plate. From the front page of the top newspaper, his own face looked up at him.

"Well, Henry, I guess we showed Mr. Roosevelt a thing or two."

19

"Yes, Senator, I believe we did. What happens to the Court bill now?"

"It vanishes into committee. Never to be seen again."

Henry frowned to denote grave pleasure and then withdrew, leaving the Senator to read about himself. Tactfully Henry had put the *Washington Tribune* on top.

"How does it feel?" Diana took him by surprise. "To be so praised! So noticed!"

"No more than I deserve." He was gay. "About once a decade I am properly appreciated." Across the table, Diana seemed to his nearsighted eyes like a great pink rose in a shaft of golden morning light.

"*We* appreciate you every day and in every way. Are you going down to the Hill?"

"Could you imagine me *not* going down there? I want to gloat."

Henry brought Diana's breakfast and listened discreetly as he served her. "Has the President made any comment?"

"Not so far. I doubt if he will. He's fled up the river on a yacht."

The telephone in the kitchen rang and slowly Henry went to answer it.

"Did you enjoy last night?" He looked at the rose blur which seemed to contract and then to expand.

"Yes, I like the Sanfords. Especially Enid. I wish I looked like her. She looks like . . . she looks like Fate."

"And how does Fate look?"

"Like Enid. Dark, severe, voluptuous, all at the same time. Men fall for Enid."

"For Fate?"

"No, just for Enid. I wish they fell for me."

Burden frowned. He knew that Diana believed that she was unattractive and, feeling herself so, did not, in fact, attract men. He wondered how to tell her that the power to attract others was simply a trick to be learned, an act of the will. He himself had begun by studying those who pleased the crowd; deliberately he had imitated the way they spoke, smiled, walked, until at last he, too, was loved by the many. Yet

20

he had never ceased to be himself, despite the shrewd artifices of his performance.

Henry appeared with the telephone on its extension cord. "Your office, Senator. It's Mr. Overbury."

Clay's voice was excited. "You saw the morning papers? Well, New York's even better. And we had a call from home, from the Governor's office. He's running you for President!" Burden's heart beat faster. Then: "Somebody named Nillson just called. He wants to see you. It's about . . ."

"I know what it's about. Tell him I won't see him. Tell him he's a crook. Well, no, don't tell him that."

"I shall translate."

"Tell him I'm too busy. Discourage him. I'll be at the office in half an hour." Burden put down the receiver.

"Who's Nillson? Why is he a crook?"

Burden looked at the rose which blazed now as sunlight flooded the room. "An astonishing man. He sauntered into my office last week and told me that he wanted to buy a hundred thousand acres of Indian land."

"Oil?"

"What else? And he assured me that the Department of the Interior would make no fuss . . ."

"But he knew that you would."

"Exactly. He wants my subcommittee not to object to his buying the land at a fraction of what it's worth."

"Do the Indians want to sell?"

"Naturally! They're idiots."

"Then you must protect them."

"I will. And so earn their undying hatred. No good deed ever goes unpunished."

"Well, it's always satisfying to do the right thing."

"I'm not so sure. Don't be rigid," he advised her suddenly. "Don't be like me. Remember what Cicero said . . ."

"He said everything and you know everything he said." Diana mocked him and he was not entirely amused for he had little humor about himself and the fact that he knew that he lacked this most American of virtues did not make life any easier. For a public man he was altogether too sensitive and vulnerable.

"Cicero said, 'One may do some time-serving but when one's hour has come, one must not miss it!'"

"Yes, but how do you know when the hour has come?"

"For him it was unmistakable. They came with swords, and cut off his head."

"I should have thought it best never to 'time-serve.' In that case, one is always ready for the end."

"To survive one must 'time-serve.' Knowing when not to, *that* is the secret to being great."

"You are great."

He was touched. "Daughters always think that about their fathers."

"But you are. Because you are not afraid to be . . ." She paused and he wondered which adjective she would choose: strong, wise, honest? It must be "honest," he decided, trying to influence her decision by telepathy. But she chose "unpopular," a small virtue which could easily turn to vice. The Senate was filled with men who reveled in unpopularity (outside their own states of course); these showmen were never so happy as when they had contrived to get the wall as close as possible to their backs. He hoped he was not of that company.

But before he could explain himself they were joined by his wife and her mother. Small and brown with bright eyes and uncombed hair, Kitty Day took her place at table, wearing an old wrapper, to the disgust of Diana who said, "Mother, *why* do you have to look like that in the morning?"

"Like what, dear?" Kitty was impervious to all criticism. Burden had met her during his first political campaign and in less than six months they were married. She had been loving and he had loved as best he could which was not much, for his days were full and often he was away from home for weeks at a time. Yet when he returned, she was always there, affectionate and gentle, and maddening for she was socially artless with no sense of the effect she made on others. Worse, she had in recent years developed a most alarming habit: she had taken to saying exactly what she thought or, more precisely, what she was thinking.

"Anyway," said Kitty, cutting her daughter short, "the cardinal must be fed." Crumbling toast, she crossed to the windowsill. "Good morning! You look very nice today." She talked to the bird who pecked at her hand greedily, without fear.

Father and daughter watched this display with fascination. Kitty's absorption in what she was doing made everything else seem idle and purposeless. When the bird was fed, it flew away. "See you tomorrow," said Kitty as it vanished among trees. "And be careful. Stay off those high voltage wires." She did not lapse into baby-talk or any special voice when she talked to animals. "I hate those wires," she said to her husband in the same tone she had used to the bird. "Can't you do something about them?"

"The Senate is powerless," he began, hoping to make a play on the word, "but I suppose we could put up signs. 'Hot wire. Do not perch.' Something like that."

"They don't read," said Kitty evenly. Then she asked her usual morning question. "What's in the paper?"

But before he could summarize the news, Diana said, "Mother, you might at least read *one* paper, today of all days. Father's going to be President, they all say so."

"Well, that's very nice," said Kitty softly, turning to Burden. "Yes, that *is* nice, people wanting you to be the President. Perhaps I *will* read just one paper." She took the nearest newspaper and held it a moment as though not certain what to do next. Then she let it rest in the butter. She turned to her husband. "Who called you just now?"

"Clay, at the office. And I had better be on my way." Burden rose and shouted, "Henry!" There was no response because whenever Henry heard the call he would exchange his white jacket for a blue one and bring the car around.

"We must ask Clay for dinner one of these days." Kitty spoke with her mouth full.

"He's much too busy," said Diana, lifting the newspaper out of the butter. "He's very social this summer. He's always with the Sanfords."

"Such a nice boy. I'm sure Blaise and Frederika like

23

him as much as we do." Kitty slowly ate scrambled eggs. Burden had never known anyone to eat as slowly as his wife. The fork seldom got to her lips before some thought caused her to put it down again untasted. "And I can see why he would like their house better than ours. After all, Enid's terribly attractive and rich."

Burden did his best to stop what was coming. "Tell us, Kitty, about the new birdhouse. When will it be ready?"

"Not for another week at least. You know how slow Henry is. Of course he's as sly as they come, and terribly on the make, and Diana's a perfect fool for wanting to marry him because he'll give her nothing but trouble."

"Mother!" Diana gave a great cry, threw down her napkin and fled.

"What's wrong with Diana?" Kitty was genuinely concerned.

With a sigh, Burden crossed to his wife and kissed her cheek, inhaling the familiar morning scent of cold cream and sleep. "Nothing, dear." He could not resist adding, "Perhaps it was something you said."

"I was simply telling her about Henry and the birdhouse."

"And Clay."

"I didn't say anything about Clay, but just between us, she's crazy about him."

"Just between us?"

Kitty nodded. "I never let on I've noticed. I don't think parents should. Let the children find their own way . . . up to a point, of course."

"Do you like Clay?"

"Oh, very much! He's such a help to you. And so good-looking. I like handsome men, you know that!"

"Naturally. You married one." They laughed together at this old joke.

* * *

Beneath a sun like a bronze shield, the new Senate Office Building gleamed white in its setting of Capitoline green. As Burden approached the main door, several citizens of the Republic (at crucial moments he saw life as a Shakespeare play) stopped him to shake hands and he murmured his thanks in a voice less than audible but with an expression full of grace and mutual understanding.

Inside the building the guard, surprisingly, rose when he entered. "Nice day, Senator." Better and better, he thought, as he proceeded to the mahogany door with its simple legend "Mr. Day."

The outer office of his suite contained leather chairs, two desks, and two secretaries. Miss Perrine was young and plump, with uncontrollable hair; she was engaged to a man with a hearing aid who occasionally came to pick her up at the end of the day. Mrs. Blaine was old and in every way admirable, except for her voice. Because of a malformation of the palate, she had a tendency to honk. "The out-of-town press is *marvelous!*" She patted a pile of newspapers on the chair beside her desk. "You should read the editorials."

"I will. I will." Pushing past the swinging door of the protective balustrade, Burden glanced absently down into the savage tangle of Miss Perrine's hair, half expecting to see a family of birds poke their heads up to him, crying for Kitty to feed them. Then he went into his private office, one of the most desirable in the building, a tribute not only to his seniority but to his long membership in The Club. No one was ever quite sure who belonged to The Club since members denied its existence but everyone knew who did not belong. The Club was permanently closed to the outsize personality, to the firebrand tribune of the people, to the Senator running too crudely for President. Members of The Club preferred to do their work quietly and to get re-elected without fanfare. On principle they detested the President, and despite that magnate's power to loose and to bind, The Club ruled the Senate in its own way and for its own ends, usually contrary to those of the President.

Ever since Burden first arrived in Washington, he had belonged to The Club. They had known right off that he was one of them: subtle, easygoing, able to yield gracefully when it was necessary to yield.

25

Though he was not yet forty when first elected, The Club took him in and showed him the machinery of power; even allowed him, occasionally, to manipulate the levers. They also saw to it that he was preferred over controversial men, and given his pick of useful committees. When rivals appeared back home, The Club did its best to see that he was able to take full credit for a dam, a road, a post office, those necessary gifts a Senator must bring back to the people to ensure their support.

Between tall windows his desk was placed, back to the view. On the wall opposite the desk hung a portrait of Jefferson. Elsewhere in the room there were gavels, plaques, signed photographs—all the usual memorabilia of a public man's life; the only unusual decoration was a life-size bust of Cicero on a wooden pedestal.

As always when alone, Burden saluted Cicero. The two republicans shared many secrets. One of the best was that nearly everyone in the Senate Office Building thought that the bust was a portrait of William Jennings Bryan.

Burden sent for Clay. While waiting, he glanced at the mail. In the last few days of the Court battle his mail had trebled, and most of it was favorable. He delighted in the praise, even though it was almost invariably followed by a request for aid: I feed your self-esteem, Senator, now you feed me.

Clay entered, carrying newspapers, eyes bright with pleasure. "That's where we're headed now." He indicated the barrier of green which hid the White House from observers on Capitol Hill.

Burden shook his head, not wanting to tempt fate. "A lot can happen in three years," he said, all on exhalation.

"Just keep the momentum going, and we're in. All we have to do is keep this thing alive."

"Keep it alive." Burden murmured approvingly, fingers feeling for his favorite talisman: the flattened bullet removed from his father's shoulder after the Battle of Shiloh and kept by that sardonic and violent man as a memento of a heroic time . . . except that to his father there was nothing in that struggle but

26

discomfort and folly, whereas his son regarded the War of the Secession as the last true moment of virtue in a falling world. For sentimentalizing those days, his father had despised him. But then they had always hated one another. Now the Confederate corporal was dead and all that was left of him was this lump of metal, crumpled from having struck the no longer living bone.

"Keep the thing alive," Burden repeated, his forefinger gently feeling the fissures in the metal. Was it here that the flesh first felt the metal as it cut? Or here? Unbidden the furious face of his father materialized midway between Jefferson and the desk. For an instant he saw the tobacco-stained teeth, the mad gray eyes, the mottled red skin; and vivid in that incorporeal face was all his father's contempt for him. "You joined the bastards who cut us up. You're one of 'em, *Senator!*" How he had snorted the title the last time they met, shortly after Burden's election, shortly before the old man's cancerous death. Burden blinked hard; the face went.

Burden sat up abruptly; energy coursed through him. He gave Clay rapid instructions. Journalists to seek out. Editors to write to. Members of Congress to see. Money to be raised. He paused a moment at the thought of money.

"That's the worst of it. That's the one thing which can stop us."

Clay shook his head. "The fat cats love you."

"Today. But maybe not tomorrow. After all, no one can be conservative enough for them and . . ."

". . . and be elected President," Clay spoke almost too quickly. But he was right.

"And be elected President. But no one can be President . . . *I* can't be President . . . without their help. That's the problem. Well, at least we've got three years to raise the money . . ."

"And before then, you'll have spoken in every state." They planned; they plotted; they guessed; they hoped. But Burden knew that all too often political planning was nothing more than a form of mutual reassurance. The future was perfectly incalculable. Clay showed him telegrams of congratulations and invita-

27

tions to speak. Mrs. Blaine interrupted them several times with news. The Supreme Court (unofficially of course) was delighted, and the Vice President would like to have a word with him if he could spare the time.

Accompanied by Clay, Burden took the elevator to the basement, where they boarded the ridiculous but useful subway car that connected the Senate Office Building to the Capitol. They rode with a new Senator and three of his constituents, who were delighted to meet Burden Day. Everyone is delighted to meet Burden Day, thought Burden Day, greeting the constituents warmly, aware that the other Senator was visibly enhanced in the eyes of his people because he was acquainted with the Defender of the Constitution. Burden made a mental note to cultivate the new man.

At the Capitol, they ascended back stairs. As always, Burden took pleasure in the subterranean corridors, which smelled of stone, harsh soap and, he was positive, woodwork burned by the British in 1814. Despite the rising heat outside, the inner depths of the Capitol remained cool all summer long.

At the level of the Senate floor, Burden avoided the tourists by slipping into the Senate washroom, a noble chamber with enormous urinals. While Clay washed his face and hands, Burden asked casually, "Can you come to the house for dinner tonight?"

Clay shook his head, face covered with soap. "I have a date."

Burden nodded. He dreaded collision, feared rebuff. Yet it was his duty as a father to net for his child the husband she wanted, and though Diana had never actually said as much it was apparent that she was in love, and helpless.

Clay dried his face until the pink skin glowed like the face of a child who has put a flashlight in its mouth to amaze bystanders in the night with the blood's luminosity. Yes, Clay was handsome. Burden experienced a momentary pang. *He* was not young, as Clay was young; not desirable, as Clay was desirable. Yet he lusted, too, and craved that response which is something more than complaisance; something more

28

than tribute to solvency or to fame. A woman would burn at night for want of Clay. He became Diana, saw Clay as she saw him, and realized that she did not have a chance. Diana was plain to look at, shy but sharp, intelligent and good. How could she compete with softer beauties like . . .

". . . Enid Sanford asked me. It's at Chevy Chase. Some sort of dance for a friend of hers from New York. I said I'd go." Clay was placating. "Enid's a lovely girl." Obviously, Clay preferred Enid to Diana and there was nothing he could do about it. Burden arranged his hair so that the forelock would fall gracefully across the brow. In a moment, he would be on the floor of the Senate, and the gallery would recognize him and perhaps applaud. At least *that* was sweet. His mood improved as he set his mask.

". . . fascinating girl. But it's not easy keeping up with her. That's how I got this." Clay touched his thickened nose regretfully. "Keeping up with her at Warrenton, riding through those damned woods in the rain and getting thrown. And how she laughed. There I was bleeding like a pig and she laughed. I could have killed her."

Yes, thought Burden, he was hooked. "Rich girl," observed Burden. "All that Sanford money will be mighty useful to a young man who wants to serve his country in the highest councils of the state." Burden parodied his own somewhat ornate platform style.

Clay blushed and started toward the door. "She just wants a good time. That's all."

They went out into the corridor. "Well, come visit us one of these days. Diana hasn't seen much of you since she got back."

"I will. You know I will."

Duty is done, thought Burden, as he crossed the corridor to the door which led into the cloakroom. Clay was to wait for him in the gallery. At a certain agreed-upon gesture (placing of left hand against cheek) Clay would come and fetch him.

Squaring shoulders, breathing deeply (and wondering why his heart was beating so erratically), Burden nodded to the huge Capitol policeman who guarded the door and stepped into the world of the Senate.

The cloakroom, narrow as a corridor, ran the length of the Senate Chamber. Here, amid lockers, black leather sofas and writing tables, the Senators of his party gossiped and politicked. When Burden made his entrance, he was given a playful ovation. A Southerner in a Prince Albert gave out a Rebel yell and waved a small Confederate banner. Two New Dealers retreated to the far end of the cloakroom and pretended to study the day's legislation. Happy, Burden drank a glass of soda water and listened to praise.

"Best thing we've done in twenty years, and it's all your doing."

"President's sworn to have your neck if it's the last thing he ever does . . ."

". . . *will* be the last. Old Burden'll lick him every time . . ."

"Burden can lick the President in 1940. That's our year."

"Why spoil a good Senator by making a President out of him?"

Then they were joined by the senior Senator from Burden's state. Jesse Momberger was a lean man who wore hats that seemed like sombreros and built-up shoes that resembled boots. He liked to refer cryptically to famous Western outlaws, as though he knew more than he ever intended to say. "Well, pardner." He took Burden's hand in his own surprisingly soft one: the West had long since been won. "You're goin' to be the President. That's clear as a mule's ass at noon. Now I got some advice for you . . ."

Burden smiled and listened until a pale-faced page in knickerbockers came to tell him, "The Vice President is on the floor. He'd like a word with you, Senator."

Burden slipped away from his admirers. At the frosted glass doors to the Senate Chamber, he paused to straighten tie, arrange hair. Then giving the swinging doors a somewhat stronger push than was necessary, he stepped onto the floor of the Senate, and was home.

Careful not to look at the gallery, Burden walked up the aisle to his seat, chin held high so that he

30

would be recognized. He was. There was a patter of applause, quickly gaveled to silence by the chair. He took his seat and pretended to study the papers stacked in front of him. But in his excitement he could not read a word. Finally he sneaked a look at the gallery. There were several men in the press box, while the gallery itself was perhaps a third full, which was remarkable on a day when there was neither a debate nor a vote. Evidently the people had come to see him, and the Senate which had humbled the President.

Several Senators stopped to congratulate him, their gestures slightly larger than life: each aware of the hundreds of watching eyes.

Then Burden saw the Vice President. He was not in the chair but beside it, talking to a group of Senators. Burden waved to him and then, solemnly, he walked down into the well of the Chamber. The murmur from the galleries increased as the knowledgeable wondered what they would say to one another. The answer, of course, was nothing. At best, the Vice President's style was gnomic. In any case, Burden knew that the thing not spoken in politics is invariably the essential. Today the words exchanged were amiable, and seemingly direct. Details about the Court bill's progress in committee, nothing more. But what the exchange meant was plain to those who understood the workings of The Club. The tiny red-faced man with teeth like black pearls had allied himself with Burden Day. Power had been exerted, and as with fire on contiguous metal fragments, fusion had taken place. They were one, for the time being.

Delighted, Burden returned to the cloakroom, forgetting to signal Clay. This was better than he had hoped. With the Vice President's support in 1940, the thing was his.

Burden made his way briskly through a crowd of tourists who stopped him from time to time with fervent praise. He was halfway to the main door when Clay joined him. "What did the Vice President say?"

"He's with us. All the way." They spoke then of a committee meeting to be held that afternoon. Burden

31

would not be there. Clay was to tell the appropriate Senator to take charge. "Where will you be?"

Burden shook his head. "Invisible. I want to think. Call me at home tonight."

Under the stone porte cochere of the Capitol, Burden waited for Henry, eyes shut against the glare. The heat was literally breathtaking. He ought to stay at the Capitol where it was cool but perversely he preferred to be alone with his triumph.

"Nice work, Senator." The voice was pleasant; the associations not.

Burden turned as a man, slender and cool in brown gabardine, approached him. Reflexively, Burden's right arm sprang from his side. He recalled it just in time, making an awkward circular gesture as though exercising a shoulder. "I am waiting for my car," said Burden irrelevantly.

"What else?" Mr. Nillson was amused, quite unaware of the effect he was making. "I saw you just now with the Vice President. He must have been pleased at what's happened."

Burden turned to look down the driveway for Henry and the Packard. But neither was in sight. The amiable voice continued. "In fact, everyone's pleased with you. Did you know that the Hearst papers are going to propose you for President?"

The man was cunning, no doubt about it. Burden was unable to disguise his interest. "How do you know?"

"I never disclose sources, Senator." Mr. Nillson grinned. "You'll find that's my best quality."

Burden grunted and started to turn away again, but Mr. Nillson's voice (was it Southern? Western?) recalled him. "But I *can* tell you that the Day for President campaign will begin with tomorrow's editorial, written by the old man himself."

"That's very interesting, Mr. Nillson."

"I think you would be a remarkable President. *I* would certainly vote for you."

"Mr. Nillson . . ."

"Sir?"

"Who the hell are you?"

"A friend."

"No, you are not a friend."

"Then I should like to be. After all, we choose our friends because they are not like ourselves. I shall never be a great statesman, like you." Irony, guile, truth in delicate balance. "You live a life that I might have wanted, but as there is not time for one person to be everything, I choose my friends so that through them I can be a politician, a journalist, an artist . . ."

"A criminal?"

"Yes, even a criminal."

"But *what* do you do?"

"I'm a businessman. Now I have spoken very directly to you, Senator. I have been completely honest."

"Yes, you have. And do you know the penalty for bribing . . . for attempting to bribe a member of Congress?"

"Among my many friends there are lawyers." Mr. Nillson was genuinely amused. Burden felt himself losing control again, anger beginning to rise, also bewilderment. "I know the law's penalties. Also the world's rewards. I wish you would think seriously about what I said to you the other day."

"There is nothing to think about. I don't take . . ." Burden found himself lowering his voice automatically even though no one was within earshot, "bribes."

"Others . . ."

"I don't care what others do."

"Is an investment in your career a bribe? A contribution to electing you President, is that a bribe? How do you think money is ever raised for a national campaign? Anyway, should I invest in your future, I shall demand a good deal less of you than, say, the CIO or the National Association of Manufacturers."

"I am not for sale, Mr. Nillson." The pomposity and hollowness of his words appalled him and he wondered desperately what had become of his celebrated gift for the single withering phrase. Speechless, he stood, head filled with copybook maxims, a portion of his brain paralyzed.

"I don't want to buy you, Senator." The easy voice

was now as cold as his own. "I will *give* you the money that you need if you make it possible for me to buy what I want. That is a legitimate exchange. The word for what I propose may be strange to your ears. So I will say it to you slowly and carefully. The word is 'business.' "

Then Henry and the Packard arrived and Burden got in without a word. The car swung away from the starling-infested portico of the Capitol, gray as ash in the fiery noon.

"Where to, Senator?"

"Where to?" Burden recalled himself. "Cross to the Virginia side. Then we'll see."

Henry knew exactly where Burden wanted to go. Near Bull Run there was a field where Civil War earthworks twisted like a huge snake beneath tall grass. Here Burden liked to sit and brood about the days before his birth and wish that he had been born in time for that good war in which he might have died, like his uncle Aaron Hawkins, struck down before Atlanta at nineteen years of age, right leg shattered by a cannon ball; two days later, dead from gangrene. Thus did fate shear the balance of that boy's life.

Burden looked out the car window and watched those few abroad in the heat as they moved slowly, trying not to sweat; and simply to watch them from the relative coolness of the car made him hot. He reached in his pocket for a handkerchief and felt heavy metal; it was the bullet that had struck his father. He had no recollection of having taken it from the office. Delicately he touched the metal and wondered, as always, which part of the bullet struck the flesh.

At Chain Bridge they crossed the Potomac, narrowed by drought. On the Virginia side the woods were dense and almost cool. He rolled down the car window, breathed deeply, shut his eyes; dozed.

"Here we are, Senator." Burden awakened to find that they were parked in a country lane where the branches of trees met over head, filtering green the fierce sunlight. At the end of the lane was the field where the Confederates had built their earthworks.

"Stay in the car, Henry. I won't be long."

The field was bright with goldenrod and Queen Anne's lace, with sword grass that plucked at his trousers as he walked slowly to the place where two mounds of earth met at a right angle. With each step he was conscious of what lay beneath the ground, of the bones, the buttons, the belt buckles and misshapen bullets.

Burden was breathing hard when he finally reached his usual place atop the earthworks. Beneath green saplings, he took his seat upon a boulder streaked with lichen. From this perch he could survey the terrain where the first Battle of Bull Run had been fought. The seventy-sixth anniversary of that battle had occurred the day before, when he had won his own victory. The omen was good, except that of course the Confederates had then gone on to lose the war.

Across the field, pine woods broke the horizon, just as they had nearly a century before. A photograph made right after the battle showed these same woods burnt and splintered like so many matchsticks while in the foreground of the picture there lay what looked to be a pile of old clothes, until one saw a hand startlingly extended toward the sky, the sinewy brown fingers curved as though to seize a fallen rifle. Recalling that hand, Burden curved his own fingers in imitation of the dead soldier and as he did he realized suddenly that it was not for a rifle those fingers curved but for life, as though life was something literally to be seized and held. He shuddered and let his own hand fall to his lap, not wanting to know what it was the man had felt as the life left him.

Grass steamed in the sun. From damp earth, a haze rose. Weeds stirred in the hot breeze, leaves rustled, clouds of gnats moved erratically back and forth. At peace, drowsy, Burden balanced the bullet in his hand as he had done a thousand times before. Now, he told himself, he must think, plan for the future, devise a timetable extending from this very moment to that day in November of 1940 when he would be elected President. First he would talk to Blaise about money. Then he would go to William

35

Randolph Hearst and make it perfectly clear that . . .
His mind shifted stubbornly: despite the boldness of
Mr. Nillson's offer (and the assumption behind it)
he had never in his life taken a bribe. At worst, he
had accepted campaign money with the vague understanding that he might some day be of use to the
donor, a disagreeable procedure but the way things
are done in the Republic. Mr. Nillson, however, had
offered a straightforward bribe, which no honest man
could accept. More to the point, to deprive the Indians of their land was both cruel and dishonorable.

But what was honor? The hand that held the bullet
became a hard fist The usual answer: to do what one
had to do regardless of personal consequences. But in
practice that sort of piety was not much help. One
could not always know what it was one ought to do. If
the country was best served by the Presidency of
James Burden Day and that Presidency could come
about only as a result of taking Mr. Nillson's money,
ought he not to take the money? After all, a defender
of the Constitution who had taken a bribe was morally preferable to an unbribed President whose aim
was to subvert the Republic. Then, finally, the familiar
black question: What difference did any of it make?
Recently he had been shown the plans for his tomb
in the State Capitol. "There will be room," said the
architect comfortably, "for four people in the crypt.
Naturally, Mrs. Day will want to join you and perhaps your daughter will, too." In time no one would
know or care which dust was Bill, which dust was Joe.

Half asleep in the sun, Burden once more reviewed
the exchange in front of the Capitol and wondered
again how Mr. Nillson could have been so certain that
his victim would not bring charges against him. The
only possible explanation was that the man Nillson
was a born tempter, a bold provocateur whose instinct
told him, rightly, that it was not in Burden's nature to
make a fuss.

Had other Senators been approached? This was
worth opening eyes to contemplate. But the sunlight
blinded him and he quickly shut his eyes, returning
to the dark rose night of his own blood. Senators

seldom discussed such things. He recalled the embarrassment that they had all felt when a famous but poor member of The Club had died and his widow discovered eight hundred thousand dollars in currency in a safety deposit box. "Well," Burden had said to a colleague when this was mentioned over bean soup in the Senate dining room. "Well," the colleague had replied. Some did; some did not. He did not. He would not.

Burden opened his eyes just as a man came out of the woods carrying a long rifle. He was obviously a hunter who might at any moment decide that Burden, viewed from a distance, was a raccoon or a fox or whatever was then being shot in Virginia. To prevent an accident, Burden waved to the man who leaped back and took refuge behind a stump. Burden was alarmed. "Runaway Convict" made black headlines in his mind. But then Henry was nearby; and the man was more frightened than he. Burden waved again, smiling and nodding to show that he meant no harm.

Cautiously, the man approached. At the foot of the earthworks he stopped. "Where you from?" he asked. The accent was Carolinian and comforting to his ear. The man was young, dirty and bearded, with long hair that fell across his forehead in a wide tangle.

Burden said that he lived in Washington; the boy frowned. "Then you oughtn't to be here, sir." The manner was curiously grave.

"Why not?"

The youth was now so close that Burden could smell the sweat of his body, could examine close-to the curious costume he wore: shapeless jacket, torn trousers, boots with slits between sole and shoe through which black toes showed. He wondered if he would have the strength to call for Henry.

The boy held the rifle across his chest as though presenting arms. He grinned down at Burden. "Now you know why, sir. Don't make out you don't." He jerked his head toward the pine woods where he had come from and Burden saw that suddenly the woods were aflame. White smoke hid the sun. The sky was lurid. He tried to get to his feet but the man's body was in his way and he did not dare to touch him or ask him to move for fear of the long rifle he held.

Burden sat back against the boulder. "But there's fire," he said weakly. "The woods are on fire."

" 'Course there's fire."

Burden shrank back, trying not to breathe, not to smell the other's sweat, to avoid the oddly intimate look in the bright blood shot eyes. "Let me up," Burden whispered. "Let me go."

But the boy did not stir. Bearded lips grinned down at Burden who lay helpless on the ground, unable to move. Then suddenly the youth extended a sinewy brown hand in whose familiar curve Burden saw death remembered and death to come. He screamed and awakened just in time to keep from rolling down the earthworks to the stony field below. For a moment, he sprawled on the ground, heart beating wildly. Then carefully he touched grass, earth, stone, to make sure that he was still alive.

"You all right, Senator?" Henry stood at the edge of the field, like a black scarecrow.

"Yes, Henry!" He was surprised at the vigor of his own voice. Then he got up as rapidly as aging muscles would allow. "I'll be right with you. Go on back to the car."

When Henry was out of sight, Burden sat on the boulder and waited until his heart regained its usual slow beat. Apprehensively he looked across the field, half expecting to see the smoke and flame of that famous burning day. But the woods were green. There was no fire. It had all been a part of the mind's theatre, without significance. Yet the face of the Confederate soldier had been familiar: but then the face of death would hardly be that of a total stranger and it was indeed his own death that had raised the rifle against him. Shuddering at the nearness of his escape, he rose to go. As he did, he noticed, gleaming dully in the grass, the bullet which had struck his father. Stooping down, he dug a hole in the ground with his fingers. Then he placed the bullet in the hole and covered it up. Pleased at what he had done, he began the descent of the earthworks and the crossing of the field.

3

"Yes, sir, I'll check on him first thing tomorrow." Clay Overbury sat at the Senator's desk. "Why are you interested? I mean is there anything special you want me to look for?" Senator Day's voice grew somewhat indistinct.

Clay, holding the receiver between shoulder and cheek, lit a cigarette. "I see," he said, realizing that either he had missed something or nothing had been told him. Then the Senator gave orders with his usual clarity and, as always, Clay marveled at how the old man could keep so many things straight in his mind. He forgot nothing, unlike Clay, who was forced to make notes.

"Do you believe in dreams?" The Senator asked this question in precisely the same tone of voice he had used to give instructions for the next day's press conference.

Clay was taken aback. "Dreams?" he repeated. The Senator chuckled, a thin mocking sound in the receiver. "Neither do I," he said. "I'll see you in the morning."

"Yes, sir. Oh . . . and tell Diana I'll call her tomorrow, if you would, sir." The Senator said that he would and hung up.

Clay rang Miss Perrine in the outer office and asked her to bring him *Who's Who in America*. Then he sat back in the chair. The day was almost over. With a sigh he unbuttoned his shirt; he hoped the evening would be cool. Opposite him a last ray of sun illuminated Cicero's tragic mouth. He must read Cicero one day; to please the Senator.

Miss Perrine entered, pushed at her mass of hair to make it form a symmetrical frame to her pretty face, and failed. She gave him the large red book and waited while he looked up Nillson, Edgar Carl, b. 1881, Havre de Grace, Md.; m. Lucy Wavell 1921 (divorced 1932). No degrees listed. Directorships in a number of corporations: land development, gas, oil. Membership in one of the best of the New York clubs. That was interesting. Residence: 1106 Fifth Av., New York City. He gave Miss Perrine the book. "Check on each of these companies, will you? Ask Commerce if you need any help. Also, check with Dun & Bradstreet. Senator needs it tomorrow."

"Yes, sir." She gave him a sidelong glance which he did not acknowledge. On dangerously high heels, she tottered from the room.

In the waning light, Clay walked through the garden of the Capitol, among trees neatly tagged with their Latin names. The air was still. The furnace of the Washington day was shutting down. As Clay passed an elderly Senator, he wished him good evening, tactfully supplying his own name. The old man flashed him a smile, grateful for the identification.

At the foot of Capitol Hill he hailed a taxicab. The driver was a compulsive talker who did not in the least mind that Clay was not a listener, particularly when the subject was "niggers," a Washington obsession. Apparently, *they* were flowing into the city from the South, and as a result the streets were no longer safe to walk in.

The taxicab stopped before a restaurant on Connecticut Avenue above which, in four apartments, Clay and three other bachelors lived. The rent was low, and the location convenient: the Mayflower Hotel, where the movers and shakers met, was only a minute's walk away.

Clay seldom saw his neighbors but relations were pleasant. They were all rising men, and Clay did his best to get along with them. Early on, he had observed that most ambitious young men tend to gravitate to those who already have power; and though this was natural and necessary, too often in the process they neglected those who did not have power—like themselves—but some day would. Clay liked to think of himself as one who planned ahead. But in actual fact, he merely existed from day to day, waiting for a door to open. Meanwhile, he spun himself a wide web of relationships, just in case.

Clay's apartment was a single furnished room with

a double window overlooking Connecticut Avenue, a wide thoroughfare whose trees and low buildings made it seem more like the main street of some small town than a principal avenue of a national capital. Clay had never got over his first surprise at discovering that Washington was not a city but a town. Except for the huge and pretentious government buildings, the streets were pleasantly familiar even to a provincial's eye. In fact, the capital of his own state seemed to him in many ways more of a city than Washington with its slow Southern ways.

Clay let his trousers drop in the center of the room, flung his undershirt over a broken standing lamp which already supported a pajama top, kicked his shoes into a dark corner, stepped on the toes of his socks and pulled them off without once bending over, and kicked his drawers accurately in a high arc so that they landed on the knob of the bathroom door, from which they hung like a green and white striped banner. Then he allowed himself to fall, straight as felled timber, onto the unmade studio couch. A small breeze dried the moist flesh until his skin felt as if it were made of warm dry parchment that would tear if he moved. He did not move. The eye which was pressed into the pillow made everything look slightly double-exposed. For a moment he slept with eyes open.

A soft rapping at the door awakened him. Without dressing, he crossed to the door and opened it an inch, expecting to see one of the bachelors. Instead, he saw Miss Perrine, very nervous and bright-eyed.

"Oh," he said without enthusiasm. "Dolly."

"I was just in the neighborhood. I'm meeting Munson at the Continental, it's just a block from here, at eight, and I thought . . ."

He opened the door wide and ended her rattle. "Come on in," he said. "I was just thinking about you." She gasped when she saw that he wore no clothes.

"You'll catch your death," she said blushing but not retreating. He shut and locked the door behind her.

"In this heat? Come on, and get out of those hot clothes." He kissed her. She responded by biting his lower lip with tiny sharp teeth. He grumbled at the

41

pain. Somewhere Dolly Perrine had read that to bite means Passion. Clay had tried, without success, to disabuse her of this notion on the several occasions she had visited him, usually just before she was to meet Munson, her fiancé, who had a punctured eardrum and worked at the Mint. She was going to marry Munson because he was kind and considerate and steady; on the other hand, she could not get enough of Clay, who had casually taken her to bed the first week she had come to work for the Senator. At first she had tried to be sentimental but he would have none of it. He told her plainly that she was a big girl who did what she did because she wanted to and not because he had, with guile and promises, seduced her from virtue. "There's nothing in it. Nothing except fun."

"No love?" she had whispered, her face covered by the tangle of hair. He had replied with a hard expletive, and she had wept a little; but since he was a good lawyer, he had misrepresented nothing. He believed that each party to an agreement must fully understand his responsibilities. He also disliked telling lies, could not bear scenes, despised emotional excess. He liked neutrality and pleasure. Dolly Perrine gave pleasure. As for neutrality, he saw to it that her thoughts never strayed too far from the central idea of Munson and the Mint and the little house that they were going to buy on Vermont Avenue.

"What a mess," she said, looking about the room with the eye of the housewife she would be once her long engagement had ended and, from the chrysalis of a five-year courtship, she and Munson would together emerge into the world as a single great domestic moth.

"It's just me," said Clay, pouring a stiff shot of bourbon into a dusty glass. He seldom drank himself but he knew that whisky and Dolly went well together. With each drink she would become increasingly happy and useful in the act of love. And it *was* love, of course, though not in the way she had been taught to think of that grand passion: two superb faces projected thirty times life-size on a movie screen, offering to share with one another every thought, every dream that a pair of thirty times life-size brains could conjure up. Clay's love was for the flesh, no more. Also, the conquest was important. He could not have enough victories over women and, indirectly, over the men who did love them. Each time he took Dolly, he conquered Munson too.

Clay watched her as she undressed, a slow process involving many buttons, hooks and zippers. He enjoyed the metamorphosis between women clothed and woman nude. Clothed, she was armored and disguised, with legs lengthened by high heels, hips and breasts diminished by elastic. Naked what had been tall and slender suddenly became short and solid and one realized not only how small she was but how powerfully she was put together, unbreakable, made of earth. Compared to woman, man was a fragile nervous instrument all fire and air, no match for earth and water. Complaining about how light the room was and why didn't he ever draw the drapes, Dolly Perrine came to bed with him and they mixed the four elements for half an hour.

When Clay came out of the shower, Dolly was already half hooked and buttoned into her armor. Grinning happily, all tension gone, Clay pushed aside the disastrous hair and kissed the round mouth.

"What are you smiling at?" Dolly backed away suspiciously. "What's so funny?"

Like most women Clay knew, she was wary of humor on the no doubt legitimate ground that sooner or later the joke would be on her. Seeing the bewildered and suspicious face, Clay knew a moment of tenderness, something he seldom experienced in the sexual act. He kissed the tangled hair which was now inexorably making its way across her face, hairpins springing from the twisted depths like arrows fired by frightened forest dwellers.

"Nothing's funny. Everything's serious. I've got to get dressed. And you must put yourself in the mood for Munson." He pulled on a dress shirt.

Dolly stepped into shoes with long spike heels and said, "I don't understand you, Clay."

"I'm simple." He tied his black tie in the dust-streaked mirror.

Viciously, hopelessly, Dolly attacked her hair with

43

a comb. "Not really. In the office you're so free and easy and on the make but when I'm here . . ."

"On the make with girls?" Clay was sharp. He wanted to know exactly how he seemed to others.

"No. Senators." She got this out just as the central bang slid back over one eye, giving her a rakish look.

Clay did not allow himself to scowl. "That's what they pay me for. They put an ad in the papers: energetic young lawyer on the make to go to Washington to charm senators, small salary, large prospects." He adjusted the white double-breasted evening jacket, hoping the worn shirt cuffs would not be noticed.

"I still think it's better for you back home, better for anybody." This was Dolly's favorite theme. Washington was Versailles, glittering and corrupt, transforming simple yeomen into dandies and worse. Forlornly, she put away her mirror; the hair had won.

"Then why don't *you* go back?"

"I am back. This is where I come from, remember? Munson and I are both native-born Washingtonians." She rose, as though in pride.

Clay turned to her and started to laugh. She looked frightened. *"Now* what are you laughing at?"

"Something I just thought of. Nothing." He had indeed recalled a story one of the bachelors had told him.

"You're laughing at *me!*" The hands flew to the hair as though betrayed.

"I'm not. It's something one of the men who lives here told me, a funny story. He's British."

"What story?"

"When he was twenty-one his father gave him just three pieces of advice. First, never drink whisky with oysters. Second, never go hunting south of the Thames. Third, never have a woman before sundown because you might meet someone better later on."

"You are a bastard," said Dolly with deep feeling.

"I thought that was funny. Especially about hunting south of the Thames. I mean, what's wrong with south of the Thames?" But Dolly was already out the door.

As Dolly crossed the street, he called, "See you tomorrow." She did not look back. "Good night." Dolly continued along Connecticut Avenue. "Give my best to Munson." He could not resist this last. She broke into a run, careening back and forth on her high heels like a plump rowboat bucking a current.

* * *

When Clay had been first invited to the Chevy Chase Country Club he was disappointed by the simple wooden porch, set back from the suburban street. But once inside he felt that he had strayed into another century where rooms were vast and evocative of slow pleasures, where tall clocks seemed never to strike the hour, and manners were ritual.

Since tonight he was early, he went outside onto the terrace; here tennis players and golfers, their last games done, sat beneath striped umbrellas, drinking and chatting. They should have left by now, thought Clay severely; otherwise the scene gave him pleasure. To his right, behind trees, were the tennis courts and the swimming pool. To his left, as green and sweet as an eighteenth-century print of an English park, the golf course curved among soft hills and valleys and clumps of trees, indigo against the blue evening sky. In the darkest of the groves, fireflies darted.

"The rich have everything, don't they?" Clay turned and saw the short thick figure of the man who had sung at the party the evening before. He shook the short man's hand and flooded him with warm greetings; recalling, as he did, that he was a writer for the *Washington Tribune,* well liked by Enid. But what was his name?

"Why am I here? That's what I want to know. Will you please tell me? *What am I doing here?* In this place, with these people?" A flood of words was suddenly let loose by Clay's neutral observation that the Chevy Chase Country Club was "some place." "I loathe the rich. I hate politicians. I despise scheming young men." Clay felt a warm flush begin just inside his collar. He hoped that the guests beneath the umbrellas would not associate him with this extraordinarily unpleasant creature who was no doubt a Communist. "Most of all I hate politics. I hate the President.

I hate Congress. The Supreme Court is particularly awful. I detest the military. The Diplomatic Corps should be liquidated, preferably with poisoned canapés. I loathe Washington, District of Columbia, gem of the swampland, home of the chigger, wreathed in its poison ivy, its belly stuffed with cabbage cooked in bacon grease and indigestible Virginia hams which taste like scrapings from the keels of sunken ships. Oh, let my hate give me eloquence! Shall we have a drink."

This last was said in such a normal tone of voice that Clay almost missed it.

"Well, yes," said Clay, "I . . ."

"Could *use* a drink, I know. But for what? You were going to say 'use,' weren't you?"

"No," Clay lied, becoming angry. "I was going to say I'd like a drink."

"To think, *I* jumped to a conclusion!" His companion grinned. Clay hated him.

They entered the dimly lit bar. Each ordered a drink. Clay had made up his mind to be polite no matter what happened. Enid particularly liked this man . . . the forgetting of the name was exasperating, and put him at a disadvantage. His name was known, the other's was not, and so Clay was at a disadvantage for there was power in names.

"Why," began Clay carefully, not wanting to inspire another speech, "are you here, if you don't like Washington?"

"Because I am weak. Corrupt. Without purpose. Tempted by free drink . . . free food . . . drawn to the company of savages for whom I do an occasional trick, sing a song, tell the future, remind them that the ship of state is drunk."

"Are you?"

"No. But Rimbaud was. You have an open face, Clay. Never let life shut it. You have political ambition?"

"Yes, I do." Clay chose to use short hard words.

"I'll never understand why you people want to hold office. Now take that fraud James Burden Day."

"I'm Senator Day's administrative assistant."

The short man laughed. "Yes, I know you are. And of course you're loyal."

46

"Yes, I am."

"I said 'fraud' not to single your Senator out. The word was not used pejoratively. How could it be, in Washington? I only meant that he is like all the rest, only more successful. You wouldn't want to be employed by some sort of maverick, would you?"

The short man took a deep swallow of his drink. Clay had not disliked anyone quite so much in years. "I admit he has a charming voice, your Senator. And manner. I studied him last night at the party. He was new to me, in the flesh, that is. But I got his number quick enough. Actor! He's an actor. The way he uses his voice. The shift in accent. The ability to mimic. The mastery of the dying fall. At the moment he is playing Brutus but he could just as easily shift to Macbeth or to Lear, or, with particularly bad luck, to Timon. He can play anything but himself, having no self. Do references to Shakespeare bore you? Do books of any kind? I often find that any reference not immediately familiar, that is to say available in the morning papers, causes the people hereabouts to grow nervous, to search for the nearest exit."

"I can see why." Clay got this out very clear, and was very proud. The short man laughed contentedly. "You win! I am a bore. And I bore myself most of all, particularly in his Godawful city."

"Why don't you leave?"

"No money. I'm poor. I have to work. My job is here. Imagine going to the movies in the *daytime,* a habit more vicious than sniffing heroin, and equally addictive because I love what I see. I weep for Joan Crawford. God, how they treat her! The swine! And little Jean Arthur with that crinkly way she has of wrinkling up her nose . . . it's so real. In fact, everything I see there in those dark theatres with their smell of feet and popcorn seems to me far more real than all this!" He took in the whole empty room with a baroque sweep of his arm, which, as if by magic, produced Enid in the doorway.

"What're you two doing in there?" Enid was silver tonight, straight and slender, more than ever an Indian princess. "Come on in here, the party's started."

"I was telling Mr. Overboard how much I loved Washington."

"Overbury."

"He knows perfectly well who you are. I think we must snub you tonight, Harold."

"I have been snubbed by masters . . . and mistresses."

Clay looked at Enid sharply but she pulled him into the next room, leaving Harold alone with glass held high, proposing a toast to the legitimate government of Spain, now besieged at Valencia.

"What a perfect son of a bitch."

"Harold? Don't take him seriously. He only wants to needle people. To get a laugh. Listen . . ."

But Clay could not listen nor Enid tell, for they were suddenly stopped by a pale nearsighted young woman, glittering with beads.

"Enid Sanford! Beautiful, *beautiful* in silver. Such a nice color for you."

"Thank you, Mrs. Bloch."

"I'm giving a little party Sunday, very *intime*." The French was mispronounced, to Enid's obvious delight. "Do come, at six. It's for . . ." She named an elderly Justice of the Supreme Court. "He is so amusing." Even Clay smiled at this. As Enid once said, cripples had been known to throw down their crutches and flee at the old man's approach. "He loves relaxing among a few congenial souls." It was generally believed that the Justice was having an affair with Mrs. Bloch, a last senile outburst before the final summing up. "And he does admire you, Enid. He adores young people."

"Well, I shall certainly try, Mrs. Bloch."

"After six, any time."

"Allow me to present . . ." Enid began to introduce Clay, but Mrs. Bloch would have none of it. She had spied an ambassador; she was gone.

"I wonder how that awful Jew got in here?" Enid was thoughtful.

"According to the gossip columns, she's everywhere."

"That's because she *knows* all the gossip writers. I think she pays them to write about her. Well, she'll

48

never get to our house, and we'll never go to hers, poor thing. She should've stayed in New Jersey or wherever she came from. Washington's not for her. Now, Clay, listen, about last night . . ."

"Sorry?"

"Of course I'm not!" Enid's dark eyes reflected the flame from a candelabra. She *was* beautiful, he thought, and felt inadequate.

"Peter knows."

"Peter knows what?"

"My brother. I couldn't tell you last night. He saw us. In the poolhouse."

"Oh, Christ! Why didn't I shut that damned door?"

"Well, it's done, and I don't know what to do."

"Will he tell your father?"

"I don't think so. I don't know. He's such a liar, they might not believe him."

"A liar?" This was new to Clay.

"Always. Ever since he could talk he would say things that were awful."

"But untrue."

"Of course." A party of young people waved at Enid from the door, and made their way toward her. "We've got to decide what to do," she said in a rush. "Here comes those friends of mine from New York."

"What about your father?"

"He's here. Over there."

The friends surrounded them. Enid's cheek was kissed by girls, hand wrung by boys. "Talk to him!" Enid cried from the center of the demonstration.

Blaise Sanford was seated in a corner with two gray men, discussing—what else?—politics. In the next room the dancing had begun. Although the party was for the young, the old were on hand. Like a chorus, they sat in the deep chairs, watching their successors move through intricate dances, aware that eventually they would be forced to surrender even the deep chairs to the young dancers who in turn would have yielded the dance floor to others, younger still. How *not* to be forgotten? wondered Clay. How to retain the floor for life? That was the question ambition asked, and did not answer.

"Mr. Overbury?" A lean, gray-blond man came between him and the dance floor. "I'm Edgar Nillson, a friend . . . or would-be friend, of Senator Day."

"I know." Clay smiled a political smile and shook the man's hand warmly. "You're from New York. But originally from Maryland." Clay knew that he was probably betraying too much knowledge, but if he was, it served the Senator right for not taking him into his confidence.

"I see I am being investigated. Well, luckily there's nothing to hide. All evidence has been destroyed."

Clay laughed: very cool, Mr. Nillson, very cool indeed.

"I want to buy some Indian land but I'm afraid the Senator's not being helpful."

"How could he be?"

"I do the Indians no great harm. The price, by the way, is a good one."

"Beads, wampum, firewater?"

Nillson laughed. "You're very quick, Mr. Overbury. No, it's better than that. Actually money."

"But less than the land is worth?"

"Who can say?"

"You can or you wouldn't want to buy."

"I'm willing to help the Senator with the nomination for President in 1940."

"What does he say to that?"

"Nothing."

"How can you help him?"

"Money. Influence. And then there is our friend Blaise Sanford." Nillson drew Clay from the dancers to the chair, to Blaise himself who looked up. "Edgar! What are you doing in town? Sit down. Hello, Clay." This was cold.

"Good evening, sir," and "A little business, Blaise," overlapped as the two men sat down on either side of the publisher, chairs still warm from previous clients.

"Wish I'd known you were here. We gave a little party last night. Would've had you there. To celebrate Mr. Roosevelt's defeat."

"And Senator Day's victory." Nillson smiled at Clay.

50

Blaise looked shrewdly from one to the other. "Business?"

Nillson was serene. "I want Senator Day to be elected President in 1940."

"Not a bad idea. What do you think, Clay?" Aside to Nillson, "Prejudiced testimony."

"Of course," said Clay, "I'd like nothing better. And after today, it's possible. We talked to the Vice President."

Like most Congressional aides, Clay tended to use "we" when properly speaking the pronoun should have been "he," a habit he disliked in others but tolerated in himself.

Blaise rewarded him with a look of interest. "Have you got him?"

"Yes."

"Good."

Nillson rose. "I'll ring you tomorrow, Blaise."

"Yes, do. Come out to the house for lunch. Swimming. It's going to be another scorcher."

Nillson disappeared into the room where the dancers were, and Clay was aware that anxious men were hovering nearby, waiting for their chance to kiss hands and receive the accolade of publicity. He should go but he chose to stay.

"Who is Mr. Nillson?" Clay was bold. After all, he had nothing to lose except Enid, a million dollars, and the support of a powerful press lord.

"*Who* is Mr. Nillson?" Blaise repeated in a tone which made it clear that what he meant was "Who is Clay Overbury?" "Well, he is a friend of mine. In oil. I don't know what else. Burden and he ought to be friends. Good for both of them." Blaise looked about him as though for help. Clay was dogged.

"Sir, about Enid?"

"What about her?" The dark eyes were suddenly turned on him full force. In the scowling red face, Clay saw Enid. "What about her?"

"We've been seeing each other quite a bit this summer."

"No." Blaise was flat.

"No?"

"No, you're not going to marry her."

51

"I didn't say I was."

"And I'm saying don't even think of it."

Clay felt terror and rage in equal parts. Rage won. "And why not?" His voice shook. But from tension, he told himself, not fear.

"I don't need to answer you."

"And I don't need to be insulted by you."

"Which ends the discussion, doesn't it?"

"Yes." Clay rose, head swimming. "For the moment," he said, "that ends it." But Blaise was already signaling for others to join him. Contemplating murder, Clay entered the room where the dancers were. From a waiter he took a glass of whisky and drank it down in a gulp. The warmth was quick to come. For the first time he realized that people drank to make bearable the unbearable. Then Clay plunged into the evening, swam through the dancers and did not reach shore until midnight, when drinking was heavy, flirting obvious, and the deep chairs empty.

"What shall we do?" Enid faced him on the screened-in porch. Outside, couples walked together in the dark, their courses through the night clearly marked by the steady burning of cigarettes, unlike the darting pulsing light fireflies give.

"What do *you* want?" He evaded responsibility. Some day a case would be made, his legal mind told him, and he wanted to be able to prove that he had not used undue influence. The choice would be hers, not his. She began to make it.

"Let's go somewhere, for the night."

"The poolhouse?" He smiled.

"No, never again! Not after Peter. Let's drive to . . . to Maryland."

"Elkton?" A leading question: Elkton was where Washington couples went to be married quickly, without formality.

"Did you talk to Father?"

"Does anyone?"

"He can be disagreeable."

"He was."

"He dislikes young men. They're not important enough for him."

"For you?"

"I'm not looking for importance. It *was* the first time, you know." She had told him that the night before, during the storm, and he had been impressed, if dubious. Yet it was quite possible that she was telling the truth. Certainly he had no evidence to the contrary. Since the winter, they had met casually at parties, less casually on weekends. The night after he broke his nose at Warrenton, they made love for the first time. She had been wickedly amused by his pain, insisting that he kiss her repeatedly despite the huge bandage. But not until last night had they gone "all the way," as she put it.

"What about Diana?" Enid looked at him suddenly with her father's face.

"Diana?" he repeated, pretending innocence.

"She's supposed to be in love with you."

"I work for her father. I like her."

"Did you ever go to bed with her?"

He shook his head. "No. Not even on a rubber mattress, on the floor."

Enid laughed. "I'll never live that down, will I?" Clay, who loved her, found himself almost liking her. At moments she had a harsh straightforward humor about herself that was unlike any other girl's he had known.

"We'll give it some thought," she said finally. "Now, let's go dance. I'm awfully young, you know. Even for my age. Everyone says so." Together they went inside, where something energetic and noisy was being danced by flushed couples. Just as well, thought Clay. He needed time to win over Blaise. Also he must, somehow, tell Diana that he could not marry her. He owed her that much; he owed the Senator more.

4

Across the plain, the two moons rose, turning the tower to silver. That was the signal. He switched off the glider. Then, wrapped in the special cloak that the

Grand Murg had given him, he strode back into the city where the army was waiting.

"I don't give a damn what she wants! It's what I want."

"But Blaise, be reasonable. After all, it's done."

In the main square of the ancient city, older than recorded time, the Thark army was drawn up. When they saw him, they cheered, recognizing the cloak of the Grand Murg.

"We'll get an annulment."

"But how can you if they . . . if she . . ."

For a long moment, he looked out across the sea of cheering Tharks. He felt the power rising in him. He glanced up at the balcony where Thuvia stood, wearing the helium crown of the old empire. She waved to him. He saluted her with the Winchester rifle his father had given him for Christmas.

"I knew we should have gone to Watch Hill in June. It's all your fault, Blaise, for keeping us here because of your dreary politics. Well, now she's gone and done it. She's married one. A politician. You should be very pleased."

There was a sound of glass breaking. Peter tried to incorporate it into the fantasy, but failed. Sadly he allowed the vision of Thuvia and the Tharks to break into bits, along with the highball glass that his father had apparently thrown at either his mother or the floor. He looked through the open French window. Between his father and mother lay a broken glass, its contents staining the rug.

"Look what you've done to the carpet."

"To hell with the carpet."

"To hell with everything. That's really what you'd like." This was unexpected. Frederika usually stayed to the periphery of a scene. Direct statements of any sort were not her style.

"What do *you* suggest I do?" Blaise challenged her directly.

"Pour some water on the rug. It will dilute the stain."

"And after I've done that?"

"Oh, whatever you like." Her positive moment was gone. "But try to be pleasant while they're here."

54

"I ought to have him arrested for seducing a minor."

"She's not a minor, in Maryland, and he didn't seduce her, he married her."

Peter sat back in the deck chair, shutting out the voices with an effort of will. The day was hot. He was dressed for tennis but at the last moment he had rung his friend Scotty and told him that if they played there was danger of sunstroke. Everyone said so. Besides, he was mortally tired, too tired even to move from the fiery terrace to the pool where there was shade.

Enid had married Clay in Maryland, early that morning. She had telephoned to break the news while the family was at breakfast. Everyone behaved characteristically. Frederika had wanted to know where they had spent the night (in the car). Blaise had said that he wanted never to see either of them again, to which Enid had answered: "Don't be silly, we'll be home for lunch." Peter had decided that considering what had happened in the poolhouse, marriage was a dull ending to a splendid event. He had by now played back the film of what he had seen so many times that it was almost as if he had been a participant. But unimaginative or not, his sister's marriage was at least a break in the usual round of the family's life. For that he was grateful.

"Anyway, it's all your fault," Frederika repeated her single argument. "If we'd only gone to Watch Hill, instead of . . ."

". . . of staying here, Clay and I would never have been married. That's absolutely true." Enid was in the room, wearing a crumpled silver evening dress and silver shoes. She hobbled toward them. "I lost a heel in Elkton. It snapped right off on the steps of the house where the Justice of the Peace lives. Clay's outside, in the car. I said I'd come in first and see how things are. I see how they are." She made a face. "Father, why do you feel you *have* to make a scene?"

"I haven't said a word since you arrived." Blaise's voice was startlingly agreeable.

"But on the telephone you were awfully loud. And now, your face! Mother, what are we going to do with him?"

"You *slept* in the car?" Arrangements always intrigued Frederika.

"We sat up in the car. We haven't been to sleep at all. I better get out of this dress and change my shoes."

"No," said Blaise. Then he noticed Peter in the window. "Go away!" He shouted like a farmer to a bird that has suddenly landed on a new-sown field. Peter went away. He walked around the house, ducking through the thick boxwood until he came to the main driveway where Clay sat in his Plymouth coupé, reading the *Tribune*.

"Congratulations, I guess." Peter shook Clay's hand, noticing that the hand was sweaty and that a day-old beard somewhat blurred the classic chin. Yet despite eyes red-rimmed from lack of sleep, Clay was as handsome as ever.

"It was sudden," said Clay. "What's going on in there?"

"It was sudden here, too."

"How's your father taking it?"

"Upset. Why?"

"I don't know. Do you?"

Peter shook his head. "Maybe he wanted her to marry . . . I don't know, someone else."

"Someone rich?"

"I don't think so. I don't know. He can be peculiar."

"Well, it's done."

Enid came limping out the front door. "Clay, come on in. Oh, it's you," she said irrelevantly to Peter. "Enjoying all the fuss?"

"Not as much as you."

Enid ignored this. She turned to Clay. "He wants to talk to you." Clay got out of the car.

"Good luck," said Peter.

Enid started back to the house, stumbled and almost fell. Angrily she took off both shoes and flung them into the boxwood. "Come on," she said to Clay. "Let's see if you can handle him."

5

Handling Blaise was not an easy task, if only because it was impossible to know precisely *what* was being handled. Blaise greeted Clay politely, and offered him a drink. Then, since the first of the lunch guests were not due for an hour, he proposed that they go to the pool for a swim. Frederika and Enid were as baffled as Clay by this particular tactic.

At the door to the poolhouse, Clay had a moment's guilt. But Blaise took his arm cheerfully. "I guess you've been here quite a few times this summer."

Clay wondered if Peter had indeed told his father. But if Blaise knew anything, he was too intent on being amiable to mention it now.

"You probably know which suit will fit you." On a hat rack a dozen men's bathing suits hung. Clay took one. Blaise another. Then, still chatting lightly, both men undressed.

"Do you know Senator Barkley well?"

"Fairly well, yes, sir."

"I was for Pat Harrison myself to be the majority leader. But we must let Franklin win an occasional battle."

"Senator Day likes Mr. Barkley but he thinks he's weak."

"Rubber stamp for the President?"

"Yes, sir."

As Clay removed his shorts, he was aware of the other's sharp eyes studying him. His face was suddenly hot, as though he were blushing; perhaps he was. He turned away as he put on the suit, recalling as sensible the Bible's injunction against beholding the father's nakedness. Not only was it unnerving to see where one had come from, it was depressing to look at the body of any man past his prime and observe one's own future in the ruin.

As Clay tied the strings of the bathing suit, he glanced in a mirror and saw that Blaise was staring at him with a look of such extraordinary hatred that he could actually feel it, like a branding iron suddenly slammed between the shoulder blades. But when Blaise spoke, the voice was pleasant. "Bring your drink outside. We'll sit in the shade. Not that it does much good this time of year. All your fault, you know."

"My fault?" Now it begins. Clay stiffened, ready for the assault.

Blaise smiled. "Congress's fault, for staying in session through July."

"The President's fault, for trying to force the Court bill down our throats."

Blaise nodded; he led Clay to the deck chairs beside the pool.

"And killing poor Joe Robinson in the process. I wonder if it's true what they say, that old Joe would have been appointed to the Court, *if* he could get the bill through the Senate."

Clay was pleased to be on familiar ground. "I don't know, sir. There's a theory that the President was just using him and that as soon as the bill had passed, he'd appoint four new Justices like, well, Hutchins in Chicago, you know, left-wingers, bomb-throwers."

"You one?" Blaise turned toward Clay, who promptly felt guilt, though innocent.

"I work for Senator Day."

"Not an answer."

"Well, I'm a conservative, on my own time, too. For one thing, I don't accept Keynesian economics."

"Atrocious fellow. I've met him. La-de-dah. Probably a pansy. But he's got the whole Administration under his thumb. Except for Harry Hopkins. He's defected now. Wants to be President, silly ass. But you can't be President and traffic with parlor pinks and socialists. Poor Harry thinks 1940 is *his* year. Just like Burden."

"I think the Senator's going to make it."

"Maybe." Blaise stretched his short blunt legs; blue varicose veins coiled round the calves. "What will you do for money?"

"We have a good deal of support in the West. Some of the oil people . . ."

"I meant you. And Enid."

Clay felt stupid; he had missed a point. "My salary's enough for two."

"For Enid?"

"Why not?"

"You expect me to finance you. Why should I?"

"Why shouldn't you?"

Blaise gave him a sharp look. "Well, that's a fair question. I disapprove of this marriage because Enid's too young. She should see more of the world than just Washington. Get to know more people."

"What's wrong with me?"

"No money."

"But I will have some. And there's enough for now."

"What sort of future do you see for yourself?"

"Excellent."

"In what?"

"Politics."

"You don't make money in politics, you spend it."

"I'm not worried."

"Neither am I. Look here, if I paid you—oh, a hundred thousand dollars—would you let us annul the marriage?"

Clay laughed, in spite of himself. "I never realized people actually said things like that. No."

"You love Enid and you can't live without her?" Blaise mocked him.

Clay looked at him with a loathing that must have been perfectly apparent, for Blaise suddenly sat back straight in the deck chair, re-crossing stubby legs. "I said nothing about love, Mr. Sanford. But since you enjoy spelling things out, I should tell you that I don't intend to have an annulment in my past for political enemies to make something of." Clay grinned at the older man, in a way which he knew was winning, at least under the proper circumstances. "You'll have to think of something else . . . sir."

Blaise was silent. He sipped his drink. He studied a rotten tree stump which had been converted by ants into a vast and intricate city. "I dislike being *had*." The colloquialism was odd on Blaise's lips. "I know what you are. Poor boy from the provinces who comes

59

to the capital to make his fortune. Then marries a rich girl and lives happily ever after, on her money. Only, *she's* not happy. Well, I swore it would never happen to Enid."

"What did you want for her?"

"Someone like me."

"With money?"

"With family."

"You are a snob, sir."

"I have never denied it. And let me tell you, this city is Calvary for the snob, for anyone with values, having to put up with all these clowns and medicine men who've tricked the people into voting for them . . ."

"Not all are clowns."

"The ones who are not are even worse. They want power for its own sake. Like Franklin."

"Like you."

"I am here because it amuses me to stir things up." He looked at the tree stump. "I suppose you've already gone to bed with her. Is she pregnant?"

"Not as far as I know."

Blaise sprang to his feet and in one swift movement crossed the brick terrace and dived into the pool. Clay followed, more slowly, aware that his sides were streaked with nervous sweat. He did a jackknife from the diving board, straightening out sharply just before he hit the water, eyes open to the cool green blur which, he knew, automatically slows the beating of the heart. He swam the length of the pool underwater. Reluctantly, he came to the surface, to find Blaise sitting on the edge of the pool, watching him.

"I was on the Yale swimming team." Blaise paid him back for the showy display on the diving board.

"I was never on any team. I had to work my way through school. I stoked furnaces."

"Bully for you."

"I wasn't boasting."

"I was. Enid is a . . . generous girl. I don't know why she married you but it was probably because she wants to give you something she thinks you need, like money."

"I need it, but not that badly."

"You won't get it."

60

Clay wondered what would happen if he were to strike his father-in-law. It would be a satisfying thing to do. Subsequent relations, though cool, would at least be honest. But he controlled his temper. He stretched his arms; flexed muscles instead. "You've still not given one good reason why you're so much against my marrying Enid."

"I'm against it because, damn it, I don't want to make it easy for you."

"Make what easy?"

"Everything. The game you're up to. You mean to rise and I don't want you to."

"Why not?"

But Blaise did not answer. He got to his feet and went back to the poolhouse. Clay called after him: "Is it because *you* didn't rise? Because you couldn't?" Clay was bold. "Because you were too rich to fight like the other boys?" But Blaise had disappeared into the changing room.

Clay waited until he was certain that the other was dressed. Then he returned to the poolhouse. Blaise was combing his thin hair. He ignored Clay, who dressed quickly. As they were about to leave, Blaise turned to him. "I acquired power on my own."

"You had money to start with."

"How I got power is immaterial. What matters is that I have it and you want it."

"Not your sort, no."

"All sorts are the same, as you'll discover. Well, it's not going to be easy, is it?" He was genial. "Now for lunch, and the spreading of good news." He smiled. "Senator Day is joining us. And I told him to bring Diana. I thought you'd like that." As Blaise led Clay between the rows of boxwood, he took his arm with a show of affection that would have impressed a bystander.

6

"I told you, I have all sorts of friends." Mr. Nillson beamed at Burden.

"So I see." For the moment he was trapped on the terrace with his tempter. At the edge of the lawn, under an elm, Clay and Diana faced one another. She was pale and silent. He was vehement in whatever it was he was saying.

Lunch had been a disaster. Clay had tried once or twice to warn them of what had happened but Blaise saw to it that he was never given the opportunity. The announcement, when it came over dessert, was altogether shocking. Burden had got up quite involuntarily, wanting to go to Diana who sat across the table from him. But if she needed comforting, she did not show it. Once on his feet, Burden had no choice but to go to Clay and congratulate him. By then everyone was up from table.

In the drawing room, Blaise played his favorite role of toastmaster. The speech: 'I won't say I wasn't surprised. I was. We all were. But that's the way people do things nowadays. Actually, we should all be grateful. Because now no one has to buy them a thing. No silver. No presents. No nothing." There was laughter at this. Enid, Burden noticed, looked tired and grim. Clay was tense. Only Blaise appeared oblivious to everything except his own enjoyment of the situation. He wished the young couple a long and happy marriage. Toasts were solemnly drunk. Then the party moved outdoors onto the terrace.

"As a matter of fact, one of the reasons I'm here is to talk to Blaise about you."

"That's kind of you." Burden had wanted to leave right after lunch, but Diana must be allowed her talk with Clay, leaving him at Mr. Nillson's mercy.

"We're about to start a Day for President campaign."

Burden stared at Mr. Nillson with that look of amused disbelief which witnesses before Senate committees invariably found alarming. But apparently nothing alarmed Mr. Nillson.

"We will probably set up our first organization in Washington. With a few celebrated names on the stationery, like Blaise. Not me, don't worry. I shall be entirely in the background, as always—the unofficial treasurer." He emphasized the last word with a little grin. "With two hundred and fifty thousand in the kitty, your campaign would be nicely launched. Of course that's only a beginning."

Diana had turned from Clay. He seemed not to have finished what he was about to tell her. He reached out a hand as though to draw her back but she was walking swiftly across the lawn to the terrace. Blaise's son stopped her on the steps and said something; she tried to smile. Burden saw the pain and excused himself. He crossed to Diana and the boy. "Shall we go?" he asked.

"I think so, yes. Where's Enid?"

Peter shrugged. "Gone to bed, I expect. They were up all night."

"Tell her how . . . glad I am."

"I will."

Burden took Diana's arm protectively. He was surprised to find himself enjoying the situation. "Father Comforts Jilted Daughter." Life often seemed to him like a series of old prints with such titles as "Statesman at Bay." "A Death in the Family." "Honor Betrayed." It was difficult at best to feel anything about others. But he tried, for he truly believed that one ought to be good. In any case, no one could fault him for not making the effort. Unfortunately, though he loved his daughter, he liked Clay, and that made things difficult, particularly now when Clay, breathing hard, stepped between them and the door to the drawing room. He had run the length of the terrace.

"I'm sorry, Senator. Not giving you any warning. But it happened so suddenly. We didn't plan it."

"Obviously." That was too cold, Burden decided. "I know how things are. She's most attractive. Congratulations."

Clay was nervous, and Burden was pleased. In their somewhat complex relations it was always Clay who was cool and Burden who tended to shift this way and that as emotions swayed him. But Clay was hardly cool now and Burden realized that he was afraid he might be fired. For a moment Burden had toyed with the idea. It would certainly gratify Diana who had a vindictive streak known only to Burden, who saw himself in her. But Clay's job was safe; Burden could not do without him.

"I'll see you Monday." He smiled vaguely at the young man. Then he and Diana went inside to say goodbye to their hostess. But Frederika was not to be found. She was upstairs, said the butler, with Miss Enid.

"Telling her the facts of life, I'll bet!" Blaise burst in on them. "What do mothers and daughters talk about at such times?"

"I don't know," said Burden, "having never been a mother or a daughter."

"Diana, what do they say to one another? You're a daughter. Tell us the secrets of women."

"I don't really know. I've never been married. So I haven't been talked to. I suppose it's warnings women give to one another."

"Warnings about what?" Blaise seemed really to want to know.

"Men. What else? The common enemy." Diana's voice almost broke.

"Well, well, what have we here, Burden? An enemy of man?"

"She exaggerates." Burden tried to maneuver Diana to the front door but Blaise would not let her go.

"I'm sure *you* won't surprise your father the way Enid surprised me."

"I'm not awfully good at surprises. Anyway, I'm not apt to. It's not as if there were anyone interested in me."

"Come now," Burden said, growing alarmed. "You have your beaux." He turned to Blaise. "And I hate them all, don't you? Yet why should a young man who likes one's daughter seem such a threat?"

"Well, the threat has become reality in this house." Blaise was suddenly hard. "I hope you have better luck. Both of you. Oh, here's something Ed Nillson wanted me to give you. I don't know what it is. Probably a mash note. He admires you tremendously." Blaise gave Burden an envelope.

"Thank you for lunch," said Burden. "And the surprise," he could not keep from adding.

"It was not exactly *my* surprise." Blaise helped them into the car, which Henry had brought around. "But we must take what comes." As Burden and Diana drove off, Blaise remained in the driveway, waving as though he were never going to see them again.

"He was unexpectedly cruel, I thought," said Burden finally, realizing that they must soon come to the point.

"He's in love with her. Why shouldn't he marry her?"

"I didn't mean Clay. I meant Blaise."

"I didn't notice, I'm afraid." She kept her face turned from him as they drove through the green Virginia jungle.

"You wanted to marry Clay." Like a surgeon who must operate without anesthetic, Burden made the first incision swiftly. The skin broke. The patient gasped, but survived.

"Yes. You might say that I did."

A quaint way of putting it, Burden thought; one might *say* anything. "What did he tell you just now, on the lawn?"

"I don't remember."

"I'm sorry. It's not my business, I know."

Diana looked at him, eyes dry and bright; the patient was running a fever. "No. I really mean I don't remember. I couldn't concentrate. He kept talking and I kept thinking: he's married Enid, and what do I do now? I suppose he said he was sorry. I don't know. He was nervous, and Clay is never nervous."

"The money must be irresistible."

"No!" Diana was vehement. "I'm sure it wasn't for the money, or not very much. I'm afraid it was for Enid. Look at her! Who can compete with that?" And then the patient had a relapse. The sobs were small, more like an attack of hiccups, thought Burden, no longer the skilled surgeon of the heart but a kindly

65

general practitioner, offering a shoulder for a girl to cry on, only to be rebuffed.

Diana pulled away from him, covering her face with her hands. Not until they crossed Chain Bridge did she put them down. In silence they drove beside the malodorous canal where horse-drawn barges moved slowly through the summer haze. Just before the first of the tumbledown Negro shanties at the edge of Georgetown, she said, "You won't do anything, will you? To Clay?"

"Fire him? No. I need him."

"I wish you would."

"Fire him?"

"Yes!" The jaw set. How like his father she was! The blood *does* continue! Nothing dies, ever. The thought intoxicated him. He would continue. "You don't mean that. You're not that petty."

"I do mean it, and I am that . . . furious. I would like to see him dead."

"Diana . . ." He tried to recall the name of Medea's father.

"I'll get over it. I'm sorry to make such a fuss."

"Did he ever . . . say that he wanted to marry you?"

Diana stared through glass at the dark rose brick of Georgetown. "Yes," she said to the window. "He did. Last Christmas. At the Sulgrave Club. Before a dance. I was wearing my first black dress. The one Mother didn't like. 'You look thirty years old,' she said, 'and in mourning.' But I thought I looked rather good. So did Clay apparently. We were to marry as soon as Congress adjourned, this spring. But Congress went on, and on, and Enid got him, in July."

"We'll adjourn next week, I think." Burden was deliberately irrelevant. "Shall we go North somewhere? To Maine? Would you like that? Bar Harbor?"

But Diana was no longer listening. She had withdrawn inside herself. The patient was now in coma, and nature must do the rest. Like all medical practitioners, he relied ultimately on the body's recuperative powers.

Then Burden realized that he was still clutching the envelope Blaise had given him. He opened it, expecting to be shocked. He was. The letter contained

66

a check drawn on a New York bank to the amount of two hundred fifty thousand dollars, made payable to the "James Burden Day for President Committee," and signed by Edgar Carl Nillson, Treasurer. He glanced quickly to see if Diana had noticed the contents of the envelope; she had not. Quickly, he tore the check into tiny pieces, and threw them like confetti into the street.

He would be the President but without the help of Nillson. If he was not true to himself, he was nothing. Old saws occurred to him. He recalled the McGuffey Reader he had studied as a child, on every page a moral lesson. Despite later knowledge, he still believed it all. Honesty is the best policy. A stitch in time saves nine. Every man has his price. No. *Not true!* He crumpled the envelope and with finger and thumb shot the wad straight at the bronze statue of an admiral. Full steam ahead! That was more like it. And then on January 20, 1941: *I, James Burden Day, do solemnly swear . . .* I will be good.

TWO

1

"OH, VERY GOOD! Very, *very* good!" Mrs. Foskett beamed. Short fingers tapped the upturned cards, as though sending them messages by code.

"What is very good?" Burden looked at the display of cards. A queen of diamonds was the only face card. He recalled that diamonds meant wealth.

"You have been very worried about money."

"Isn't everyone?"

"No, not eveyone. Not by any means. Some very poor people never worry about money and some very rich people do nothing else. Oh, I could write a book!"

"Don't, Mrs. Foskett! Ever!" He played at alarm but there was always the genuine fear that Mrs. Foskett might one day spill the beans, and there were some most distinguished beans to be spilled. At least a dozen Senators that he knew of came to her old brick house in California Street to have their fortunes told. One member of the Cabinet never made a move without first telephoning Mrs. Foskett to find out whether or not the stars were auspicious. It was remarkable how many sophisticated men were superstitious. He himself did not actually believe that the future could be charted since tomorrow was an abstraction which, literally, did not exist. Yet often one needed hints as to how to act, and he had found that many of Mrs. Foskett's intuitions had been extraordinarily useful; nor was he alone. She was by far the most succesful of a considerable tribe of fortune tellers, handwriting analysts, and astrologers who had taken up lucrative residence in the capital of a nation as yet uninspired by a new religion.

68

"Your money situation will improve quite soon." She studied the cards a moment. "Before the end of the year, I should say." Burden kept his face a mask. He tried never to give her clues.

"Also . . . oh, this is good! In the next three weeks there will be news which will please you very, very much. It has to do with . . ." She frowned, as though puzzled. She gave him a swift look but he was non-committal. She shuffled the cards expertly; then the brown fingers turned up certain cards. "It concerns your career so I suppose that must mean your campaign for the nomination next year. You see, there it is, the ace in combination with . . ."

"*Will* I be nominated?" Never before had he asked her such a direct question.

"Goodness! You do want to know everything. Well, it's not for me but for the cards to say. And you know how they are. Sometimes they are right *on the nose*. Other times they don't seem to make any sense at all." She stopped and looked at what she had dealt. "Someone close to you is causing you great grief."

This was almost true. Diana had moved to an apartment near the Library of Congress where she was now working. When she did visit Rock Creek Park, she was dutiful but uninformative. He had no idea whom she saw or what she did. Wanting to avoid Clay and Enid, she had abandoned all her old acquaintances, taking up instead with obscure New Dealers attached to the various new agencies.

"Your daughter must be very careful about her health. Particularly the kidneys. You must tell her to have a thorough medical checkup immediately. I don't like the look of these cards at all. Not at all." Mrs. Foskett gathered in the deck. "That's it, Senator. I know how irritating it is not to find out immediately what one wants to know. But we must be patient. Meanwhile, I'm working on your horoscope, where some very interesting things are beginning to show up, very interesting indeed! I particularly like the look of your Sun. It's a *good* Sun. I'll be in touch with you when I know more."

Mrs. Foskett led him to the front door. He paid her, feeling as always that he was leaving a whorehouse. "I suppose you'll be going to the garden party for the King and Queen?"

"Didn't the cards tell you that?" He could not resist this.

"Not a word from the cards but I read your name on the British Ambassador's list this morning in the paper."

"Yes, I'm going. We're also going to the dinner tonight, at the White House." He wondered why he had added that. It sounded as if he were boasting. In any case, he had been invited not because the President wanted him but because protocol required his presence.

"How exciting! I must say I haven't seen Washington so steamed up over anything since the Prince of Wales came to town, remember? I was there the day when he planted a tree at the Cathedral. What a handsome boy he was, and how badly he turned out. Cancer. They'll do it every time if they haven't got a good Moon. You have a good Moon, Senator, a *steady* romantic life."

"You will make me blush, Mrs. Foskett!"

"Oh, Senator, if only I could! Well, give the Queen my regards. I like the way she does her hair, so courageous."

* * *

Pennsylvania Avenue was already roped off for the parade from Union Station to the White House. Burden had not been asked to be in attendance at the station when the President and Cabinet received the King and Queen. But he did not in the least mind. He was doing quite well as it was. Tonight would be his first White House dinner since the Court fight two years before. It would be amusing to see all the contenders gathered in one place for the President had, no doubt deliberately, seen to it that nearly everyone who wanted his place in 1941 would be at the White House, except young Mr. Dewey.

Burden entered his office to be told that "Dewey is leading Roosevelt by four per cent in the Gallup Poll!" Clay was exuberant. "The President couldn't

70

run for a third term even if he wanted to. The Republicans would lick him."

"The country's going conservative. No doubt of it." Burden looked at Cicero, as though for confirmation. The telephone rang. Clay answered it. "Yes, the Senator's here. No, he's not available. He's going to the garden party. Yes. I'll tell him. Thanks." Clay put down the receiver. "Man from Hearst. They want to talk to you about the Gallup Poll. They'll call back tomorrow, for an interview."

"In which we shall say nothing while suggesting everything." Burden had not been so contented in years; he wondered why. Today's pageant? Mrs. Foskett? The Gallup Poll? For the moment all things conspired to make him happy and he was not one to quarrel with providence.

He went to the closet and took out morning clothes. "Unbearable to have to wear this costume today."

"I'm glad I'm not going."

"Is Enid?"

"I don't think so." Clay promptly changed the subject; he never discussed his marital life with Burden, who was duly grateful. He disliked confidences. "I'm going over to the House Office Building. One of the Texans is 'pourin',' for all those who weren't invited to the Embassy."

"Find out what they think of Garner." The collar was much too tight. He scowled at himself in the mirror.

"I plan to."

"And me." Burden smiled at himself in the mirror.

"That's why I'm going. I think that of all the conservatives we've got the best chance."

"They called me a radical when I first came to town." Burden adjusted the morning coat. It was too snug about the hips. "I wanted to nationalize the railroads and smash the trusts. Well . . ." He sighed, wondering which had changed the most since 1914, the world or himself.

Miss Perrine appeared at the door. "Mr. Overbury, your wife's on the phone."

"I'll take it in here."

"You *do* look nice, Senator." Miss Perrine smiled at her employer.

"Thank you, my dear. I suppose I do look nice, by Senatorial standards." She giggled and shut the door behind her. "Unhappily, Senate standards are not the highest," Burden added for Clay's benefit but Clay was talking to his wife.

"That's all right. No, I understand. I'll see you later." Clay hung up and said, "She *is* going to the garden party. Well, it's historic, I guess."

Burden often speculated about Clay's marriage. On the surface, all things were as they should be. They lived in a small rented house on N Street. They had a daughter named Alice Frederika. They had everything except money, for Blaise had not relented.

Just as Burden was about to inquire, tentatively, how matters stood at Laurel House, Clay said, "I forgot to give you your new speaking schedule." He left the room.

Just as well, Burden decided, staring at his favorite quotation from Plato which, framed, hung on the wall. It was from one of the letters: "Each of us is born not for himself alone. We are born partly for our country, partly for our friends. The various contingencies that overtake our lives also make many demands upon us. When our country herself calls us to public life, it would perhaps be strange not to respond, since one must otherwise at the same time give place to worthless men who do not enter public life for the best motives." The sentiment of course was aristocratic. Plato had suffered too much from democracy to find in the people's voice anything more inspiring than an animal's roar. If only because of this, Burden found him congenial. They would have liked each other. Burden fancied that he might even have helped Plato to understand the Tyrant of Syracuse and of course Plato would have taught him—did in fact teach him —that the unexamined life was not worth living. And though there were limits to how much examination any situation could bear, Plato had got him into the habit of scrutinizing his own motives. He knew of course that he was inclined to give himself the benefit of much doubt, employing arguments hardly worse

72

than some of those which Socrates used to propound to the amazement of simple questioners who seemed never able to follow up a dialectical lead; even so, Burden was afflicted with conscience, a unique disadvantage, he knew, in a man who wanted to be President.

Clay returned with several papers clipped together. "It's shaping up beautifully. You'll follow the President all through September. Wherever he speaks, you'll speak, a few days later. He visits the West Coast; so do you. He stares at the Grand Canyon and talks about conservation; so do you."

Burden studied the list, his pleasure in so many speaking dates somewhat diminished by the thought of crowded smoky auditoriums, clutching hands, endless introductions.

"It will certainly annoy Franklin. No doubt of that."

"Do you think he'll talk to you tonight?"

" 'How are you, Brother Day!' " Burden mimicked the famous voice with all its resonant artifice. "And that will be all, except an occasional glare from those chilly eyes. He does hate, you know."

"Well, he is hated."

"Not by me."

Clay looked at him with genuine surprise. "You really don't hate him, after all he's tried to do to us back home?"

"Look what I do to him in the Senate. Anyway it's hardly personal. At least not on my side. Two ideas are set upon a collision course, that's all. He believes government must do everything, and I don't see how it can do much more than it does if we're to keep any sort of private freedom. Neither of us is really *right*, but I think that what I believe is closer to the good life, to the original idea of the country, than what he believes, or is."

"But perhaps he's closer to the way people are now."

Burden studied Clay thoughtfully. Then he nodded. "That's my nightmare, of course. The wheel does turn in the night, without one's knowing it."

"Maybe you ought to make a few liberal-sounding speeches. Not *too* liberal of course. . . ." Clay was always practical and Burden wondered if he believed in anything at all. It had been his experience that, contrary to legend, young men are seldom idealistic. They want the prizes, and to rise they will do whatever needs doing, echoing faithfully the rhetoric of the day. Idealism comes late in life, if ever. After all, politics was largely twisting and turning merely to survive, and in the process even the simplest goal was lost sight of. Disgust with one's own kind was inevitable while eternity mocked them all. Since President, Senators, and Britannic Majesties were so much stuff for worms, what did any of it matter? That question he knew to be the origin of true evil, for there was no answer to it, other than to say that the wise man did not ask it.

Burden gave last minute instructions to the staff. Then putting on his top hat, he left the office.

Henry started the car. "The British Embassy, Senator?" he asked for the pleasure of asking.

"That's right, Henry. You look very handsome, Kitty." Burden gave his wife a kiss. She was at least presentable. For some days she and the ladies of her bridge group had debated what she was to wear to the garden party and how her hair was to be done and should she or should she not dye. This was the question currently debated among the ladies of Washington. New York women were already dyeing their hair, which was to be expected. Now honest women must face the challenge. To date, only a few had succumbed; and those few tended to be not the fading beauties but the eccentrics who had nothing to lose. Better a head of green hair than to be thought a nice grandmother nodding over her cards.

"I won't dye," said Kitty firmly. Burden took this to mean "die." Sooner or later Kitty said everything that was on her mind.

"I hope never!" He took her hand.

"Of course the new hairdresser wants me to let him change me to auburn, I think he said, even though my original shade was chestnut. But I said no very firmly. I happen to know that Gladys Mergendahl's sister in Oklahoma went *insane* as a result of hair dye. You see, the dye seeps through the skull and affects the brain."

"I like you as you are." This was true. He could not imagine life without her.

"I wish Diana had been invited. Goodness, the King and Queen! I never thought I'd ever meet and talk to such people. Did you ever think you would?"

"Of course," said Burden, who had never thought that he would not. Then he wondered what Kitty would actually *say* to the King or, worse, to the President. He would have to keep an eye on her.

As they turned into Massachusetts Avenue, the crowds began. For over a mile people lined the avenue, staring intently at the chauffeur-driven cars which contained their masters.

"Diana's been talking about New York again, about going there to live. She can't be serious but you know how she is once she gets a bee in her bonnet. She's even talked to Ed Nillson about finding her a job in New York. He was very concerned."

"What sort of job?" Burden turned away from the crowds, suddenly alert.

"Anything. Ed wanted to know if he should. Such a nice man. So kind. So few people are. I told him not to do a thing until we'd talked to her."

"We'll talk to her." Though what to say was another matter.

A sweating policeman poked his head through the car window. "Got your invitation, Senator?"

Burden flourished the invitation from Their Britannic Majesties.

"Everybody and his brother are trying to crash this thing. Will you look at that, Senator?" The policeman indicated a long line of limousines slowly creeping up to the Embassy's porte cochere, while at the iron gates that opened onto Massachusetts Avenue, people clung to the railings—like monkeys, Burden thought, trying to force their way into a gilded cage. The policeman motioned for Henry to drive on.

"Many are called," said Burden, taking Kitty's hand in his own. "But we were chosen."

Harold Griffiths threw open the door to his office. "Come in, come in. He sits there." Harold imitated an ancient retainer showing off the workroom of genius. "Yes, at that plain desk, on that old typewriter, he wrote those savage reviews which thrilled a generation, and made the movies art. Notice the view: Ninth Street, with its burlesque houses and shops devoted to the sale of pornographic literature and odd devices calculated to give pleasure to twisted minds." Harold whinnied alarmingly. Then: "Why aren't you at the garden party?"

"Not invited." Peter sat on the edge of the desk and studied the film studio handouts. Harold's job was very glamorous indeed.

"Lies, all lies," said Harold comfortably; he put a hat on the back of his head. "I wear this only in the office. To remind myself that I am a journalist."

"You are a bit of a movie yourself, aren't you?" Peter enjoyed Harold.

"It's impossible to see twenty movies a week and not be affected. I close doors like Kay Francis." Harold darted to the door; then, half smile on his lips, hand over the knob, he leaned back against the door and slowly shut it. "To denote skepticism, I suck in my cheeks . . . so!" He drew in his cheeks. The effect was properly droll. Peter laughed. Encouraged, Harold became Captain Dreyfus on Devil's Island. As he staggered toward the door to the prison, eyes blinking in the unaccustomed sunlight, the door was flung open to reveal a woman in a great hat and white gloves who said, "Harold, are you all right?"

Harold's voice cracked; he had not spoken to anyone in twenty years. "Free . . . free!" Actual tears flowed down his face.

"Oh, honey, do shut up, will you?" Hat and gloves were not charmed. "I can't find the city editor and he's supposed to have my invitation to the garden party, if it's come, which I don't know . . ."

"This is Helen Ashley Barbour." Harold said the name reverently, and Peter recognized the *Tribune's* society editor, a lady of formidable presence, uncertain syntax and perfect ubiquity. The relict of an obscure Southern Congressman, she had managed to get herself invited at one time or another to almost all the great houses of Washington, except that of her employer. Frederika thought her vulgar.

"How do you do, Mrs. Barbour?"

"Not at all well, as you see. Am I supposed to be covering the garden party or not? That is the question. It certainly comes under Society but of course it also comes under News, and Heaven knows all the press is going to be there. Maybe Blaise will cover it. He's always threatening to write something for the paper. This might be a good beginning for him."

Peter enjoyed the drop of acid in the honeyed torrent. Harold did not. "This is Peter, son of Blaise," he said.

Mrs. Barbour took it very well. "I should have known. You have your mother's features, you lucky thing, such a marvelous face she has! But now just look at you, all grown up. Look at him, Harold! He's taller than you."

"Everyone is taller than me, even you!"

"You're in your, let me see . . . *second* year at the University of Virginia. Oh, I know everything about you. That's my job. I adore Charlottesville. In fact, I used to have a beau there when I was a girl in Atlanta. Of course that was during the siege. Well, I can see you're no help, Harold."

"I never am."

"So nice to see you again, Peter. So very very nice. We must have a real chat one of these days." Mrs. Barbour left the office, and Harold observed, "If you were going to build a Washington society editor from scratch, you couldn't do better than that."

"I liked the gloves."

"I like everything. What do you think they'll have you doing?"

"Who knows? Father said I was to work at the paper. That's all. I suppose I'll be an office boy."

"Start at the bottom, inherit the top. That's America."

"I'd hoped they would let me work with you."

"Movies in the morning are for the old and the failed. What do you really want to do?"

"Be old, be failed."

"Naturally. But en route?"

"I don't know. Politics maybe. I can't decide."

"I don't suppose the Académe of the Blue Ridge is much help."

"It's not so bad." Peter was used to defending his university against the charge that it was a country club. It was one, of course, but a good club, and between parties he found there was quite enough time to glut himself with books. He was now reading D. H. Lawrence. After the first surprise that he had by mistake selected the Lawrence who knew nothing of revolts in the desert, he found that he enjoyed very much learning about women in love.

"What a burden, to be a rich man's son."

"Is that from a movie? Or do you mean it?"

"Both. Movies are life, after all, with the point made simple. No. You're in a position where everything is possible, which naturally means that nothing is particularly enticing."

"I wouldn't say that," said Peter, who often did say exactly that in long sessions with his roommate, an earnest youth who believed that very soon the Lord would come with a sword and wrathfully judge all men, thrusting sinners into the fiery pit of hell where he himself was bound to go because of masturbation and one encounter, while drunk, with a girl from Richmond who had, he swore, robbed him of his precious virginity. But when not in the grip of religious mania, this young man was both shrewd and ambitious. He planned to make a fortune by the time he was thirty. Peter had no doubt that he would, and he envied the other's sense of purpose. He himself had none, beyond pursuing girls in Washington with his friend Scotty. Twice he had been successful. He had enjoyed the sex; but he had not enjoyed the long conversations which, sooner or later, got around to the subject of marriage, causing him to flee. Unlike Scotty, who was always what he called in love, Peter was wary with girls. Only once was he able to make himself believe that he was in love. But whenever the girl laughed she made a curious snorting noise at the back of her nose and after a dozen meetings he came to dread her laugh, knowing that with it, inevitable as death, would come the snort. So he had given her up and not loved again.

"How is Enid? I never see her any more."

"Neither do I." It was true. Enid was entirely removed from him now that she had crossed the line that separates the children from the grown-ups. "I suppose I'll see her this weekend, at the house."

"With Clay?"

"With the baby."

"I'll never understand why your father wasn't pleased to have Clay for a son-in-law."

"I never know how he'll react to anything. But then, I don't know him very well." It pleased Peter to speak coolly of his own father. The shocked response of his more innocent contemporaries was worth a few insincerities.

But Harold would have none of it. "Oh yes, you do. Now I must analyze the art of George Brent." As Harold approached the typewriter, he became not George Brent but George Arliss, the weight of high office burdening aged shoulders. Peter watched appreciatively as Cardinal Richelieu sat down in his chair of state, picked up an invisible feather, and began to intrigue.

* * *

The crowd was so dense at the Treasury Building that Peter could not cross the street; could not, in fact, move at all, as the people milled about him, eager to catch a glimpse of the King and Queen, who were soon to pass from railroad station to White House. Cardboard periscopes were raised high. Box cameras were set. To avoid the crowd, he climbed up on the railing of the Treasury and was promptly rewarded

79

with a glimpse of majesty. The King and the President sat side by side in the back of an open car. The crowd cheered politely. The President waved, his large pink face dwarfing the King's which was, in any case, hidden beneath the cocked hat of an admiral.

That was all there was to it. The crowd began to break up, and Peter wondered if they were satisfied. It seemed impossible but one never knew. The people, as such, never seemed quite real to Peter. They were so out of things; and yet they seemed perfectly content to be irrelevant. Pushing through overheated irrelevancies, he entered the Willard Hotel.

Diana was waiting for him in the lobby.

"It was so stupid of me, asking you here. I'd forgotten all about that damned parade."

"I watched it, saw the King."

"How was he?"

"Small. What's so urgent? Why couldn't you tell me on the phone?"

"Because I couldn't. Someone might have been listening in. Do you have any money?"

"About twenty dollars."

"No. I mean *money*."

"No. Oh, maybe two hundred dollars. Why?"

"I thought you were rich."

"My father's rich. I'm not."

"Nothing at all of your own, before he dies?"

"You ask the most intimate questions." Peter was embarrassed; sexual candor was already fairly common in his set but money was never mentioned.

"Because I must know."

"There's a trust fund, when I'm twenty-one. But I don't know what the income is." Peter knew exactly. He would have thirty thousand dollars a year. The trust had been created when he was born by his Grandmother Delacroix. A similar trust had been made for Enid but with the proviso that she receive no income until she was twenty-five. Their grandmother had believed that if a girl is married for her money, a number of years spent waiting for that money will make her situation absolutely plain to her. But their grandmother's considerate malice had failed to destroy Enid's marriage. She spent whatever she

80

liked and then forced Blaise to pay her debts. That she was poor did not in the least distress her.

"And I thought you were already rich. Well, you'll like him anyway. He's in the bar."

"Who's in the bar? And what are you talking about?" Peter was not used to the new Diana. Living alone had changed her for the better. In five minutes she had not blushed once; in fact, she had made him blush.

"Billy Thorne." Diana paused dramatically.

"Well?"

"Oh, you know who he is! Spanish Civil War. He lost a leg and wrote a book about the Lincoln Brigade, about the Americans who fought against Franco. He's a hero, and now he wants to start a magazine, a political magazine."

"Only there's no money."

"How quick you are!" Diana chuckled. Peter liked her. But he was less certain about Billy Thorne whose wooden leg creaked noisily when he moved. He was thin, small, and not at all heroic, except for a thundering bass voice.

"Too bad about the money," he said to Diana after she had told him the bad news. "But we'll manage somehow." He gave Peter a sharp suspicious look as though Peter were holding out on them.

"I don't have a penny," Peter said. Then, deciding that he had sounded too apologetic, he added: "And if I did, I'm not at all sure I'd want to put it into a political magazine. What sort of politics, by the way?"

"Liberal," said Diana.

"Socialist!" boomed Billy Thorne, causing several businessmen at the next table to turn around.

"But I'm hardly a socialist," said Peter who currently believed only in the divine right of kings, on condition of course that *he* was the King with a blue uniform covered with gold braid, a cocked hat, and no huge pink-faced President to tower over him as he rode in triumph through the streets of Washington. Actual power he would cede to anyone who allowed him to be figurehead.

"Peter's a reactionary," said Diana.

"His father certainly is. Worse than Hearst."

Peter was irritated. He turned to Diana. *"Your* father is hardly apt to free the serfs."

Billy Thorne roared his approval, alarming a waitress. "He's got you there!"

Diana flushed. Yes, she was still Diana. She stammered. "He's conservative, of course, but he's awfully liberal about a lot of things."

"Name one!" Billy winked at Peter, who wondered what the stump looked like. Did the bone stick through the skin? But of course not. It would look like a healed gash, still red and shiny. He tried to imagine the way the leg looked as it was torn off. He saw blood, heard Billy screaming. Very nice.

Diana continued to defend her father. She explained that to be nominated for President one needed the support of every kind of person; besides, the United States was a highly conservative country, which is why a magazine that would give the views of the enlightened Left (she did not much like the word "socialist": too narrowing) was definitely needed. She had more or less regained her ground by the time she finished. Billy showed a certain rudimentary caution in not continuing to tease his patroness (mistress? Peter wondered).

Billy grunted. "Anyway, it's needed. Something more adventurous than *The Nation,* more alive, for the young!"

"I thought magazines were published in New York. Why do you want to start one here?"

"Because Billy's got a job with the Department of Commerce. He's in statistics. He can't give up the job until we're under way." Peter saw Billy Thorne plain. A clerk working in a large room filled with desks where the other clerks helped him add up endless rows of figures. There was a drinking fountain in one corner of the office where the clerks regularly gathered to chat about baseball. Peter could taste the white conical paper cups with that curious lime-lemon flavor from the glue, or was the taste in the paper itself? Billy Thorne had suddenly ceased to exist for Peter except as a column of numbers to be added up.

"I want to quit. I will quit, just as soon as we get rolling. I came here because of the New Deal. But that's all over."

"All over?" This would be news to Peter's father.

"Of course. Next year there'll be either a conservative Democrat elected or a Republican, and that'll be the end of it."

"But suppose Roosevelt runs for a third term?"

"He won't," said Diana quickly, reflecting her father's hope.

"Even if he does," said Billy, "he's washed up as a liberal. He never was much of one anyway."

"And what," asked Peter, "is a liberal?"

Billy told him at length. The voice boomed. Barricades materialized in the streets. The proletariat got their bread at gunpoint. Medicine was socialized. Inheritance taxes ended the great fortunes, while natural resources were nationalized. The rich went to work; the virtuous poor had long vacations. And at the center of this fierce leveling and raising, Billy Thorne stood, directing operations, wooden leg creaking, voice booming. Meanwhile the businessmen at the next table fled, no doubt to report to the House Un-American Activities Committee that the enemy had seized the dining room of the Willard Hotel.

When Billy finished his speech, Peter saw that Diana was ecstatic, and he decided that she was either in love or out of her mind, assuming that both were not the same.

"And that's why we need a magazine," Billy added. "Some place where we can see to it that the right things get said and done."

"But how can you be so certain you're right?" Peter was mild. "You think it's correct to take my father's money away from him. He thinks it's wrong, and so do I . . . selfish reasons, of course."

"If it benefits all the people to confiscate your father's money then it ought to be confiscated."

"But will it really benefit them?"

"He's hopeless!" Billy roared. "Read Keynes, read Lenin, read Marx!"

At that moment an official from Commerce entered the bar and Billy Thorne called out to him. Peter used the introductions to say goodbye. Diana walked him to the door.

"I'm sorry I got you into this."

"It's all right. He's . . . interesting." That was the best Peter could do.

Diana smiled, suddenly mischievous. "Poor Billy *does* rub people the wrong way, but he's awfully brilliant. I'll send you his book about Spain. The reviews were wonderful, at least those that weren't written by fascists."

"Well, I hope you get your money."

"So do I. There's a chance Mr. Nillson might help out. He was going to give me a job in New York but then I met Billy. Now I'm going to stay."

"You're not going to marry him, are you?"

"I don't think men like Billy get married."

"Doesn't he believe in it?"

"Something like that. He's the most stimulating person I've ever known. Oh, all right. I can tell you despise him." She laughed. "If you like, we can try again. You're going to be here this summer, aren't you?"

Peter nodded. "We'll try again. I'll call you." Diana went back to her revolutionary and Peter went out into Pennsylvania Avenue.

The crowd was gone. Traffic was normal. He found a taxi and gave the driver Enid's address. He had not seen her since the Easter vacation. Since her marriage and his own translation from adolescence to manhood, they were seldom together. Yet difficult as she was, of all the people in his life he cared most for her; and he often wondered if she continued to feel the same attraction for him that he could not stop feeling for her even though between them flowed the never-to-be-spanned river of their common blood.

3

The Texans were making a lot of noise when Clay arrived. Although the host was notoriously committed to the New Deal, he welcomed Clay with a large hug and introduced him to those few he did not already know.

"We have been pourin' for quite some time." The Congressman steered him to a desk on which bottles and glasses had been set. Everyone was in shirtsleeves, including a member of the Cabinet, who turned away when he was told that Clay was Burden Day's assistant. But though Clay was in enemy territory, as the son-in-law of Blaise Sanford he was the object of a certain amount of deference. That he had not seen Blaise a half dozen times since the wedding was not public knowledge.

The Texans were in a happy mood, arguing about everything. The Vice President particularly concerned them. Despite the fact that he was also from Texas, few thought he should succeed the President.

"Anyway," said one of the Congressmen, "you could never sell a man like him to the country."

"Because he's from Texas, that's why." Laughter at their common predicament.

The Congressman shook his head. "You couldn't sell him because he lends money in that bank of his at *twelve* per cent. Now I ask you, who's goin' to vote for a man who charges stockmen *twelve* per cent?"

"Any Republican," said Clay. He was rewarded with laughter. Despite his connection with Burden, he got along well with the Texans, if only because working politicians tend to be tolerant of one another, realizing that one man's conviction is another man's heresy, which was why it was helpful not to have too many convictions. In any case, the fiercely doctrinaire were seldom elected to the Congress. But they did get appointed to various agencies. Clay detested the New Dealers, particularly the member of the Cabinet who had just snubbed him.

"Regular son of a bitch, ain't he?" An elderly Congressman indicated the Cabinet member.

Clay was alarmed that his dislike had been so apparent. He used one of Burden's favorite lines, "You might say that he has every characteristic of a dog, except loyalty."

The older man chuckled. "Only thing is, he *is* loyal to the President, which shows what kind of yellow dog he is. Well, thank the Lord we won't have him around much longer, or any of that crowd. Next election and back they all go to New York City where they belong, doin' good."

"If the President doesn't run again."

"He won't. Come over here." Clay was drawn to a corner of the room. He recognized in the other's broad smile that the time had come for politicking.

"Now then," said the Congressman, voice pitched so that none but Clay could hear. "I'm for Burden." If this was true, Clay was startled. The Congressman was known to favor Secretary of State Cordell Hull. Assuming that the declaration was not true but merely a gracious prelude to something else, Clay nodded and waited.

"Lot of fellows here in this room *might* support him if he'd make a little effort to woo 'em." Clay wondered just what it was the old man wanted in the way of wooing. No politician ever spoke for another politician. "They" usually meant "I." The Congressman mopped his brow with a red bandanna; no doubt a useful prop when he was on the hustings. Clay tried to visualize the district his companion represented: oil, cattle, cottonwoods, Indians.

"For instance, there's been some concern about Burden's dealings with a certain Ed Nillson."

"What about them?" Clay blinked his innocence.

"What about them?" The sly red face was thrust suddenly into his. Inadvertently, Clay stepped back, into a table.

"Nothing much to tell." The metal top of the table pressed hard against Clay's legs. "Ed came to the Senator, oh, a couple of years ago. He wanted to help out. And he has. He's been invaluable to us." So far, all that Clay had said was perfectly true.

"You know, I got some Indians in my district." The Congressman's voice was dreamy. "They are the salt of the earth, those fellows . . . fact, I'm one-eighth Indian myself." Ever since the rise of the humorist Will Rogers it was fashionable for Westerners to claim a drop or two of Indian blood. They could then pretend to be "original Americans."

"Now, these good people whom I have the honor to represent . . ." A slightly sardonic smile took the edge off the pious words, usually delivered straight with hand on heart. ". . . sold off a large section of land to a company whose owner is one Edgar Nillson."

Clay nodded. "I heard about that deal. There was a bit of commotion over at Interior but it was finally O.K.'d."

"A great deal of commotion, of hue and cry which didn't stop until a certain Senate subcommittee, without a peep, allowed the desperate deed to be consummated, allowed those rich lands to go for a mess of pottage to one Edgar Nillson, who then became, as if by magic, treasurer of the James Burden Day for President Committee."

Clay felt sweat form at the temples. "I'm not sure I understand you."

"Our friend Burden was the chairman of that Senate subcommittee."

"But he was also out of the country when the committee read out the bill. I remember, he was in Canada and . . ."

"That's right. But just before Burden went to Canada, he phoned one of the Senators on the subcommittee and told him how important it was that Mr. Nillson be allowed to buy that Indian land. Now though the Senator to whom he confided these instructions has since gone to his reward, his secretary, a true gem and a recent addition to my staff, just now told me how they used to have in his old office this recording device which was attached to the Senator's private telephone, a truly infernal doodad which could spell the ruin of us all."

Clay's hands went cold. His stomach contracted. His career in politics was ended before it ever began.

"Now I have the means of obtaining this . . . what should I call it? *Piece* of conversation which I firmly believe should not be floatin' around as a possible source of embarrassment to my good friend and maybe next President, no, sir. We don't want the wrong people gettin' ahold of it."

"It could be misinterpreted." Clay played the game. He had no choice.

"You bet your ass it could be." The Congressman beamed, revealing broken teeth, brown from chewing tobacco. "Now I happen to have a friend who has an interest in a few skimpy acres at the edge of Mr. Nillson's development and it seems to me that it might be a fair trade if Mr. Nillson bought that land—at a reasonable price of course—receiving in addition to those acres, which contain who knows what mineral treasure, the record of Burden's conversation."

Not as bad as Clay had feared. "Okay." Clay was equally to the point. "I'll talk to Ed this afternoon."

"Tell him to call me at home. I've been livin' at the Alban Towers since my wife passed on and I gave up the big house. It was just too lonely without Li'l Tyke—that's what I called her, Li'l Tyke—she was the tiniest thing with those big eyes. Oh, I do miss her!" The Congressman poured himself bourbon. "I'll be waitin' for Ed's call."

"It'll come. And when you two agree . . ."

"Which I'm sure we will. He's a good old boy, Ed, and my friend is not unduly greedy."

"I'm sure he's not. Anyway, once you two settle the price, let me know. And I'll collect the . . . recording."

"You don't want Ed to have it?"

"No, I do not."

The Congressman laughed. "Can't say I blame you. Well, as long as he don't *demand* it—and he's the one who's payin'—it's yours. The Alban Towers will find me every night. I don't go out no more. At my age, what's the use? I'm just markin' time till I join Li'l Tyke, at the good Lord's pleasure. Nice to do business with you, son."

Clay then said hello to a Congressman from Oklahoma and gravely discussed with him whether or not Cordell Hull, a Southerner, could be nominated for President. As they talked, Clay recalled Burden's casual dismissal of Nillson just before he went to Canada. "I don't want anything to do with that man." Then, a few months later, Nillson formed the Day for President Committee. Yet Clay had suspected nothing, and that was what most alarmed him. He had been fooled by Burden. It was unbearable. After all, if he could not understand a man with whom he had worked for half a dozen years, could he understand anyone?

"Bright young fellow," said his host at the right moment, taking him by the arm. "I just made a bet that in ten years you'll be with us here on the Hill, as an e-lected o-fficial."

"Or I'll be in the White House, working for President Day."

"Well, that is outside the venue of my bet. I tend to put my money on a sure thing."

"You don't think the Senator can be nominated?"

"I don't *want* him to be nominated."

"That's not the same thing."

"No, it is not. I will say that I'd rather see him than Garner or Farley or Hull or McNutt."

"But not as much as Douglas or Hopkins or Jackson."

"That's about it."

"The Senator's right between the two groups. Maybe you'd take him if you couldn't get one of yours nominated and you didn't want one of theirs."

"As a compromise, Burden would be all right. But hell, who's compromisin'?"

That was that. But the exchange had been useful. Burden had not been ruled out.

At home Clay telephoned Nillson, who did not sound in the least surprised. But then, he never displayed any emotion stronger than bland interest.

"These things happen from time to time." The voice from the receiver was serene. "I'll give him a call."

"Will you . . . uh, buy the land from him?"

"What else?"

"Do you think he'll make copies of that telephone recording?"

"Why should he? Once I buy the land, he's in *my* pocket. He can't use anything against me that I can't use against him. What a world we live in!" Nillson actually sounded amused by what had happened. Clay found him more than ever impressive.

"Incidentally," said Nillson, "I don't think you ought to tell Burden about this. It would just worry him and do no good. But use your own judgment. You know him better than I do." It was then agreed that Clay would pick up the recording, once it had been paid for. With a few soothing words, Nillson rang off.

Thoughtfully, Clay went upstairs. He looked into the nursery and beheld his daughter asleep on the floor of her crib. In a chair the colored nurse was asleep, a movie magazine on her lap. Clay watched the two for a moment. The nurse's mouth was open; saliva made a gleaming viscous trail across the caramel chin. His child did not look much better. Fat and fair with a skin mottled from prickly heat, she lay curled like a dog among her toys, breathing heavily, mouth ajar. Mildly depressed, he went into his own bedroom.

Enid's clothes were everywhere. He cursed silently. Confronted by her untidiness, Clay had become neat, forging a new weapon in the war between them. And their marriage was a war, no doubt of that. Like enemy commanders surveying a battlefield, each studied the other for signs of weakness. The first shot had been fired at Elkton, their Fort Sumter, when she had blamed him for her heel breaking off and he had countered, logically, that if she were to watch where she was walking . . . So it began, with a broken heel. Since then neither had let up for more than an occasional truce in order to shift troops, extend supply lines, bring up big guns. Yet the marriage was happy, even though, like all the women he had ever known, Enid did not satisfy him sexually; nevertheless, unlike the others, she never ceased to interest him and though he continued his adventures, he was always happy to return to her, knowing that for all her wildness she was entirely his. He was aware that it was irrational of him not to allow her the same freedom that he allowed himself, but he had been brought up to believe that women were not like men and that they could be faithful *if* they were in love and so despite all the quite considerable evidence to the contrary, he based their marriage on the fact that she, in love, would never stray and that he, equally in love but male, would on occasion find other pleasures while reserving for her the essential self.

Suddenly exhausted by the heat and the day, Clay flung himself on the bed as though it were Enid, threw his arms about a pillow which smelled of her, and slept.

In the Senate dining room Nillson and the old Texas Congressman were having lunch with Dolly Perrine, who was nude. As Nillson cut his steak into small pieces, she attempted to seduce him, but he ignored her, as did the Congressman who was putting silver dollars into a shoebox while repeating over and over again: "How proud Li'l Tyke would be!" To which Dolly would reply in a flat voice, "It's long distance, Senator. It's the Governor's office." Then Clay joined the party; he lay on his back on the table, aroused by Dolly, who promptly turned her back on him and clutched the stolid Nillson, who continued to eat his lunch. Then the Congressman suddenly noticed Clay. With a glad cry, he started to undo Clay's trousers as though searching for a cache of silver dollars. "Oh, how proud Li'l Tyke would be!"

Why a cry, Clay awakened to find Enid, smiling wickedly and tugging at his trousers. "For Christ's sake!" He gasped, pulling himself away from her. "Don't!"

"Who were you dreaming of?"

"None of your business. What time is it?"

"Late. I'll bet it wasn't me."

Clay sat up. "As a matter of fact, it was a Congressman from Texas. I was having some dealings with him."

"There's a hell of a situation down on the Hill!" Suddenly Enid was in bed beside him, and though she still wore her long dress from the garden party, they made love, twisting and turning, in one of those spontaneous moments of truce which made the war, when it continued, all the more meaningful.

Later, Enid lay full length in the bathtub, among bubbles iridescent in the day's last light. "Well, it was awful, the garden party. The Queen looks like an upstairs maid. He's rather sweet but tiny. They're both so tiny. I towered over them." Enid splashed her elegant breasts; her body shone like bronze. "You know those MacDonald girls, the ones from Berryville who were in school with me? Well, a few years back they had a London season and they were presented at Court wearing ostrich plumes in their hair and looking like the cat's meow. They even sent

91

everybody pictures of their triumph and we were all so jealous. Well, no longer. Everybody's been presented. No fuss. No feathers."

"How was your father?"

"Complaining about the heat, like everyone else. The poor King and Queen spent most of the time on the porch. But it was hot even there. The rest of us just milled around in the garden. I think he wears makeup. The King. He looked awfully brown and sort of smooth-looking."

"Like you." Clay stroked one brown smooth breast. She pushed his hand away. "Listen, I said I'd go to dinner tonight with the Davises in McLean. They were there, at the Embassy. You don't mind?"

"Without me?"

"Father's coming, too."

"Then I'd better not."

"You're not furious?" She looked at him from under heavy brows, suspecting ambush.

"This is the third time in a week you've gone some place without me."

"But it's so uncomfortable when Father's there."

"Father wasn't at that thing in Georgetown on Tuesday. Also . . ." Clay moved easily from charge to charge while Enid prepared her defense with customary skill, relying, as always, on the unexpected counterattack for which he was seldom prepared, despite a thousand days of marriage. In fact, at times he still could not believe he was married. Sometimes he awakened in the night and when he saw the sleeping Enid beside him in the bed, her hair like a dark stain on the pillow, he would experience a sudden panic: What am I doing here? How was the trap sprung? Is this sentence for life? But then he would light a cigarette and in the brief glow of the match remind himself that of all the girls he had known, only she had never bored him.

"Peter said so, too."

Clay had missed what must have been a particularly damaging bit of evidence. "Peter?" he said, as though weighing that young man's reliability as a witness.

"Yes, he was here today."

Enid allowed the case to rest while she got out of

the tub like a sleek water animal and picked up a crumpled towel from the floor where she had dropped it after her morning bath, and wrapped herself in the moldy folds.

"I want a drink," she announced and left the room. Clay followed, without will. What the rabbit must feel for the snake, the audience for the demagogue, Clay felt for Enid, as he followed her down the narrow stairs to the living room of their rented house. Enid always roared the word "rented" at visitors, wanting no part in surroundings so unlike those of Laurel House. Unlovely paintings of Naples under glass; dark mahogany; old chintz; a blond-wood coffee table with many rings of different sizes, tribute to the rented pantry's diversity of glasses.

Enid made herself a martini. She had just discovered martinis and she could, she declared, drink any amount without getting drunk, which seemed to be true. Drink merely made her lively, happy, loving, and it was then that Clay liked her best, at parties, when every man was attracted to her and she was entirely his.

"Peter dropped by. I didn't even know he was in town. That place really is a country club." Clay sat in his usual chair, feet on the coffee table, while Enid sipped at her martini, eyes glowing. "Oh, I *needed* this! That sun! Those people! I wouldn't be the Queen of England for all the tea in China!"

"What did Peter want?"

"Nothing. A friendly call. I try to discourage him, but he doesn't take the hint. He is good-looking, though." Enid picked up a silver cigarette box (a wedding gift from the staff of Senator Day) and studied her own reflection, which Clay thought odd, for Enid seldom looked at herself. Lack of personal vanity was her most startling trait.

"He's going to work on the paper this summer." She put down the box, and he realized that it was Peter she had been hoping to find reflected in the smoky silver. Clay was immediately on guard. Brother and sister were an alliance he did not understand.

She hoisted long legs onto the pale coffee table. The legs resembled dark expensive polished wood while the table seemed ordinary flesh. "I hope you realize that if he hadn't seen us that first time, in the poolhouse, I'd never have married you."

"Thanks." Clay looked at her with sudden distaste.

"I didn't mean it like *that!*" She was contrite. As usual, she was most wounding when she did not mean to be. She crossed his ankles with her own: pushed one foot beneath his trouser leg and tickled the hairs with her big toe. "I'm glad what happened finally. But, God, he's a little sneak!"

"It was an accident."

"Accident? In a pig's eye! Who would be out in the middle of a thunderstorm in the middle of the night unless he'd been *following* us?" Enid denounced her brother; and Clay defended him. For one thing he liked Peter; for another, the boy was an important strategic position in the war, and the side that held him commanded a good deal of the terrain.

"Anyway Peter said that Father said last night at dinner that you and I would be divorced long before I was twenty-five."

"Good old Blaise." Clay groaned. "What a family!"

"I guess we are awfully intense." Enid stirred the martini with her forefinger. "But Father will come around."

"Who cares if he does?" asked Clay, who cared the most. The more he saw of the world, the more convinced he was that without money, a very great deal of money, he could never obtain any of those glittering prizes the Republic bestows so generously upon the rich, so haphazardly upon the poor. But as long as Blaise was irreconcilable, Clay's career was at a halt.

"Oh! Peter said something about your old girl friend." He let that familiar cannonball drop out of range. "Apparently Diana's involved with a Communist who wants to start a magazine."

"A Communist? Are you sure?" Clay was alert.

"Of course I'm sure," said Enid, obviously trying to recall what Peter had said. "They wanted Peter to put money into it, as if he had any, though he'll get his before I do. And . . ."

Clay stopped her. "This could be serious. For the Senator."

Enid looked at him blankly. The problems of others, including her husband's employer, never seemed quite real to her.

"Are you absolutely sure that Peter said he was a Communist?"

"Yes, that's exactly what he said, but then Peter's such a liar you can never tell."

"I'd better call the Senator." Clay stood up.

"Oh, don't go!" Enid was like a child, not wanting to be left alone. "I never see you when that awful Senate's in session."

"You could have seen me tonight."

Aware that she had exposed an entire division to certain defeat, Enid hastily abandoned all positions, threw wide her arms, causing the towel to fall from her shoulders; then, acknowledging total defeat, reverted to their private baby talk. "Kiss dear puppy dog and tell her you don't mind her being bad, bad, bad!"

Clay kissed her, said he did not mind her being bad, bad, bad, and as he tasted her ginny mouth, grew excited and might have forgotten to telephone the Senator if the nurse had not chosen that moment to enter, carrying the baby in her arms.

"For Christ's sake!" shouted Enid. "Why don't you knock? Why do you *creep* like that?"

"That's all right, Annie," said Clay soothingly, pulling himself together. But Annie had fled, with Enid's curses ringing after her. "Cut it out!" Clay spoke sharply, the spell broken. He was himself again. "You don't want to lose her like you lost the others. You can't shout at people like that."

"I can do any damned thing I please!" Enid drank the remains of the martini from the silver shaker; then she wrapped the towel about herself and went upstairs. Clay knew that the next day she and the nurse would again be giggling together. No matter how badly Enid behaved she never bore a grudge. She also spoke to everyone with the same degree of intimacy and lack of reticence, and though this candor was part of her charm, Clay had learned never to tell her anything that he would not want his worst enemy to know. As for the new nurse, she was still fascinated and thrilled at being treated as an equal. But she was

95

not yet prepared to pay the price of Enid's intimacy: the sudden rages, the elaborate insults, the alarming cruelty. Yet Enid was always genuinely hurt when her victims later reproached her with what she had said. "But you don't understand, I absolutely love you!" Perhaps they didn't; and perhaps she did.

Clay tried to telephone the Senator. Mrs. Day answered the Senator's telephone. "Burden's taking a nap. He's worn out after the garden party. It was so hot! And then we're going to the White House tonight. Is it very urgent? Should I wake him?" Clay said that it could wait. Then he wished them a good evening in the enemy's country and hung up. Moodily he opened his briefcase, began to work, lost track of time, and was not aware of Enid until she made a loud noise, causing him to drop some papers. "Don't do that!"

"I love it when you jump, like an old maid. Do I look all right?" Enid looked all right and he told her so. But she did not listen. She was as impervious to truth as to flattery. "Listen," she said, "I feel awful, saying I'd go to this party and leaving you."

"It's all right."

"Of course it isn't all right. I just get carried away and say yes when I should say no. Half the time I don't make any sense, anyway. If you want me to stay home, I will."

Completely vanquished, he told her to go to the party. He would stay home and work. She said that puppy dog was bad, bad, bad. He agreed but insisted that he would not have her any other way. She left saying how sorry she was and he duly noted that the only time Enid could ever bring herself to say that she was sorry was when she was not. He added this useful new weapon to his armory. Their war was love. Or their love was war. Either way, only in battle did they truly meet. He could not imagine life without Enid.

4

At a signal from the President's wife, the ladies rose. Led by Mrs. Roosevelt and the Queen, they left the men in possession of the State Dining Room. As the usher shut the dining room door, Burden moved from his place just below the left curve of the horseshoe-shaped table toward the center where President and King sat. The empty chair on the King's left was swiftly filled by the Vice President, who exuberantly patted and prodded the little King, to the President's obvious annoyance and Burden's amusement. The knives were out between the President and his Constitutional if not political heir.

Brandy was served; cigars appeared. Burden sat down between Blaise Sanford and an Englishman whose name sounded like Lord Garbage. They complained of the heat.

"The President refuses to put in air conditioning." Blaise chewed his cigar. "Says it's bad for his sinus. Sinus, hell! What about the people that work here? What about us? Cardiac cases, that's what we'll be."

"Maybe he doesn't care." Like the others, Burden found it an effort not to stare at the President, who looked fit if somewhat overweight, the famous smile flashing on and off as though controlled by a master switch. Earlier, when Burden and Kitty had been presented, the President had given him the widest of smiles and then turned to the King and said in a stagy whisper, "He wants to live here, too!" The King looked faintly unsettled.

Later Burden discovered that the President had been making the same little joke about all his rivals, most of whom were present—Hull, Vandenberg, Farley, as well as the fragile Harry Hopkins, who had already maneuvered himself close to the magic center of the table. It would be a scrap but Burden was increasingly confident. According to the Gallup Poll, Hull was the party's first choice and he was the second choice, but since Hull was a Southerner and could not be nominated . . . Burden visualized himself at the head of the table; then he recalled his vow; no daydreaming. He tuned in on Blaise.

"Of course maybe he *wants* us to have heart attacks. Some of us anyway." Blaise chuckled.

Lord Garbage smiled and turned to Burden. "You must come here often, Senator."

"Never!" Blaise answered for Burden. "They hate each other," he said in a voice loud enough to be heard by the President, who did not hear because his full attention was concentrated upon the Vice President, now kneading the King's shoulder as though it were dough. The President's smile was set; the cold gray eyes glared. Full of bourbon and gay malice, the Vice President ignored that withering gaze.

It was explained to Lord Garbage (who seemed to have something to do with the Foreign Office) that although Burden belonged in the President's party they were political enemies. "I can't fathom your politics," said the Englishman.

"You should give it a try," said Blaise coldly, reflecting Burden's own irritation with those British who took pride in not knowing or, worse, pretending not to know how the American political system worked.

Lord Garbage was apologetic. "One ought to know of course. It's just that we're so used to party loyalty. I mean in Parliament you *have* to follow your party leader or you get out."

"We don't follow," said Burden, "and we never get out. Voluntarily."

"But sometimes we drop the party leader," said Blaise ominously, puffing blue smoke into Lord Garbage's face.

"It *is* hot," said the Englishman. On all sides Burden saw faces flushed with heat and wine. He was suddenly seized by a sense of unreality, recalling the other Presidents who had sat in this same room wining and dining the magnates of their day, all forgotten now. They come and they go, he thought, comforting himself. Nothing mattered but the moment. Then he noticed the newly carved motto just below the mantel on the main facing of the fireplace: the pious

98

hope of John Adams that "None but Honest and Wise Men ever rule under This Roof." Of course it mattered who governed. He pulled himself together. The trick was to avoid being overwhelmed by the swift rushing moment; to act as if the future did exist, as if one might indeed by doing good affect the lives of the unborn. But watching the President at the head of the table, Burden saw only vanity in that conceited face; nothing else, certainly no trace of *virtus,* to use Cicero's word, that moral goodness which does not translate as "virtue."

Blaise and Lord Garbage were discussing friends in England. Lord Garbage (that *couldn't* be his name) was assuring Blaise that an old friend had not really gone insane. "He just doesn't like people, which is perfectly normal. He lives alone in the country. And reads Carlyle to the pig."

Burden gave this his full attention. "The pig?"

"Yes. He used to read Gibbon, but he didn't like the style."

"Your friend?"

"No, the pig. Actually our friend rather likes Gibbon, and I don't think he's at all keen on Carlyle, but the pig finds Carlyle soothing. So what can he do?"

Blaise laughed delightedly. "Burden, you must get to know the English. They're not like us."

"Fortunately for you," said Lord Garbage who might or might not have been making fun of them. Yet Burden did not at heart dislike the British, differing from many of his Senatorial colleagues who resented England's eminence. Southerners still recalled with bitterness England's betrayal of the Confederacy, while in the Northern cities any politician with not much to say could always count on the Irish to applaud if he threatened to punch King George in the snoot. Burden looked at King George's long distinguished snoot and felt protective. The King seemed so fragile, so distinguished, so perfectly undeserving of anything but courtesy. Burden decided that this year he must definitely go to Europe and in the course of his travels propose himself for an interview with Hitler. Hitler would receive him at Berchtesgaden and Burden would begin by saying that he was speaking not for the Senate but for himself, and for world peace. The Chancellor would be attentive as Burden outlined a course of action which would take into account Germany's *legitimate* interests while maintaining the good will of the Western powers. As Burden spoke, Hitler would take notes, muttering "Ja, ja," from time to time.

"I think there will be war this summer." Burden's reverie was shattered. He turned to the Englishman whose tone of voice had not changed at all; he might have been giving a review of the pig's reading list. Blaise frowned. "I don't think so."

Lord Garbage blew smoke out large curved nostrils. "Mid-July is our guess. The little man will do to Poland what he did to Czechoslovakia."

"And what will *you* do?" asked Burden.

"I rather think we'll fight, this time."

"How?" Blaise was scornful. "The Germans have ninety-five hundred planes ready for combat. How many does England have?"

"None, I should think. Part of the charm of being a democracy is that one's always unprepared." He smiled. "How many planes do you Yanks have?"

"We don't need any because we're not going to fight anybody." Blaise was firm.

"Yes, I read your newspaper. But Hitler has already said first France, then England, then America."

"He's just bluffing, and who wouldn't? The way you people give in to him, he'd be crazy not to try for more."

Burden stopped listening as the familiar arguments went back and forth. He knew them all. Essentially he was isolationist. He saw no reason for the New World to involve itself once again in the sheer bloodiness of the Old. But he also knew that it would be difficult to stay out, particularly with a President who had an itch to perform on the world stage. Like Wilson, thought Burden, looking toward the President who was now whispering something into the King's ear. Yes, that was how Roosevelt saw himself, whispering to monarchs, obscuring domestic failures with foreign pageants. It was all too plain.

There must be no war. If only because the President would then run for re-election, and who in the party could stop him? Burden looked about the room at his peers, not one of whom could defeat the President at a convention. All that they could do was pray that the Europeans would keep the peace until the next convention which was (he counted on his fingers) fourteen months away.

"No," he said, to reassure himself, "I agree with Blaise. Hitler's too smart to begin a war . . . This summer," he added, native caution not allowing his thinking ever to be entirely wishful.

"I hope you're both right," said Lord Garbage politely.

There was a commotion at the magnet's center. The President's son was wheeling his father away from the table and, as always, Burden was reminded with a shock that the enemy was a cripple whose emaciated legs were locked inside heavy metal braces. It was distressing to watch the President get up and sit down. Yet he himself seemed not to notice his infirmity. Only once had Burden seen the President disconcerted by it. As he was walking laboriously to the rostrum to accept a second nomination for the Presidency, someone accidentally knocked him off balance, and like a tower he fell almost to the ground before aides caught him, the pages of his speech fluttering in the air. As much as Burden despised the man, he did feel a certain pity for one who governed a powerful nation but could not walk unaided.

Blaise took Burden's arm and they joined the procession from the dining room into the white marble entrance hall where, at the far end, in the East Room, the ladies were gathered, waiting to be joined. There was to be music.

Blaise's views were much like Burden's own. "There can't be a war. Hitler's not that stupid. But even if he is, the English won't fight. Too decadent. Reading Carlyle to a pig!"

"Don't forget that if there is a war, our host will be here another four years."

Blaise shuddered. "Don't even suggest such a thing. But if he does run again, I'll support . . . *you*, Senator." Blaise clapped Senator Vandenberg on the shoulder. The Senator looked surprised, then pleased. "Arthur, I pray that you get the Republican nomination." Vandenberg indicated that his own prayers were not entirely dissimilar, and he winked at Burden, a fellow member of The Club. For a moment Blaise paused at the door to the Red Room.

"Ed doing a good job for you?"

"I think so. Don't you?"

"First-rate is my impression. But . . ." Blaise frowned. Burden's heart missed a beat. He was about to die at a White House reception.

"But," Burden repeated, surprised that he could still speak.

"One of the columnists. You can guess which one. He's out for your scalp. He thinks there was some hanky-panky between you and Ed over an oil deal. Was there?"

"None." On those rare occasions when he was forced to tell a large and deliberate lie Burden knew that he was totally convincing.

"I don't think so. I said it was unlike you. But I also said that if you *were* up to anything, you'd cover your tracks!" Blaise gave him a long shrewd look; then both men laughed and went into the East Room.

Beneath the huge central chandelier, Burden found his wife already seated. She looked uncommonly vivacious, even young. He sat beside her and took her hand. "Isn't this the limit?" she exclaimed.

"The veritable limit," he intoned.

"I talked to the Queen."

What had she said? Again Burden's heart skipped a beat. Was he about to crumple to the floor, the last thing his eyes saw the crystal chandelier above him? "What about?"

"Oh, her children, and Diana. You know, just talk. And how hot it is! She finally allowed she was really dreadfully warm."

"So am I." Burden's collar felt like a metal band drawn tight about his neck.

"You know, she's awfully nervous."

"She doesn't seem to be." Burden looked at the Queen who sat now between President and Vice President.

"But she is!" Frederika Sanford could not resist the interruption as she took a seat in front of them. "I watched her during the receiving line. She was clutching a lace handkerchief. By the time we went in to dinner it was *in shreds!*"

"It must be a strain," conceded Kitty. "Being always on display like that. Nasty immoral things. *We* know about royalty back home."

"What?" Frederika could not believe that she had heard aright.

Burden quickly intervened, as Kitty beamed, unaware that once again her unconscious had joined the party. "How's Enid, and Clay?"

"You see Clay more than I do. You probably see more of Enid, too. I don't know. I supose they're getting along well. Enid brings the baby out to the house, a sweet child. Blaise adores her."

"I think it's awful the way Blaise treats Clay." This was from Kitty's conscious as well as unconscious mind.

"Now, Kitty . . ." Burden's life had been devoted, on the whole successfully, to avoiding this sort of personal confrontation.

". . . is right." Frederika broke in with more than usual force. "When you think what Enid *might* have dragged home! A Communist or a lounge lizard or a Jew." Frederika interrupted herself. "They're Jewish, you know." She indicated the King.

"Oh, no!" Kitty was genuinely anguished.

"He is, anyway," said Frederika, happy to be the first to shatter Kitty's illusions about British royalty. "Prince Albert's father was a Jew. I suppose that's why the King gets on so well with our Franklin Rosenfeld."

Burden looked about uneasily to see if anyone had overhead Frederika. But in the general noise of people being seated her voice was lost. He noticed Harry Hopkins hovering near the President. It was rumored that Hopkins was dying. But dying or not, ambition was by no means gone. He was running for President, too. Earlier in the evening, Burden had teased him for having bought a farm in Iowa, "a nice place," he had told the press, "to bring up my daughter." This bold bid to present himself as a simple Midwestern farmer had caused much amusement in Washington where Hopkins was regarded as a stateless person whose only constituency was the President.

"Everyone is to be fingerprinted. It's hair-raising." Burden turned around. A member of the Cabinet, full of whisky, was talking to a White House aide, unaware of Burden's interest in what he was saying. "Somebody at Justice, probably Hoover, got the bright idea that every government employee should be fingerprinted, and the President bought it."

"Well," said the aide cautiously, "I don't know that he bought *all* of it . . ."

"Yes, he did! He's already told my department to start fingerprinting, even though I said it was a goddamned invasion of privacy. Hitler stuff."

Burden wondered if this might make an issue. Of course the conservatives in their fear of Communism saw spies everywhere and they would probably approve of fingerprinting everyone, except themselves. But Burden was surprised that the President had favored the idea. He himself disliked it. Every man should have the right to hide.

"Blaise thinks he should have his nose fixed. That's the only thing he's said about him in months."

"Whose nose?" asked Burden.

"Clay's. It was broken riding. Blaise thought it looked better the other way."

"I like it the way it is," said Kitty loyally. "I like Clay very much."

Then a fat woman sang. The voice was not pleasing and Burden switched his attention to the back of the President's large balloon-like head, the hair sparse and gray, the scalp pink. He seemed unusually gross next to the demure little King who resembled an ambulatory creation of Madame Tussaud. Despite his vow, Burden wondered if he would ever sit in that chair. Only the day before Nillson had said yes. "You have great appeal. You're a hero in the South and the Midwest. Yet you're not too conservative for the big city types. You can certainly lick Dewey."

"But if *he* runs again?"

"Then all bets are off. But it's not likely. Unless

there's a war." Let there be peace, prayed Burden, as the fat soprano sat down to applause, her last shrill note lingering on the heavy air.

"She has a sweet voice," said Kitty. "For such a fat person."

"Common as Paddy's pig," said Frederika, for whom the worst was yet to come. Marian Anderson stepped forward to sing. "A *colored* woman!" exclaimed Frederika. "Wouldn't you know it?" she whispered fiercely. "Aren't there enough *white* singers in the country?" Burden pretended not to hear. He shut his eyes while Marian Anderson sang. When he was very young he had gone to bed with a colored whore and had been depressed to find that she was no different from a white woman. But there were those who preferred black to white, and found a difference. The first time Burden visited Nillson in his hotel suite, he found a slender high-yellow girl lying on the sofa. She had got up, unabashed, and put on her shoes. "I told you it wasn't the waiter."

Nillson was not at all embarrassed. "Come in," he had said to Burden.

"I'm sorry. I should have rung from downstairs."

"No damage done. Miss Morgan was just leaving. She's an old friend. I knew her mother. Say hello to Bess when you see her, dear."

"I certainly will. Goodbye." She kissed Nillson's cheek as formally as a schoolgirl acknowledging a friend of Mother's; then with a little nod to Burden, she went into the bedroom just as the waiter arrived. The whole thing was handled with such cool dispatch that Burden wondered if he might not have dreamed it all. But he had other things to worry about.

Nillson began with: "Blaise wants us to be friends because he wants you to be nominated for President in 1940. He thinks I can help."

"I think so, too," said Burden.

It had been altogether too easy. There had been no drama, no brimstone, no document signed in blood, no angel desperately signaling through Venetian blinds: *Don't do it!*

Burden would accept a long-standing date to speak in Ottawa. While he was gone, a complaisant Senator would allow the land sale to be approved without discussion. Should there ever be criticism, Burden could quite honestly say that he had taken no part in the subcommittee's decision. Meanwhile, the James Burden Day for President Committee would be established in Washington, with a treasury of two hundred fifty thousand dollars to be raised by Nillson, "from many sources, all legitimate."

The money was duly raised, and wisely spent. The results were gratifying. To the conservative press, he was the only statesman capable of preserving the Constitution while keeping the peace, and Blaise, for one, was certain that Burden's nomination was 'in the bag.' But despite Nillson's extraordinary tact ("I've always wanted you to be President, even before we met"), Burden suffered guilt over what he had done, even though he knew perfectly well that either one played the game according to the rules or not at all. Only once in his career had Burden tried to change the rules. During his first political campaign he had been shocked to find that votes were being bought for him. When he had tried to dissuade his campaign manager, he was told, "But this is how you win elections."

"I'd rather lose." He could still hear his own voice, thin and righteous.

"What *you* want don't matter one hoot in hell. You're just the candidate, and a pretty feeble one at that. Over a thousand people in this district expect to be paid their two dollars come election time and we have no intention of disapointing them." Burden had given way. Since then he had been generally if not happily resigned to the way things are. Rather like Mrs. Roosevelt, who had once told him how in her innocent youth she had gone to her husband and said, "Franklin, they are *buying* votes right here in Dutchess County!" And the President had laughed and told her, "Don't worry, dear, the Republicans buy them, too."

The question, finally, was at what point one drew the line. Neither the President nor Burden was responsible for the corruption of the voters. Even so, was it right to continue the corruption? The question

106

was fatuous. One did what one had to do to win, and that included selling votes as well as buying them. When he took Nillson's money he had sold his vote, which was morally no worse than the accepted practice of buying one. He comforted himself with the thought that what he had done was precisely what any other politician would have done.

"But I am not *any* politician," he said to himself, as the applause for Marian Anderson began. He believed in honor. Had he been born in time, he would gladly have given his life for the Confederacy. The fact that the South's cause was neither wise nor just would have made him fight all the harder; and had that bullet struck *him* at Shiloh, he would have exulted in the pain, unlike his father who saw no virtue in anything human, saw mankind as brutish, cruel and doomed and so became himself brutish, cruel and doomed to go mad. Yet his father had been marked with a white jagged scar that extended from collarbone to left shoulder and for that honorable ensign Burden would have given his life.

What had possessed him, Burden wondered, to bury the bullet? What god had he wanted to propitiate? Temporary insanity, he decided, and the first chance he got he would drive out to Manassas and dig it up. He would need his talisman in the days ahead. Meanwhile to end the reign of the wicked President, a thousand wounds to self-esteem was a small price to pay for victory in a war no less significant than the one in which his father had been scarred.

Suddenly, through the sound of singing, Burden heard thunder; the heat wave had broken, tomorrow would be fair.

Three

1

"HAPPY NEW YEAR." Clay kissed Kitty Day's up-turned face.

"Happy New Year to you, too. Where's Enid?"

"At a party. Where else?"

"Oh, what a shame! I'd hoped she'd come tonight. We never see her." Kitty led Clay into the living room where Burden, Ed Nillson, and Judge Hooey, the state Democratic chairman, sat beside a dying fire.

"Clay came alone," said Kitty, "Enid's gone off gal-livanting."

"Just as well. This is a business meeting." It was Nillson who drew Clay to the fire, as Kitty excused herself.

"I'm sorry it had to be so late," Clay began, turning to Burden who said, "Couldn't matter less. Besides, the Judge had a dinner party."

"Saw your mother last week," said the Judge, eye-ing Clay as though hoping he would plead *nolo contendere*. Clay's mother worked in a bank in the state capital, her widowhood made supportable by a small pension and the nearness of Clay's sister, whose four children gave her much to complain of, and in the complaining, joy. "No *discipline* at all! But just what you'd expect if you don't provide them with a *sense of values* . . ." She herself was stern with a sense of values, derived, she maintained, from the con-templation of Henry Clay, a remote cousin, for whom she had named her only son. Every week, dutifully, she covered many pages of pale pink paper with small pointed writing, inspiring him to succeed.

"You ought to write her more often," said the Judge, putting Clay on the defensive. This was not going to be easy.

"I know I should. Mom's such a good letter writer." He turned to the Senator. "It's true, what we heard. The White House is drawing up the legislation right now."

Burden shook his head. "I'm not surprised. That speech should have warned us. 'If your neighbor's house is on fire . . .' " He mimicked the President with his usual accuracy.

"What legislation?" asked Nillson.

Clay told him that the White House was preparing an Aid to the Democracies bill to be presented in both House and Senate; it was a way of giving money and arms to the British. As Clay spoke, he kept Judge Hooey in his peripheral view and wondered if he would make trouble. It was hard to tell. The Judge sat very small and self-contained in the big armchair beside the fire. He seemed not at all interested in what Clay was saying. To the Judge Europe was small potatoes compared to the Fourth Congressional District, where the Republicans were gaining strength, or the Third, where they ought to be gaining strength, or the First, where an unexpected candidate had suddenly materialized, upsetting the machine which the Judge with such patient care had assembled over the years in order to keep random happenings in the electoral process at a minimum. The Judge profoundly hated a surprise on election day.

Burden was against any aid to the British. "For one thing they're bankrupt. Even Lord Lothian admits it. And if that's true, we're just throwing good money after bad, because even if they win, they'll never be able to pay us back."

It was Nillson who answered. "We can't afford to let Hitler win." Clay was intrigued: Nillson never disagreed with the Senator.

"How can we stop him?" Burden was gloomy. "Joe Kennedy says the British have had it. I think he's right."

"I'm for helping them anyway." Nillson was unexpectedly firm. Usually when he sensed disagreement, his enigmatic smile would suddenly flash and in its radiant cover, he would shift ground with lightning speed. But tonight he did not take so much as a single step toward safe country.

It was the Senator who was forced to give ground. "Perhaps you're right, Ed. Who knows?"

More and more, Clay had noticed that Burden had come to defer to Nillson. It had all begun with the President's announcement that because of the situation in Europe (France defeated, Britain beleaguered) he would seek a third term. This meant that though the James Burden Day for President Committee continued to function, its goal was no longer the Presidency but the Vice Presidency. A week before the convention, the Senator had gone to the White House without appointment, the result of a telephone call. Clay never knew what was discussed but the Senator had returned in a good mood and told his supporters not to push too hard at the convention, indicating that he was the President's choice for Vice President even though it was plain to Clay, if not to the Senator, that the President would never accept Burden Day or any conservative as a running mate. Their only hope would be to get so much Presidential support for Burden on the first ballot that Roosevelt would be obliged to take him for Vice President. But Burden had held back, and the President, winning renomination with only token resistance, chose the dreamy Henry Wallace to be Vice President. When Wallace's name was announced to the convention, there had been a violent uproar and even the most loyal of Roosevelt's admirers had been angry. In his room at the Blackstone Hotel surrounded by placards, "A New Day with Day," the Senator had struck the radio a blow. "The son of a bitch," said James Burden Day, and Clay never knew whether he meant the President or Henry Wallace.

The Senator took little part in the election. He attended a few rallies in his own state but neglected to endorse the national ticket. Clay was certain that Burden had voted for the curious but likable Wendell Willkie, who had taken the Republican Party nomination by storm and then gone on to campaign as a New Dealer.

Through all this, Nillson remained loyal or at least

110

attentive. He dissolved the committee in a business-like way. All outstanding bills were paid, and the troops let go. Hope ended, or was deferred. Despite the Senator's disappointment, Clay knew that he was already looking forward to 1944. So was Nillson; to Clay's surprise, Nillson still acted as if the prize might yet be gained. He continued to be a part of their lives, always obliging, except just now. But the Senator was not about to quarrel. He gave his tragic half-smile.

"Affairs of state can wait. The house is not burning *yet*. We can keep our garden hose for ourselves." With a gesture, he dislodged the celebrated forelock from across his forehead. "Gentlemen, we are here to discuss the special election in the Second Congressional District. And Clay."

Clay was exultant. One way or the other, his life would change.

"As you know, Judge, Clay has had his eye on that seat for some time. He's known in the District. The fact is, he was born there. And for some years now, unknown to me, he's been keeping that seat warm." The half-smile became a whole one. "Now that our old friend McClure has been raised to the Federal bench, the seat is empty, and Clay would like to fill it. But . . ." Burden turned to Judge Hooey and opened wide his arms as though to embrace him. "He will not, he cannot, he must not make a move in our state without you."

There was a long silence. Logs popped in the fire. Wind sounded in the trees outside. Clay felt a sudden draught, as though somewhere a door had opened. The weather forecast had been snow.

The Judge pushed his chin down hard against his collar; the celluloid vanished beneath loose folds of flesh. Upon this one man's will, Clay's future depended. At last the Judge spoke, a single word. "Jesse?"

At first Clay thought he had merely cleared his throat. But the Senator was quicker than he. Jesse meant Jesse Momberger, the senior Senator from their state, a political wonder who supported the President as often as Burden hindered him and yet managed

111

somehow to keep in the good graces of the conservative majority of their state.

"Jesse will bestow the blessing, when the time comes."

"They like Jesse in that district," said the Judge, as if he wished it were not so. He turned to Clay for the first time. "You know you're going to have to fight a good man who wants that seat and by rights should have it."

"Yes, sir. I know that. But I'm prepared to fight for it."

"These damned Johnny-come-latelys," the Judge murmured to the fire, and Clay's heart sank. "I can't help you," said the Judge finally. It was the Senator who got the range again just as Clay pondered suicide.

"But you won't help the other man?"

The Judge grinned suddenly, a ghastly sight, dentures huge and implausible. "That's right. I won't help nobody."

The Senator chuckled. "You are the cleverest old fox ever to trick a hound dog." As always, Clay marveled at the ease with which the Senator dealt with backwoodsmen. He never patronized, never seemed to curry favor, never got a signal wrong. Working so closely with Burden in Washington where he was not always wise, Clay tended to forget that his employer was their state's craftiest politician.

The Judge turned to Clay. "All up to you."

"Thank you, Judge." Clay took the Judge's limp hand and shook it warmly.

"You ought to win." The Judge was flat. "Now I got to go get my beauty sleep. Long past my bedtime. Oh." He stopped, halfway to the door. "Got a rich wife, ain't you?"

While Clay prepared an answer, Nillson came to his rescue. "Yes, he has."

"It'll cost you maybe twenty, thirty thousand. Lot more than the old days, when me and Jim started." The Judge was one of the few men to call the Senator by his first name.

"I think Clay can manage," Nillson was obviously amused.

The Judge grunted. "He better. It's also considered usual to give the first year's salary to the party, kind of investment, you might say, in the future."

"Of course," said Clay, much too quickly.

"Well, that seems to be that," said the Senator, slipping his arm through the Judge's arm and steering him toward the hall. "I can't think why I'm doing this. I don't want Clay to leave me. If I had any sense, I'd conspire against him." Clay could not hear what the Judge said to this, for they were out of range. Clay dried his sweating palms against his trousers.

"Nervous?" Nillson saw everything.

"That's a tough old bird."

"Apparently. I haven't much experience with these grass-roots types. What *will* you do for money?"

"I'll manage somehow." Clay was not yet ready to reveal that since Blaise was still hostile, his only hope was Nillson.

"The Judge is with us!" The Senator entered the room with a gust of cold air. He was jubilant, as though the victory were somehow his.

"Thank God!" Clay was fervent.

"You know what he said at the door? He said, 'I won't do him a bit of harm.' That's the endorsement we wanted."

"How can you let Clay go?" Nillson asked suddenly. Clay turned to him, scenting danger. "He must be like a right arm."

The Senator gestured, a matter usually of aesthetic pleasure to Clay. With most men a gesture was simply a sudden movement of the body, an involuntary jerk or tic, but the Senator's gestures were superbly revealing in their studied art. He exhibited his talent now. The head tilted to one side, inner despondency; arms fell straight to the sides, palms out, acceptance; then the entire body sank into the armchair beside the fire, resignation as the long years drew to a golden close, without regret.

"They must all go, sooner or later." The words were superfluous. Clay loved the old man, exactly as he was meant to.

"But you *could* make it tough for him." Nillson

winked at Clay to show that he was not serious, proving that he was.

"Never!"

On that sharp word, icy air flooded the room.

"Hello, Clay. I didn't know you were here." Diana stepped back, ready for flight. But it was Clay who wanted most to avoid the encounter.

"I was just going."

"No, stay!" bellowed Billy Thorne. He was drunk.

"Billy, I think we better go upstairs. They're having a conference."

"Conspiring against the people, Senator?" Clay marveled at Billy's gift for striking the wrong note. It was hard not to dislike him. The Senator's wince was visible to every eye except Billy's.

"Unlikely, my dear Thorne, since I was elected by them." The Senator never called his son-in-law anything but Thorne. Clay found it remarkable that he spoke to him at all. On the day before Christmas, Diana had quit her job and married Billy. On the day after Christmas Billy announced that he had been fired from his job at the Department of Commerce. No one knew why. The indigent newlyweds were now living in the attic.

"Washington is filled with elected officials who are devoted enemies of the people. Think how many members of Congress represent not people but oil! Great geysers of bubbling prehistoric oil, the property of hard-faced men who worship profit. And how are you, Mr. Nillson?" Clay found Billy's death wish awesome.

"Trying to compose my hard face into a gentle mask," said Nillson. "Diana, come give an old man a New Year's kiss!"

"You are good!" Diana embraced Nillson warmly. "We've been going to New Year's parties. I didn't realize it was so late. We'd better go up, Billy."

But Billy would not let bad enough alone. "Senator, I made a bet at the White House that when you denounce Lend-Lease, you'll say 'Let the British pull their own chestnuts out of the fire.' "

"Is my style so predictable?" The Senator's voice was even. His was an old hand with hecklers.

"In a word, yes." Billy poured himself a drink. The others watched him with the fascination audiences usually reserve for an acrobat working without a net. "You will oppose the bill, of course?"

"I wasn't aware that such a bill exists." The Senator gave him a wide-eyed look.

"It exists, all right; we're . . . they're working on it right now at the White House."

Reluctantly, Clay admired the deliberate confusion of the pronoun. Billy had many dealings with the New Dealers but precisely what his relations were to any one of them no one knew, and it was the not knowing that gave him authority in political drawing rooms. It was too easy to dismiss him as a liar; also dangerous because whenever one did, sure as fate, Harry Hopkins would take Billy's arm at a party and the two of them would go off to talk privately in a corner. Billy was thought to help write the President's speeches. At the moment, his principal claim to attention was as editor of *The American Idea*. For two years a handsome mockup of the magazine had made the rounds, but for lack of money the first issue had yet to appear. On occasion Billy sounded discouraged; Diana never. To publish *The American Idea* was her dream and she would not let it go. Unfortunately, potential sources of money were quick to dry up under the hot radiance of Billy's uncharm. Nillson, the last hope, had only recently turned them down.

On orders from the Senator, Clay had tried to find out what had happened at Commerce. But no one would tell him. To the direct question: Is he a Communist? the Department declined to answer.

Billy swayed on his wooden leg, drink in hand, while the Senator lectured him on the Constitution. "Legislation originates only in the Congress. Those bills which have to do with finance—and Lend-Lease is one—must originate first in the House of Representatives. At no point does the Constitution allow the Executive to initiate legislation."

"But it's a lucky thing the Executive does. If it didn't, where would the country be? Where would *you* be? Every line of the Day-Mortimer Act was drafted by the Department of Agriculture, and your only contribution was putting it in the hopper, doubt-less unread."

That does it, thought Clay. The Senator went white. Clay filled in. "That doesn't happen to be true, Billy." Clay stressed the diminutive's last syllable. "I know because I helped the Senator write the bill. The only contribution Agriculture made was to let us use their statistics."

"Not the way I heard it," said Billy.

"We are all misinformed from time to time." The Senator had regained control. He was cool. "Actually, I've never introduced a bill prepared for me by the Executive. After all, if we don't legislate, we have no function."

"It may well be there is no function for a Senate like the one you were elected to."

Nillson got to his feet. "Burden, I must go. Clay, I gather I was invited here to bestow some sort of blessing. I do so." They shook hands warmly. "Diana, courage." Nillson kissed her cheek. He turned to Billy. "I hope you find a job soon, Mr. Thorne." The insult was given in precisely the same tone that the others had been told good night. For a moment no one could quite believe what had been said. Nillson was at the door when Billy, with a roar, caught his arm.

"Because I happen to be honest . . ."

Abruptly Nillson pulled his arm free just as Billy took a step toward him. Off balance, Billy's artificial leg buckled under him and he fell backwards onto the floor. For a moment no one moved. Then Diana hurried to help him up. As she did, like a magician's trick, the leg grew longer and longer until Billy finally pulled it back into place.

"You son of a bitch," he said to Nillson, who said, "Good night," and left.

Clay helped Diana put Billy on a chair. The Senator made no move to help. Once the leg was again secure, Billy was himself again. "That man should be in jail! The stuff we have on him . . ."

"I think we'd better go up, dear." Diana turned to Clay. "How nice to see you again." She was unexpectedly formal. He wondered if she had married

Billy on the rebound. If she had, he was twice guilty.

"You must come to dinner," said Clay. "Both of you, with Enid and me."

"We'd like that." Decorously, Mr. and Mrs. Thorne withdrew for the night, leaving Clay alone with the Senator, who threw up his hands, putting into this gesture all his high mimetic art. "What am I going to do with him?" It was the first time he had ever revealed to Clay the extent of his horror at Diana's marriage.

"Find him a job, I suppose. Anything to get him out of the house."

"I've tried. But he won't take just any job. He wants to stay in government, but that's . . ."

"Impossible. I wonder why."

The Senator smiled his beyond-tragedy smile. "We shall discover that when I am up for re-election and my opponent announces that my son-in-law is a Soviet agent."

"I don't think even the Russians would want him. Why *did* she marry him?" A stupid question; the Senator's reproachful look was like a blow. Quickly Clay added, "I mean politically. She was always a conservative, wasn't she? Like us. Then suddenly she takes up with all those New Dealers, and marries him."

"Normal reaction to her father? I don't know. I suppose he has some hold over her, having lost a leg . . ." He paused. Both pondered the false leg. The Senator walked Clay to the front door. "I'm very pleased about the Judge," he said.

"So am I." Clay turned to the Senator, suddenly affectionate. "You did it all."

"Hardly. And don't forget Ed Nillson. He'll be helpful."

"But in exchange . . . ?"

The Senator looked at him blankly. What a superb actor he was, thought Clay. "Exchange?" The Senator said the word as though he had never heard it before.

"Will I have to . . . to do anything for him?"

"Oh, I shouldn't think so." The response was smooth. "Naturally he's interested in keeping the oil depletion resources allowance on the books, but so are

117

you. There will be no . . ." He smiled as he selected the obvious phrase: ". . . conflict of interest." The two men shook hands warmly. Then Clay got into his four-year-old Plymouth coupé and drove through the cold drizzle of the New Year to his own house.

It was two in the morning and Enid was not home. She came and went as she pleased and usually he made no complaint. She liked to go to parties; he did not. So she went her way and he went his. The arrangement was reasonably satisfactory except on those occasions when he wanted her, like tonight, and she was not there. Feeling deprived, he undressed, got into bed, and promptly fell asleep, one hand on his genitals like a child.

He dreamed of water, and awakened to find that it was a quarter to five. The light in the bathroom was on, and water was being run. Half angry, half lustful, Clay went to the bathroom door and opened it to find Enid douching herself.

"I thought you were asleep." She spoke first.

"No." The marriage ended. "Who was it?"

"This *is* pretty awful, isn't it?" Her tone was matter-of-fact. "I'm sorry."

"Anybody I know?"

"I don't think so." Suddenly she was angry. "Well, don't just stand there, looking at me."

"What do you want me to do, beat the hell out of you?"

"You couldn't, if you wanted to."

He struck her, giving her pleasure but himself none. Then he took a blanket and in the dark made his way downstairs to the living room. Still in the dark, he wrapped himself in the blanket and lay down on the sofa. He decided to pretend that he was still asleep and dreaming, but the sounds of a toilet flushing, of a door slamming, of footsteps crossing the bedroom overhead, made it impossible to pretend that he was anything but wide awake, with a life in need of mending.

By artificial light the colors were lurid and unconvincing, as though the flowers had been made of bright paper and gleaming wax. Marveling at the warmth within this narrow world of glass (snow fell outside), Peter made his way between two parallel rows of wooden tables which converged at the far end of the greenhouse like an exercise in perspective. On the tables a thousand plants were set out in pots. He paused at the gardenias, his favorite flower ever since he was a child and Frederika had built the greenhouse because "It will be such a saving, really, to grow one's own flowers." Of course it had been, as she intended, a useless luxury but it had given Peter almost as much pleasure as it had the old gardener, a courtly Virginian who always wore a straw hat indoors and kept his shirtsleeves neatly rolled and gartered. It was he who explained to Peter the Latin names of the plants, as well as the proper English names; gardenia was the wrong word but Peter used it anyway. Delicately, so as not to bruise the thick white petals, Peter touched the fullest blossom on the largest plant. Among the dark green of leaves it shone like a white star.

"There you are! But get away from those gardenias. I can't stand the smell. They make my head ache. I don't know why Mother's so keen on them. They remind me of dancing school! Remember Mrs. Shippen's? When each boy had to bring his date a corsage consisting of two wilted yellow gardenias. My God, it's hot in here."

Enid fanned herself with a small evening bag. She wore black which was unusual for her, but the effect was ominously splendid. Like a jeweler's black velvet foil, she set off the flowers. She seemed not at all nervous even though she had been most urgent that Peter meet her here the moment dinner was over. But now that they were together, begonias between them, she merely sipped her whisky and soda, frowned distractedly and said, "That girl from New York, you're not really going to marry her?"

"No. What gave you the idea I was?"

"Mother. Who else?"

"I don't plan to marry anyone, just yet." This was accurate. Peter noticed that whenever Enid raised the glass to her lips the hand trembled slightly and with each swallow she would shut her eyes tight as though trying to exchange the outside world for a more manageable one within. Trouble with Clay, he had already decided, pleased that she had chosen him to confide in because for some years he had felt a certain restraint on her side, and could not guess its cause. Their lives were different, of course. He was still a college boy, member of an anonymous horde sought after by hostesses with daughters and no one else, while Enid was what Helen Ashley Barbour called a "young society matron," occupied with going to parties and raising her child.

"Don't ever get married!" Enid opened her eyes wide.

"Ever?"

"It's Clay," she added disjointedly, putting her drink down among the roots of a plant with green-red leaves.

"What's wrong?" Peter was obscurely excited at the thought of Enid's marriage going wrong. Like an old admirer who sees a chance of getting back the beloved, he offered sympathy.

"It happened. In the bathroom." She looked about distractedly.

"What happened in the bathroom?"

"I caught them. Clay and this girl. Making love."

"On the floor, or in the tub?" Peter was momentarily diverted by the logistics.

"In the bed!" She was irritable. "They had gone into the bathroom. You know . . . after . . . and I caught her, using my douche bag." Enid spoke evenly now, control regained. "I said, 'Well, this is a mess, isn't it?' and the girl just stared at me, mouth open, and Clay said, 'Yes, I guess this is a mess,' and I said, 'I suppose we better get a divorce,' and he said, 'We'll talk about that later,' and then I said, 'You might at least have gone somewhere else, not used *our* bed!' "

"What did she say?"

"Who? What do you mean, what did she say? She didn't say a damned thing, the bitch, she just stared at me, with my own douche bag in her hand. I hope she's pregnant." Enid plunged her hand into the jungle and pulled forth the whisky and soda. Eyes shut, she drank.

"Who was . . . who is she?"

The beautiful eyes opened, made adjustment to the confusing world outside. "A girl. South American. I don't know. Somebody's wife. A diplomat's wife. Clay thought I was spending the day out here, New Year's Day. Remember? But I had a hangover and went home early and found them and now . . ."

"But if it's just a girl, why are you so bothered?" Peter accepted the lenient Washington view that men were promiscuous and women monogamous and each invariably ran true to type. Where he was not usual was in his willingness to accept the fact that the way things are is neither shocking nor undesirable.

"Listen, it was *my* bed they made love in! Don't you know what that means to a woman? If it was someplace else, a hotel room, or the back seat of a car and I never had to know about it or if I did know about it I didn't have to . . . react, I might be able to say, oh, what the hell, but in my own bed, with the baby in the next room! It was too much."

"Does he want a divorce?"

"Of course not. But I do. I can't go on living with him. Not now. It's so damned unfair!" There were tears. He took her in his arms. She clutched him about the waist, her face against his dinner jacket, sobbing hoarsely. He was perfectly happy.

But the storm passed. She pulled away. "Sorry," she said. Her eyes were red. She straightened her hair, fixed her face in a compact mirror. "You're getting fat," she said, chilling him.

"I'm not," he said automatically as they again became brother and sister: yes you are, no I'm not. But she was right. He had gained ten pounds since the beginning of the fall term. He needed exercise. Once the warm weather started, he would play tennis. In the spring he would be in shape again. The ball would skim the net. He would show her.

"I don't know what to do!"

"Have you told Father?"

She shook her head. "He'd be only too pleased. Besides, he's up to something. Father and Clay, they're together right now."

Peter had been startled to find Clay at dinner; and said so. No one had any explanation to offer. According to Enid, "It just came out of the blue. We hadn't talked all week, Clay and I. He's been sleeping downstairs on the couch. I insisted on that. Then this morning he said, 'Your father's asked us to Laurel House, for dinner.' 'Both of us?' I asked. 'Yes, both of us,' he said with that ice-cold look he has when he really hates you, and he hates everybody . . ."

"Oh, come on."

"He does. Particularly you. He thinks you're just another rich-boy dilettante. He's said so a thousand times."

Peter was stung. He had thought Clay liked him. In any case, he could not bear for anyone to call him a dilettante since that might very likely be his fate. But then he would not graduate from the university until June. After that, there would be time enough to determine just who he was and what he could do. He would be great of course; he had no choice.

But Enid was unaware of his distress as she recounted her own. 'I think he must have called Father. Told him something. To turn him against me."

"But what?"

"I don't know. That I was the one having an affair, something like that. Clay's capable of anything."

"Then you go tell Father the truth . . ."

"About what?" Frederika's question was more than usually well-timed. She stood in the doorway to the greenhouse. "What are you two doing in here? I saw the lights were on."

"Talking, Mother." Enid reached for her glass and finished the drink. "Come on," she said to Peter. "Let's face the music." She hurried past Frederika, who looked after her, bewildered.

"Face what music? What's wrong?"

"Enid's dramatizing herself, that's all." Peter decided not to tell their mother what Enid had said. "Trouble with Clay, I suppose." He gave her that much, certain it would not interest her, but it did.

"I thought so." Mechanically, Frederika removed a dead leaf from the nearest plant. As she got older she spent more and more time in the greenhouse or out of doors, creating terraces and floral borders, rock gardens and tree-lined vistas.

"What made you think so?"

"It's perfectly plain, just looking at them tonight. Then when Clay phoned Blaise yesterday I knew something had happened."

"Clay phoned Father?" Enid was right. There was a conspiracy.

"Yes, and the next thing I knew, Blaise had asked Clay here for dinner tonight." Frederika switched off the greenhouse lights. Snow swirled against gray glass. Peter felt for the stem of the largest gardenia blossom, and pinched it off. Holding the flower between thumb and forefinger, he followed his mother back into the drawing room.

"What's that for?" Harold Griffiths pointed to the flower.

"Luck." Peter was cryptic. He set the flower on a side table. Already one petal had started to turn yellow. "They don't last," he added.

"The greenhouse. I'd forgot. What an excessive display of wealth."

"Envious?"

"Yes."

"Good." Exchanges with Harold were not always so direct nowadays. With each year Peter found Harold increasingly predictable in his wit. They sat side by side and watched the other members of the party maneuver about the room. Enid held forth at the fireplace where their mother reigned beneath a Boldini portrait of herself, wearing lace. Blaise sat in a corner with Clay.

"When was the ban lifted?" asked Harold.

"I don't know. I couldn't have been more surprised to see Clay at dinner."

"It's a pity, in a way. There was something so awe-inspiring about your father's forbidding his son-in-law to set foot in his house. It was such splendid . . . corn." Harold had obviously surprised himself with the choice of word but he did not retract it, pleasing Peter. "Now he's spoiled everything. Like Lionel Barrymore in the last reel, making up with Garbo."

"But this is hardly the last reel."

"My boy, I've misjudged you. . . ." While Harold imitated Lionel Barrymore, Peter noticed that there were still pecans in the nut dish. He thought he had eaten the last one before dinner, but there beneath the cashews were a half dozen unbroken pecans, glittering with salt. He ate them, two at a time, delighting in the first hard dry crunch followed immediately by a soft release of oil. So absorbed was he by the pecans that he did not hear the beginning of a sentence which ended ". . . or would he be too afraid?"

Peter swallowed hard. "What do you think?" Always a safe response; Harold enjoyed explaining things.

"I think it was politics that brought them together." Harold was still talking about Clay and Blaise. "Enid's a bit strange tonight, isn't she?"

"Strange? No. She's always the same." The last pair of pecans were ground to a salty pulp and swallowed. Mouth dry, he asked Harold about the paper.

"I'm bored with it. I'm bored with everything."

"With movies?"

"Am I bored with life? No, not yet. It's these damned politicians that depress me. Grinding away, as though what any of them did ever mattered. They're interchangeable, the lot of them." As Harold began his familiar diatribe, Peter noticed for the first time that, properly speaking, there were no politicians at all in the room, a tribute to the international crisis: the French Ambassador, a British economist, various journalists returned from abroad with grim warnings and dark hints about "certain elements" at home that wanted war or appeasement, depending upon the politics of the journalist. Blaise listened to all of them and said little. Until the election, the *Tribune* had been isolationist but now Peter suspected that it was only a matter of time before his father would support aid for England.

Peter watched his father watch Clay. Again, uncharacteristically, Blaise was listening and Clay was talking fast. He wondered if Clay would now win Blaise. It was not impossible. Peter had always thought that his father had reacted violently to Clay simply because his daughter's marriage had brutally reminded him that he was aging, losing, dying, despite the fierce will to prevail that beat inside him like a second heart.

"So what will you do?" asked Harold suddenly. A compulsive performer, he knew instinctively when his audience's attention was flagging. "Go to work for the paper?"

Peter felt sudden panic, as he always did at the thought of the future and all the grave decisions yet to be made. "I don't think so. Not on Father's paper anyway. What could I do?" Two summers of desultory work on the city desk had made him despair of journalism. As for the business side, he was hopeless, which was to say not interested. Yet Blaise had taken his son's mediocre performances in stride; in fact, Peter suspected that he was really pleased for if Peter were entirely to fail, that would mean one less youthful rival. His father must be disappointed.

"Perhaps I'll go to New York." Peter was vague. New York had always represented freedom, danger, the actual world, as opposed to the safe familiarity of Washington.

"*You* can, of course," said Harold bitterly. "You have money."

"When I'm twenty-one. In September." For half his life, Peter had looked forward to his twenty-first birthday as the moment when he would be able to lead any sort of life he wanted. But now that he had almost attained his majority, he had begun to grow alarmed. He would be free, but to do what? He had no idea. At the university, he had recently become interested in American history. Grateful for any sign of interest from one of his golden charges, the instructor had suggested that he do graduate work and obtain a master's degree while continuing to study the career of Aaron Burr, whose portrait hung in the library at Laurel House. But Peter could not endure the thought of another moment spent in a university. Aaron Burr

125

could be investigated at the Congressional Library where Peter now spent a good deal of time, making notes and talking to Diana, whose recent marriage continued to appall him.

"I've got to get something to drink," he said, abandoning Harold. On the console just behind his father, bottles were displayed. As he poured himself soda water, Peter heard Clay mention "special election" and he realized that at last his brother-in-law was about to make the great leap onto the political stage.

"Peter." Blaise looked up at him. "Sit down. Join the family conference."

Peter sat down. 'Family conference': Clay was doing very well indeed. But he did not seem happy. Nor young. But then Clay was at least thirty (to Peter middle age), and his face was set for life, unlike Peter's which was still unformed.

"Clay's done me a good turn tonight." Blaise smiled, a rare sight.

"What was that?" Peter was curious. It must have been excessively good for Blaise to lift the ban so suddenly.

"Information."

Clay looked exhausted and Peter wondered if adultery was really so tiring. "State secrets?" asked Peter, just as Enid's laugh sounded hoarsely across the room.

"They won't be secrets tomorrow." Blaise ignored his daughter. He seemed unusually pleased but Peter could not tell whether with himself or Clay. "After all, I'm a newspaperman," he exaggerated. "Clay's just told me about an interesting meeting the President had today with certain Senate leaders in which he tried to sell them H.R. 1776, known to our readers as the Lend-Lease bill, or Give Away America, a bit at a time."

"I thought the press should know what he's up to." If Clay was concerned about the ethics of what he was doing, he did not show it. In fact, he seemed perfectly indifferent, which Peter knew would make an excellent impression on Blaise, who was as impervious to moral nicety as he was to charm. Possessing neither himself, Blaise suspected these qualities in others. The thought that Clay and his father might yet be allies somewhat disappointed Peter who liked his passions raw. Apparently not even hatred was sacred.

A member of the last Polish Embassy to Washington presented himself to Blaise to say good night. The Pole was tall, and wore a monocle; his wife was equally tall, and also wore a monocle. They were accompanied by a small pale woman whom Peter recognized but could not identify. While the Poles thanked their host profusely, their pale attendant admired the room. "This is my first time here," she said, as though the house were not merely a house but some sort of sight to be ticked off a list.

"Really?" Blaise looked at her blankly. "But you're from Washington, aren't you?"

"Oh, yes. I'm Irene Bloch."

She pronounced her first name as though it were French, and Peter knew exactly who she was, and realized the significance of her appearance at Laurel House, for his mother was severe to climbers and merciless to Jews, except for a handful of Rothschilds and Warburgs who, she often noted with surprise, were "just like anyone else." Peter's own anti-Semitism had been worn down at the university by his friend the instructor in history, but despite his new liberalism, Peter found himself resenting Irene Bloch in the drawing room at Laurel House. There had to be some standards in society. Jews could be intellectually stimulating but they were not the way people ought to be. They tended to look wrong and behave badly, like Mrs. Bloch, who had got the Poles to bring her to a house where she knew she was not welcome.

Blaise was brisk. "Good night, Mrs. Black," he said, carefully getting her name wrong. Then the Poles, unaware of their mistake, departed, Laurel House forever shut to them.

Suddenly Enid materialized. Peter saw alarm in Clay's eyes. That proved he was guilty.

Enid stood, glass in hand, swaying slightly. She had taken too much whisky which was unlike her. Ordinarily she held her liquor well.

"Well, Daddy, how do you like Clay now?"

"We're having a talk." Blaise was neutral.

"Has he told you all about running for Congress and how much he needs your money?"

127

"Money has not yet been mentioned." Blaise was serene.

"It will be. Don't worry."

Clay stood up. "Come on, Enid. Let's go."

"Go? I'm not going anywhere with you. I'm staying here. Can I stay here, Daddy?"

"If you want to." Blaise was cold. "But since Clay is your husband . . ."

"No thanks to you. You've done your best to make us miserable." This new tack promised rich drama. Suddenly protective, Clay took her arm but she pushed him to one side.

"Don't touch me, you son of a bitch," she said to her husband, bringing Blaise to his feet with a roar. "You're drunk! Get out!"

The room was silent. The guests had heard. Enid gave her father a long look. Then she turned to Clay and said, "Take me home."

Attended by Frederika, Clay and Enid left the room. Talk began nervously. Though father and son were facing each other, Blaise's eyes were on his daughter's back.

"Do you think," said Blaise at last, as though Peter were not his son but a visitor to be diverted, "that the Lend-Lease bill can pass the House?"

Peter played the part of a guest. "I think so. Yes. By a comfortable margin."

"I think I'm in favor of it, properly amended," said Blaise, still staring at the door through which his daughter had passed. Watching his father, Peter realized to what extent Enid had outraged male comity. Blaise, aroused, was merciless, and if he chose to be punitive there would be no one to help Enid except Clay, who would not, and Frederika, who could not. No one will come to her aid except me, thought Peter, taking a mint from the nearest silver plate; through bitter chocolate the mint stung. Blaise said that he would personally write an editorial, endorsing H.R. 1776, but with suitable amendments because "We don't want Franklin giving away the whole country, do we?"

"No," said his son. "We don't."

Burden sat at his desk in the Senate Chamber, holding in his hand H.R. 1776. The roll was being called. Voting on the bill had begun early. The galleries were packed. Just above him sat Kitty and Clay while Blaise Sanford presided imperially over the press box. Even the most frivolous of the Senators was aware that this was an important moment. Faces were grave, voices solemn as the "Ayes" and the "Nays" rang out in the green-lit Chamber.

It had been a discouraging month for the isolationists. One outspoken Senator had not helped the cause by accusing the President of wanting to 'plow under every fourth American boy.' On the other hand, the cause of intervention had not been much helped by the insouciant testimony of Wendell Willkie who, explaining his sudden conversion to aid for England, referred to his recent speeches denouncing the New Deal warmongers as "campaign oratory."

Nevertheless the bill which had been drafted at the Treasury and given to the majority leader of each House to introduce was certain to pass. Helplessly, the American First Committee raged. Important hostesses spoke bitterly of secret alliances between Roosevelt and the British. Catholic priests declared that Hitler was, after all, the last stout shield against Stalin, the Antichrist. But to no avail. The bill would pass.

"Mr. Clapper." They were approaching the 'D's.' Burden thought for a moment of the consternation in the Chamber were he to vote "Aye." He would make the headlines but lose the coming election, even though he suspected that at heart the citizens of his state were not so isolationist as their Congressional delegation. The people tended to be unreliable on issues they did not ordinarily think much about. Although they disliked Europe on principle, a few newspaper stories about the rape of Belgian nuns and they would want to stand up to the bully.

"Mr. Chavez."

No, Burden could not vote "Aye." He was too closely identified with the isolationists. Yet, in a way, he wanted the British to win and Hitler to fail—unlike certain of his colleagues who hated Engand and secretly supported Hitler for reasons that did not bear close scrutiny. At the most Burden had wanted to amend the bill, to limit the President's power to give away arms and materials. But his amendment had failed and he was conscious of having played no significant part in the great debate. A year ago, he was the President's conservative successor, courted by all. Now he was one of ninety-six Senators. Suddenly in need of solace, he looked up at Kitty who gave him a little wave.

But there was no disguising the fact that at a time when he should be leading the Senate, he was not. Of course, no one else was either. The day before the Bill was to be presented to Congress, he had gone to the White House with a group of Congressional leaders. Not once during the meeting was Burden consulted. Except for Senator Barkley, who talked political strategy, the others were as silent and acquiescent as he.

At the end of the meeting Burden shook the President's huge hand and said, "I had a splendid time in Chicago." The President looked at him blankly. Burden could not resist a twist to the screw. "Mr. Wallace was an excellent choice, not popular perhaps but I'm sure what you had in mind all along."

The President was saved by a Senator from Texas who made him vow solemnly that the battleship *Texas* would never be given to the British. The President so swore.

Burden had, of course, been outmaneuvered at Chicago by the President. Once the first shock had passed, he rather admired the way in which it had been done. In a private meeting at the White House, the President had been friendly, apparently candid, entirely plausible. In so many words he had said that taking into account the importance and restiveness of the conservative wing of the party, his running mate would almost certainly be a conservative. The President had mentioned several possible choices, of whom the first was Burden, who fell crashing into the sort of trap he himself was so expert at laying for others: seeming to promise favors he had no intention of bestowing in order to keep the would-be recipient in a cordial and optimistic frame of mind. Having left the meeting convinced that he would be selected Vice President, Burden had not pressed his own campaign for the Presidency. If he had, he might seriously have hurt the President at the convention and dramatized the split between Left and Right. But he had done nothing, just as the President wanted. Thinking of that day in the Blackstone Hotel when he had heard the news on the radio, Burden's blood pressure rose so that he could hardly breathe. Fortunately, at that instant the clerk called his name and he shouted "Nay," relieving the pressure in his throat and evoking, as reward for vehemence, applause from the gallery. A small recognition was better than none.

The final vote was sixty in favor of Lend-Lease to thirty-one opposed. The President had won again.

The day was bright but chilly. Spring was late. Ordinarily by March, daffodils and forsythia would be in bloom. But this year the winter had lasted longer than usual. The lawns and gardens of the Capitol were brown and bleak. With Clay beside him, Burden made his way to the Senate Office Building. The anti-Nazi, pro-British pickets had all gone home, and only the America First banners were still forlornly displayed by angry youths and well-dressed matrons in cloth coats.

"Pretty much what I predicted," said Burden.

"We never had a chance." Clay was perfunctory. Burden suspected him of wanting America to join the war. None of the young men knew what modern war was like. He did. As a new Senator, he had toured the battlefields of France and seen corpses rotting in the mud and dangling from barbed wire; he had heard shells whistle and explode; he had smelled poison gas. It was not like Shiloh where a man with a gun could fight for his honor on equal terms with another man so armed and so inspired. It was not the same thing now. Not at all.

An America Firster waved a placard angrily in

Burden's face. "I'm Senator Day." Burden smiled pleasantly, hoping the youth would realize that they were allies.

"It's you Jew bastards who want a war!" shouted the zealot.

"Oh, dear." Burden hurried away, followed by the amused Clay. "Heaven protect us from our admirers."

Not until they were in Burden's inner office, with Mrs. Blaine as buffer between them and the mob of reporters wanting statements and partisans wanting comfort, did Burden at last summon up the nerve to say what he had wanted to say all week. Standing now at the bust of Cicero, holding the *New York Times* in his hands as though it contained notes for a speech, he said, "Is it true that Enid has left you?"

Clay's answer was prompt. "No. She's gone to New York for a few weeks, to visit friends. That's all."

Burden was relieved despite the fact that he knew he was not entirely above enjoying the misfortunes of those he loved. He put down the newspaper and turned from Cicero to Clay who now sat on the edge of the desk, balancing a letter opener as though it were a dagger. "I'm glad. But you should do something to stop the rumors."

"What are they?"

"That you . . ." Burden was embarrassed. He was not one to discuss sexual matters with anyone, particularly another man. ". . . are having an affair with a girl and that Enid caught you *flagrante delicto,* as it were."

Clay's expression was stony. "Who is the girl supposed to be?"

"A Brazilian, I believe. A diplomat's wife. Look, I'm only repeating what I've heard and if *I've* heard it everyone's heard it because I don't exactly move in . . . youthful circles, or amongst embassies." The "amongst" rather pleased him, suggested a courtly old-fashioned statesman with a face like Emerson and the habits of a saint.

"Well, it's not true." Clay paused, as though pondering what to say. Burden took it for granted that he was lying. "But that doesn't help, does it? Truth has

132

nothing to do with reputation, and that's what we're talking about, isn't it?"

Burden nodded. "You're going to have a tough fight. If Enid wants to make trouble, she can lose you the election."

"Don't think I don't know that." Clay looked suddenly wretched, and young.

Burden, wanting to be compassionate, was harsh.

"The family is sacred out there on the hustings, particularly in your district with all those wild-eyed Baptists, wallowing in the thought of sin. You're going to have to run as a good clean family man."

"Is it worth it?" A cry from the heart, but the heart lies, too, thought Burden, who said, "Of course it's worth it. What about Blaise?"

"We *seem* to be on good terms. He even asked me to Laurel House for dinner."

"Did you talk to him about the election?"

Clay nodded. "He's interested. Or so he says."

"But if Enid should tell him about your indiscretion . . ."

"I think she has told him."

"And he's said nothing?"

"Not to me. For some reason, he seems angry at *her.*"

"A strange man. If I were you . . ." Burden paused. He was reluctant to give advice, particularly good advice, since this was the sort most resented. ". . . I should cultivate your father-in-law. And apologize to Enid."

"Apologize?" Clay looked at him coldly.

"You want her to divorce you?"

Clay did not answer.

"Of course you don't. Certainly not now when you're just beginning."

"I seem to be in a trap."

Burden managed not to say that the trap was of Clay's own devising. Any married man who brought a girl to his house was a fool. He wondered if perhaps he had overestimated Clay. But then, aware of the other's wretchedness, he was gentle. "When in doubt, do nothing. I'm sure if Blaise is on your side, Enid will come around. After all, there is the child." That was what one always said, thought Burden, who as a lawyer knew that the welfare of children was the first weapon and the last consideration in any power struggle between parents.

Then Burden gave Clay instructions: he was to meet a pair of constituents at Union Station and escort them to the house in Rock Creek Park, where Kitty would take over. He would join them no later than six o'clock. "Now I'm off to the doctor."

"Anything wrong?"

Burden, who had never felt better, could not resist an enigmatic smile. "Blood pressure, too much sugar, hardening arteries, nothing more than the usual pleasures of being sixty." He waved goodbye. As he left the office, he remembered ever so slightly to shuffle.

Once in the street, Burden walked briskly to the nearest taxi stand and gave the driver an address in Georgetown. He felt extraordinarily elated, thanks to the cool March day, the political hopes deferred but still alive, and the sense of a body still capable of taking and giving pleasure, even though his blood pressure *was* high and his arteries probably hardening.

Whistling tonelessly (he had no ear for music), Burden paid the driver, tipping him well. "Thanks, Senator." Usually he was pleased at being recognized, but not today. Nevertheless he tapped the man's arm affectionately, vowing to himself that next time he would give a different address and then walk to the house before which he now stood: eighteenth century rose-brick, with shutters and classic front door newly painted black. After looking first to left and right, Burden walked up the steps and rang the doorbell. A white-jacketed Negro butler admitted him, smiling broadly, happy to see Senator.

Burden followed the butler up the staircase to the second floor where he was shown into a paneled study whose shelves were filled with rather too many leather-bound books. A fire burned in the Adam fireplace. Before it, a table was set for tea. The effect was rich and careful; somewhat too careful for Burden's taste, used as he was to Kitty's haphazard arrangements.

She entered the room, slightly breathless, arms outstretched. "My dear!" she exclaimed in her careful

134

voice from which almost all source of origin had been removed. "You are early. No, on time. On the dot. And I'm late." She kissed his cheek; he responded to the scent she wore. Yes, today everything would work properly. He was certain of that, aroused as always by her manner (attentive if careful) and her figure (well and carefully made). Best of all, he liked her paleness. Either she wore no makeup or what she did wear was so discreetly applied that she seemed like . . . like a camellia, a word which unexpectedly conjured up the image of a bright pink flower. But of course there were also white camellias.

"Do sit down. Let's have our tea." Burden sat in his usual place on the sofa beside the fire. She sat next to him, poured tea and knew without asking one lump or two, milk or lemon. For a year they had known a perfect if occasional intimacy. Occasional because they thought it best only to meet when her husband was not in the city; though the husband was indifferent, Burden preferred to have his tea secure in the knowledge that they would not be interrupted.

They spoke fondly of the absent. "He's in Jersey City today. At the other emporium." She stressed each syllable of the word "emporium," simultaneously mocking and emphasizing the source of her considerable wealth. The husband was indeed a merchant prince, and Burden was impressed by him. Fortunately the prince worshiped the princess and allowed her every freedom, knowing that she would never compromise or embarrass him; and he was right. She was superbly shrewd. Only the most malicious of Washington ladies would have interpreted these occasional afternoon meetings in Georgetown as anything but an open friendship between a would-be lady of fashion and a famous Senator of known discretion. At worst their meetings might be thought political. It was a useful thing for a shopkeeper to be able, through his wife, to influence a Senator who rather carelessly governed the District of Columbia through a minor Senate committee of which he was, he admitted, without pride, the altogether too indolent chairman, much criticized by civic organizations. Happily, whenever they met at tea, no mention was ever made of such knotty problems as home rule for the District or the sales tax. Only great world issues were threshed out between the watercress sandwiches, carefully rolled, and the chocolate-covered leaves of pastry from Hubert's.

"What a blow it must have been to you, the final vote!" She looked at him tenderly, narrow eyes like an icon gleaming.

"I expected it. We never really had a chance. I was counting on being able to amend the bill, not give Franklin such a completely free hand to play at being Santa Claus. But . . ." he shrugged.

"On the other hand, I am glad, in a way, you know, about helping England." He adored her at that moment. Her diffidence was such a contrast to the usual Washington lady who made speeches when she disagreed with a Senator's politics. But not his mistress. *She* was apologetic. Quite suddenly he kissed her cheek, almost losing his balance for in moving toward her, he slipped into the trough between the thick cushions. Luckily the teacup did not spill.

"You are . . ." He wanted to give her a compliment but his heart was beating so rapidly from the narrow escape that he could think of nothing suitably elaborate and so he said, "looking so well today." Then, to compensate, he took her hand and kissed it, as earnest of what was to come. He was still amazed at having found so late in life something so profoundly satisfying. More to the point, at a time when he thought himself altogether free of the demands of the flesh, he had become like a boy again, or almost.

Lovingly, on cue, she recalled their first meeting. How he had impressed her! For his part, he could not recall when he first met her. It had seemed to him that she had always been very much around town. Then one day, shortly before the Chicago convention, she had asked him to tea. Tired as he was and distracted by all the confused maneuvering for the Vice Presidency, he had joined her in the rose garden at the back of the house and after drinking iced tea full of mint, they almost became lovers.

He frowned slightly, biting down very hard on a cucumber sandwich. At first he had been embarrassed. But her tactfulness had saved the day. She had been, in every sense, marvelous. Since then their encounters had been a bit like Russian roulette. Neither ever knew whether or not he would be capable of the act, but this uncertainty, instead of demoralizing him, added piquancy to the lovemaking. In any case, she was so good about everything; so sensitive; so entirely appreciative.

Thinking of lovemaking, Burden experienced a sharp tug of desire, all senses suddenly heightened. This was going to be a memorable encounter, he told himself. No doubt of it. He could hardly wait for her to lead him into the bedroom with its fourposter bed and the view from the window of a copper beech, one of whose branches occasionally tapped on the windowpane, reminding her that it needed pruning, reminding him of a world outside, well lost.

"And how is Clay?" She had first to go through the usual catechism of how was this one and have you seen that one. She was not to be rushed. He told her that Clay was in good spirits, but she frowned. "I wonder. I saw them the other night, at Laurel House."

Burden was astonished. He had the impression that she was not known to the Sanfords. "Were you *there?*" he asked, for once almost tactless.

"Yes, after dinner. For a moment. With friends. I do like Blaise, and of course the house! *Ma foi!*" Burden was always impressed and only a little put off by her occasional use of French phrases, acquired, she once said, during a summer in Paris, at a school for *jeunes filles*. Although Burden knew no French, his ear was good and he could tell by certain flatnesses and odd nasalities that her pronunciation was not precise. But he loved her ambition. So few Washington women made the effort to learn anything. They drank hard, laughed loudly, knew all sorts of disreputable gossip about the great, and there it ended: village women inhabiting not a city but a supervillage.

"I had the impression that she . . . that Enid was somewhat in her cups."

"I can remember when women never drank in public." Burden pursued a tangent; a bad habit, he knew, a sure sign of age.

"*I* never drink." A quick careful smile kept smugness to a minimum.

Burden continued to recall early days in Washington. "Before the war, there was no such thing as the cocktail party. There were tea parties, and that was it. Some of the grand houses served wine, of course, and after dinner the men might drink but not the women. Enid was drunk, you say?"

"I don't know her well enough really to say but I *think* she was. There had obviously been some sort of trouble between her and Clay." She looked at him shrewdly, knowing that he knew.

"Trouble?" Native caution exerted itself, even with her.

"I've heard it said—you know how people will *say* anything—that Clay has been involved with a woman who's married, a South American."

"Oh, I doubt that." Burden wondered if Clay might not be, unexpectedly, a fool. No woman was worth the loss of a vote, much less a career.

"I was told that after I left Laurel House there was a dreadful scene and that Blaise struck Enid in front of everyone."

"Struck her? Oh, I doubt *that!*" Blaise was hot-tempered but he was also daughter-dazzled, like himself. Burden tried not to think of Billy Thorne; his blood pressure was already too high.

"But he did. People who were there saw it happen."

"People often exaggerate. What did Enid do?"

"She left with Clay. Most upsetting."

"I should think so." Suddenly exuberant, he put his arm around her, kissed lips, neck. She returned his embrace with so much fervor that a hairpin came loose in the sweep of hair that covered her right ear. But, uncannily, she knew it was loose and fixed it with one hand while she pushed the tea table away with the other.

Burden leaped to his feet, muscles unexpectedly supple. Sex *was* rejuvenating. Bernarr Macfadden was right. He was light-headed with desire. "I can't wait," he said.

Her face went suddenly pale. As he reached out to

138

take her, her eyes grew round with horror. She stepped back, as though in the presence of an executioner.

"What's wrong Irene?" His own voice sounded faint and far away. What *was* wrong? he asked himself as his face turned to ice and he fell slowly, leisurely toward the floor, catching at the cloth of the tea table on the way down and pulling the plates and saucers after him. For a long moment he lay at the bottom of a pit, with the not uncomfortable sensation that he was, literally, floating away on a vast tide. From far above him the white face shone and he heard a voice through the noise of the blood's surf. "Quick! It's the Senator. Call a doctor! He's fainted!" Perfectly at ease and not in the least alarmed, Burden floated away. If this was death, he thought languidly, it was easy.

Four

1

THROUGH BARE WINTER trees, a white sun. The bridle path was thick with decaying leaves, slick and dangerous, hiding rocks. Peter's horse suddenly stumbled, hoof striking stone.

"Be careful!" said Diana, irritating him.

"What do you mean, be careful?"

"Well, there are rocks," she said diffidently.

"Nothing to be done about them. We break our neck or we don't."

They had come to a stream, a tributary of Rock Creek. Carefully the horses forded the shallow water. Breathing fast, thighs holding tight, Peter waited for the slip and sprawl of the horse and the breaking of his skull. But the horse was a placid gelding not in the least prone to desperate adventures. Safely they reached the far side of the ford where picnic tables, set permanently in a grove, provided a sad prospect on a December day.

Relieved at the successful fording, Peter was suddenly happy. "What a good idea, to go riding."

"I love it. Especially in the park, this time of year. No people." Diana had recently acquired an aversion to people in crowds, noncontagious agoraphobia, she would say, shying away from strangers.

"And a sunny day. We must be near your father's house."

She pointed toward an iron-colored hill, dense with brown trees. "Just there, on the top. How Father loves that house! He built it himself, you know. Before the crash."

"How is he feeling?" Peter acknowledged the existence of no house but Laurel House.

"Physically, he's all right. Whatever it was the stroke did to him went away."

"What's wrong, otherwise?"

She frowned. "The world, I suppose. He doesn't much like it."

"Do you?"

"Hardly. But I'm in it. I don't think he believes that he is, anymore."

"I think my father's running him for President in '44."

"That's over." She was emphatic.

"How can you be so certain?"

"Times change." She was ruthless. "He no longer matters to people now." She was also loving. "He is very good, you know. And as much as I disagree with his politics, his instincts are the right ones."

"Don't tell Billy that."

"Billy." She said her husband's name neutrally. Her cheeks glowed in the cool air. Mounted, in jodhpurs, Diana looked uncommonly healthy and except for Enid he enjoyed her company more than that of anyone else he knew. For one thing, they were entirely used to one another; for another, the fact that they had never been lovers made being together pleasantly potential.

"Does Billy like his job?" asked Peter, hoping she would say no.

"Oh, yes." She spoke too quickly. "We're so grateful to your father." After a year's unemployment, Billy Thorne had gone to work on the *Tribune* as a rewrite man. At almost the same time Peter, a bachelor of arts, had gone to work in the advertising department, where he was given the task of selling space, an activity he found as empty as it sounded. But since he had no alternative in view and it was not considered right to do nothing, he sold space and lived on his income. Ordinarily, he would have gone to Europe. But there was no longer a Europe to go to. Hitler had absorbed most of it. Only the Iberian Peninsula was unoccupied and that was to be invaded once Russia surrendered. Since the German Army was only thirty miles from Moscow, the absolute end of Europe was near. Like so many of the American magnates, Peter's father vacillated between despair at Hitler's continuing success and terror that Hitler might fail in Russia.

"Does Billy seem to like what he's doing at the paper?"

Peter told her, correctly, that he seldom saw Billy, "but everyone thinks he's capable."

"Oh, he is."

"And unbearable."

"Oh, well, there's that of course." Diana sounded more weary than hurt. Some women, Peter had noticed, reveled in having a husband no one likes. But not Diana. She had wanted to be the wife of the editor of *The American Idea,* and settling for so much less had not increased her love for a difficult man.

As they rode across the main road, they saw two cars stopped; a radio blared in one, while the occupants of the other gathered about and listened. Peter's horse shied at the noise. Angrily Peter spurred him forward.

Not until they returned to the rental stable at three o'clock and gave their horses to the groom did they learn that the Japanese had bombed the American naval base of Pearl Harbor, in the Hawaiian Islands.

"We're in the war now!" Diana's first response was jubilant. Like Billy and all the New Dealers, she was eager for the United States to join the war.

"Yes, we're in the war now," Peter repeated, gauging his own response as best he could. First there was shock. It was inconceivable that a small clever country like Japan, known only for its manufacture of small clever toys that fell apart, would strike at God's country, which had given birth to the automobile, the skyscraper, Boulder Dam, Jefferson's serpentine wall at Charlottesville, cellophane and the hamburgers Diana and he had bought for lunch (advertised as "Not the best but better than the rest"). All this could not fail. Yet suddenly he saw Japanese soldiers among the California orange groves and Nazi troops along the Potomac. The prospect of national defeat was infinitely thrilling. In the hills of the Shenandoah Valley, he would organize a guerrilla force in order to harass the mechanized Nazi convoys as they proceeded from Washington to Norfolk and the new German Sea. But then he saw himself dead among the Blue Ridge Mountains, and that pleased him not at all. Hopefully he added a musical score to the scene and a grave narrator's voice: "Heroism took on a new meaning when Peter Sanford, alone, unaided, stormed an enemy position . . ." A quick cut to himself armed with rifle, hand grenade, gas mask . . . no, the gas mask covered his face. He tore it off.

"Let's go see Father." Diana was businesslike. Peter decided that if anyone could give a new meaning to heroism, it would be she.

The Senator and Kitty were staring furiously at the radio in the upstairs study.

"It can't be true!" said Diana.

"I'm afraid it is." The Senator looked up, very pale. "Hello, Peter."

"Would you like some coffee?" asked Kitty. "Did you two have a proper lunch? I'll bet you didn't. I'll bet you ate something greasy, from a store."

"Oh, Mother, do shut up, please!" Peter and Diana sat down in front of the radio.

Kitty, however, was not yet finished. "Children eat so stupidly nowadays. And just look at them! Peter's fat as a pig."

Through the world crisis, Peter experienced a sudden flash of rage. He knew, as did everyone, of Kitty's strange habit but that did not make her pronouncements any the less wounding. He *was* overweight and he hated it but food was such a pleasure, and since girls seemed to find him no less attractive, he continued to eat as much as he liked, distressed only on those rare occasions when he looked in the mirror and observed the rounded belly and the hard but unmistakably overdeveloped breasts. Yet he had gone riding nearly every Sunday this winter and in the spring he would play tennis regularly. No one could say that he was not doing his best to keep in trim.

". . . President has scheduled a meeting of the Cabinet for this evening, as well as a bipartisan meeting of Congressional leaders."

"I'd better go down to the Hill," said Burden, standing up. "They'll want me at the meeting."

". . . to address a joint session of Congress some

143

time tomorrow. The President is expected to ask for a declaration of war."

"And he'll get it. The thing he's always wanted." The Senator positively snarled at the thought of that delinquent President who had so cunningly involved his country in a war whose end was in no way calculable.

"Who would have thought it!" The news had finally got to Kitty and, briefly, she was concerned with something outside the family round.

The Senator switched off the radio and got to his feet. "I'll be at the Senate Office Building." He kissed Kitty.

"Shall I come?"

This was obviously unexpected, and the Senator appeared to be touched as well as surprised. "No, dear. Thank you."

"But suppose they bomb Washington?" Kitty looked faintly troubled. "They could, couldn't they?"

"Of course not." Peter answered without thinking. He turned to the Senator. "I mean it's not possible, is it?"

"Depends on the position of their carriers and the risks they're willing to take. But it would seem to me that if they could do what they've done to our largest naval base, they can probably do pretty much what they please to undefended cities. You see," he gave the smallest of smiles, "we are not ready. For all this talk . . . and hope . . . of war, we have nothing to fight with. As we used to say on the Chautauqua Circuit, the President has reaped the whirlwind."

On this high note, the Senator departed. Unable to compete with such drama, Peter told Diana that he would take her home. Solemn at the thought of history being made, they left the house, refusing Kitty's offer of coffee and upside-down cake. For Peter, this refusal of pastry was to be the beginning of a new and austere time in his life; he would replace sloth and greed with vigor and abstinence, and so write a chapter in heroism.

2

At the Senate Office Building there were a number of Senators and aides. No one quite knew why he was there. After all, war or no war, it was Sunday and there was nothing anyone could do but sit by the radio and wait for the news. But like soldiers assigned to some redoubt that must not fall, certain Senators converged upon Capitol Hill and took up positions, speculating darkly on the fate of a nation so rudely and apparently so successfully challenged.

In response to a journalist in the downstairs corridor, Burden said, "Naturally we are all behind the President. This Sunday there are no isolationists or internationalists. Only . . . Americans." The small hairs at the back of his neck rose. He had thrilled himself. It was a superb if dangerous moment for all of them.

He was stopped by a familiar figure just opposite the door to his office. "Hello, Senator."

"Oh, hello!" He had forgotten the old man's name but he did recall that thirty years earlier he had been a power in the Senate and one of the most awesomely impressive men Burden had ever known. Now, frail and diffident, the old man haunted the Capitol, as though searching for his early self. Like all former Senators, he was allowed the courtesy of the floor and often when the Chamber was nearly empty, he would sit very straight at his old desk, listening solemnly to a dull speech. To Burden's chagrin he still could not recall the other's name, and so he compromised by calling him "Senator," that sonorous title each would carry, in office or out, to the grave.

"I was just in the neighborhood," began the old man.

"Come in, Senator. Happy to see you." Burden, wanting company, any company, led the grateful ghost into the inner office.

"Now whose office was this?" The old man pondered, white brows drawn together, making deep

145

grooves in the pale forehead. Burden was at the telephone, ringing Clay.

"Could it have been Mr. Vardaman, of Mississippi? Yes, I think so. Yes, I'm sure it was his office." He chuckled. "Wore his hair long, all the way to the shoulders, he did. A fine looking man, if you didn't object to the long hair." The old man sank slowly into one of the leather armchairs. He wore the frock coat and striped trousers of an earlier time; on the right lapel, a fragment of dried egg resembled the rosette of a foreign order.

Clay was not at his room in the Wardman Park Hotel. Burden debated whether or not he should telephone Enid. Deciding not to, he telephoned Blaise.

"Well, the bastard's done it! He got us in the war." Blaise's voice sounded thick as though he had been drinking. "I'm looking at the wire now. We've lost the whole Pacific Fleet. There's nothing between Japan and Los Angeles. Nothing! Not a boat, not a gun. Oh, he's a military genius!" Burden asked for other news, alarm growing. Apparently the Japanese were attacking the Philippines, Malaya, Guam, Wake Island and Hong Kong and neither the British nor the Americans seemed able to resist. "We've lost the Pacific. We'll be lucky if we can hold the line at the Rockies. I'll talk to you later." He hung up. Burden's head swam. This could not be true. Then Clay rang to say that he would be right over.

"Very different from 1917," said the old man placidly. "Of course, Mr. Wilson had been conniving for a war too, just like Mr. Roosevelt. Remember the Sunrise Conference or was that before you came here? No, you were here then. Yes, I remember distinctly. That fellow will go far, I said to Senator Lodge, and I'm happy to say I was right. You've certainly stayed the course, and kept the faith."

While Burden tried to telephone the majority leader, the old man talked of the First War and Mr. Wilson's perfidy, as though it were yesterday: then he spoke of the present and how times had changed. "Look at the Senate now and just think what it was then! Aldrich, Jim Reed, the first LaFollette. We had orators then. True debate." The old voice grew suddenly firm, becoming what it must have been in those halcyon days before the public address system when a politician's unaided voice had to be able to fill the largest hall like sounding brass. The majority leader's line was busy.

The door to the inner office opened and Jesse Momberger looked in. "Thought you'd be here. I'm not interrupting, am I?"

"No," said the old man, aware that the moment had come for ghosts to be exorcised. He rose and took Burden's hand in his papery one. "You must come see us soon, Senator. We're at the Congressional Arms, the wife and I. It will be like old times, when we used to discuss monetary reform. Remember? Only now I've really got the problem licked. I've had the time, you see, to think it through. No more fiat money, no paper. Only copper and platinum coinage. *That's* the key to sound finance." Gracefully, he left the living to their turmoil.

"There but for the grace of God," said Momberger, "go I. Or you."

Burden shook his head. "When I leave this place, I'll never come back. Too painful."

"They all say that, and they all come back. If there's a more useless article than a defeated U.S. Senator, I've yet to see it on display. You got the call yet?"

Burden shook his head. "I've been trying to get through to the majority leader. All the lines are busy."

"Nothin' from the White House?"

"No. But I'm standing by. There's a meeting of Congressional leaders at nine tonight. So I am preparing."

"Funny, I never thought this would happen." Momberger rested one hand on the head of what he took to be a poor likeness of his old friend William Jennings Bryan.

"I wonder if *he* did, the President."

"He's a mean cuss but I don't think he'd lose the whole fleet deliberately." At heart Momberger was a New Dealer. As a result, relations were often strained between the two Senators, for the President saw to it that all patronage was funneled through the senior Senator, a situation that would not make easy Burden's fight for re-election in 1944.

"Even Franklin miscalculates on occasion." Burden

was neutral. He could afford to be. The President was directly responsible for the greatest defeat inflicted on the United States since the War of 1812. He might yet be impeached. "We must all rally 'round," said Burden.

They sat in silence, with time suspended, as the winter afternoon came to a close and there was nothing anyone could do but wait for the President to lead them into battle.

"How're you feelin', by the way?" Momberger sounded like a concerned friend but Burden knew that he was merely an interested politician.

"Never felt better." This was almost true. "It wasn't really a stroke." This was not true. "But what they call a temporary blockage in the brain, like a spasm." This was euphemistic. "I had difficulty speaking for a week or two, and that was the end of it." The end of it! He still awoke in the middle of the night, panicky lest an artery had burst in the lobes of his brain, depriving him of speech, sight, movement, or, worst of all, creating hell beneath the skull's curve, since he knew now that all the agony and terror of which man is capable can be created simply by a drop of blood seeping into the wrong passage of the brain.

Clay entered with a sudden burst of sound from the corridor behind. "Hello, Senator." He shook hands warmly with Momberger who said, "Howdy, Congressman!" Momberger seemed to like Clay and had already given him tacit support in the special election.

"Not Congressman, *Captain* Overbury, Army of the United States." Clay turned to Burden, as though in apology. "It's all arranged."

"So fast?" was all that Burden could say.

"I've been in touch with the War Department for the last six months, just in case. Well, this is the case."

"Then you're *not* goin' to run?" Momberger was suddenly alert.

Clay shook his head. "How can I, when there's a war?"

"Good boy." Momberger turned to Burden. "We better pass the word on to the Judge."

Burden nodded. "I'll call him tonight."

Momberger crossed to the door. "Tell me what

148

the President says." He was gone and Burden knew that within minutes, national disaster or not, his colleague would be on the telephone to the Judge, proposing his own candidate for the Second District.

"Are you seeing the President?"

"I assume so. According to the radio, all Congressional leaders are to be briefed at the White House tonight. Better get me the Far East file."

Clay put the file on Burden's desk. "Also that memorandum I made right after I talked to Ambassador Kurusu." Burden shook his head with wonder. "Just think, he was in there with Hull, talking, while Pearl Harbor was being bombed. Fantastic people!"

Clay spread papers on the desk as Burden asked, "What are they saying at Laurel House?"

"That it's a plot. What else? Blaise thinks the President blew up the ships himself."

"Maybe he did! Was Enid there?"

Clay frowned. "No. She's at home, as far as I know."

A Senate page appeared at the open door to the inner office. In a rapid singsong he said, "Senator, majority leader says there'll be joint session Congress tomorrow twelve-thirty. President will speak." The boy was halfway out the office when Burden said, "Come back here, son." The boy stopped. "Is that all the majority leader said?"

"Yes, sir. Same message to all Senators. President speaks tomorrow, twelve-thirty joint session." The boy was gone.

Burden frowned. "Clay, you better check with Senator Barkley's office and find out just when and where we're supposed to meet tonight."

Wanting comfort, Burden telephoned Ed Nillson in New York. But Nillson gave none: he was glad that the United States was at last committed, to which Burden replied, suddenly fervent, "I want no war, of any kind, ever. Nothing is worth a man's life."

Nillson made a dry crackling noise in the receiver. "May I quote you, Senator?"

Burden laughed, too. "No, you may not. But I do mean it."

"But surely Hitler should be discouraged. And how can that be done without war?"

"I don't know the answer. No one has ever known it." Distressed by the resonance of his own unexpected despair, he changed the subject and told of Clay's enlistment.

"A good idea," said Nillson. "He'll make a better candidate if he's been a soldier, with a good record."

"But suppose he's killed."

Clay returned, unaware that it was his death that was being considered. "Let the future take care of itself." Nillson was cool. "How are *you* feeling, by the way?"

Burden gave the usual answer and rang off. He looked expectantly at Clay, who said, "I'm afraid you're not on the White House list."

"*Not on it?*" Burden was astonished. "But Senator Austin is going and I certainly outrank . . ." He stopped abruptly, refusing to reveal his pain. "Well, that's Franklin's revenge, I suppose."

Clay nodded. "Senator Barkley was apologetic. He said you'd understand that it wasn't his doing."

Burden said good night to Clay and left the Senate Office Building. In the cold twilight, he saw the old anonymous Senator making his slow way toward Union Station and his hotel, where he lived, no doubt, in small rooms filled with piles of yellowing *Congressional Records,* scrapbooks that smelled of old paste and signed photographs of forgotten celebrities. Depressed, Burden beckoned to Henry who opened the car door with a flourish.

"The White House, Senator?"

"No. Home." As Burden settled back in his seat, he realized that what disturbed him was not so much the President's insult as the fact that he had not anticipated it. One could not survive for long in politics with senses so impaired. Do I begin to fail? he asked himself, and nowhere in his mind could he with much conviction sound the negative.

If Enid was surprised, she did not show it. Wearing an old silk kimono, she sat alone in the sitting room, painting her nails with a solution that smelled like model airplane glue and looked like blood. "We'll come home." She frowned at the nails, not at him.

"I guess you heard the news?"

"News?" She looked at him blankly.

"About Pearl Harbor."

"Oh, that. Yes. It's awful. If you've come to see the baby, you can't. She's gone to bed without supper. Children need discipline." She spoke defiantly as though she expected to be challenged.

"I came to see you."

"Well, that's nice. How's Daddy?" Malice gave unexpected life to her face.

"Doing nicely. I'm going into the Army."

"You'll look sweet in one of those white suits with that thing about the neck, like gym clothes for girls."

"That's the Navy." Clay had no idea what response he wanted from her. Doubtless a protestation of love which he could then reject coldly or accept warmly. At the moment he was capable of either.

"Anyway, you'll have a good time. Men always do. Do you like this red?" She displayed her talons.

"A bit bloody."

"My mood exactly. I'm going to Harold Griffiths's tonight. Are you? No, I guess not, since he'd never ask us both together. He just phoned to say he's going to be a war correspondent if Daddy will let him. Imagine Harold in a war! It's too silly!" She took a sip from a half-finished glass of whisky and Clay realized that she was drunk.

"Drinking alone?" Automatically, he added to the brief.

"You're here. That's not alone, technically anyway." She finished the glass. "Fix me another," she ordered, indicating the bottle on the coffee table. "This stuff isn't dry yet." She waved her hands in the air to dry the lacquer while he made her a drink.

* * *

"Listen," she said, taking the glass. "I don't want a divorce. Do you?"

"No. I never did." He had to say this; and yet, in a way, he meant it.

"Then why did you move out?"

"How could I stay? Besides, you wanted me to."

"I did not! Why do you say things like that?" She stared at him reproachfully. "You moved out just to spite me. Father put you up to it, and don't say he didn't. He's getting back at me for having married you. Oh, he's sly as they come, and never forget it and never start thinking *you* can manage him like that Senator of yours, because you can't. Not Daddy. He's managing *you,* to hurt me. Why don't you come with me to Harold's tonight. It ought to be fun."

Clay had never got used to her sudden changes of mood, not to mention her dazzling dialectic. Starting with a false premise, she could build such a logical case that by the end she had almost made the premise itself seem true. Even more virtuoso were her sudden revelations, always egocentric, usually false, and yet often perceptive. On the face of it nothing was more absurd than that her father should take up with him to get back at her. But Blaise was mysterious and passionate. Enid had deeply offended him by marrying Clay (or so it had seemed), and now by taking Clay's side against Enid he could at last get back at her. For want of a better theory, Clay accepted Enid's; otherwise there was no understanding Blaise, who supported him while believing Enid to be the injured party . . . Clay had told no one the truth about the adultery on the excellent ground that it is not the aggressor but the victim the world despises and fears. The more Enid told her story of Clay's adultery "in my own bed with the baby in the next room," the less sympathy she was able to evoke even from those strangers whom, after three martinis, she took into her confidence.

"No. I can't go to Harold's. I've got work to do. For the Senator."

"I was in Bloch's today. They've got some marvelous clothes for children, much cheaper than Woodward and Lothrop's. Is the Senator still seeing Irene?" As usual, Enid mocked the name, stressing the terminal "E" as did all her set, to whom Irene Bloch was a source of constant diversion.

"I don't think he ever saw much of her." Clay did not believe the popular story that there had been an affair between the Senator and Irene and that in the act itself he had suffered a stroke. The Senator's own story seemed more likely; he had gone to tea with Mrs. Bloch, a new acquaintance, and promptly fainted.

"No use protecting him! Everyone knows, the old goat! Serves him right. What on earth could he see in her, aside from the money? Oh! Did you know that her husband doesn't mind at all who she goes to bed with as long as it's someone important? Isn't that disgusting? But then the town's full of that sort of thing nowadays."

Clay could not resist this opening. "You mean it would be less disgusting if they were not important, just sexy?"

"That's not very nice," she said mildly, holding her dark gold drink up to the light. "Why do you keep harping on poor Ernesto? I said I was sorry."

"But that's the one thing you *never* said!"

"I certainly did! Don't tell me I didn't. *I* tried to make up. But you distort everything so. I mean, let's face it, your pride was hurt."

"At the time you gave the impression that not only were you not sorry but it was all somehow my fault that you got laid by that spick."

"Charming. Well, I never said it was your fault, though you were certainly as responsible as I was. I mean, let's face it, it takes two to make an adultery between man and wife." Enid had now reached the stage in her drinking when argument became obscure and syntax difficult. "Anyway, you know exactly what I mean. Obviously if you were never going to go out with me at night I was bound to meet someone sooner or later who did like to go out and have a good time, unlike you who spend all your time conniving, unsuccessfully . . . well, until recently unsuccessfully since God knows you and Daddy are up to no good, two of a kind, really, except you don't have his balls. In fact, you don't have any balls at all, which I noticed very early on." She took a deep swallow.

He reminded himself to be tolerant. "You're drunk." At least that true statement was a legitimate counteroffensive in their war; never a knockout blow but always good for a diversion.

"That is no excuse," she said firmly, more muddled than usual. "You can't get out of it that easily. Let's face it, I wanted a man and what did I get? A secretary. Somebody's secretary! And why, did I get somebody's secretary?" She paused for emphasis; and promptly lost her train of thought. Clay answered for her.

"Because it was the first time you'd ever gone to bed with a man because that's the way you were brought up and so because Peter saw us in the poolhouse, you married somebody's secretary. . . . Let's face it," he added, happy at having caught the style.

"Very funny." She swung her legs onto the coffee table. The dressing gown fell open. She wore nothing underneath. But she was not trying to be seductive. It was part of her character that she had no physical sense of herself.

"Anyway," she organized her thoughts with an effort. "Anyway what's done is done and it's all water under the bridge what happened between Ernesto and me. Besides, he's going back to Argentina, with that wife of his, who is a marvelous girl who can't help the way she looks though they say there's a new operation now where they put this silver thing in your chin or where your chin ought to be and then stretch the skin over it so it looks like you were born with a normal chin, but the operation would scare me to death. . . . I mean, suppose something went *wrong?*"

Clay got to his feet. "I've requested active duty. I don't suppose I'll be in Washington much longer."

She looked at him thoughtfully. "Ernesto thinks there's a better than fifty-fifty chance that the operation will work so Flora will have the new chin *before* they go back."

"Oh, Christ!" It served him right for soliciting sympathy: soldier off to the wars was really not his style.

"Well, what do you want me to do? Knit you a sweater?" The voice was hard and the enunciation, which had begun to slur, was suddenly precise. A phenomenon of her drinking was the speed with which she could seem to sober up when she wanted to. With some surprise, he realized that she hated him for what he had allowed her to do to him.

"No. I just thought you'd be interested. That's all."

"Well, before you go marching off, I want you to give me permission to sell this house. Don't worry, I'll split with you."

"Where are you going to live?"

"I'm looking for something in Georgetown."

"O.K. I'll write you a letter."

Suddenly she was on her feet. She threw her arms about him. "Oh, damn it! Why do we act like this?" She started to cry. "I don't know why I say what I say. I want you back. If you want to, that is. If you want to, I will." The words came out jerkily. But though he wanted to tell her that he did love her still, a freezing pride made him mute, punishing not her but himself. And so by saying nothing, he gave each the most pain.

Enid stepped back. "Well," she said through tears, "that's that. I seem to've got nail polish on your sleeve."

"That's all right." His voice was hoarse. "I'd better get back to the hotel."

"Of course. You know I never said anything to Father about what happened."

Clay wondered if this was true.

"Did *you* say anything?" She looked at him suspiciously.

Clay shook his head. "Not a word."

"I wish I could believe you." She dabbed at her eyes with Kleenex.

He lost all patience with her. "If you never said anything to anyone, why does everyone think I'm the one who's been carrying on, with some South American's wife?"

"You know how people are." She gestured vaguely. "Use plain alcohol or lighter fluid to take the nail polish off."

They parted without physical contact. As he drove through the cold darkness to the hotel, he wondered if Enid had been telling the truth. *In vino veritas* was, he knew, a demonstrable fraud, since the truly devoted liar is never so uninhibitedly inventive as when drunk. Some day he would have to ask Blaise, his new and unexpected friend.

4

The leisurely pace of prewar Washington was now replaced by a positively New York surge of people coming and going, particularly women hurrying to do manly jobs: their short skirts revealed knees, while mountainous hair fell to padded shoulders, despite urgent warnings that long hair, by getting into machinery, not only slowed down production thereby delaying America's inevitable victory over tyranny, but scalped its owner. The hair, however, was necessary to maintain a femininity compromised by so many hundreds of thousands of women fitting altogether too easily into the jobs of absent husbands and lovers. It was the army of women in the streets (the servicemen he took for granted) that most astonished Peter when he returned to the city on a warm June day, after intensive training as a rifleman in the swamps of Florida. Influence had saved him from a more active participation in the war. Now assigned to the Pentagon, he had every intention of surviving a war which so far had failed to interest him.

The taxicab stopped in front of a large house on Connecticut Avenue. Duffel bag slung over one shoulder, he entered the building, the property of a lady who had recently lost a husband who, unknown to her, had lost her fortune. But the lady believed in survival, too, and with Frederika's help she had converted her house into the District Club, a successful venture thanks to the excellence of the cook, the resolute exclusiveness of the board of directors, and the need for just such a place where the gentry of Washington could give discreet parties or simply have a quiet lunch while charting the course of a love affair or, more likely, threading the maze of government bureaus in pursuit of treasure.

Peter's duffel bag was taken by John, a butler long known to him. "You look mighty nice in your uniform, Mr. Peter," said John, perfunctorily playing the part of family retainer. It seemed as if all the butlers of his generation had gone to the same school where ante-bellum charm was applied to them like spar varnish. But when Peter asked how business was, John showed an unexpectedly commercial side.

"We turn 'em away at lunch," he said with some satisfaction, hiding Peter's duffel bag in a closet. "Then most every night there's at least a couple parties. Of course we get a lot of *new people.*" John betrayed his schooling by the pinched way in which he said "new people." Although the city's leaders were entirely the creation of the voters—at least to begin with—there had always been a division between "us" and the new people, who of course might be very nice but only time would decide whether or not "they" would translate to "we." Time of course was not on the new people's side. The voters were fickle. Many new people were forced to return to the provinces; while others moved on to New York and the big money. Yet of those rejected by the voters, an astonishing number remained in Washington to practice law, to lobby, to live the good life and eventually become "us," or "cliff-dwellers" as they were known to the prosperous class which existed to serve them as realtors and insurance salesmen, doctors and morticians.

"Mrs. Sanford isn't here yet." John showed him into the sitting room, empty at this time of day. Over the mantelpiece hung a portrait of the dead husband who had squandered the fortune. He looked as if he had enjoyed the going of the money. His widow's maid, an old German woman, put her head in the door to say how glad she was Mr. Peter was home from the war, and still alive. Peter, who had come no closer to the enemy than Tallahassee, Florida, did his best to look doomed but the poignancy of early death did not really interest anyone in a city concerned almost entirely with shortages. "Madam says we cannot stay in business this winter unless that *liebe* general who was here last night helps us get more oil!" She disappeared.

On an English hunt table, magazines were filled with photographs of the Battle of Midway, in which the Japanese fleet had received its "first defeat in three hundred fifty years." What, Peter wondered idly, had happened in 1592? There were also aerial photographs of Cologne burning, the result of a Royal Air Force raid in which a thousand bombers had done to Cologne what the Luftwaffe had done repeatedly to London. Obviously the Allies would win the war, but when? He saw himself putting pins in a map forever, a sergeant (clerk non-typist) for the rest of his life or certainly youth.

Happily the longest period of his life was over, and already half-forgotten. Basic training in Georgia, cretinous Southern non-coms, shouting commands in a non-language. *Missed the Saturday dance, heard they crowded the floor*. Jukeboxes blared in country stores converted to dance halls for the pleasure of a million recruits. Bright-eyed, long-haired girls danced together until they were cut in on. *Gonna buy a paper doll that I can call my own*. Then the furtive tugging and feeling in the warm night. *Only a páper moon*. Venereal disease films, in which diseased penises dangled from troubled youths as kindly but stern doctors explained the arcane workings of the foreskin and the necessity of prompt *post coitum* attention to the exposed glans and urethra, all in technicolor. *Don't sit under the apple tree with anyone else but me*. The jolting train rides with shades drawn. The betting: four to one it's New York. No, L.A. *Got* to be West Coast. Why? Look, we got our suntans, right? Well, they can't send us to no place cold. Why not? Laughter. Troops in summer uniform had indeed been sent to winter while those with parkas and thick wool clothing had gone to summer. Situation normal, all fucked up. Peter applied to officers' candidate school, and was rejected: eyesight not good enough, though adequate to fire an M-1 rifle and remain in the infantry. Queen of battles. But he was found useful in Intelligence. Promoted to sergeant, he put pins in a map of Europe after reading Intelligence reports, based on dispatches from the *New York Times*. Germans now attacking Sevastopol. *Roll out the barrel*. Weak coffee in the mess halls. Food bad except for pork chops. He once ate twelve while on twenty-four hour K.P. which, despite the grease and the noise, was preferable to being night fireman and sleeping on a cement floor beside furnaces constantly in need of stoking. Again the small towns. The bars. The girls with too much hair and bold shiny eyes. *They're either too young or too old*. And as it must to every American fighting man, clap came to Peter Sanford, and the cure was by no means as disagreeable as the kindly but stern doctor in the film had said it would be.

"But you're thin!" With those welcome words, his mother embraced him. "You're not sick, are you? You look pale as a sheet!"

"Never felt better," was the usual response; and accurate, too. The old fullness of breasts and thighs had gone; he was hard to the touch. Waist: thirty inches. Height: six feet. Weight: One hundred seventy pounds. He would never be fat again.

"Lunch, that's what you need. What *I* need! I've been shopping. It's hell with all this rationing. And apparently we've lost all those rubber places in Asia. Blaise is furious."

They went into the garden where the lunchers sat beneath trees whose leaves made a green dappling light on white tablecloths. He recognized perhaps a dozen of "us"; the rest were "them," for the most part in uniform.

While Peter ate rolls and butter, Frederika waved to friends and received the homage of various generals and admirals, introducing each to "my enormous son," and Peter felt a certain pride in being, if only through family, one up on the world of military rank in which he was so obviously one down.

"Your father's in Watch Hill this week. I told him he could open up the house by himself because I was not about to leave town with you coming home." She beamed at him; he beamed back at her. They were fond of one another. Unfortunately, they had nothing much to talk about. Since neither had ever given the other serious cause for distress, true intimacy had not occurred, nor was it apt to in a family where the normal passions of childhood had been visited not on parents but upon servants. It was Peter's theory that Blaise's interest in Enid began only when she married Clay. Since then father was exquisitely aware of daughter, and as they sparred, each waited hopefully for that sudden opening through which familial love might find its ultimate expression, with a knockout.

The first course arrived: avocado containing crab meat. The crab was good but there were too many tiny membranes that got caught between his teeth. The Russian dressing was neither too bland nor again too peppery.

"You have no idea the wires your father pulled to get you to the War Department." Frederika took it for granted that influence was a thing to be used quite openly.

"I can imagine," said Peter who chose not to imagine Blaise at work to make his life more comfortable.

"I think he tried for a commission, too."

"That's too much."

"*I* thought so." She was direct. "But I think it irritates him, your being only a soldier, a sergeant."

"But I like it." Peter did enjoy being merely a sergeant, particularly now that he would not have to live in barracks. More rank would have meant more involvement in a war that he refused to acknowledge. He had shut it out. And though he was bored working in an office, he did not in the least crave action. For one thing, he was certain that he would be killed. This set him apart from most of his contemporaries, who seemed quite unable to visualize their own deaths. But he could imagine his altogether too vividly, and so chose life. Let others do their duty.

"Clay's coming home on leave. He's just been promoted to . . ." She interrupted herself. "What . . . *what* are we going to do with Enid?"

Peter was flattered to be included at last in the ranks of grown-ups who must always *do* something about someone.

"You must talk to her!" Frederika acted as if she had thought of a marvelous solution. "Yes! She listens to you. She never listens to me and as for Blaise, they hardly speak." She gasped. "My God, it's Mrs. Bloch!" Peter watched with amusement as Irene Bloch crossed the garden, head held high; she was in enemy territory, and she knew it.

"She's everywhere, that woman!" Frederika was genuinely anguished. "One of the reasons we started this club was to keep her out."

Irene Bloch joined a table of generals and their ladies.

"That seems a frivolous reason for starting a club." Peter found his mother's passion touching.

"Also," Frederika added, for no reason, "she's having an affair with Burden Day."

"I don't believe it! He's old."

"Sixty is not *that* old." Frederika's hand flew to her throat to hide the years. "As you'll find out for yourself." She spoke again of Enid, while Peter ate his avocado and found it stringy. But the main course was splendid: breast of chicken folded to make a cutlet. As his fork speared the browned surface, hot butter spurted from the interior.

Apparently Enid was seeing too much of a Naval officer. She had not answered any of Clay's letters. Clay was now willing to divorce her but she refused to discuss the matter with anyone.

"Is she drinking?"

Frederika, unexpectedly, went on the defensive, a mother prepared to commit perjury. "What do you mean, drinking? Of course she drinks, like everyone else."

"Well, she seemed to be doing more than her share last winter."

161

"Oh, everyone does, now and then. It's the . . . tension," she said vaguely as Lucy Shattuck kissed her cheek and Peter rose, still chewing, and Lucy said, "Frederika, isn't this one a little young for you? Unless it's Peter. My God, it is! And I'd hoped your mother had become a Victory Girl, doing her bit for our boys!"

Of the tough Washington ladies, the sardonic Lucy was the one who most amused Peter. Her husband was one of the leaders of the Republican Party, a fund raiser and optimist. Lucy was a pessimist. "We are doomed this year, as usual."

"That awful Roosevelt." Frederika's response was automatic.

"I think he's immortal. Anyway, that's what I tell Lawrence: you may just as well face the fact that we are doomed to a century of dreary social workers, like Harry Hopkins. And speaking of darling dreary Harry, did you hear what happened last weekend at Middleburg?" She told them, eyes glistening. History is gossip, thought Peter sagely, but the trick was in determining which gossip is history.

As soon as Lucy paused for breath, Frederika indicated Mrs. Bloch. "She's here."

"Well, so she is. Big as life and twice as rich. I've ordered Lawrence to be nice to her. We must *wring* the money out of her, for the party."

"Only Burden Day gets her money, and the Democrats."

"Old goat," said Lucy Shattuck. "He's going to have a primary fight, by the way. They say Roosevelt's backing someone against him and . . ."

"So *vindictive!*" Frederika checked in.

"Absolutely savage, if you disagree with him. The knife is always out, isn't it?" Lucy looked to Peter for comment, causing him reluctantly to put down a spoon containing homemade vanilla ice cream with a dense chocolate sauce, and declare, "He treats others as he fears they would treat him, given half a chance." Then the spoon made it to safe harbor.

"It's a shame," said Lucy Shattuck narrowly, "that my Elizabeth is so young." She turned to Frederika. "I want her to marry a very great deal of money." She patted Peter's hand warmly. "You're just what we have in mind."

Frederika frowned as she always did at the mention of money. "Peter's much too young . . ."

"Elizabeth is younger, only fifteen." Lucy got to her feet. "You'll be at Enid's party tomorrow night, won't you? It's only her father who snubs her, isn't it?"

Peter paid Lucy Shattuck the tribute of putting down his spoon. She was sharp, no doubt of that.

"Yes, of course," said Frederika brightly, and it was plain to Lucy Shattuck as well as to Peter that she knew nothing of her daughter's party. "It's for Harold Griffiths," said Lucy. "He's going to the Pacific . . . to be a war correspondent."

"I know." For once Frederika came in too late; her timing deranged by the news. In any case, Lucy Shattuck was gone.

Frederika turned to Peter. "It's up to you," she said, sending him into battle, shield and all. "You must talk *sense* to Enid."

But Enid was not about to be talked sense to. For one thing, she was not drinking. For another, she was happy. She embraced him warmly. "You've lost weight! And about time!" Then she showed him about her new house, small but comfortably furnished. She had a gift for decoration which she often talked about commercializing. It had always been her dream to have a shop with a handful of devoted employees and a large ledger in which she kept invoices and outvoices or whatever one keeps in ledgers. According to Harold Griffiths, "While everyone else tries to forget their origins in trade, Enid is atavistic. She wants to go back to the family origins and keep a shop, to know that when the cash register rings it is not for every man but for herself."

"It *is* nice," she said, sitting on a sofa beneath a bay window which looked out on a walled garden. *"House and Garden* is coming to take pictures this week which ought to be good for business. I'm quite serious about working. I've even got a card." The card rested on a coffee table which had once been a nineteenth-century sled. "Enid Sanford, Interiors."

"What happened to your last name?"

Enid frowned. "I'm not using it. That's all over. I've taken up painting again, too."

"Clay's coming home on leave. He wrote Mother."

Enid sipped Coca-Cola. "I'm going to divorce him."

"All because of what he did with that one girl, the South American?"

"But that was nothing! Since then, the things I've heard! You know, people never tell you a damned thing until something happens and then they never *stop* telling you. Anyway, we weren't right for one another, not really. He tried to make up just before he went into the Army and I said that I would only if he gave me his solemn promise that he would never put me in that sort of position again. Well, he wouldn't."

"Wouldn't promise?" Peter was skeptical. The man always promised.

"Oh, let's not talk about it. Stay for dinner. A few friends. You don't know them. Washington's really changed. It's full of new people who are fun."

The people were indeed new to Peter, if not fun. An Army Air Force brigadier general and his wife, a Navy captain (married but with a girl friend), and Joe Bailey, a divorced Navy captain, who was Enid's lover. They all drank too much, except Peter, who drank beer, and Enid, who drank Coca-Cola. The conversation, which had been as banal as Peter had anticipated, just before midnight suddenly turned fantastic.

"Easiest thing in the world." The Air Force general's naturally ponderous manner had become leaden with drink, while his wife, though she never spoke, from time to time would punctuate his slow discourse with occasional shrill cries, whether of appreciation or despair Peter could not determine. "And you wouldn't need more than maybe one regiment of M.P.s."

"If you don't mind, I'd use Marines," said Joe Bailey. "They're tough and they wouldn't ask questions."

"Well, maybe you're right. We'll put you in charge

of that phase. Send in the Leathernecks!" The general's wife shrieked briefly into her bourbon. The other couple looked pleased.

Enid said, "But that's only for the White House. What about the rest of the country?"

"That's the simplest part. You see, we have our chain of command," said her lover. "Everyone's trained to take orders from the echelon above, no questions asked. So once we nail down the White House and the Pentagon . . ."

"That's where we'll need your second regiment," said the Air Force general. "We make our move on a Sunday. And while we're putting the Chiefs of Staff under house arrest, you'll be locking up the President. Then on Monday, bright and early, we hold our press conference at the White House and explain what we've done, and win the war."

"What *have* you done?" Peter wondered if he himself might not be mad.

"Saved the country," said the general quietly. "From your New Deal Commies."

"It's up to us!" Enid was splendid. "There's no one else."

Joe Bailey nodded. "You see, Peter, the point is," he swished whisky and ice with a flourish, "the Japanese are the real enemy, not the Germans. Fact, you might even say we're on the same side as the Germans because they're against the Commies and so are we, excepting for maybe a handful of New Dealers."

"Who will have to go." His Naval colleague looked stern.

"Tell him about the message, the one your friend in Intelligence got from Switzerland!" Peter had never seen Enid quite so exuberant. He wondered if it was love or simply the prospect of treason.

"If we help Hitler in Russia, *he'll* help us with the Japanese. And in a proper geopolitical division of the world, we get Asia and he'll keep Europe, and everybody's happy."

"You see," said the General thickly, his tongue grown suddenly too large for his mouth, "once they're gone, your White House gang, it will be like the country was before, a real country with real values." His wife cried agreement.

Then Joe Bailey flung himself upon the piano and played romantic ballads while Enid sang along with him, in a loud contralto.

When Peter left, the others were still drinking. At the door he turned to Enid. "Are those jokers serious?"

"Serious about what?"

"This taking over of the Pentagon, locking up the President."

"Well, *something* has to be done!" She was vehement. "We all know that. I mean things can't go on like they are. Why, do you realize that we are *losing* the war? Well, no, you couldn't know that because they're keeping it from the people, with censorship and everything. But we are losing and there's only one person who can save us."

"Your friend Captain Bailey?"

"Don't underestimate him. Let's face it, he's quite a guy in a country of weaklings. But it's not Joe. It's MacArthur."

"Is he in on this, too?"

"If I told you, you'd just blab to everybody. You never could keep a secret. Anyway, I'll see you tomorrow. I'm giving a party for Harold. He's off to the wars." She kissed his cheek.

"All right." Peter started to ask her again about the conspiracy but a sharp cry from the general's wife discouraged him. "Good night," he said. He paused in the open doorway. "What does Father think of 'quite a guy'?"

"We're not speaking," said Enid. "You ask him. He's your father."

"Yours, too."

Enid gave a mirthless laugh. "I'm not so sure of that."

"Idiot!"

"I mean, how can you tell, unless you were in the room?"

A cardinal fell, an arc of scarlet against green. Bees hovered in the garden. Through the deep woods of the park came a cool breeze.

"Not an easy time, not easy at all." In a most easy mood, Burden sat in a deck chair, feet up, wearing a golfer's cap to shield his head from the bright June sun. Beside him, in a straight chair sat Sam Biermann, the Washington correspondent for the state's leading Republican newspaper. In a long relationship, there had been many difficult moments. Partisan editors often cut Sam's copy in such a way that the essential paragraph of praise was left out; they had even been known to change the text in order to traduce the junior Senator. Burden always accepted Sam's excuses, having no choice because he needed him. But he often wondered to what extent the other did indeed admire him. If Sam had flattered him less he might have trusted him more.

Sam wore string ties, and chewed cigars with teeth as yellow as the somewhat distressing elk's tooth which hung from his watch chain. "Do you anticipate any trouble in the 1944 primary, Senator?"

During the interview proper, Sam always addressed Burden formally, a warning that whatever he said was copy. Later they would chat intimately, and use first names.

"Off the record," said Burden, somewhat mischievously, making the interview difficult, "a hell of a lot. Franklin's pushing a certain fellow whose name we both know. And the old WPA crowd are already working for him."

"Then you expect that this man will enter the primary against you?"

Burden nodded. The thought of battle did not displease him. He was going to win. He said so, for quotation, with the usual modest qualification that naturally everything was dependent upon the good folk of the state. As he intoned pieties, Sam nodded gravely and though he took no notes, Burden knew that he would be accurately quoted.

"Your health . . . ?" The polite, embarrassed question to which he was now accustomed.

"Never better!" Burden gave sudden resonance to his usual soft conspirator's voice. "Funny thing about a stroke at a *relatively* young age." He congratulated himself upon that boldness. "It forces you to take care of yourself. Which I do now. Regular hours, sensible diet. Also it makes you wonder about what really matters, after all." He continued in that vein, convincing himself that he had undergone a sea change. But of course he had not. He was more than ever puzzled by the body and he never ceased wondering to what end this complex mechanism had been created, its terminus so implicit in its beginning. Until he had puzzled that out, he preferred not to go. Yet his old terror of extinction had lessened considerably since he had discovered how easy death was: like bath water down the drain was the inelegant metaphor which had occurred to him when he regained consciousness in the hospital with Kitty beside him. He had greeted her somewhat formally, and then slipped easily into darkness. Later, as easily, he returned as though from sleep with only a slight headache and the muddled sensation of having been trapped in a particularly confusing dream to memorialize his brief attendance upon the dark angel.

Released from the hospital, Burden found that now daylight was everything to him, and he took to rising with the sun and walking barefoot through the damp grass, as though he were a boy again and part of the cycle of growth rather than of decay.

Political plans? "Win the war, of course. Also clear up some of the debris of the New Deal. No need for pump-priming when the pumps are needed for a real fire." Burden hoped Sam would get that one straight. A constant danger was Sam's love of the qualifying clause, the informative aside which spoiled the point.

Then Burden embarked on the one matter that did concern him and which, with an election approaching, ought not to. "The way the government has rounded up the Japanese on the West Coast is one of the most shameful, flagrant abuses of the Bill of Rights in the history of the country." Never having made a speech on the subject, Burden was bursting with untried rhetoric. "Many of them are fourth, fifth generation Americans, no more security risks than you or I. But even if they were, then let them stand trial in an orderly manner. Don't put them in concentration camps, without due process of law."

"Concentration camps?" Sam looked startled.

"Yes, concentration camps. There's no other description for it."

"You want me to use that phrase *exactly,* 'concentration camps'?" Sam looked mournful, like a croupier taking the last of a friend's life savings.

For a moment, Burden's sense of survival struggled with his sense of justice. To his horror yet secret pride, justice won. "Yes," he said, "concentration camps are what they are, so that's what we'll call them."

"Are you planning to hold any hearings in the Senate?"

Burden nodded. "Judiciary Committee, as soon as possible."

"This is not what you'd call a popular issue." Sam looked wretched. He had spent a quarter of a century cultivating this particular Senator. He obviously could not bear the thought of having to begin again, at his age, with a new Senator.

"American citizens are being deprived of their Constitutional rights. They are being treated in the same way the Communists treat their unpopular minorities. I'd rather *lose* the war than have us turn into that sort of country."

Sam was close to tears. "You really mean you would rather *lose* the war than . . ."

Burden laughed, and said the magic phrase: "Off the record." Same sighed with relief as the suicidalist stepped back from the window ledge. "But you must say how strongly I feel about this abuse of justice, and how particularly ironic I find it that an administration which prides itself on its liberalism should have committed the most illiberal act in our history."

Sam nodded, almost happy. That was more like it. One could defend the right even of Japanese if the issue was plainly partisan. The Senator might yet be saved.

Then through the screen door of the side porch, Diana appeared, accompanied by an Army officer. It took Burden a moment to recognize Clay. Greetings were warm. Clay looked lean and hard and somewhat ill at ease, as though he might inadvertently break something, clumsy from too much physical strength. Diana was equally uncomfortable; obviously she was doomed to love Clay hopelessly for life, like a Victorian heroine. Burden was rather proud of her madness which seemed to reveal strong passion, if not strong character.

"I see she's taken my place," said Clay.

"Oh no, not really." Diana spoke too quickly. "I'm just helping out at the office."

"Because, she maintains, I'm too cheap to pay for a new assistant." Burden winked at Clay.

"You mean, let the government pay?" said Sam hopefully.

Burden played up to him. "She's not on the government payroll."

"Wonderful." Sam was admiring. At one time Jesse Momberger had four relatives working in his office, all drawing government salaries. When questioned by Sam, he had said, "Hell, I'm a good family man." The voters had agreed; nepotism had not hurt him.

"When are you replacing Clay?"

"After the election. As if I could," said Burden fondly. "Maybe the war will end. Maybe he'll come back."

"If only it would. If only I could." Clay responded in kind. Then he told them that he was on final leave before being sent overseas. A captain of infantry, he has been assigned to a division in Hawaii. Presumably he would be involved in the Pacific campaign. "But they tell us nothing."

"Do you still have an eye on the Second Congressional District?" Sam came to the point.

Clay hesitated. Smoothly Burden answered for him.

"Let's say we're keeping our powder dry." The interview at an end, Sam departed, escorted by Diana.

"How does it look?" From force of habit, the two men reverted to their old relationship of conspiring politician and devoted accomplice.

Burden frowned. "Not good. Primary fight."

"Republicans?"

"Don't know yet. Doesn't get easier, this business." But then he recalled that he was an old man saying farewell to a young one, on the eve of battle. The role had possibilities. "Has it been . . . difficult, Army life?"

"No. Rather lazy. But now I'll be with a division headquarters, and that ought to make a difference."

"War Department help out?"

Clay smiled. "It's not as if I had connections."

Burden laughed, as a matter of form. "Actually, I suppose I am a handicap to you."

"Fortunately Blaise is not."

Burden was suddenly jealous. "I'm sure Blaise can do anything." He praised his rival. "The Administration is terrified of him. But," he questioned his rival's sincerity, *"will* he do anything?"

"Who knows? Anyway, it's academic. There's nothing I want. Now we'll see what happens out there."

Suddenly in the green garden, there was a tumbling of bodies in gray. The sound of arms stilled the chatter of birds. The bullet struck his father, tore gray cloth, white skin, red flesh, shattered the bone. Burden clutched his left shoulder, felt the bullet burning.

"What the matter, Senator?"

Burden let go his arm. "Neuralgia," he said easily, and asked for news of Enid.

"I think I'm going to divorce her."

"You divorce her? Or the other way around?"

"Me divorce her. She's living with . . . practically living with a Navy captain."

Burden squirmed in his seat. This was not at all the sort of conversation one ought to have with a young warrior departing. "I see," said Burden, hoping Diana would return. There were details in the lives of others which he took no pleasure in knowing.

But Clay was obviously bent on giving him pain.

"I've got to make up my mind before I go. Before I leave tonight. I'm seeing her this afternoon."

"Does she want a divorce?" Burden went through the expected catechism.

"She does if I don't. She doesn't if I do."

"At least you know where you stand." Burden asked the next question. "Do *you* want a divorce?"

"I think so. There's not much point in living the way we do now, with me in a hotel and her in the house, with the child, and that Navy bastard."

"Then you really want her back." Burden was blunt. "In that case, make up with her."

"It's not that easy. She's not easy to make up with."

"Clay," Burden detested those who for emphasis addressed other men by name, but now he must be as emphatic as possible, if only to end this dialogue and regain the vision of soldiers wounded in the garden, first his father and now Clay, gold curls clotted with blood, blue eyes glazed with dying. Ah, the sweetness of it! and the honor. "Clay, you cannot be divorced, *by* her if you want to represent the Second District in Congress. You might conceivably divorce *her* and be elected, but why make a difficult election more difficult?"

"The alternative is that I live in a hotel while she lives in our house, having affairs? Don't you think the voters will find out about that?"

"But you're not in a hotel, you're in the Army. You're going overseas. You're going to be legitimately separated from her. And who knows what she'll be like, what you'll be like in a year or two?" Burden was a devotee of inaction, always the best course in private matters. He had yet to break off with Irene; he had simply not gone on and as a result there had been no recriminations, no final scene, only a mutual sympathy on the rare occasions when they met on neutral ground in someone else's house. He doubted if he could ever return to that room where he had so unexpectedly fallen into the pit and, lying among the cups and saucers and spilled tea, saw his own death plain.

"Then," with finality, "there is Blaise. You'll need

him. But will he help you if you're not his son-in-law?"

Diana and Kitty returned. Both made a fuss over the departing soldier who did depart at last, led by Diana through the rose garden to the driveway. Kitty looked after them a second. "I wish she had married him."

"Ah," said Burden in wistful agreement.

"Instead of Billy."

"Ah!" Burden struck a richer chord. Upon a light wind, the scent of roses.

"I wonder if Clay's sorry he married Enid. He ought to be. He has far more in common with Diana. Made for each other, they were. Now she's nothing but a Communist married to a cripple. Oh, it's sad! It *is* sad, what life does."

6

"How does Billy like the paper?"

"Very well. How is Enid?"

"Oh, fine. She's living in Georgetown."

"That's nice. We're out on Wisconsin Avenue now."

"Do you like working in the office?"

"It's interesting, yes. Except for the constituents."

"They can be hell. How is Mrs. Blaine? Miss Perrine?"

"Miss Perrine is married now. They miss you."

Clay got into his car. Talking to Diana had never been easy. It was now impossible. The fact that neither could look the other full in the face did not help matters. "Be careful," she said. "In the war, I mean."

"I shall. Take care . . . of your father." They shook hands. He started the car. She turned to go back to the house, then turned again to wave goodbye as he circled the fish pond in the center of the driveway. He waved to her, and then trees separated them as he drove down the wooded driveway to the main road. At least he had not married her and spent a lifetime trying to make conversation. Even Enid was better, or at least different, unexpected.

"You could be killed!" She was vehement.

"That would solve everything."

"I'd never forgive myself if they killed you, never! I'd feel it was me somehow that had done it. Joe likes you, you know."

"Why?"

"Because he was very impressed by something I told him you said. Joe is a marvelous judge of people and of course he plays the piano like nothing you've ever heard." Enid took a long swig of Coca-Cola from the bottle. She had been, she declared, on the wagon for some weeks. "Until the war is over. That's my war effort."

"I don't suppose you'll stop seeing him while I'm gone."

"If you want me to, *really* want me to, I will." She looked at him very straight. Unlike Diana, she always looked him in the eye. Her gaze was most constant and candid when she was lying. He wondered if she was lying now.

"I really want you to." Clay fell into the familiar rhythm.

She sighed. "You are the most selfish person I've ever known. All you can think of is your own convenience. If you'd ever thought of me for just one moment, this would never have happened." She indicated the drawing room. "This" was apparently the Georgetown house.

He raced through the next few moves. "If I'd taken you out every night to parties, you'd never have gone to bed with Ernesto. But because I preferred my career, which is a failure, to being with you twenty-four hours a day, you went to bed with Navy Joe. Yes. Yes. Yes."

She looked at him reproachfully. The game was sacred. Neither was allowed to skip moves. "If you're going to take that tone," said Enid, taking it herself, "why did you come here at all?"

"To leave you the car and say goodbye to the baby."

"She's out, with the nurse. At the zoo. They'll be gone until five. You could always come back of course.

I don't need the car. I suppose you want free garage space."

Both found a good deal to be said about his motives for wanting her to have the car while he was overseas; the subject was far from exhausted when Blaise arrived.

"Quarreling again?" Blaise looked cool and compact in a summer suit, the red face not shiny with heat but merely red, his usual ensign.

"Daddy! You're supposed to be in Watch Hill!"

"Well, I'm not." Blaise kissed Enid's cheek amiably, eyes on Clay. "Off to the wars?"

"Yes, sir. Tonight."

"Hawaii?"

Clay nodded. He had planned to telephone Blaise at Watch Hill that night, to say goodbye and seek a father-in-law's blessing. Now Blaise had materialized in the flesh.

"I had to fly down. Lord Beaverbrook's arriving."

"At least he's not here to see us." Enid moved close to Clay. "This is quite a reunion. Peter back in Washton, and all of us together."

"Until I go." Clay was flat.

"Until you go. Yes. It's awful, Daddy. Do you realize he could be killed? Can't you keep him home, like Peter?"

"He doesn't want to stay home. I made him the offer. He's stubborn." Blaise grinned at Clay. The male world closed ranks.

Seeing herself shut out, Enid retaliated. "Listen, Father." When Daddy became Father, Enid meant business. "He wants a divorce."

"That's not exactly what I said . . ." But Clay lost the initiative.

"Yes, it was. And I think it's silly. Don't you, Father? At this point? With the child and Clay going off anyway to have a good time in Hawaii."

"Yes, I think it's silly." Blaise was calm. He turned to Clay. "We don't want to lose you."

Clay was grateful for that sign of interest. He might yet win the game against Enid. Thought of victory inspired him. "If Enid were only more discreet, I wouldn't mind so much, the way things are." His bold-ness was rewarded.

Enid was on her feet, with a tiger's spring, impress-ing even the old tiger, her progenitor and fellow carnivore. "Discreet! He started it! I didn't!" Her voice rose but she did not lose control. Clay watched her, fascinated, as she presented her case to the appellate court, not faltering once in the presentation, leaving no loophole through which truth might pass. As she described his adultery with the imaginary Argentine, he realized with a shock that she really believed what she was saying. He watched Blaise nervously: did he believe her? Enid paced back and forth in front of the fireplace, the Coca-Cola bottle clutched in her hand like a weapon. But luck was with Clay, for with a loud, "Hi, baby!" Joseph Bailey, Captain, United States Navy, burst into the room, arms filled with phonograph records.

Enid came to a halt. Blaise stared in disbelief at the newcomer. Clay said, "I'm the husband," taking the match if not the game.

"I brought Enid some records." Joe placed them on top of the Capehart phonograph. Enid put down the Coca-Cola bottle, a queen relinquishing her scep-tre. "Daddy, this is Captain Joe Bailey, a friend of mine."

The two men shook hands and with a small thrill Clay saw in Blaise's eyes the same fury directed at Joe that had once been reserved only for him. "Just passing by. On my way to the office." Blaise's silence spread through the room like news of plague. But Joe did not immediately get the point. "Enid's told me a lot about you," he said to Clay, affecting ease, not realizing that the funeral bell had already begun to toll. Enid watched her father with the fascination of a child soon to be punished.

"Not too damaging, I hope." Clay had begun to en-joy the situation.

"Not at all. Not at all." The Captain turned to Blaise and opened his second front. "We were all pretty thrilled, sir, with that editorial last week about con-taining Communism, after the war. It was crackerjack stuff."

Clay was not certain what it was that set Blaise off but he suspected that "crackerjack" might well have been the detonator. Blaise laughed. It was not the artificial booming laugh he sometimes affected to make others ill at ease. It was a genuinely merry laugh, charming in its spontaneity. Enid was shattered by it. Her hands clutched air, as though seizing invisible Coca-Cola bottles. The Captain was mystified. "I don't think I see the joke, sir."

"Nothing. Nothing." Blaise touched one eye with a stubby finger, dislodging a small diamond of a tear. "I gave him the sack, that's all. The man who wrote that editorial."

"On what grounds, sir?"

"Grounds?" The old dangerous scowl began its lengthening and deepening between brows that ought to have bristled but instead looked as if they had been painted on, bold and black, like Enid's. "We are allied with the Soviets. We need them for the war with Japan. We must not undermine them. It is too soon to start talking about containing Communism."

"It is never too soon." The Captain was now somewhat dark in the face. Ideological passion and embarrassment made his voice quiver.

"Apparently not in the . . . Navy, is it?" Blaise indicated the uniform as though it might as easily have been that of a movie usher.

"Some of us look ahead. We'd always thought of you as one of us."

"One of *you?*" The contempt was perfect. "I think what all you young fellows need is a bit of war duty, like Clay here. Washington's a demoralizing place unless you've something important to do." Having shot the Captain down, Blaise gave wings to Clay. "Want a lift? I've got the car outside."

Enid returned to life. "I want to talk to you a moment, Clay." She turned to the ruined Captain. "I'll see you later."

"Of course." Joe's voice reached for its original note of triumph but did not make it; without shaking hands he withdrew, a half-wave to the room his only tribute to the master he had met.

"Father, could you wait for Clay outside?"

177

"Whatever you say, my dear." He kissed her averted cheek and left the room.

"He seems very nice, your Navy captain."

"Oh, shut up. Listen, do you want a divorce or not?"

"It's up to you." That was the usual answer. Enid's hand shook as she poured herself a drink.

"Well, I don't. There's the baby, though God knows you pay no attention to her. Joe takes her everywhere."

"I thought he'd be too busy containing Communism."

"You and Daddy can laugh all you like but they're taking over the country." Enid launched into a fierce incoherent attack on those elements which were conspiring against American virtue but then, characteristically, something she said reminded her of herself and abruptly she allowed the Republic to fall into Red hands while she saved their marriage. "I'll stop seeing him, if you really want me to, though he's a real man and they're hard to come by and I don't mean that he's my lover or anything like that."

"He isn't?"

"I didn't say he wasn't," she said, careful in her illogic. "The point is I do need a man around, to take me out, cope with things, and the baby needs him, needs a man to look up to, to do things with her. It's very hard on her having no father and me trying to be both parents when, let's face it, I'm not any too good at being a mother."

Against his will, Clay found himself liking his wife; her sudden bleak honesties about herself were endearing. "All right," he said. "We postpone decision until I get back, if I get back."

"You mustn't go! I mean *go,* yes, to Hawaii or some place like that. But not where there's fighting. What on earth would I do if you were killed?"

To this obvious rhetoric there was altogether too much answer. He was soothing. He kissed her. Arm in arm they went down the brick steps of the house to the long Cadillac in which Blaise sat, quietly reading a newspaper. The chauffeur opened the rear door. Blaise looked up from his reading. "All set?"

Enid threw her arms about Clay as if he were certain to be killed, and perhaps he was, he thought, gently undoing her arms and climbing into the back seat. The chauffeur shut the door. Metal and glass separated him now from Enid, whose lips continued to move though he could not hear what she was saying through the closed window and the sound of the engine starting.

As the car pulled away from the curb, Enid took a long swig from the glass she was holding and ran back into the house. He wondered if he would ever see her again.

"She started drinking again, didn't she?"

"Drinking? I don't think so. She was on Coca-Cola, wasn't she?"

"There was Scotch in the glass when she came outside." Blaise's manner was that of the impersonal recorder. "No divorce?"

"No. At least, not now."

"Good." They both were silent as the car left Georgetown and turned into a broad avenue lined with low buildings each with a false wood or brick façade like the main street of a Western town. They passed "People's Drug Store" (yellow letters on black), one of a city chain almost as ubiquitous as the "Palace Laundries," whose color motif was purple and gold or the green and white one-story brick huts known as "Little Taverns." These visual points of reference made the city home to Clay, who had grown entirely used to the slow-moving, languorous town with its long empty vistas of columned public buildings and unexpected slums where Negroes lived in somber brick houses built in those summery days when McKinley reigned and Mark Hanna ruled. Elsewhere, there were the elegant tree-lined avenues, broken by circles designed to keep the dreaded mob at bay with cannon, the work of men who could not foresee to what extent the mob would govern not in the streets with musketry but in the Capitol itself, going through the motions and sometimes the reality of ruling themselves, leaving the circles to their betters who put up palaces and feared no one, not even the President they accused of wanting their ruin.

"Sorry to go?" Blaise's voice was low.

Clay nodded. "But it's something I've got to do." He had not intended to strike the heroic note.

Fortunately, Blaise did not hear it: his ear attuned only to the practical. "You must go, if we're going to get you in Congress."

Clay turned to look at Blaise. "You know, I'm very grateful for the way you're helping me, after all this business with Enid."

Blaise looked away, apparently shy. "Enid's difficult. I don't like what she's doing with herself. This drinking. That Navy fool."

"I suppose I'm to blame for a lot of it." Clay's tentative lead was promptly followed up.

"Yes, you are. And I can't say you handled it very well. But it's done and that's that. I will say that I was very impressed when you rang me up and wanted to talk but then never said one word against Enid. I admired that." As you were intended to, thought Clay, grimly pleased that his desperate strategy had worked. "What I don't like is the way *she's* blown this thing up out of proportion. Anyway, let's hope all will be forgotten when you come back home a hero."

Clay laughed. "That's not easy to guarantee, being a hero."

"I've told Harold Griffiths to keep an eye on you. He'll be in the general vicinity."

"We're not exactly buddies."

"What possible difference could that make?" In the cold voice, Clay heard power. "If you do anything notable, Harold will write about it and I'll publish it. You see, I want you to go far."

"Why?" Such a simple statement invited a straight question.

"We talked about this once, years ago at Laurel House." Blaise was precise. "I said I didn't want to make things easy for you to rise. I had my reasons then; I have them now. They are personal and perhaps not particularly attractive." Blaise looked away. "I told you then that though I was a *rich* boy," the husky voice managed skillfully to italicize the pejorative word, "I had wanted much the same things you do, and got them. In my way, which won't be half as satisfactory as yours." He frowned. "If the Republicans had

180

won last time—never had a chance, but if they had— I was going to be Ambassador to Italy. Interesting post, nice life, and then there was Mussolini to deal with, which might have been worthwhile." For a moment Blaise spoke of Mussolini as though he regretted not having conducted President Willkie's embassy. Then he turned back to Clay. "You see, that would have been second-rate."

"To be Ambassador to Italy?"

Blaise nodded. "For *me,* second-rate." He stated it as fact. "But that's all I could ever get because I have no future. Except to go on as I am, which isn't bad." He gave his sudden smile. "But you do have a future. And it could be remarkable. Do you realize that?"

"Yes." Clay could equal Blaise's proud candor. "I've always known it."

Blaise laughed. "Good! You're like me, only not being a rich boy you have a better chance."

"Not having money I have no chance at all for anything really big." Clay was to the point.

"You will have what you need, don't worry."

Reflexively, Clay could not help but wonder *why* Blaise was helping. Certainly not for Enid's sake for it was now plain that Blaise had exchanged daughter for son-in-law, as if he could not hold both simultaneously in his affection or perhaps "interest" was the better word since Blaise seemed not to care about anyone. Depending upon mood, he spoke with equal politeness or disdain of wife, son, daughter.

For the present, Clay knew that he had obtained Blaise's interest; he must make the most of it. He spoke casually of money in politics, of how difficult it was for men like Senator Day to become presidential. Mention of Burden caused Blaise to sit up straight and kick the jump seat back into place. "Nillson!"

"What about him?"

"You! You have any dealings with him?"

Clay kept his voice steady, forced himself to be cool. "A great many dealings. After all, he handled the Senator's finances in 1940."

"Notice anything funny?"

Clay shook his head. "Nothing. I mean, naturally

181

we got around the law that limits campaigning, but . . ."

"No. No. Between him and the Senator, anything shady?"

"If there was, I never knew about it." In matters like this, truth was almost always a mistake. "What have you heard?"

"They're going to indict Nillson. The government. Some kind of fraud. Don't know the details. I got it from our financial man in New York."

"The Senator's not directly involved, is he?"

"No. But to the extent that Ed raised money for him, he's involved."

Clay was relieved. Apparently it was not the Indian land sale. "Guilt by association?"

"Poor Burden. He's got a tough primary coming up."

"You'll support him?"

Blaise nodded. "But I'm glad you're on your own now. He could be in trouble." Blaise offered Clay a cigar. Both men took their time lighting the tobacco. When smoke filled the car, Blaise opened a window and said mildly, "I liked Ed." Clay noted the use of tense. "Belonged to the same club. Bad time for us." Blaise chuckled. "Whitney was a member, too. And he went to jail. Capitalism doesn't look so hot, does it?"

"Maybe they won't nail Ed."

But Blaise was tired of the subject. He turned to Clay, the whites of his eyes dark gold and the irises as black as the pupils. "We're going to make it! You hear me?"

Clay was startled by this unexpected intensity. Fortunately, before he had to respond in kind, the car stopped and as chauffeur and hotel doorman contended for the honor of opening the car door, Blaise put his hand on Clay's thigh and gripped him hard, causing pain. Tears came to Clay's eyes but he did not pull away. In some obscure way he was being tested. Son of a bitch sadist, he thought, as the powerful fingers continued to pinch hard the muscle of his leg. Then the chauffeur opened the door and the hand was withdrawn. But the pain continued. Blaise shook his hand perfunctorily. "Keep in touch."

"I will." Clay got out of the car, his leg tingling.

"Oh . . ." Blaise called him back.

"Yes, sir?"

"Don't get killed."

"I'll try not to." Both men laughed. Then Blaise was gone, and Clay was left with the depressing thought that he might not live to complete the grand design Blaise had so temptingly revealed to him. But the appearance of a familiar figure dispelled all doubts. The good omen was Miss Perrine. "Only I'm Mrs. Fallon now. But I'm still working for the Senator, because we need the extra money. Munson's still at the Mint." She smiled brightly and accepted an invitation to come to his room for a drink, after she had delivered some papers to one of the Senator's constituents.

Five

1

"IT IS THE closest thing in Washington to a salon,"
said Sergeant Aeneas Duncan to Warrant Officer
(junior grade) Peter Sanford, as he led him into Dupont Circle.

Peter chose to be perverse. "But what is a salon?
And do we need one in Washington? And why go
to the 'closest thing to'?"

Patiently Aeneas explained to Peter that here, at
least, there was conversation, almost on a par with that
of New York, the city from which Aeneas had entered
the Army so that he might kill Nazis. Instead he had
been sent to Washington to think up ways of en-
couraging troops grown bored and weary after three
years of war. Before enlistment, Aeneas had taught
philosophy and written dense critiques of literature
and politics. Though forty-five and in bad health—
he wheezed with asthma, smoked too much, and was
for all military purposes blind—he had been accepted
for duty and assigned to an office next to Peter's where
he produced an enormous amount of writing, much
of it mimeographed. He was not happy with Washington but he did his best to make do in what he
regarded as a provincial city and like a Chekhov character, he spoke wistfully of his exile from the true
capital. To him, Washington did not exist. Despite a
passion for political theory, he had no interest in
actual politics. Until the system was entirely changed,
there was no use, he declared, in even acknowledging
the present power structure. But though the name
and function of the chairman of the House Ways
and Means Committee were strange to him, he read
Locke, quoted Hume, and explicated Marx. In any
case, "They'll be gone soon enough," he would say

balefully whenever Peter questioned him too closely. But whether swept away by revolution or simply withdrawn by history's tide, he would not say.

Often, as Aeneas talked, Peter found himself wondering what it was like to be so entirely preoccupied with moral nicety. It was this quality in Aeneas which most attracted him. Aeneas took nothing lightly. Everything must be weighed upon the fine scales of a moral sense that never slept. At first Peter found this seriousness sufficiently refreshing to imitate it, and he took to analyzing not only deeds but motives, not only the visible effects of action but the incalculable aftereffects as well. He got so he could play the game; yet in the playing he soon realized that for himself it was sport and not, as with Aeneas and his friends, the true purpose of life. At first, Peter was troubled by what he took to be his own lightmindedness. While Aeneas's court was in constant session, his own was in permanent recess. He simply could not make final judgments. The stupidity and malice of others amused rather than alarmed him, except of course when he was the victim, in which case he knew that he was apt to behave quite as stupidly and maliciously as anyone else. But left to himself, he assumed that others were governed entirely by self-interest. This did not distress him as it did Aeneas who saw with irritable clarity the misdeeds of others and, worse, regarded himself, if not without tenderness, at least with a suspiciousness which gave him no peace.

Aeneas found Peter baffling. "You are stupid," was his constant refrain but then the true pedagogue, he would proceed to enlighten Peter who enjoyed learning; only occasionally would Peter reedress the balance and assert himself by taunting Aeneas with his ignorance and actual politics and non-Marxist history. But Aeneas, not eager to be told anything he did not really know, merely quoted Hegel: He knew what he knew.

Since Aeneas, recently divorced, was alone in the city, he often spent his off-duty hours with Peter. Reversing the usual roles of native and visitor, Peter saw only Aeneas's New York friends. Most were writers assigned to the Pentagon; some were said to be celebrated, though all were unknown to him. In any case, he enjoyed their fierce disdain for everything he had been taught to value. Most of them had been Communists until the Hitler-Stalin pact. All were socialist, delighting Peter, who had only known of such people at second hand. Since he had denied any relation to the infamous publisher, none suspected who he was. As a result, he learned terrible things about his father.

Suddenly, after a year of Washington, Aeneas discovered the natives. "You know, there are some interesting people here, simply as specimens of course. The sort you read about in novels by ladies with three names, or in Henry James who was a bit of a lady himself. There's one in particular I like. She's the Old America at its best, if that's not a contradiction in terms. She only invites people to her house who can read without moving their lips. That means none of your beloved politicians."

But Aeneas would not say who *she* was, beyond: yes, she was well known. No, she was not political, not really. Yes, she was rich. And married. And old. In any case, it amused him to surprise Peter, who was surprised only to find that Aeneas like everyone else was a social climber. But then he reminded himself that motion was life. All men must climb, particularly those born at the top who must make the fascinating but perilous journey down, a treacherous business since a single misstep could mean a terminal fall.

Somewhat reluctantly, Peter agreed to go to the house of this paragon, realizing that if he knew her, the game was up and his newfound friends would know him for what he was, son of a fascist beast.

In Dupont Circle, Aeneas was also having second thoughts; he was not at all certain if Peter would fit in. "The rich are pretty bloody, you know," he began uneasily. "If you're sure you feel up to her . . ."

"I'll do my best." Peter was humble. Aeneas and the New Yorkers believed that his father was a minor functionary in the government. As a result of this necessary lie, he had for the first time in his life the sense of being entirely himself, with no need to defend or deprecate a celebrated father. It was an exhilarating sensation. Until now he had not realized just how much of his life had been taken up with discussing or, worse, deliberately not discussing Blaise and the *Washington Tribune* and his family's maze of connections.

Aeneas stopped in front of a large yellow palace with an elaborate iron-grilled gate. "This is it," he said.

"Millicent Smith Carhart!" Peter could not hold back the name. The masquerade was about to end.

Aeneas was startled. "You know her? But of course you would," he answered himself. "How could anybody living in Washington *not* notice this place? In those days the rich felt they had to be conspicuous." Generalizing, Aeneas rang the bell.

A maid admitted them. For a moment she seemed to recognize Peter who quickly pulled off his cap in such a way as to mask his face.

"Madam is in the library," said the maid, obviously not much liking the look of either of them. Peter started toward the library.

"That's right," said Aeneas, "it's in there. Let's hope she doesn't assign a topic. Sometimes she does."

"I thought you said this would be conversation, not a seminar."

"Is there a difference?" But Peter was not about to play Glaucon to Aeneas's wise man of Attica. He was too busy preparing himself for Millicent Smith Carhart, whom he had known all his life.

Everyone knew Millicent. She was the niece of a somewhat shadowy President who had reigned in the serene years before the century changed. As a young girl, she had lived with her widower uncle in the White House and acted as his hostess. Lacking conventional good looks, she had resolutely made herself interesting by, among other things, marrying a British peer. Unfortunately, her belted earl, as she called him, was addicted to *le vice anglais,* and though this might have interested Millicent, it did not please her. Finally, after an otherwise uninteresting dinner party at the American Embassy, she had, in her own phrase, belted the earl. She then returned to Washington, and built a palace on Dupont Circle with the fortune left her by the President, who had died unexpectedly rich. Millicent lived alone until the earl died when, to everyone's surprise, she married Daniel Truscott Carhart, a dim New Englander who interested no one but Millicent. Speculation as to just *how* he interested her continued for many years. But now that each was seventy, it was simply assumed that he must once have been amusing and that she generously kept him on, as an extra man at dinner. His only function in Washington was an obscure link with the Smithsonian Institution to which, it was rumored, Millicent had left herself, as part of the national heritage.

The drawing room was intended to be impressive, with elaborate *boiserie* and Chinese screens but like Millicent it had a seedy look of grandeur not quite achieved. The curtains were faded and torn; the chairs wobbly and in need of repair; the inevitable silver-framed portraits of royalty tarnished.

Millicent's servants had grown old with her: they had even become like her in the sense that they regarded the house not so much as a place to be kept up as a shrine to be tended. A portrait of the house deity hung over the mantel. The late President had been a stubby thick-jawed man with anxious eyes and curly sideburns. His administration had long been forgotten, yet here, in this room, Peter was conscious of the nineteenth century as he was nowhere else in Washington and he pondered what the city must have been like in those days of slow travel, twelve-course dinners, and interminable speeches. But Millicent gave no clue to the gilded age of her youth. In manner she was entirely modern. But then she had always been contemporary, and were it not for the obvious decay of her house and husband, one might have thought her eternal in her bright enduring middle age.

"Mr. Duncan, how good of you to come!" She seized Aeneas's hand as though it might bring her luck. Millicent was tall; she had the President's heavy jaw but the pebbly eyes were her own.

Aeneas was nervous. "Mrs. Carhart, I hope it's all right but I brought a friend."

"Of course. Of course." Millicent took Peter's hand in both of hers. But when she heard "Peter Sanford," she embraced him, to Aeneas's astonishment.

"For heaven's sake, what's a child like you doing in the Army?"

"Grown up, Mrs. Carhart. Child no longer."

"Time!" Mrs. Carhart shouted the enemy's name. "Where's Blaise? Frederika?"

Hobe Sound, Peter reported; but they would be at Laurel House in a few days, for Christmas.

"Will they give their New Year's Eve party this year?"

"Oh, yes."

"Then I'll be there. That's really the only time I'm ever invited to Laurel House. I'm not grand enough for them. To think, *in the Army*. Daniel!" She called to her husband, a large, placid man whose face was stained with liver spots. "It's Peter Sanford! And Mr. Duncan, the critic I told you about, or should I call you Captain?" Aeneas merely shook his head, bemused at the change in Peter's estate. Before Aeneas could begin to question and accuse, Mr. Carhart took Peter around the room, while Millicent introduced Aeneas as the 'famous critic' to a number of people who had never heard of him. Yet Millicent did her best to create a salon. Not that Peter had any clear notion of what a true salon was except that in addition to several brilliant talkers, there would have to be a large number of superb listeners, carefully educated to appreciate every allusion and nuance the speakers made. But he had never been in such a place. At the houses he knew, only the politics of the day was discussed; other subjects tended to confuse and bore.

"I think your sister Enid's coming for tea, too." Mr. Carhart spoke slowly as he moved Peter toward a long lace-covered table where tea and coffee were being served by two elderly maids in gray uniforms. As they poured, their hands shook but they did not spill a drop. When Millicent said tea, she meant tea. There would be no alcohol served to anyone, which did not distress Peter, who was thrilled by the vista of food: thin-sliced bread and butter, as well as cucumber, watercress, and chicken sandwiches; also, on time-darkened silver plates, pyramids of chocolate-coated leaves and pale macaroons.

Life was good. He asked for tea, devoured a chicken

sandwich, and said that he had not seen much of Enid lately. "They keep me pretty busy at the Pentagon," he invented. The chicken sandwich needed salt, which meant that the butter was fresh. He tried a hot rolled cheese sandwich: superb. Butter had been used to glaze the toast; inside, cayenne gave definition.

"Will the war ever end?" asked Mr. Carhart politely. Expecting no answer, he vanished. It was a question to which no one, this week, had the answer. Until very recently the wearisome business seemed near its end; then both Germany and Japan had got a second wind. In the case of the Japanese "a divine wind": kamikaze pilots flew their planes directly at the enemy, themselves dying in the explosion. In Europe, the Germans had unexpectedly stopped the Allied advance in a violent action which the newspapers referred to as the Battle of the Bulge. Casualties were high. Peter had received letters from friends with the First Army who reported that things were rough; they praised his foresight in remaining at the Pentagon. But he refused to feel guilty. He had made up his mind to survive, and so far he had.

Diana approached. He swallowed hard, gulped tea, shook her hand.

"I didn't know *you* were one of Millicent's." She was amused.

"I was brought here." He thought she looked uncommonly pretty. "Where's Billy?"

"Who knows?" She was abrupt. "There's been a row."

"Worse than usual?"

"Much worse. Apparently he testified against Ed Nillson. Father's furious. I'm furious."

"Who's Ed Nillson?"

"He raised money for Father in 1940. He's an oil man . . ."

Peter vaguely recalled a recent newspaper account of an oil man being charged with some shady doing.

". . . he's being tried in New York. And Billy testified against him. He even got the White House involved. He couldn't have been more proud. After all that Mr. Nillson's done for Father, for me. It was too . . . lousy. I don't suppose I could get a drink. No, it's a serious tea." She took a cup from one of the maids, spilled half of it in her saucer, drank the rest from the cup and seemed somewhat restored.

During this, Peter ate a small star-shaped sandwich: tongue with a dash of mustard. He ate another, and asked, "What're *you* doing here?"

"Mr. Carhart. I'm after him. For the magazine."

"Still looking for a backer?"

Diana nodded, face suddenly stern. "I'm going to get this magazine published or die . . . from too much tea. I've had tea with every dowager in Washington."

"Dowagers are not apt to support a socialist magazine. Goes against the grain."

"I don't tell them that at this stage. I tell them that *The American Idea* will be devoted to art, beauty, truth . . ."

"Things they secretly deplore . . ."

"But must admire. And of course anti-Communist. We are, too. That always goes over well. Only . . ."

"They don't invest?"

"They don't invest. Mr. Carhart's almost our last hope."

"I don't suppose Billy is much help raising money."

"None. But he is a marvelous editor. No, really. He's got together some wonderful contributors."

"*There's* a possibility." Peter indicated Aeneas. Diana was impressed. Clutching a chocolate leaf in his left hand, as provision during a long circuit of the room, Peter led Diana to Aeneas, who knew Billy by reputation, and agreed that there was indeed a place for *The American Idea* in the literary world.

"Of course I'll write for it. I'll write for anything that pays. How much do you pay?"

"Oh, we haven't any money yet." Wanting to seem gay, Diana merely sounded discouraged. "But of course we *will* pay," she added quickly. "As soon as we've raised enough for at least six issues. But it's not easy."

"Not easy! What about your young friend here? The capitalist wolf in his golden fleece pretending to be an innocent lamb." Aeneas affected a hearty tone but Peter saw that he was angry. Fences would have to be mended.

Peter turned to Diana. "If you want me to, I'll tackle Mr. Carhart." He wanted very much to do something for Diana, because she was angry at Billy, and if he could be of use to her now . . . The pavan would continue. Sooner or later all hands touch. She was delighted, delighting him.

Halfway to Mr. Carhart he was stopped by Lucy Shattuck. Like all Frederika's friends she presumed that she knew him as well as she knew his mother. "Peter! Look at you, all filled out!" He pulled in his stomach; in his hand the chocolate leaf had begun to melt. Lucy introduced him to a Naval officer who turned out to be a movie star assigned to the Pentagon. The actor looked smaller than himself, and unexpectedly prim. The ladies of Washington could not get enough of him. To their astonishment he was a "gentleman."

"*He*'ll never live through another term." Lucy was emphatic. The "he" of course was the President who obsessed them all. Yet for some reason people had accepted the fourth term more easily than they had the third, doubtless realizing that in bloody times it was only suitable that the son of morning reign over them. Peter himself found the aging Lucifer tedious and redundant; whenever he came upon his photograph in the newspaper he quickly turned to another section in order to avoid the sight of that haggard glaring face, with the curious dark splotch above the left eyebrow which looked always as if there had been some sort of flaw in the newspaper's system of reproduction, a drop of ink that spread from year to year, edition to edition.

The actor demurred. "Not that I'm a New Dealer," he said softly, in the voice which had given so much pleasure to so many millions—among them Peter, who wished suddenly that this were all a film and each had been assigned an exciting part already memorized. "But I was at the White House for dinner only last week. And I thought he was in great form. And very funny about Dewey. I must say I laughed, even though I voted for Dewey." Somehow the thought of a movie star voting was distasteful to Peter, who longed for the hero to say in that celebrated steely voice, "All right. Stay just where you are. I want the diamonds." Then with his funny half-smile, he would turn to Peter and say, "O.K., Pete, you cover the back room." But the voice was ordinary, not steel; the manner a mere echo of the screen self; the half-smile inauthentic. Lucy, however, was thrilled. Like most Washington ladies, she never went to the movies, but she did know about movie stars. Though it was considered good form to make fun of them, they were much in demand at parties: they dressed a room.

Lucy rendered the star the high tribute of sharing important gossip. Apparently the President, though dying of inoperable cancer, was having an affair with the Crown Princess of Norway who had stayed much too long at the White House. "Of course Mrs. Roosevelt couldn't care less, but Missy LeHand went out of her mind with grief because he is absolutely mad about this woman." Peter noted with some amusement that even the cynical Lucy accepted the feminine convention that men were always "mad" about women when it had been his own observation that men were seldom mad about anyone.

"Then, on top of everything, he gave her country a submarine chaser!" As Lucy roared with laughter, the top of her nose moved up and down. "Isn't that just like him? Other men give their mistresses a diamond bracelet but *he* gives his a submarine chaser!"

Across the room Peter saw Irene Bloch being greeted warmly by Millicent. He wondered if this was a new alliance. "Mrs. Carhart has the most interesting guests," observed the actor carefully.

"A grab-bag, I should say," said Lucy a bit too sharply since two of the bag's contents stood before her. "I mean," she qualified, "it's not like the dear old highbrow days when I wasn't allowed in the house and Henry Adams used to lecture. That was before his wife died, of course, poor woman: *he* wasn't easy. Now Millicent's taken up with the common folk, like us." But the folk present were neither common nor in any way related to one another except that each knew that in this room he stood, if only briefly, upon the last of the bridges between nineteenth century Washington and the new imperial city whose fleets and armies now ranged the earth from Borneo to the Rhine.

Peter glanced at the stout President above the fireplace and wondered what he would have thought of this new American empire so unlike the old Republic whose jovial steward he had been. The change in the country, as reflected by the city, had been so sudden that Peter was not surprised that so few people seemed to notice it. Overnight everyone took it for granted that without design and by God's election, the American Empire existed to rule the world. Not as if we *wanted* the world, the magnates grumbled, as they seized bases and trade routes, but who else can stop the Nazis and the Japs? Who else can keep the peace, through war?

"I must say, this war is terrible!" Lucy sounded as if she had given the matter more than usual thought. "I was with Millicent in Maryland last weekend. She has the most beautiful place there," Lucy explained to the actor who said yes, he knew. "And that Mrs. Osborne came over for the afternoon, you know the one who is always trying to preserve old Georgetown?" Peter said yes, he knew. "She wanted Millicent to join some committee or other, so while we were discussing the ins and outs of the matter, it was that very warm day . . . Sunday, like spring . . . and we were sitting outside, down by that awful pond of Millicent's which is so full of weeds that I call it the gumbo. Anyway, the outside telephone rang and Millicent answered it and the call was for Mrs. Osborne who took it. Well, she hadn't listened for two minutes when she stepped back from the phone, got her foot tangled in the extension cord, and *fell* head over heels into the pond. Luckily, Millicent is strong as an ox and she pulled her out. So there the poor thing was, soaked to the skin, teeth chattering from shock, and plastered with leaves, and she told us how her son, that nice tall boy Scotty—"

The hand that held the chocolate leaf shut into an icy fist. "Was dead," Peter sounded the words in his head an instant before Lucy Shattuck said, "—was killed, shot in the head at Saipan. He was a Marine."

Lucy continued to talk but Peter no longer listened. He shut his eyes, tried to evoke Scotty, got a black-and-white negative, tried again, got a blurred likeness of Scotty roller-skating at fourteen, wearing corduroy knickers; tried once more and got full color. Each was thirteen. They were in a bathroom at Laurel House.

Peter had no practical knowledge of sex. Scotty volunteered instruction. Both lay down on the cold tile floor. Half his life later, Peter could still feel the grip of that callused athlete's hand.

As Scotty went about his work, he described how the previous summer he had seduced a girl of seventeen, a great victory. At the time Peter did not believe him (later he discovered that Scotty never lied). But true or false, the story made him envious, for that day on the bathroom floor he was convinced that he would never be able to have a girl, or even himself. Only in dreams was he potent.

"It isn't going to work," he said at last, but Scotty merely grinned, black hair falling over his forehead as he methodically continued. Suddenly, feeling odd, Peter tried to pull away. "That's enough," he said. But Scotty would not let him go. Then, with a sense of being torn apart, Peter felt his life go. "Jesus!" He struck away the other's hand. Scotty shouted with laughter. Like a meteor drawn into a planet's orbit, Peter fell toward Scotty and with a gasp crashed against the smooth long body and died, to be reborn minutes later when Scotty pushed him away, eyes glittering with delight. "Well, that's how you do it. But next time not all over me."

The look in Scotty's eyes at that moment was the only thing he could recall, as the voice of Lady Shattuck continued, far away, like a bad telephone connection.

"Come on," said Diana, taking his arm. "Excuse me, Mrs. Shattuck." She pulled him away from the fatal messenger.

"Come on where?" he asked, wondering how he could still speak. He caught a glimpse of himself in a mirror and saw with disgust that he looked the same as ever: nothing revealed the inner pain, except the melting pastry in his hand. But the pain was real enough; it was simply that his response was inadequate. He could not rise to tragedy or sink to grief. Instead, newsreels played through his head. Marines hit the beach. Movie dialogue boomed in his ears. "But he's only a kid, Captain! You can't send him out on that patrol!" When he tried to visualize the moment of Scotty's death, he was rewarded with a still photograph of

Scotty pitching a baseball beneath palm trees, while a nearby jukebox played "All the Things You Are," rendered in Scotty's own flat never-to-be-heard-again bass.

"Mr. Carhart's ready. He's in the study."

"Ready for what?" Peter wanted not to go on, to stop where he was. It's been quite enough, thank you. And then he would pitch to the floor, a bullet between his eyes.

"Here's the mockup." Diana gave him the dummy issue of *The American Idea*. "Now go on. In there." She pushed him toward the door.

Mr. Carhart was standing at his desk on which had been arranged a series of charts containing thousands of little boxes, some blank and some written in. "Genealogy," he said amiably. "I've traced the Carharts back to Robert the Bruce, in two lines."

"That must be interesting, sir." Peter held *The American Idea* stiffly in one hand. In the other melted chocolate threatened to drip onto the Turkey-red carpet. To his disgust he realized that he was now dramatizing not the death of Scotty but his own grief.

Fortunately Mr. Carhart's reputation as a bore was not exaggerated. Not only did he, like the greatest bores, have a series of set numbers, not anecdotes so much as annals, but he could also be spontaneously dull. He was exactly what Peter needed.

"I'm all right, as you can see, through the nineteenth and most of the eighteenth century, a few holes here and there, of course, but the Carhart line is clear. Then in the seventeenth century we have a few little problems." He frowned: large problems obviously. "There is a connection with Sir Thomas Browne which is quite exciting but depends entirely upon this lady here." He poked one of the little boxes. "*Who* was her first husband? And are we kin to her children by him or to those by the second husband?"

While this question was being threshed out, Peter looked for some place to deposit the chocolate, a risky business since Mr. Carhart, not wanting the attention of his victim to stray, was apt to pivot about and fix with a cold stare the listener who had dared fidget or yawn even with mouth shut.

But at last the set piece ended, and Peter gave Mr. Carhart the issue of *The American Idea,* and made him a speech.

Mr. Carhart appeared impressed. "We could do with something like that. As my friend Henry Adams used to say, 'Washington is a cultural desert.' I used to wonder why he stayed. It must have been torture for him, living opposite the White House and knowing that *he* would never live there, unlike his grandfather and great-grandfather, who did of course live there." Trust Mr. Carhart to explain that. Peter was becoming restive: a sign that he was responding to the Carhart treatment. He was being bored to life again.

" 'Let's be vulgar and ask the President,' Henry Adams used to say, which always made Millicent furious since of course her uncle was the President." It was Aeneas Duncan who had pointed out to Peter that like the medieval Roman nobility, each of Washington's important families was based upon a single important man. In Rome he was a Pope, in Washington a President or notorious legislator. And long after this celebrity was quite forgotten, he continued to be worshiped at the home altar, for he was sole source of the family's honor and root to their pretensions. Millicent always referred to her uncle as The President, as though there had not been thirty others.

"I don't," said Mr. Carhart finally, after a long reminiscence of an afternoon with Henry Adams in which, it developed, nothing was said that in some way did not touch upon the Carhart genealogy, "invest in this sort of thing. But," the small dull eyes almost twinkled behind gold-rimmed pince-nez, "I'll take the first subscription."

Fuck you, thought Peter, scraping his left hand under the chair, vengefully dislodging the chocolate, not caring if Mr. Carhart saw or not. But his crime went unnoticed. For just then Millicent put her head in the door. "Come on you two, do your stuff. Peter, your sister's here."

Joe Bailey pounded Peter heartily. "How's a boy?" He explained in his rich voice while Enid said, "You're fat again! And what's that on your hand?" She saw everything. "Chocolate! The way you eat." She pro-

197

duced Kleenex; gratefully he took it and cleaned himself.

"What're you doing here?" each asked the other at the same time. Both laughed, acknowledging if nothing else their likeness of response. Peter said business with Mr. Carhart. Enid said Joe wanted to meet Washington society. "Though God knows why! Let's face it, Millicent's the dullest woman alive, and tea is all we'll get!"

As always, people were drawn to Enid and Peter let her go. She had been drinking but she was steady on her feet and she spoke distinctly. Nevertheless, Joe Bailey held onto her, as if he feared she might fall.

"Who's the girl?" Aeneas was beside Peter.

"My sister."

"That was a lousy thing to do, stringing me on like that."

"I wanted you to love me for myself."

To save honor, Aeneas took the negative line. "About as worthless a group of people as I've ever seen. Stalin was right: the undesirable classes do not liquidate themselves."

"But what about the conversation? This is a salon, after all." As Peter teased, he was conscious of an obscure distress, something to do with Scotty, other than the fact of death.

Aeneas bitterly denounced the golden world he had been so eager to reveal, and, wanting to keep his friendship, Peter agreed with him until Diana joined them, anxious for news. Peter was blunt. "Nothing doing. He won't give a penny."

"Oh, no!"

"Why don't you use your money, the Sanford millions?" Aeneas took heavy revenge.

"I don't have the millions. They're my father's and I don't think this is quite his sort of thing. But," he turned full face to Diana, "I'll see that it gets published. That's a promise."

Diana looked at him with some curiosity. "Do you really mean that?"

Peter meant it. The time of drifting was at an end. The years in school and in the Army were all so much time forever wasted. Now he must put a stop to the drift by doing something that was not only worth doing for itself but would please Diana, particularly now that she had fallen out with Billy. But he put the ignoble secondary motive out of his head. He would do this thing for its own sake, like Scotty, who had died doing something which, in the moment's frame at least, was meaningful. But that was maudlin, he told himself severely, and not true. To die for any thing was just as bad as to die for nothing. He had meant to survive the war and he had survived. Now he must pay the price for this sensible caution and use his life properly. On the verge of self-congratulation, he reminded himself that he was not noble. He did only what he wanted to do, and no more. He turned to Diana. "Come on, let's go." He surprised himself more than he did her.

"All right," she said. "I'll get my coat. I'll meet you in the hall."

"I know her husband. He's not the easiest man to deal with." Aeneas looked at him shrewdly.

"Luckily, I don't have to deal with him." Peter said good night to Aeneas, keeping the lines of friendship intact if frayed.

As Peter crossed to say goodbye to his hostess, he heard Enid say to Irene Bloch, "Really, I'd love to come see your new house. I hear everybody goes there now. I never did understand why they were all so down on you for so long." Irene Bloch went, if possible, whiter than usual, a drift of snow beneath Enid's cruel sun.

"Oh, yes." Irene was bright. "Oh, yes," she repeated, somewhat desperately, hoping for a change in the weather, which Peter provided.

"Hello, Mrs. Bloch."

"Ah, Pierre!" She turned to him, took both his hands in hers and would not let him go. "You must come, too. A little party. *Un petit cocktail.*" Wanting her to win, Peter could not help wincing at being called Pierre. Enid winked at him, pleased with herself. The little cocktail was for a Middle European foreign minister, exiled by Germans. Wanting to make up for Enid, Peter said that he would be happy to come. He tried to undo Mrs. Bloch's hands but she clung to him, fearing Enid.

She talked quickly, filling every silence in order to keep Enid at bay.

"We don't see enough of you," she said gaily, and Peter wondered who was "we." He barely knew her and only horror at his sister's behavior made him suddenly an ally. "But I know how busy you young men are with this awful war! You do all the work, too, I'm sure, for *you* never go out and the generals are out to dinner every night."

"That's lucky because . . ." Enid's fangs were bared to draw snow water.

But Peter deflected her. "I do nothing at all, Mrs. Bloch. I wish I did." The idea came to him. "I'm about to publish a magazine. Why don't you invest?"

"But I should love to!" Reminded of the merchant prince's wealth, she was herself again. She let go Peter's hands. She even indulged in a second thought. "I mean if I approve of it, naturally!" With a small laugh, she avoided commitment.

"Oh, you'll approve!"

"I'm sure she will," said Enid. "After all, it's social, isn't it? A magazine like *Town and Country?*"

But her victim was already on the wing. Over her shoulder she said to Peter, "Come and see me. Almost any afternoon." She was gone.

Peter turned to Enid. "You are awful," he said, which made Enid laugh until her eyes filled with tears.

Joe Bailey materialized. "How's my girl?" He struck a deep note on the rich organ of his voice.

"Oh, your girl is just fine but she could do with a drink. I can't take much more of this old maid's tea party. Peter's found a new friend, one of the chosen people, Irene Bloch!" Enid's voice filled the room. At the fireplace Lucy Shattuck gave them a knowing smile.

Suddenly Peter was aware that his head was aching and that if he did not soon release some portion of his grief and rage he would burst. He turned on Joe. "How is the revolution coming?"

"Revolution?" Joe Bailey looked at him blankly.

"The take-over of the White House, the elimination of the Commies, the return to a cleaner, simpler, more godly America, dedicated to the small rural farm, baseball and slavery?"

"Don't get smart-aleck, mister!"

Enid started to say something but for once decided not to. His inner pressure somewhat lessened, Peter said good night to Millicent and joined Diana in the hall. In the taxicab, without consulting Diana, he gave the driver his own address.

Not until after Diana had left at midnight did he recall what it was that had been troubling him all evening. The year before, when Scotty was home on leave, they had got into a pointless quarrel about a girl each knew. As a result they had parted coldly, in a Hot Shoppe drive-in where Peter had eaten two hamburgers and two orders of French fried potatoes. Pride had kept them apart for the rest of Scotty's leave. Now Scotty was dead and Peter realized that never once in all the years they had known each other had he told Scotty that he liked him. Lying among tangled sheets that smelled of Diana, Peter scowled, gritted his teeth, vowed he would not make that mistake again.

2

From far away, Burden heard his own amplified voice fill the room. He was making a speech to an audience which laughed at every joke. It was exactly his sort of group: prosperous farmers come to Washington for an annual lunch, held this year in the new Statler Hotel with himself as guest speaker. He told an old joke: loud laughter. He cast down his eyes, simulating modesty while trying to read the notes he had made on the menu. As the laughter continued, he took a quick sip of coffee and noticed that his slab of ice cream had not been taken away. It was now liquid. Disgusting.

Suddenly the laughter stopped. Burden tried to start again but all that he could think of was melted ice cream. He had gone blank. For an instant he did not know where he was or what he was doing in front of so many strangers. He had literally lost himself, as he had done from time to time in public over the years. Fortunately, his moments of aphasia were brief and seldom noticed.

Desperately Burden reached for the menu; read "Boeuf à la Washington." That was no help. Panic increased; the audience was watching him curiously, wondering why he did not go on. He looked at the back of the menu, saw several scribbled words. One was "Luzon." He was saved. With MacArthur's recent landing on Luzon, the reconquest of the Philippines had begun. Restored in time, he made the eagle, if not scream, at least discreetly flap its wings, for flag-waving was out of fashion, which suited his temperament rather more than it had that of his opponent in the recent primary, a passionate New Dealer whose campaigning had been full of the "Remember Pearl Harbor!" sort of thing.

Burden had chosen quite a different tack. Low-keyed and sweetly reasonable, he had reminded the voters that in the thirty years he had been their Senator, the state had grown prosperous. But where another politician might have labored that essential point, Burden simply made it and moved on to describe how, during his lifetime, the United States had become a world power and (echoing Pericles) he told them what a marvelous yet dangerous thing it was to be great. To his surprise, this part of the speech invariably struck the collective nerve. As he came to it, he could see people lean forward, eyes suddenly wide, wanting to hear every word. At such moments, he knew a pleasure which made altogether bearable the harrowing process of election.

Burden had not planned to mention the danger of world power to the farmers, but since they had reacted so well to his tribute to MacArthur, he decided to continue. But he had not got two sentences into Power when he realized that he had spoken too long. He should have quit with Luzon. Drastically, he shortened Power; sadly, too, for he was grateful to it. Power had been particularly effective against his Republican opponent, a businessman of crude imperialist tendencies with twice Burden's financial backing. Though it was

202

a close race, Power had finally defeated money. Burden had been so poorly financed that in the last weeks of the campaign he had been unable to pay for billboards or for radio. He had hardly been able to buy those useless but necessary advertisements in the weekly newspapers. Useless in the sense that they changed no votes; necessary because the editor invariably supported the candidate who bought the most advertising.

To Burden's relief, his connection with Nillson did not become a major issue. For one thing Nillson's difficulties with the government had not so far involved the Indian land sale. For another, though Nillson had been indicted on several counts, he had yet to be convicted of anything. As a result, neither his challenger in the primary nor his opponent in the election was able to do more than deplore the company the Senator kept.

Ironically, it was Burden's sense of justice that cost him votes. He was savagely attacked for defending the Nisei. "Nip-lover" was often scrawled on his posters. Just before election, in desperation, his Republican opponent had charged that Senator Day was a secret agent for the Japanese Government (why did the Senator see Ambassador Kurusu ten days before Pearl Harbor?). Because of this hyperbole, the Republican lost; to Burden's secret surprise, for he had been convinced that this time he would lose and if he did, he had not the slightest idea what would become of him. He had no life outside the Senate. But virtue had triumphed, and he was safe for six more years.

In a good mood, Burden ended his speech with a pleasantry. During the laughter, he dropped his menu in the pool of melted ice cream. The chairman thanked him; another speech made.

Tired but pleased, Burden proceeded through the crowded room, shaking hands, giving autographs, allowing the photographer (only one, a bad sign) to take his picture with various worthies. Then, with a last wave to the room, he crossed the lobby to the newsstand.

As he searched for his own name in the afternoon paper, a familiar voice said, "That's what I call disloyal! Reading the opposition!" It was Blaise.

Burden greeted him loudly, his voice still pitched for

public speaking. They had not seen one another since the election. "Well, what's the word from our boy?"

Burden went blank. What boy? Whose boy?

"Clay wrote me two weeks ago that he'd be on the move again but of course he couldn't say where. He's in Guam at the moment, or so my spies tell me."

"I haven't heard from him lately." In fact, except for a note of congratulation in November, Burden had not heard from Clay since the election. This was odd, since Clay was usually meticulous about "keeping in touch." Burden wondered if the Nillson affair might have made Clay reluctant to write him. The rising man wants no part of the falling one. But I did not fall, thought Burden grimly, buying a magazine emblazoned with the legend, "The Dogface War in the Pacific, by Harold Griffiths."

Blaise tapped the cover with a blunt forefinger. "Harold's a phenomenon. Damnedest thing. Outsells Ernie Pyle. Never suspected he had it in him. Pansy, of course. That's what makes him so good writing about soldiers."

"I'm surprised you let him write for anyone but you."

Blaise scowled. "Who would've guessed it? Anyway, I've got him tied up for newspapers." Blaise bought the same magazine. "You know," he said, "I'm going to be the President's guest at the Inaugural next week."

"Traitor." Burden smiled.

"Well, maybe." Blaise lit a cigar. As he did, several farmers' wives came up to shake Burden's hand and wish him well "because you think right!" to which Burden made his usual response, "May the good Lord increase your kind." Then he turned to find Blaise, cigar lit, watching him.

"You see," said Burden, "I am still loved."

"Why not?" Blaise was not impressed. "I'm going to the White House not because I like the old shyster . . ."

"You supported him last time."

"Only because I couldn't take Dewey. No, I'm going because of this United Nations business. I'm all for it, Burden." Blaise spoke as though in warning.

"I know you are." Burden was demure.

"You fellows in the Senate aren't going to make trouble, are you?"

Burden found himself enjoying the situation. "It's possible. I don't really know. A lot will depend on how Franklin handles us. Wilson treated us like schoolboys. That was a mistake."

"You behaved like schoolboys, too," grumbled Blaise. "Anyway, the President wants to play ball with you. The only reason he picked Truman for Vice President was to help out with the Senate."

"That may have been a mistake."

"You're *not* going to make any trouble, are you?"

"Trouble? How can we? Two years ago we approved a postwar international organization."

"But *you* didn't vote."

"No. But I was in favor of the resolution, because it made Senate approval of any treaty mandatory."

"Which means you boys will have the final word on everything."

"We have it anyway. Article Two, Section Two, the Constitution." Burden changed the subject. "You know, we're still keeping that Second District seat warm for Clay. I mentioned him quite a few times when I was in the district. They like him."

Blaise brightened at the thought of Clay. "That's terrific! Of course we'll have to find some way of getting rid of the incumbent, but that shouldn't be too hard. After all: the returning soldier, in uniform . . ."

"Not hard at all." Burden heard youth knocking at every door. "We'll do everything we can for Clay. Don't worry. How's Enid?"

"All right." Blaise dismissed his daughter with the first gray ash of the cigar. "Did Ed Nillson find you?"

Burden was startled. "No. Is he in town?"

"Ran into him this morning, at the Press Club. He was on his way to the Hill, to see you. Poor Ed." Blaise puffed a great blue cloud into Burden's eyes. "Did he hurt you much in the election?"

"Yes." Burden chose not to elaborate.

"I figured so. Well, at least he stayed out of jail. That's something. Good to see you, Burden."

* * *

Ed Nillson was in the inner office, acording to Miss Perrine, who looked frightened. Ed was sitting on the sofa, head in hands. But when he saw Burden he greeted him gaily. "Hope you don't mind my barging in like this. But your office is the only quiet place around here."

Burden was stung by the truth of this observation. No longer in the running for President, he was simply another Senator. But not for long. In a few days time he would be the most talked-about member of the Senate. Thinking of the card he was about to play, his mood improved and he was almost exuberant with the man who had very nearly cost him his political life.

"You look well, Ed. I've missed you. We all have."

"That's nice of you to say." Nillson was as bland as he had been that day when they first met in front of the Capitol. He never showed distress, even now when he was under indictment from a Federal grand jury, largely because "of your son-in-law."

"I know. I'm sorry. I would gladly murder him."

"What is sad is that I was doing all right with the Internal Revenue people. We were even doing all right with the Justice Department, but apparently there was a call from the White House from one of Billy's friends. And that did the trick. That's what made the last indictment possible. He has a vengeful nature."

Burden sighed. "You are not the object of it."

"If not the object, I am at least the principal victim."

"But it was me he was getting at. If you recall, Billy's revelations were made *before* the primary. He wanted to defeat me. So did the President. That's why the White House helped him."

"Not a loyal young man."

"Not loyal at all. But I survived. And so will you."

"Oh, yes." Nillson was easy. "At this moment I don't think they can get me on anything. Why, we're even clear on the land sale."

This time the "we" made Burden shudder. He examined the *Congressional Record* on his desk. "That's good to hear," he whispered.

"The fact that to this day we've never found one God-damned drop of oil on that land didn't hurt the cause a bit. Now, Burden, what I want from you . . ."

Burden stiffened. Nillson laughed. "It's not that bad. Just tell your son-in-law that if he doesn't lay off I'll see to it that everyone knows he is *currently* a member in good standing of the Communist Party."

"Have you proof?" Burden was not surprised.

"I've had proof for the last six months."

"Then why didn't you use it?"

"Because you were up for re-election. Knowing me was bad enough. A Communist son-in-law would have finished you."

Burden was stunned. If ever a man was practical it was Nillson. Yet he had allowed himself to be hurt in order to save a friend's career. Burden felt the tears start. He stammered. "You did nothing, just because of me?"

Nillson smiled. "There is a certain loyalty among thieves."

That was better. "Thieves" shocked Burden, as Nillson had intended it should. "I don't know how to thank you."

"By warning him."

"I'll do that. Don't worry." Burden felt the adrenalin flow. He would enjoy his task. So, he suspected, would Diana.

"Tell him that now that you're safe from the voters for a while, I don't in the least mind making trouble."

"I'll help you," said Burden.

Nillson rose. "Hope you're going to support this United Nations business."

"If I tell you something, will you not repeat it?" Ever since the conversation with Blaise, Burden had been eager to share his secret.

"I'll do my best." Nillson regarded him with fond amusement.

"Well, I plan to make a speech next week in which I shall renounce isolationism and support the United Nations."

"Wonderful!" Nillson was genuinely pleased. Then he smiled. "And so, by doing the right thing, you'll be back on top. That's very unusual."

"Yes, it is," said Burden, and they laughed like

schoolboys, shook hands like conspirators, and parted friends.

It was already dark when Burden arrived home. Henry opened the door for him. From upstairs his wife called, "That you, Burden?" and he shouted, as he had done for thirty years, "I'm home!" Then he went into the living room.

Sitting stiffly on a straight chair beside the fire was Billy Thorne. Opposite him on the sofa sat Diana and a stocky young man in uniform who looked familiar. On the coffee table between them were strewn papers and what looked to be a disemboweled magazine. "May I come in?" Burden asked.

Diana ran to him, kissed him. "We've got wonderful news!" The young man shook his hand and he saw that it was Peter Sanford, a likable youth, if somewhat characterless. Out of the corner of his eye, Burden saw that Billy had grudgingly hauled himself to his feet.

"Good evening, Thorne." Burden poured himself an unusually stiff drink. "What's the good news?"

"The magazine, we've got the money for it! We're putting out the first issue right now." Diana was ecstatic.

"It's being published in the spring, not now." Billy sat down in his chair with a clatter.

"Well, soon," said Diana.

Burden took his usual seat beside the fire. "Where did you get the money?" He indicated Peter. "From this young man?"

"This young man has no money," said Peter. "I got the money from a lady, Mrs. Samuel I. Bloch. I don't suppose you know her, sir."

Burden sat up straight. Irene. The tea. The falling. "But I do know her."

"Of course he does! She found him when he had his stroke, in the street." Diana was innocent. "I told you that, Peter."

"A fine lady." Burden sounded, he knew, as if he were seeking votes: a fine fellow, a good friend, a great American. He had often regretted the end of the affair with Irene. But he had had no choice. Half his life he had lived in dread of the moment when a doctor would

208

tell him that there must be no more sex, ever again. Yet after the stroke when he had been told as much, he had experienced relief as well as despair, no doubt due to the fact that for him the spirit had always been weaker than the flesh. Yet the cold knowledge that all loving was past made death seem near. Swallowing bourbon, he made up his mind: during the summer recess, he would definitely put himself in a hospital with the single request that he be restored—and he *would* be restored, for medicine was fabulous nowadays. In any case, it was unthinkable that youth could not somehow be regained. Suddenly his right eyelid began to twitch; a sign of fatigue. He finished the drink. "I like Mrs. Bloch," he said. Then he added, "Very much."

"So do we," said Peter. "She's giving us a free hand, too."

"A free hand to do what?" Burden was benign in his lack of interest. He must find out the name of that doctor in Switzerland who had successfully rejuvenated so many aging men.

"To publish a decent socialist magazine," bellowed the never-for-long-silent Billy Thorne. Burden winced at his son-in-law's voice. He could never get used to it. The period in which they had all lived together had been harrowing. No matter where Burden was in the house, he could hear Billy's voice. It got so that he even found himself growing impatient when that rasping voice was too long silent. Then there had been the constant scattering of books. In every room there would be books, left open, with elaborate marginal notes. Since many of the books were Burden's there was inevitably a scene. Finally Billy defaced a biography of Cicero. Burden remonstrated. "Terrible old phony," Billy responded, pulling down Cicero and admirer with one tug.

"Decent, naturally," Burden echoed softly.

"We've had enough of alienation. Now we want action."

"Alienation?" Burden thought he knew what the word meant but Billy made it sound as if it were some sort of political party.

"Alienation of the intellectuals." Billy always liked

to explain. "We've been alienated from American life much too long, without influence. But when the war ends, we'll have a real chance to make connection with the people, with the soldiers returning, to change a greedy society into a generous one."

Burden avoided this lurid bait and chose instead to surface at the phrase "without influence." "Surely under the New Deal, you've had a good deal of influence."

"The New Deal's finished!"

"That's true, Father." Diana joined husband in cabal against father, after first giving the father a smile to show that she was still his, despite necessary lapses.

Burden tried a flanking movement. Peter seemed a weak link in the chain of socialism. "Are *you* a socialist?" he asked.

Surprisingly, the young man laughed. "Of course not. I'm nothing. That's my function. To be nothing. Silently I shall express that point of view."

Burden realized that he had misjudged the boy. Long experience of interrogation, however, had taught him when not to follow up. He shifted his line of questioning. "Have you had any publishing experience?"

"None!" The boy seemed to regard this as a virtue. "But I've observed publishers . . ."

"At close hand. He knows what not to be." Billy insulted Blaise.

"There are so many things one ought not to be." Peter gave Billy a swift cold look which pleased Burden. It was plain that they detested each other. Diana might yet be saved. "My function, sir," he turned to Burden who saw how young indeed he was, "is to find money, and I have found it. Mrs. Bloch will finance us, in exchange for a dinner at Laurel House."

The harshness of this made Burden sit back in his chair. The laughter of the others did not much help. Yet it was true. That was exactly why Irene would give money. Laurel House was her Versailles, and not until she had taken her place within the sacred circle could she consider herself arrived. Though Burden disliked Peter's cruelty, he found the hard sense of reality refreshing, even unique in a rich boy. After thirty years among the rich, Burden thought he knew them well. He was most at ease with the self-made; after all, he was self-made, too. But the heirs were another matter. Diffident, shy, not easily fathomed (assuming there was anything beneath the surface gold), they tended to be guilty about their wealth, and Burden favored keeping them that way. But Peter Sanford did not seem guilty about anything. "Billy's the editor, of course," he was saying. "He knows about these things. Diana will . . . what?"

"Answer letters. I type well. No, Father, I really do now."

Even though Diana was not an heiress, she shared, Burden knew, many of the traits, for children of successful politicians are deferred to like princes until the day the source of their distinction dies or is defeated and if they have no money, they sink into disgruntled obscurity, occasionally appearing at Washington parties, loudly quoting what Father used to say. Diana must be spared that fate.

Burden turned to Peter. "But surely you will want to do something more than raise money." Burden was genuinely curious. He recalled Peter as a child, grave and attentive and intelligent. Now he was positively merry, inattentive and more than likely intelligent.

"Yes, sir. But that will take time. First," he looked at Billy, "I must read Marx."

"Don't. It would spoil your ignorance." Billy meant to be unpleasant but Peter ignored him.

Then Kitty entered and kissed everyone. She enjoyed kissing, touching, holding people. To Burden's surprise no one in the least minded her effusiveness, accepting it for what it was, a link to the world and a loving one at that. As she made her tour of the room, he turned to Billy and said in a low voice, "I'd like to see you a moment. In the study."

Burden excused himself and made his way to the second floor, happily aware that stairs were difficult for Billy. But Burden's pleasure in Billy's discomfort was somewhat diminished by the fact that nowadays stairs were none too easy for him; he felt as if he were continually off balance.

The study was a spare bedroom which Kitty had

never got around to furnishing. In the middle of the room a rolled carpet lay like an exhausted python; twenty years before it had proved to be too big for the room, and no one had ever thought to take it away. Burden would have been lost without the carpet's friendly presence. He sat down at the desk which was the room's sole furniture, and came to the point. He did his job briefly and well.

Billy quibbled, "The Russians are our allies."

"They were Hitler's too." Burden knew the dialectic. To every charge a given countercharge; Moscow trials, corruption of the capitalist press; liquidation of the Kulaks, lynchings in Alabama. He indulged Billy for a moment. Then he delivered the final blow. "There is *proof* that you are a Communist, and Nillson has it."

Billy shrugged. "Well?"

That simplified matters. "He will make use of it if you continue your . . . persecution." The word was too big but the thing described was no more or less than that.

"The man's a crook," said Billy, in what for him was a reasonable tone. *"I'm* not the Treasury Department. They're the ones on his tail."

"Your friends at the White House . . ."

"Couldn't care less . . ."

". . . are involved because of you. I suggest you *dis*-involve them."

"And if I don't?"

Burden noticed for the first time that one of Billy's eyes was gray and the other brown. He had never noticed this anomaly before and he rather wished he had not now when he wanted slowly, carefully, feature by feature, to erase Billy, if not from the world, from his own memory. "If you don't, you'll be fired from the *Tribune.*"

"I'll be leaving anyway, to work on the magazine."

Burden was ready. "But it's a socialist magazine, isn't it?"

"The Soviet is, as you must've heard, a socialist state."

Burden continued, "I'm quite sure that if the editor of *The American Idea* was known to be an active member of the Communist Party, there would be no Mrs. Bloch, no Peter Sanford, no money at all to publish a magazine, and probably no audience beyond those few who read the *Daily Worker*." That was it. Billy did not surrender without self-justification. But he did surrender just as Kitty called them to dinner. He would lay off. Burden was satisfied.

As the two stumped and tottered down the stairs, Billy said, "I'm surprised that somebody with your experience could ever have got mixed up with Ed Nillson."

"He is a good friend. I don't know all his business arrangements but I believe him to be honest." Burden had no choice but to lie.

"You can't be that dumb."

Only the fact that Burden was two steps ahead of Billy on the steep descent kept him from responding childishly and in kind. Instead he ignored the insult. "Ed's indictment almost cost me the election."

"A lot of us had hoped it would."

On the ground floor, Burden turned furiously on Billy, who took the last two steps in one, loudly banging his wooden leg against the newel post as he did. "You little swine," was the best Burden could do.

"Why, *Father!*" exclaimed Billy, and he burst out laughing.

"What's so funny?" Diana came in from the drawing room.

"Your father," Billy continued to laugh. Burden managed a smile, aware that he had, after all, won the war.

Then Peter and Kitty joined them, and they all moved into the dining room. As they did, Peter asked him about the United Nations, restoring Burden's good humor. He did not answer the boy directly. He spoke in generalities, not wanting to give away the game.

As they took their places at table, Kitty said, "It's roast beef." Then she added for her own benefit, "If it's not horse. Nowadays you can't tell."

3

"Poor Father!" Half dressed, Diana sat on the edge of the bed, newspaper in hand, while Peter made coffee in the closet where a hot plate and a miniature refrigerator qualified as kitchenette in wartime Washington.

"Why 'poor'?" He started to open the refrigerator. Then stopped. Since Scotty's death, he had forced himself to lose all interest in food.

"Well, look." She held up the newspaper. The headline: "Vandenberg Rejects Isolationism."

Peter did not understand. "What's that to do with your father?"

"But this was to be *his* day." Anxiously she riffled pages, found what she was looking for halfway through the first section. "And here he is, *buried* absolutely buried alive!"

Peter poured coffee for two and brought the cups to the bed. "What are you talking about?"

Diana showed him the newspaper. A small headline said "Senator Favors UN." Peter glanced at the story, Burden had renounced isolationism. "But what's wrong with that? You ought to be proud of him."

"I am. But don't you see? *He* should have got the headline. He's been working on this speech for months."

"Well, his timing was bad."

"He didn't know about Vandenberg. How could he? Oh, he has the worst luck!" She reached across him to pick up the telephone, splashing coffee onto the sheets. He put his arm around her. The Senator's line was busy. She put down the receiver. "This will kill him."

"I doubt that. He's pretty tough." Peter pulled her down beside him and absently they made love as she discussed her father and pondered fate while through the window, the orange winter sun sank behind Dumbarton Oaks.

"We've got to get ready." She tried to sit up; he held her tight.

"There's time. Just as long as we're there before Irene." It had taken a week of negotiation before Frederika consented, without grace, to invite Irene Bloch to dinner. "But remember, I'm only doing it because she's helping you."

"If *you'd* help us, you wouldn't have to have her to the house."

"I don't have any money," Frederika declared, with what sounded like pride. "And neither," she added insanely, "does your father." He chuckled, remembering.

"What are you smiling at?" Diana was pleasantly jealous of his interior drama, wanting always to be included. He told her. She smiled, too. "It would be nice if your father helped."

"He won't. I wouldn't want him to anyway."

"Why not?"

With forefinger Peter drew a pentogram on her stomach. "Because he *is* my father."

"But you have a good relationship, don't you?"

Peter acknowledged that his relationship with his father was good because neither had ever had much to do with the other. "But I often wonder what he's really like, under all that tycoonishness."

"A very peculiar family." Diana had observed this before. "You all try to be so self-contained."

"Not all of us. There's Enid." The orange sun disappeared and the sky went black. Neither much wanted to discuss that turbulent girl, who the previous week had been arrested for drunken driving on a back road in Virginia (no one knew what she had been doing there). Her arrest had been featured widely in all the papers except the *Tribune*, which had not mentioned it.

They made love as if they had been married a long time yet still desired each other. But then, they had known each other a lifetime and their lovemaking could be considered simply a progression in a friendly relationship. Lately Peter found himself, to his disgust, using jargon words like "relationship," picked up from Aeneas and his friends who, to a man, were addicted

215

to the opulent vocabulary of psychiatry, a pseudo-science now in vogue, even more than phrenology had been during the previous century. But though Peter found touching the belief of the simple in these new mysteries, he was alarmed when intellectuals attempted to redefine art and life in terms borrowed from the mental therapists, who meanwhile, like the early church fathers, warred with one another, each maintaining that his was the truth and all else heresy. The first victim in these stormy quarrels had been the English language. Eager to illuminate interpersonal activity, words were made up exactly as if this elaborate game were a science in which new things heretofore unknown must be named. One of the great discoveries, the Vinland of the bold voyagers, was "relationship," a word Peter personally found less appealing than the as yet uncoined "connectionship" or "loveship."

"*Now* what are you smiling at?" She pulled herself up on one arm.

"Erotic pleasure. Normal reflex of the aroused male."

"No, it's not. They scowl."

"Are your eyes always open? And who are 'they'?"

"I've watched. I meant Billy, I suppose."

Peter was delighted. It had been agreed that he never mention her husband. Now she—not he—had broken the taboo. "Does he know, do you think, about all this?" Peter found himself for some reason pointing at the refrigerator.

"Oh, no! He would certainly have had a lot to say if he did. No, he's quite pleased with everything. He thinks he can manipulate you nicely, so he's in a friendly mood."

Peter ignored this deliberate goad. When the time came he would manage Billy. But managing Diana was something else again. "You ought to divorce him."

"Maybe. Some day."

"Not that I believe in marriage." This had been said before.

"Nor do I!" Diana spoke with more than usual vehemence. Then she was on her feet, straightening her garter belt. "We've got to go."

Peter was pleased to find that his uniform, which

216

had been too tight for him, now hung loose, the result of two weeks of not eating. He would be thin
again, once and for all. Between the shock of Scotty's
death and the creation of the magazine, Peter had
ceased to be his old passive self, reading books in
order to find out who he was or listening by the hour
to Aeneas and his friends, hoping that their conversation would suddenly turn to him and someone at
last might tell him who and what he was so that he
would know how to fill the coming years. Now of
course he knew. He was a publisher, like his father.
The irony was pleasing.

"What are you reading?" Diana combed her hair
while examining an open book on Peter's desk.

"Ten things at once, as usual."

"No . . . this." She looked at the title page, squint-
ing in the twilight. "Walter Map. Who's he?"

"Twelfth century. Historian. Poet. Author of—as
you can see—*De Nugis Curialium*. I ought to pretend
I'm reading him in Latin. But I'm not."

Diana turned the pages. She stopped at one of
Peter's underlinings. She read aloud, " 'When I have
begun to rot, the book will begin to savour . . . it will
be an age of apes (as it now is), not men; they will
scoff at their present, and have no patience for men
of worth. Every century has disliked its own modernity; every age from the first onwards, has preferred
the previous one to itself.' " Diana stopped, shut the
book, unwillingly impressed. "You do read everything."

"I want to know everything."

"Except what everybody else knows, like Marx and
Freud."

"Since everyone knows those things, why should I?
Anyway, they can always explain them to me. They
like that."

"I didn't know the word 'modernity' was used
then."

"I don't suppose there is any idea older than the
modern. I rather like the part about the 'age of apes.'
We should have called the magazine that."

"A bit pointed, don't you think? Besides, apes don't
read."

"That's my fear. Let's hope Irene is willing to spend a great deal of money."

They finished their dressing in semidarkness. Then like two shadows, they came together, and Diana unexpectedly asked, "What do you feel about growing old?"

"I can't wait!"

"Do you mean that?"

"Of course. I want to be middle-aged. To be entirely myself, all there, for better or worse. But thin," he added, and she laughed.

"I don't think I shall mind being old either." Diana was thoughtful. "Yet why are the middle-aged so eager to seem young when here we are—here I am—not able to make anything out of it at all?" She was bleak.

"Thank you," he said, both amused and hurt.

"Oh, *you!*" She laughed and he realized with sudden pain that he was more taken with her than she was with him. Fortunately, it was not his nature to despair. As they left the apartment, he knew that sooner or later he would cause her pain and thus eliminate the difference.

* * *

Frederika greeted them warmly. "Diana! You do look lovely. How's Billy? Why couldn't he come?" While Diana explained, Frederika said in a low voice to Peter, "*She* isn't here yet."

"Oh, she'll come, don't worry." Peter found his mother's horror not only enjoyable but impressive because it was so impersonal. Frederika had nothing at all against Irene Bloch. But two thousand years of Christian teaching had done its work. Because Irene Bloch had torn the sacred flesh and smeared herself ecstatically with the blood of the Lamb, she was unclean and ought not to dine at Laurel House.

"Thank Heaven, they all speak English," said his mother, identifying for him a number of guests, including a Russian with steel teeth. "It's not like it was," she added, but he could not tell if she was sorry or glad. Since the start of the war, the Congress

218

had declined socially. Senators were seldom seen at Laurel House. The men who mattered now were the chiefs of those bureaus that stabilized prices and increased production. These czars, as the press called them, were courted by all. Several were present in Blaise's drawing room, to the delight of the other guests, mostly foreigners on missions. Of the old Washington, only those 'good mixers' the Shattucks were present. They could get on with anyone.

"There's the young publisher!" exclaimed his father, with as much contempt as affection in his jovial voice.

"And there's the . . . *senior* publisher," said his son, not about to be trampled upon, even by so venerable a rogue elephant.

But Blaise affected not to hear. He turned to the men he was talking to, all foreign except for a recent addition to the President's Cabinet, new to Washington.

"My son's not really a soldier, in spite of the uniform. He's a magazine publisher. Tell them what kind of a magazine." Blaise grinned wolfishly at Peter, who knew that he did not mean altogether to be unkind.

"The magazine," said Peter, in a clear schoolboy voice, "is somewhat longer than it is wide and printed in two columns on rough stock paper." He stopped and smiled at his father. "I think that about describes it."

The others chuckled uneasily, not certain how their host would respond. But Blaise laughed without malice. "That is about it, gentlemen. Only it's pinko!"

"Socialist, yes," said Peter, as though describing a type face. "But not doctrinaire."

"Aren't they something, these kids? They never know when they're well off. Here he goes and publishes a magazine with capitalist money that wants to do away with capitalism."

"At least it's not *your* capitalist money." Peter wanted that straight for the record.

Blaise looked annoyed for the first time. "No, it's not mine, and never will be. It's . . ."

But the source of Peter's capitalist backing had entered the room. Irene's evening dress was much too vivid, too personal, too fashionable for the subtly calculated dowdiness of a Laurel House dinner. Everyone stared. She paused a moment at the door. Then, seeing Peter, she came toward him just as he started toward her.

Both were intercepted by Frederika beneath the chandelier. To Peter's surprise, Frederika was effusive, Irene serene. So far so good, he thought, heart pounding, wishing Diana would swiftly join them and divert attention. For a silence had fallen on the room.

Peter was never certain how Irene did it but in a matter of minutes she had maneuvered herself in front of Blaise, and made her first error. She interrupted him. Holding out her hand, she said, "Good evening, Mr. Sanford." Too late, Frederika said hurriedly, "Blaise, you remember . . ."

Blaise slowly took Irene's hand and said, "Good evening Mrs. Black. Nice you could come."

"Bloch!" exclaimed Irene merrily, making her second error. Peter was sweating now.

"That's right," said Frederika. "The department store, the one I love so. You know, Bloch's."

"Sorry. Of course." Blaise let Irene's hand fall.

Irene, well-launched upon disaster, made her third error. She looked about the room. "My," she said in a loud voice, "I haven't been here in . . . oh, *pas depuis longtemps.*" All eyes were again turned upon Irene. Peter looked at Diana; her eyes were shut.

"What?" said Blaise in a voice quite as loud as that of his guest. And, as Peter knew she would, Irene repeated the French. The Europeans smiled among themselves. Entirely unaware of the effect she was making, Irene translated the French for Blaise. Before she could do herself more damage, Frederika took her arm and led her away. Across the room, Lucy Shattuck folded her lorgnette, and said something to her husband who smiled: a new Washington legend had been born.

Diana joined Peter, too late. "Why didn't you *do* something?" she asked unreasonably.

"Do what?" Inspired by Irene, he gave the Latin

for " 'Those whom the gods wish to destroy, they first make mad.' " Then he translated it.

"Thanks, pal." Diana was in a bad mood. "Now that your father's royally snubbed her, there goes the money."

"Luckily I don't think she thinks she's been snubbed."

"She may be awful but she's not stupid."

"But that's the point. Don't you see? Father's behaving exactly the way she would want him to behave. If he were friendly, she wouldn't be impressed and if she weren't impressed she wouldn't be here and then there really would be no magazine."

Diana was dubious. Put Peter was certain that he was right. He joined Irene, who had gone, instinctively, to the Europeans who had smiled at her French. She was telling a Frenchman, "I used to see a very great deal of your Ambassador Claudel. Do you know him?" Only by reputation, it seemed. "He was not popular in Washington, *hélas*. He used to read his poetry after dinner and if there is anything we Washingtonians dislike more than poetry, it is poetry in French. We are barbarians."

This went over well. Irene might yet pull through. Peter offered aid. "He also served bad food, which was tragic since your Embassy is the only good French restaurant in town." Peter's pleasantry fell flat, and Irene gave him a swift compassionate look as if to say, better leave this sort of worldly badinage to your elders.

"Do you admire St. Jean Perse?" she asked the Frenchman, who again knew of him only by reputation. "Naturally you've *read* him." The Frenchman looked uncomfortable. In her element now, Irene quoted St. Jean Perse in French and despite the extraordinary accent, she clearly knew her stuff. Peter slipped away.

On Peter's left at dinner sat a girl with black hair, pale skin, long dark eyes, and a voice so low that he had to strain to hear it. "You don't remember me, do you?"

He said he did not, noticing an empty place across the table: Enid had not yet arrived.

"I'm Elizabeth Watress." The name meant nothing. "I'm Mrs. Shattuck's daughter." Peter recalled that Lucy Shattuck had first been married to a New Yorker named Watress, who played polo and drank heavily; one day, capriciously, he turned Lucy out. In a matter of weeks she had married Laurence Shattuck and moved to Washington. Since Elizabeth was younger than Peter, she had never come his way. "Except one weekend when Mother brought me here, before the war, and I met you but you wouldn't remember. I was rather awful. But I did distinguish myself. I went riding with all of you, and the horse, he was called Antic, ran away." Peter did remember this episode. "It was your sister Enid who grabbed the bridle and stopped the horse. If she hadn't, I'd probably have been killed. She's coming to dinner, isn't she?"

"She's held up in town, she'll be late." Peter was perfunctory in his excuses. Actually, he was relieved Enid was not at dinner; like a cat with a bird, she could not have resisted mauling Irene.

He found Elizabeth so attractive that after the first course, instead of turning to the lady on his right, he continued to talk to her, while drinking consommé with tiny flecks of some liver-tasting substance, all served with twisted sticks of pastry; virtuously he ate only one stick and drank no sherry.

Elizabeth did not enjoy college. "It's not for me, I'm afraid. I want to start life right now. This minute. School is just a postponement for a girl, unless you're very brainy, and I'm not."

As they talked, he looked from time to time to see if Irene was getting on. She very definitely was. She was explaining Washington to the new member of the Cabinet, who seemed impressed. Suddenly Elizabeth asked him about the magazine. He was surprised. "You've heard of that?"

"Oh, Mother and her friends do nothing but talk about it, and you." He was flattered to think that he was a subject of interest to the grownups. He had not yet got out of the habit of thinking of himself as a boy, to whom adults were indifferent. "But then they love talking about your family and Laurel House."

That took away some of the pleasure. Only as a part of Laurel House did he really engage anyone's interest. That must change.

"Well, it's to be socialist." Automatically, he gave his spiel, watching her face as he did. She listened raptly, not in the least alarmed.

"I can't wait for the first issue," she said at last.

"Neither can I," said Peter. The evening was not over yet. Irene could still go under, taking the treasure with her.

"I'm very stupid," said Elizabeth unexpectedly, helping herself to salmon but not touching the green sauce, Peter's favorite. "You must cure me of it."

"I doubt if you are. But I'll cure you anyway." Her laugh was particularly beguiling, low and genuinely amused.

But then from his right the lady's voice said sternly, "I haven't seen you since you were in diapers." Peter dutifully turned to one of his mother's friends, helping himself as he did to salmon although for Scotty's sake, he took no sauce.

After dinner, Blaise proposed that the men immediately join the ladies: there was, he said, something he wanted to tell everyone. Peter had seldom seen his father in such a good, positively puckish mood.

"Ma foi," said Irene at the door, "what can it be? Unconditional surrender?"

"Ours or theirs?" Diana nervously clutched at Irene as though to steer her through a particularly stormy sea, but the adventuress, launched, had no further use for either of the small tugs that had so recently guided her through treacherous shallows to the sea itself. She slipped from Diana's grasp and took the arm of the new Secretary. "You will be a great success in Washington. I can always tell." Peter and Diana exchanged their by now familiar conspiratorial look: had they won?

"This will appear tomorrow in the paper." Blaise's loud voice silenced the room. Peter sank into a chair. On the low table beside his chair was a silver dish containing chocolate coated mints; he took this as an omen. He had not intended to eat anything more, yet the mints were unmistakably there. Hell yawned at his feet.

"... by Harold Griffiths." What was by Harold Griffiths? He asked Elizabeth who, by some magic, had come to light on a straight chair beside him.

"A dispatch," she whispered. "From the Philippines. I love his writing, don't you?" Peter shook his head. He preferred the old Harold and wondered what had gone wrong.

" 'Dateline Pacific.' " Blaise's voice became dramatic as he read Harold's staccato sentences. " 'Dawn. We came ashore. They were ready for us. There was a machine gun nest to our left. Bullets whizzed like mosquitoes swarming. Only *their* sting was death!' "

Peter hit the beach and fell full-length, burying his face in the wet coarse sand, the mosquitoes ... no, the bullets crisscrossed above him and all around him—Harold's prose. He would not move, he decided, ever.

" 'Lingayen Airfield is our target. I turn to the major. His face is young but when you see his eyes you know he's been to hell the hard way.' " Peter chose to go to hell the easy way. He ate one of the mints.

" ' "We gotta take the airfield." He cut his words short like that. No fancy talk. Just simple statement. But when I said, "You're outnumbered, why don't you wait for reinforcements?" he just shook his head. "We got our orders." And that was that. I was scared. But then, I'm not a hero. I'm just a witness, a witness to bravery.' "

Peter felt his face grow hot with embarrassment for his old friend who had once borne such sardonic witness to Washington's folly. Harold must be perpetrating an elaborate hoax.

" 'Brave men don't talk much. They just get the job done. Like that major. A brave man. One of the bravest I ever saw. He gave the order to attack. It was like the Fourth of July when those Japs opened fire on us.' "

Suddenly Peter understood his father's strategy.

" '... the hangar exploded. Hair and clothes on fire, the Nips ran screaming out onto the runways ...' "

Fire. Wrapped in the cloak of Nessus, he ... No! No literary references ever again, for Scotty was dead.

" 'He went into the burning hangar. When he came out he was carrying the young private, who was still alive.' "

What young private? The thought of Hercules in agony—of himself in agony—had made him lose a vital part of the narrative. But whatever he had lost, it was plain that the major could easily win the war in the Pacific, for " 'In those minutes when that handful of brave men faced the elite of the Jap Army, I knew what intestinal fortitude really was. But then when the major ran into that burning hangar in order to save the life of a plain ordinary G.I. Joe, I saw something else. I saw a hero. As I sit now on the beach writing these words, General Krueger is recommending to the President of the United States that the Distinguished Service Cross be awarded to Major Clay Overbury.' " Blaise's voice broke at the name.

Applause filled the room. Peter looked at Diana; she had shut her eyes tight; was it the flames she saw or the President's medal? Not for a long moment did Peter realize that what at first sounded like his own inner voice was Elizabeth whispering in his ear. "So proud! Your own brother-in-law. Isn't Enid lucky?" Peter ate the last mint.

Six

1

BURDEN AND DIANA sat in silence as Henry drove them through the red-brick slums where Negroes lived in what Burden still believed was a happy, mindless abandon despite all evidence to the contrary. But on this watery April morning the Negroes were like everyone else, somber, mindful, restrained. They sat on the stoops of their houses and talked without smiling while their children played among ash cans in dusty yards. History had seized them all, black as well as white, and the flags of the Republic were at half mast.

At first Burden had not believed the page who had come running into the Senate barbershop to say, "He's dead! The President's dead!" But it was true. The glorious enemy had died on Thursday morning at Warm Springs in Georgia, while posing for a portrait. The last words were, "I have a terrific headache," (or "damnedest," depending upon whose account one read) and so with the breaking of a vein in that large head all the splendor had come to an abrupt end.

When Burden heard the news, he had leaped from the barber's chair and though the Senate was already adjourned, he hurried toward the Chamber, still wearing the barber's white cloth about his neck. Not until he was in the Senate cloakroom did he realize that he must resemble some togaed Senator, arrived too late at the Theatre of Pompey. He tore off the cloth, and gave it to a page. The Senators still on hand were as stunned as he. Some had hated the President; some had wanted his place; all envied him. Now he no longer mattered. But in death as in life he had triumphed for none of them would ever take his place. He had seen to that. Now there was a new President, and Burden was old.

The buzz of gossip during the next two days was

diverting. The President had had many strokes before the last one. At Yalta he had been catatonic, and Stalin's doctor had reported that he would soon be dead. There was also scandal. At the moment of death he had been not with his wife but with an old mistress. So many rumors. So much grief.

All spoke of Lincoln; like that paladin, Roosevelt had died at a time of victory in war, cut down at the zenith while lilacs bloomed. Whitman was quoted solemnly as the city recaptured the mood of that long ago April day when the black cart was drawn through crowded streets and the people wept. Even Burden in Rock Creek Park, thrilled by the springtime mourning, held a single cluster of purple lilac to his face until the tears came for he was allergic to new pollen. Later, seriously, he did almost weep for his own past when, on Saturday, it was put to rest in the rose garden at Hyde Park. O Captain! my Captain! how I hated you, and hate you still, for without you I am incomplete. Now what is left? wondered Burden, as the car stopped in front of Union Station.

Diana took his arm protectively, as though he had become suddenly fragile and enormously valuable to her. He was grateful for any attention. "You're good to come," he said.

"I look forward to seeing him again," she answered, as if she meant it.

They made their way through the waiting room, crowded with servicemen carrying duffel bags and foot lockers, all set in motion by lunatic mimeograph machines issuing orders by the mile. Fortunately the war in Europe was almost over; soon the armies would disperse and the young men would stay at home where they belonged and leave the traveling to decrepit Senators.

Inside the station, at one of the iron-grilled gates, the police had roped off a small area where stood Blaise and Enid and Peter, surrounded by photographers. Opposite the gate, a newsreel camera unit had been set up. As usual, Blaise had seen to everything, thought Burden, straightening his forelock. Then, ready for the camera to record, ready for history to begin, he greeted Blaise.

Diana joined Peter at the gate, and while Burden exchanged pleasantries with the excited Blaise, he watched the young couple and wondered, as usual, whether or not their interest in one another was simply the result of publishing that magazine of which he had grown so heartily sick or something more serious, as he hoped. Peter himself he found disconcertingly smooth, without edges, nothing to grasp; but despite this elusiveness, he was certainly preferable to Billy. Although Burden had been taught to disapprove of divorce, he would have preferred to see his daughter a scarlet woman, with himself as pimp, than married to Billy Thorne.

"I didn't think Clay had it in him, did you?" Enid's voice was clear, the words unslurred. Only the slowness with which she spoke and the smell of gin upon the breath betrayed that she was drunk.

"To be a hero?"

She nodded, too precisely.

Burden was firm and conventional. "Of course I thought he had it in him. He's a courageous young man."

Then the lights for the newsreel went on, and the photographers aimed their cameras like rifles. Prematurely a single flashbulb went off. The servicemen in the immediate vicinity paused in their shoving and pushing to catch a glimpse of the celebrity, whoever he or, better, she might be.

Then the iron gates opened and Clay appeared, suitcase in hand. Flashbulbs popped and sizzled. Burden went blind. He put out his hand as directed, and felt Clay's hard dry hand close over his own.

"Welcome home," he said, voice lost beneath Blaise's roar: "That's right. Get a good shot with the Senator. Stand back now. Don't shove. Let the newsreel people have a crack at him. All right. Now move over here."

Obediently Burden started to move, only to be shoved to one side. "Not you, Senator. Just the Colonel and his wife." Burden scowled, forgetting cameras: for this rudeness, there must be revenge. But then this was Clay's moment, not his; he smiled again and, as reward, regained his vision.

Clay was standing a few yards away, facing the cameras. Burden was startled at the change in his appearance: gone the soft curve to the jaw, the smooth cheeks, the red lips. Now a man's face looked upon the world, the flesh sunk to its mature level and the lines deep. Most striking of all, beneath pale brows, thicker than he recalled, a stranger's eyes reflected unnatural light and in their brightness Burden saw the glory to come. He shuddered, for none of it was his.

"Come here, Enid." At least Clay's voice was the same. He held out his hand. But Enid seemed not able to move. She stared dumbly into the lights, mouth ajar, disoriented.

Blaise intervened. Roughly he took her arm, tore her up by the roots. "Here she is!" He dealt his daughter like a playing card.

Clay took the card but not the game, for just then Enid, dazzled by the lights, got in the way of the sound boom which pushed her hat rakishly over one eye. The effect was comic. A spectator giggled; giggling turned to laughter. Blaise hurried to Enid's side. The hat was readjusted.

Everyone made helpful gestures except Clay, who did not move; he stood where he was, as though waiting for a train to arrive. Then Burden caught his gaze and with a smile offered encouragement. But either Clay could not see him through the lights or for some reason of his own chose not to respond. He stared at Burden without expression until Enid joined him, and said in a careful voice, each syllable precise, "I'm so glad that you are home again, safe and sound."

"Now *kiss* him," muttered Blaise, eyes garnet with rage. Enid kissed her husband, as the cameras turned and the legend continued.

2

"It's obscene!" Having decided on the word that morning, Peter had held it in readiness all day, allowing it to rhyme with other words spoken though the word itself must not be delivered until, alone with Diana on the fifth floor of the Union Trust Building in the two-room office of *The American Idea,* he could drop the pile of newspapers at her feet and declare *"Obscene!"*

"Every newspaper?" She looked vaguely unhappy, as if a shoe pinched.

"Every single one." Peter kicked the pile of newspapers. Across the floor an endless series of photographs of Enid and Clay embracing; there was, apparently, no visual record of the tipped hat.

"Father's done it." Peter sat heavily in the Morris chair from which he presided at editorial meetings of *The American Idea,* muddling print orders, misrepresenting advertising revenues, losing subscription lists and otherwise keeping, as he put it cheerfully, "on the bottom of things."

This time it was Diana who asked "Why?" and it was Peter who said there was no explanation of his father's behavior, "unless he's mad, which is possible."

"He's not mad. He's running Clay for Congress. And I know why."

"Tell me."

"Mischief. Pure mischief. What would annoy Enid more? Or you?"

"You overestimate his interest in me."

"You underestimate it. Because he dislikes you doesn't mean that he lacks interest. Quite the contrary."

That hurt. It was one thing for him to dislike his father—normal, even—but quite another for his father to reciprocate. But then Diana was merely theorizing in the manner of Aeneas Duncan. "Besides, he's in love with Enid. Anyone can see that."

"Clay?"

"Your father. That's obvious."

"Only to Freud." Peter was quickly bored with this sort of analysis. But Diana never tired of it. Peter said exactly what he thought was true. "I believe he's sick of her. He's embarrassed by her drinking, and he's right. She is a mess."

"But *you* love her, don't you?" Diana challenged him.

He refused to be baited. "Someone must," he said neutrally, as Aeneas joined them, asking for Billy.

"Billy's at the printer." Diana, the wife in name, answered for Peter, the publisher in fact. Relations between husband, wife, and lover had been surprisingly good during the six weeks they had worked together on the first and second issues of a publication which, as one critic put it, "fills a definite need," though precisely what the need was Peter had never dared ask himself for fear the answer might be that he simply wanted an excuse to be with Diana. He *was* with her every day, and to his surprise Billy had shown no jealousy, even though Peter was positive that he knew exactly what was happening while Diana was certain that he did not.

Aeneas worried them with his latest insight. He had decided that the Administration's insistence on the unconditional surrender of the Axis powers had been absolutely necessary to win the war. Peter and Diana and Billy disagreed, each in his own way. As a result, their days were spent arguing whether or not the magazine ought to print Aeneas's closely argued defense of his position. They were repeating themselves happily when there was a knock on the door. Aeneas opened it to reveal Clay. "Can I come in?"

Diana blushed. Peter leapt to his feet. Abruptly, Aeneas stepped back as though he anticipated assault. But Clay was affable. "I came here to get these notarized." He held up a manila envelope, as though he expected not to be believed. "There's a notary public down the hall. Then I saw your door. So I came in. I hope it's all right."

"Marvelous." Peter wondered at his own heartiness. "Sit down. Here's the first issue . . ."

". . . seen it . . ."

". . . and the second. This is Aeneas Duncan."

". . . read your piece. I hadn't realized that Trotsky was such a . . . well, such a force still."

"Well, of course . . ."

"Who's been collecting my publicity?" Clay indicated the newspapers spread out on the rug like a fan. "Diana?"

Now pale, she shook her head. "Peter. But we're all impressed. A hero."

"It's great to be back," Clay observed conventionally, the first true note in what so far had been dissonant prelude.

Politically he was the enemy. That was plain. But

Peter was not entirely certain why. After all, to be ambitious was not in itself a fault.

Aeneas of course disagreed. "It must be difficult to take." He looked at Clay suspiciously through clouded glasses. "All that sickening stuff."

"What stuff?" Clay seemed genuinely puzzled.

"Of the sort that sob sister writes, what's his name . . . ?"

"Poor Harold." Peter supplied the name and Homeric epithet.

Aeneas nodded. "How can you stand being written about as though you were some kind of soap-opera hero . . . no, worse than that, as if you were the soap itself, to be sold in quantity, as something it's not."

"Oh." Clay's expression was pointedly blank. Peter watched with interest as the quick if rather ordinary mind of his brother-in-law came to grips with what apparently was a new thought. Obviously a wide range of response was possible. Clay evaded choice. "Harold does sort of overwrite, I guess, but . . ." He tried to let it go but Aeneas was relentless.

"Yes, yes. We all know that. Harold Griffiths has made illiteracy an art form. Even so . . ."

Peter had long since given up defending his old friend Harold to his new friends. They were right. Harold's reports of the war were peculiarly dreadful. But soon he would be home (the last "Dateline Pacific" was from Manila. "The Pearl of the Orient is in ruins. The Nips went on an orgy of destruction . . ."), and Peter could not wait to find out whether or not Harold was deliberately mocking them all.

Aeneas was saying that it was wrong to say something is what it is not. To which Clay's response was a puzzled "Of course, but . . ."

"But even worse is not to *know* what is real and what is illusion. When you deliberately confuse people with something false . . ."

"But *who* is confused?" Clay's voice was suddenly sharp.

"The public." Aeneas was equally sharp.

"Why? Don't you believe what Harold wrote about me?"

"I'm sure it's true, what happened . . ."

232

"Then what is confusing?"

"The style, the manner in which you've been presented, as a kind of cheap fiction hero . . ."

"I've no control over that."

"I was not criticizing you."

"Then who? Harold?"

"All of them!" Aeneas indicated the newspapers on the floor with a contemptuous wave. "Everything they touch withers, becomes *kitsch*."

"I'm sure *The American Idea* will set us all straight." Clay smiled sweetly at his brother-in-law and Peter smiled back, susceptible as always to the man who had seduced his sister in the poolhouse, after having made Diana love.

"Mr. Sanford has certainly done a marvelous job," said Diana, drawing her own knife. "With the press. And everything." This last twist to the blade caused Clay to sit up straight in his chair, eyes bright with pain.

"Blaise has been quite a help." He turned to Blaise's son. "He keeps a lot of people off my back."

"I expect you'll be running for Congress next year, with all this publicity?" Peter could hold back no longer. He joined in the sport.

But Clay was suddenly easy. He had got their range. "Who knows? I've been away a long time, overseas." With a word, he reminded them of his warrior status. "I've kind of lost touch. That's why I think I may practice law. Make some money. After all, Blaise is not *my* father."

Clay rose to go, holding the manila envelope in front of him like a warrior's shield to protect his crotch.

"You're fortunate." Peter was cold.

"Aren't we all?" Clay was amiable to the end. "To be alive," he added, ruining his moment. Aeneas snorted and started to speak, no doubt wanting to declare for the tragic sense, but then he thought better of it, allowing Clay to depart with the vague comment to Peter that "Enid's O.K., all things considered."

When Clay had gone, the three enemies of the status quo avoided looking at one another, each somewhat embarrassed, Peter decided, like people who had caught one another weeping at a bad film.

"What is it?" Of the lot, only Diana had a true grievance; yet she was the one most genuinely puzzled.

"Slickness, emptiness, a vacuum . . ." Aeaneas began.

But it was Peter who concluded, "It's quite simple. He has *all* the luck. And that is unendurable, for us."

3

Careful to make no noise, the colored maid opened the door. The room was dark, cavelike, redolent of cigarettes, stale perfume, Enid.

"Enid?" As Clay spoke, the maid withdrew, not wanting to be present at the premature waking of her mistress. But it was two o'clock in the afternoon, and Clay had come to have lunch with his wife, who had been most friendly on the telephone: "No reason why we can't be friends, after all this time." But the putative friend was snoring as Clay drew the curtains and let in the day.

In a tangle of sheets Enid lay curled like a bronze foetus at the center of the bed. On a chair her clothes were neatly arranged, always a sign she had been drinking. Sober she left clothes on the floor; drunk she was obsessively neat. On the night table a half-finished glass of whisky was placed exactly in the center of an ashtray. Next to the whisky a vial of pills, for sleeping.

Enid stirred, moaned softly; then pushing the dark hair from her face, she looked up at him with bloodshot eyes. "What the hell are you doing here?"

"Lunch. Remember?"

"Listen. Go in the bathroom and bring me an Alka-Seltzer and two Empirins. I have the most God-awful headache. You're too thin. But it's sexy," she said to his back as he went into the bathroom, noticing with a certain pain the historic douche bag which had changed their lives.

Enid drank the mixture, belched softly: made a face, sighed, stretched and smiled. "Sit down." She patted a place on the edge of the bed. He pulled up a chair instead. She seemed not to notice. Except for the red eyes her face was as clear as a child's. She had even remembered to remove her makeup the night before and her face was still streaked with vestiges of cold cream.

"I was fried last night," she said, using a euphemism he recognized as being popular among the people she considered *fun*: officers of the regular Army and Navy, engaged in a perpetual party. "I was celebrating your return."

"I'm sure."

"Why don't you move in here? You can use the guest room."

"Wouldn't Joe mind?"

"He likes you. Now listen. I want to talk to you about Joe. *Ellen!*" She suddenly shouted the name, nearly deafening him. "That damned nigger is slower than molasses on a winter day, but I'm devoted to her even if she does tote."

Molasses materialized nervously in the doorway; to be given an order for coffee, for *two* coffees ("that'll be your lunch") and orange juice with vodka. "I need a hair of the dog. In fact, I could probably manage the whole pelt."

Enid gave him her slow mischievous smile and against all common sense he was aroused. He crossed his legs. She noticed everything when she chose to. "Well, well." She stretched again. Then she said neutrally, "I want to marry Joe."

"All right."

"Is that *all* you have to say?" She frowned, suddenly irritable.

"What else can I say? You want to marry him. Go ahead. Get a divorce."

"I want custody of Alice. *Complete* custody. Light me a cigarette, will you?" She held up her right hand and demonstrated the tremor, almost proudly, like a child showing off double-jointedness. Clay lit the cigarette, gave it to her. She puffed strenuously; ashes fell on the pillow; she continued. "I don't think a baby should be torn in half just because the parents couldn't make a go of things. Besides, she doesn't like you."

As always, Clay marveled at Enid's unerring ability

235

to go too far. The desire to give maximum pain invariably overcome whatever shrewdness she possessed. She never gave herself a chance to win.

"If she doesn't care for me," said Clay evenly, "it's because of you."

"You're the one who walked out, not me. So naturally I'm the guy who's got to make a home, be father as well as mother . . ."

The maid entered with a tray. "Put it there, honey." Like so many Washingtonians, Enid's accent became deep South when addressing Negroes. "Baby's off havin' lunch with the Claypooles, isn't she? And then goin' on to the zoo? My, she is social, isn't she?" Enid positively cackled, like Aunt Jemima. The servant acknowledged that all this was so and departed while Enid, still clucking softly, seized the vodka and orange juice with shaking hand and drained it. The hand shook less perceptibly at the end of the drink than at the beginning. "That was good. Drink your coffee. Now what shall we do?"

"You go to Nevada, get the divorce. Mental cruelty."

"Won't that be tough on you? Won't that shock those unspeakable rednecks you hope will elect you?"

"Probably. I don't have much choice."

"No." She took a long drag on her cigarette, began to cough, waved frantically, "Kleenex! Top drawer!" The top drawer contained Kleenex and a small revolver. After the coughing and the wheezing she said, "A woman alone needs protection in this part of town. Niggers all over the place and getting uppity."

"*You* are nervous?" Clay was startled. Enid never locked a door, had no fear of the dark, of anyone.

"Yes. Now put it back where you found it. I get custody. Yes or no?"

Clay visualized the daughter he hardly knew. Blond hair like his, dark eyes like Enid's; and a furious temper according to Blaise, who adored the child. "Always have grandchildren," he declared. "Skip the children, if you can." Clay skipped the child without regret. "You can have custody," he said.

"What's wrong with you?" She was indignant. "What sort of father are you? No wonder she hates you. You're a monster. You have no feelings at all." She denounced him for some time but the marriage was over and he no longer, even in reflex, played the game of suit countersuit. He was finished not only with his wife but with the child he did not know. He let her go and Enid took her, after a long tirade which ended with, "How long are you going to stay at Laurel House?"

"Until I decide what I'm going to do."

"Funny. You end up out there in my old room and I end up here, out in the cold."

"Doesn't seem too chilly. You have Joe."

"I suppose Father has great plans for you. I've never seen such publicity. You know, if you gave me half a chance I wouldn't marry Joe. We could stay together."

Clay got to his feet. The tactic was familiar, and he ignored it. "I've got to go. Thanks for lunch."

"You are a bitch." She spoke without rancor. "I must say you and Father make a perfect couple. I hope you'll be very, very happy together."

"Thank you, Enid." Clay crossed to the door just as Joe entered.

Each recoiled. Clay recovered first. "She's all yours. I've agreed to a divorce. Custody of the child. Everything."

Enid's voice came loud and clear. "Joe, why don't you break every bone in his body?"

"Now, dear," mumbled Joe, smiling at Clay, pleading for sympathy. "You know I've been reading all about you the last few days. Really swell, what you did."

"Joe, *don't!*" Enid's cry was from the heart.

"Thank you, Joe. Goodbye." Clay slipped past his successor and left his marriage behind him.

* * *

That night Clay went to bed early in Enid's old room, from which—between trees—the poolhouse of legend was visible. By the light of a dim lamp, made dimmer by insects attracted to the bulb like planets circling a dangerous sun, Clay studied a file of newspaper clippings Burden had sent him from the state. It was taken for granted that he would enter next year's primary and win, bringing "credit to the state."

A rap on the door. Blaise entered, wearing a white Chinese silk dressing gown on whose back was embroidered an elaborate dragon. Clay made a move to get out of bed, to come to attention. Blaise waved him back into place. "My God, it's hot up here. Well, we'll be off to Watch Hill soon."

Blaise sat down in the chair, on whose back hung Clay's jacket, ribbons vivid even in the half light. Like a doctor in attendance upon a patient certain to survive his ministrations, Blaise asked for symptoms. "What did Enid say?"

"A divorce. She'll get it. I gave her custody of the child."

"That will look bad." Blaise frowned.

"The whole thing looks bad, but what can I do?" Clay had already accepted a limit to his political career. He could be divorced and elected to the House from his district, at least next year when he was still wreathed in military glory. But anything beyond the House would be difficult. After all, no divorced man could be a candidate for President, and though he hardly need worry about that now, the thought was there, lodged in his mind, the necessary motor to any action; there was no point in pursuing a career in politics if the ultimate prize was not, at least theoretically, obtainable.

Blaise, too, was concerned with precisely the same thing. "There must be some other way," he murmured, taking the press clippings from Clay's lap. "Shame you're not running in the whole state instead of that one lousy district."

"*My* district," said Clay with mock pride. "Where I was born. I'm one of them."

"Your neck is not so red."

"Neither is theirs. After all, we were civilized. We lived in a suburb." But Clay did not mention that during his childhood the streets of that suburb had not been paved, and there was no running water in the house. The family used an outdoor privy, buzzing with flies. According to his mother, her husband was handsome "but worthless, not a good provider. You see it was the war that brought us together. I was young and impressionable, though I already knew typing and shorthand, and he looked so romantic when he came home

238

from Plattsburgh in his uniform. He never went overseas though naturally he said he had when he was drinking." Clay remembered nothing of the man except one twilight evening when his father started to paint the house. He could still recall the broad strokes of thick odorous paint transforming gray boards to white. Of his father's appearance he could recall only a tattooed forearm. Not until he was grown did he learn that the tattoo was a tribute to "Agnes," which was not his mother's name. One day when Clay was four years old, his father got into the automobile he had constructed from junk and drove off; to town, he said, but the town he had in mind was not the one where he had been working as a hardware salesman. He never came back, to the delight of his wife and to the momentary grief of his son who must now decide whether or not to disappear from the life of his own child. The day before when his daughter had been visiting Laurel House, he had tried to pick her up and she had run away. Frederika had said, "It takes time. After all, you've been gone most of her life."

But Clay had been chilled by the child's response. Unreasonably, he could not bear to lose the idea of her even though the fact of her moved him not at all. He was conscious that it was *my* daughter that mattered, not *her* father, but there was nothing to be done about that.

Blaise believed that the war would last at least another year. Clay said that he thought that the worst was still ahead. "With the Germans defeated, the Japs will only fight harder."

The kamikaze plane circled the ship. Then, as in a nightmare, the plane came at them. For an instant, Clay saw the young pilot, mouth wide, shouting or screaming, praying or singing, he could not tell. Then the explosion rocked the ship and he was thrown against a bulkhead. But he had lived; the ship had not sunk; the kamikaze pilot had died in vain, and the invasion of Luzon proceeded according to plan.

"We're so stupid." Blaise denounced the late President's policy of "unconditional surrender," which had so effectively kept the German Army from capitulating while strengthening the fanatic element in Japan.

239

"Yet he thought of himself as a superb international statesman, like Wilson. Well, he was right. He was every bit as disastrous as Wilson."

"But he did get *his* League of Nations." Since the war began, Clay had come to admire the elegant, ravaged old President who continued to pursue, even as he was dying, the high business of reassembling the fragments of broken empires into a new pattern with himself at center, proud creator of the new imperium. Now, though he was gone, the work remained. The United States was master of the earth. No England, no France, no Germany, no Japan (once the dying was done) left to dispute the Republic's will; only the mysterious Soviet would survive to act as other balance to the scale of power. Clay thought he understood the shape of this new world. In any case, he did not regret the passing of the old America, unlike Burden, who truly believed his own rhetoric and was moved by his own sentimentality. Burden wanted to bring to all of those without the law that sense of common dignity which was, he believed, America's peculiar gift to the world. But to Clay there was no dignity of any kind in the race of man, nor was the United States anything more than just another power whose turn at empire had come, and in that empire he meant to wield power entirely for its own sake. In this he resembled not Burden, the flawed idealist, but the old President who had prevailed by mingling cant with shrewdness in such a way as to inspire his followers and confuse his enemies none of whom quite realized what he was up to until, by dying, it was suddenly plain to all but the totally deluded that the author of the Four Freedoms had managed by force of arms and sly maneuvering to transform an isolationist republic into what no doubt would be the last empire on earth. Clay thought him great.

"I'm afraid Burden didn't play his cards too well," remarked Blaise. It was well known that Burden had expected to be part of the American delegation to the first United Nations meeting at San Francisco. But just before he died, the old President had rejected him, while any hope of being appointed by the new President was dashed by "that damned thing Burden said the day the President died, did you hear about it? He called Truman a first-rate second-rate man." Blaise chuckled. "Announced it to everybody in the Senate cloakroom. Needless to say little Harry heard it before nightfall and that was the end of Burden."

Blaise puffed on his cigar. Smoke wreathed the lamp, slowing the death dance of insects. Clay studied Blaise, trying to divine his mood. One had to proceed carefully with him, assuming nothing, wait for the weather report to be verified before venturing out: hail had been known to fall on the clearest day.

Blaise looked at him through cigar smoke, as though counting ribs against some inventory. Protectively, Clay pulled the sheet high on his chest. Suddenly Blaise pulled a magazine out from under a stack on the night table. It was *The American Idea*. He turned to Clay. "What do you think?"

"Lively." Clay was neutral, waiting.

"Communist! The whole lot of them. Like that Aeneas Duncan. I had him checked. But . . ." Blaise let the magazine drop to the floor. "I'm all for it."

Policy was now established. Clay could respond. He did. "Wonderful for someone like Peter . . . to have something to do . . . that's different." Clay made the expected noises.

"He's clever. Watch out for him."

Clay was taken aback. "Why?"

"A hunch. That's all."

"Enid?"

"Yes. He'll take her side no matter what."

"But what side is there to take? I go. She stays as she is."

Blaise was oblique. "Met a fellow from New York, very brainy. Couldn't have been more impressed with Peter's magazine, said it was better than *The New Republic*. He meant that as a compliment."

"Peter's clever," Clay repeated. That was the now-agreed-upon characterization for his soon to be lost brother-in-law.

"Funny. I thought he'd be just another playboy and I was ready for that. Wouldn't have minded at all, if he did it in style. Sometimes I wish I had stuck to horses and women and having a good time. Naturally

241

I'd never tell him that. You can't. Anyway, *she* put a stop to it. She launched him."

"Diana?"

Blaise nodded. "Your old girl friend." He brushed aside smoke with a thick paw to get a closer look at Clay, who realized how vulnerable he must look, stretched out like a victim awaiting sacrifice, the golden chest ready for the stone knife's cut and the baring of the living heart, to be torn from the body as offering to the sun. "She's clever," said Clay, unhappily aware of the inane repetition.

"Whatever she is, she's after my son and I suppose he could do worse. *She* did worse. That one-legged bastard. Why didn't *you* marry her?" The stone knife tapped at a rib.

"I told you that day at the pool. Enid."

"You really liked Enid? Or me?"

"Meaning your money?"

"Is that me?"

Clay sat up straight (the victim struggled); the sheet fell to his waist (the victim struck back at the executioner). "That's what *you* said that day, not what I said, when you offered me money to get lost."

"Just a test."

Clay had no choice but to pretend to believe Blaise. As he cajoled, sweating nervously, he found it harder and harder to breathe in the close room, blue with cigar smoke and full of the cloying odor of night-blooming jasmine.

"You're right." Blaise nodded in response to whatever it was Clay had said, his gaze shifting thoughtfully to the victim's pubic hair, which in the heat of the struggle had come into view. Clay pulled the damp sheet over himself. Blaise came to the point. "Divorce is political suicide in that state of yours. Not to mention later."

"I have no choice."

"If you agree I can have her declared insane and committed to an institution for life."

A rapid series of images raced through Clay's mind. Enid dressed for a garden party, with a ladder in one stocking. Enid holding out bare arms which smelled of lemon. Enid hobbling on one high heel; the other

242

broken. Enid among twisted sheets that smelled of love and cigarette ashes. Enid drunk and shouting, "Let's face it!" Well, now they were about to face it, all of them. Blaise waited for Clay to answer but Clay deliberately chose not to. The other must take all responsibility.

Blaise sounded uneasy when at last he broke the silence. "I know it's drastic. But she's hopeless. She really is. I sent her to a psychiatrist last spring. Did she tell you? Well, she went to him half a dozen times, then stopped. He gave what's wrong with her some name, of course. And he's willing to see to it that she is . . . well, put away. There's a place not far from here, in Maryland, where he says they've had good luck with her kind of case." At least a half million dollars, Clay decided, carefully disguised as a new annex to a hospital; although a straightforward cash payment could not be ruled out. Blaise was direct in these matters.

Clay prolonged the next silence until he had the satisfaction of seeing Blaise's hand tremble as he stamped out the unraveled stub of a now-dead cigar. Then Clay asked, "Committed for *life*?"

Blaise nodded.

"But aren't there review boards? Wouldn't they let her out eventually? After all when she doesn't drink, she's perfectly normal."

"That's the point. She's not. He says she's not."

"*One* doctor's opinion?"

Blaise shifted uneasily. "Others will be called in."

"And concur?"

"Yes."

"It's been arranged?"

"Yes. For her sake."

"And ours?"

"Clay, she is sick. You can't deny that. And if she isn't put away, she'll only suffer, kill herself . . . you know what she's like."

"And so with a wife declared insane . . ."

"We won't say she's insane. Just that she needs help."

"I could never remarry, could I?"

Blaise's response was swift. "Do you want to? Is there somebody?"

"No, I meant in theory."

"No, you couldn't. Ideal situation, isn't it? Married but single. Free but safe. Well?"

Now Clay was master and Blaise must learn to bear the unfamiliar chains of slavery. Clay looked at Blaise, saw the black eyes large with fear. Power at last, thought Clay; and he continued to stare until the older man's eyes watered and he looked away.

"All right," said Clay.

They agreed to act immediately. Papers would be drawn, medical testimony sought. "Should be all over in a week or two. Poor girl," added Blaise, not without feeling, Clay noted, but also not without the self-consciousness of a man professing to feel something he knew others would think eminently natural.

"Yes. Poor girl." Clay coolly mocked him. Then master dismissed servant: "Tired . . . need sleep . . . busy day." To which: "Yes, of course . . . damned sorry . . . busy day."

Blaise left, and Clay turned out the light. For a long time he lay awake in the hot darkness of the room, aware that at last everything was possible. Enid had lost. Yet he himself was perfectly in the clear, for Blaise not he had dealt the final blow.

4

On the eighth of May, Germany surrendered and Blaise celebrated as though he were the victorious leader of the nation, not the small colorless President who had never once set foot in Laurel House nor was apt to, despite the fact that fate had placed him so ludicrously on high.

"No one will be at the White House today," exclaimed Elizabeth Watress, looking across the lawn at the pavilion put up especially for Blaise's "open house." "*They* are all here, including that gruesome Mrs. Bloch."

Indeed *they* were all present, converging upon the tent which contained a bar, Blaise, Frederika and the military hierarchy whose day it was, since indirectly (very indirectly, thought Peter sourly) they were responsible for the victory.

"Oh, look! There he is. I must meet him. Oh, please!" Elizabeth turned to Peter, arms extended in appeal. Invariably when they went out together, there was some celebrity she "must" meet. "What will you do with him once you've said hello?" Peter teased her. "Ask for his autograph?"

"I shall look into his eyes and think: this man is a hero, an authentic hero."

"But then what will you do?"

"You are cynical!" She gave him her slow handsome smile. Then her voice dropped. "Doesn't *anybody* impress you?"

Peter shook his head.

"It's living here that's done it, surrounded by all this." She looked out across the Sanford lawn, her hunger obvious.

"Very early," Peter began, aware too late of the pedantry in his voice but unable now to alter the emerging sentence, "I saw the difference between what these people seem and what they are, which is . . ."

". . . is often fabulous." She broke his stately line impatiently.

"*What* is fabulous?" With relief, he became Socratic inquisitor.

But Elizabeth preferred direct statement. "What you're saying is that they are *all* phony, which isn't true."

"No more phony than the rest of us, I agree. But their scale is so much larger."

"But that's what makes them marvelous. Anyway, *I* admit when I'm impressed while somebody like you . . ."

". . . a true phony denies the shiver of excitement he experiences when he shakes the horny hand of a man who was killing Japs a few weeks ago."

"I don't believe you're that cynical. I can't believe it."

"But I am. People who profess virtues do not necessarily lack them."

"That's hardly a virtue . . . *There he is!*" She gasped as Clay appeared on the terrace. "Stop him!"

Peter called to Clay. He joined them, his rows of ribbons diminishing Peter, who, for lack of other clothes, still wore his uniform even though he was soon to be separated from the service, on the valid ground that with one of the two wars ended, there was no need at all for him or for any of the other dissidents to continue at the Pentagon, their wastebaskets regularly studied by intelligence officers, eager to crack the code in which Aeneas's poems were composed.

Elizabeth was cool. Clay was warm. Each appeared as his own opposite, which was as it should be. Elizabeth spoke not at all of heroism. Instead she told in a hushed voice of her love for Enid and asked where she was today. Peter wondered how Clay would handle this. Straightforward: "She's been a bit under the weather lately. She's at a clinic now, having some tests."

"Poor Enid. I'd love to see her."

"Easy to arrange. I'm sure she'd like to see you." Clay turned to Peter and each inquired about the other's military status. Clay would leave the Army as soon as he had completed a bond-selling tour of the country.

"Will the tour include your home state?"

Clay was unabashed. "Yes. As a matter of fact, I end the tour in the State Capitol, in the rotunda, receiving a citation from the governor."

"You are shameless." Peter ventured humor.

"Not entirely." Clay maintained his equable smile.

"How wonderful." From Elizabeth, a sigh.

"What?" Clay had not yet discovered how to listen to Elizabeth. Those phrases others spoke loudly, she tended to whisper. But she never repeated; she simply went on. "There's to be a book about you, I read . . ."

"Not a book really, a long piece in a magazine. It's pretty dull. But useful." Peter admired Clay's directness. He seemed genuinely unimpressed with himself, as he realized that the sort of publicity he was getting— though necessary to a political career—was in itself nonsense. That he was actually a hero and deserving of praise never seemed to occur to him.

"Book . . . propaganda . . . whatever, it's so rare to meet anyone definite, who actually exists." Peter listened with some awe to an Elizabeth he did not know. "Who knows just what he wants." In a rush she had become eloquent. This was Clay's moment, no doubt of that, and Peter could think of no way to spoil it, short of announcing to everyone, "My father and my brother-in-law want to commit my sister, who is not mad, just messy. She drinks too much and she makes scenes but she should not be put away."

But then Peter had already made that speech to his father, shortly after Enid had told him, hysterical but sober, what they planned to do with her. Blaise had heard him out. His response was surprisingly reasonable. It was up to the doctors to decide what was to become of Enid. He hoped she would not be put away. But she did need help, didn't she? And Peter had been forced to agree. Meanwhile she would go into a clinic for tests.

Only that morning the tests had been completed and Blaise had rung Peter (an astonishing thing to do; neither ever telephoned the other). "It looks like she's all right. She may need a few months of drying out, but that's all." When Peter asked about the divorce, his father had hesitated before answering. Then he said, "I don't think Clay ought to leave her in the lurch just now. Maybe later, when she's well. But that's their business. Anyway, Enid's coming home today, and we'll see how she is."

Peter's suspicions were allayed. After all, Enid had always had a paranoid side to her and fantasies of persecution were consistent with her madness, and that she was somewhat mad Peter never doubted. Who was not? The night before, quite alone, he had devoured an entire jumbo Hershey chocolate bar, weighing at least a pound, and as a result slept fitfully, and woke up sick. Virtuously he had skipped breakfast, and now refused to enter the tent where food was. Enid needed alcohol; he needed food; each demanded more than the normal amount of assurance that all was well. They could of course blame Blaise, Frederika, Washington,

247

life. And at one time or another Peter had blamed each but only halfheartedly, for he had accepted early in life that there were no specific villains. One was what one was, and there was no malice in eternity.

"Yes, I would like something to drink." Elizabeth whispered to Clay. She turned to Peter, and mocked him with a splendid smile.

"You win," said Peter graciously, to both of them.

* * *

Sun seared the canvas roof, and despite large fans the interior of the pavilion was hot. Burden took refuge in front of a life-size swan carved in ice. Waiters circulated with trays of glasses, and a number of people were already quite drunk. With Mussolini and Hitler gone, Japan would soon fall and life would begin again.

"Senator Day!" He did not recognize the plain woman with bright eyes and large unsuitable hat. "Helen Ashley Barbour," she drawled helpfully, used to not being remembered. Burden told her how much he enjoyed her column.

"Aren't you the nicest thing!" She was effusive. "I can't tell you what an idol you are of mine!" I'm a Jeffersonian Democrat, too! Unlike my employer, who is a perfect angel but gettin' awful do-goody lately." She indicated Blaise who stood beneath crossed American flags at the back of the tent. "But we're *old* Washington, aren't we? My husband was in the House in . . ." Burden recalled Mr. Barbour with a favorable phrase as the flow continued.

"I can't get over the way the town's changed, can you? Since the war began and all these new people arrived it's got so you can't get a hotel room for love or money or go to see a show or eat out. Why, Harvey's is jam-packed for every meal. That's my favorite place. The Occidental was my husband's. They still have his picture on the wall. No, I'm afraid our lovely gracious Southern city has been engulfed by all these . . ." She opened her arms wide to take in all the guests as though to crush them, but instead of malediction she wisely chose to give a tactical blessing: "these charmin' peo-

ple who've opened our poor eyes to so many things un-
dreamed of in our philosophy."

"Such as?" Burden got one phrase in, as he looked
about the pavilion. One of the most rabid of the old
New Dealers was talking to Blaise, his manner significantly meek now that the source of his greatness had
been removed by that extraordinary *accident* (there was
no other word) which now occupied the White House.
Burden knew that he was being unfair to the new President, whom he had liked well enough in the Senate. Yet
there was no getting around it, Roosevelt's revenge on
all of them had been in character. Aware that he might
not live out his term, he had shattered in death as he
had in life the hopes of better men. He had eliminated
them all, friends as well as enemies, by the elevation
of a mediocrity who could now take pleasure in observing his splendid betters fade, one by one, as new
men emerged. I shall but hate thee better, Franklin,
after death.

"Music . . . Churchill . . . foreigners . . . Queen
Wilhelmina . . . diplomats . . . theatre . . . *everything!*"

"I suppose the city has changed." Burden stemmed
the tide. "Lord knows it's crowded."

"Where is Mrs. Day?"

"Home. She's not a party girl."

"Adore her! My idea of a truly great lady, but in
our old Southern tradition, not like those highfaluting
Yankee ladies you can't tell apart from the English.
And Diana, how is that pretty girl?"

Aware that anything he said was for the archive,
Burden indicated that Diana's marriage was superbly
happy and that she was at this moment working . . .

"On her magazine, I know! I like to fainted when I
saw that first issue, so *extreme* politically . . ."

Frederika materialized. "Mrs. Barbour, what a surprise!" She made no effort not to sound surprised.

"Oh, Mrs. Sanford, I've never seen such a gatherin'!
And this tent, and all these lovely appointments!"

"Blaise wants to see you, dear." Frederika turned to
Burden. "Excuse us, Mrs. Barbour." Frederika pulled
Burden away, leaving Mrs. Barbour in mid-sentence.
"She wasn't invited."

"But she works for Blaise."

"I hate gossip writers, even ours." At that unpropitious moment, Irene Bloch darted out from behind a pair of admirals. "Dear Mrs. Sanford, what a glorious *fête!* I came with Admiral Cheyney," she added carefully.

"So happy to see you." Frederika, meaning to smile, frowned. "Peter is here," said Frederika, her face a tragic mask.

"I know. I've seen him. What a success he had had with *our* magazine. Have you seen it, Senator? But what am I saying, of course you have, because of Diana, *une jeune fille très raffinée.* But don't let me keep you from your guests, Mrs. Sanford." Graciously, Irene turned back to her admirals, as though the day were entirely hers, even to the victory in the West.

"It's just no good," muttered Frederika, holding tight to Burden's arm as they approached Blaise. "You can't keep *anybody* out nowadays."

"Not if you hold an open house. It's your own fault."

"Peter's fault. I've accepted her for him."

"For which we're duly grateful. Diana is also a beneficiary of Irene's wealth . . . and social ambition."

Frederika stopped a moment and looked Burden full in the face. "Is Diana getting a divorce?"

"Not that I know of." The truthful answer sounded false.

"I've heard she was. I've also heard . . ."

". . . that Peter and Diana . . . ?"

". . . yes. He's too young. Here's Blaise."

Burden was unexpectedly hurt. Did she mean that Diana was not good enough to marry Peter? He put the thought out of his mind. Of course she meant only what she said but even so he was, he knew, unexpectedly touchy lately, insisting on prerogatives, suspecting slights where none was.

Fortunately Blaise did not treat him as a falling star; at worst he seemed to regard Burden as a sun in momentary eclipse, to be propitiated in the knowledge that once the lunar shadow passed there would be light again. With a gesture Blaise shooed away those lords in immediate attendance and drew Burden close to him. Just behind them one of the fans slowly stirred the warm air.

". . . bond tour . . . governor . . . all set . . . what about you?"

Burden said the expected. "I'll be there, of course." Indeed he would. He was still one of the masters of the state's political machinery. No star could rise above the flat horizon of that volatile region without his blessing, real or feigned. In any case, he could not afford to be ignored even though the choice of candidates was no longer entirely his as it had been in the years before the war, when a word from him to half a dozen leaders meant a seat in the Congress for some eager (but not too eager) politician whose total loyalty he could then count on for all of one term of office.

"We're trying to fix it so he's unopposed in the primary." The "we" was like a dagger in the back. What right had Blaise, a Washington publisher, to speak of "we" in referring to political arrangements within Burden's state?

"But how is this to be . . . done?" Burden was mild. "The incumbent will want to remain where he is. A most ambitious man, not old either."

The word "old" had begun to obsess Burden. In his last race, he had been called old, even though to himself he was exactly the same as he had been the day when he first arrived in Washington with two suitcases made of wicker and a reservation at a hotel midway between the station and the Capitol, where, on a bright afternoon, trembling with tension, he had been led down into the well of the Senate by a Senator long since dead, to take the oath of office, as Kitty watched proudly in the gallery, wearing a huge hat with a bird on it and puffed sleeves of striped bombazine. Old!

"I think we've taken care of him." Burden writhed again at the "we"; he kept smiling. "There's a Federal judgeship. He wants it. Now my spies tell me the President will appoint him but only if you and Momberger . . ."

"Of course I'll recommend him," said Burden, who was already committed to someone else for the judgeship in question.

"Good! Good! Knew we could count on you!" Blaise pounded his shoulder. "Momberger's no problem. So, there it is. Our boy is in!" Burden tok final solace in the knowledge that no one in life was ever "ours." Time would break Blaise.

*   *   *

Below the terrace, an outcrop of rock marked the beginning of the cliff's precipitous fall to the river far below. Here Harold Griffiths, war correspondent, brooded, heavy face resting upon two small fists, as Peter approached, careful to make no noise, wanting to startle. He succeeded. Harold leaped to his feet, eyes wide with alarm.

"Peter! God, never do that!" He held one hand to his heart while shaking Peter's hand with the other. "In the jungle when somebody did that . . . it was for real."

"Our jungle is for real, too," said Peter, matching the other's theatrical grimness.

"It was our lives there." Harold had always been quite impervious to any irony but his own.

"Ours, too. As well as sacred honor pledged and fortune committed. What a long time!" He looked at Harold fondly, confident that beneath the awesome façade of the G.I.'s Homer he would soon find the old friend who had once played stout Falstaff to his dour Hal.

"I've got malaria," said Harold with irritable pride, and he did look ill, the whites of his eyes bronze, the face livid.

"You wanted to go to the war."

"I'm not complaining," he complained. "I'm glad I went. Best thing ever happened to me."

"To the *Tribune*, too. You're famous."

"I know." Harold nodded gravely and Peter wondered if perhaps the old Harold had been murdered and in his place an impostor had set up shop as shrill journalist. But Peter was careful to be tolerant. Bad prose or not, Harold had been in the midst of death for two years and stronger men than he had come back not at all themselves, old personas erased by what they had witnessed in the damp heat of jungles.

"Somebody had to tell what it's like. And I happened to be the guy. That's all." The new Harold tended to speak in short sentences, reminiscent of Hemingway.

"Like Ishmael, you were there." The new Harold's terseness made Peter want to be elaborate, true Corinthian as opposed to sham Doric. "But now the wars are ending, what next? You can't go back to what you were."

"The war's not over yet." Harold looked across the Potomac as though by some cartographer's error the green chiggery hills of Maryland had become the mainland of Japan. "I'll go back where the fighting is. Where they are, I am. Right to the end."

"Like Ruth amid the alien corn, you follow the troops."

This penetrated. Harold turned to look at Peter and for the first time seemed actually to see him. "You've . . . filled out," he said, indicating Peter's thickset torso which, despite a strenuous diet, continued to expand autonomously.

Peter gave him the round. "Yes, I'm getting fat, like you." But in actual fact Harold's paunch had been reduced by fever. He was now thin and fragile-looking; only the huge lion's head remained unchanged.

Yes, Harold had read the first issue of *The American Idea* and, no, he had not liked it. He attacked the contributors, denounced all Communists (even as he had once defended them). Then, obsessively, he spoke of *them* and their sacrifice. Rapidly he dictated for Peter's benefit a half dozen columns until Peter said, "You *have* found religion," arbitrarily putting "30" at the foot of what was by no means the final column. "But when the war does end, what will you do?"

"It's bad luck to make plans when you're out there."

"But at the moment you're not out there, you're here and I'm sure Father's trying to tie you up for life, but to do what?"

"To write a column. Politics. *'Dateline Washington.'* " The response was quick. Despite his commitment to war, Harold was ready to be converted to peacetime uses.

"Politics! But you . . ." Not wanting to say "know nothing," Peter quickly shifted to ". . . couldn't care less about politics. 'What is more trivial than a United

253

States Senator?' you once asked James Burden Day, and did not stay for an answer."

"A lot has happened to me since then." Harold looked out across the Potomac, chin held high, like Douglas MacArthur. "I found out what was real."

"Senators are real?"

"They're real because *they* are real, the little guys who get pushed around. And I feel kind of responsible for them." Harold indicated the opposite shore, proudly assuming the responsibility for the inhabitants of Rock Springs. With wonder Peter realized how time had altered their roles. Prince Hal was turning into King Cole while Falstaff had become Polonius. Amused and appalled, he listened to the somber jester discuss just what it was he felt for the G.I.s, the subject of the book he was writing. Would Clay figure in the book? Yes, he would.

"I hope you realize what you've done, writing about him the way you did."

"I did nothing. He did everything. I just told the story." Harold's style in print was bearable since one could at least laugh out loud, but face to face the dead-pan monotone was unendurable. Peter wanted to shake the little man, restore him to his senses, assuming of course that the sympathetic companion of before the war had indeed been the true Harold, a puzzling point since it was quite possible that even then this solemn melodramatist had been the reality, waiting impatiently to be revealed by large events.

"He was like a figure out of legend, like a knight in a tapestry of jungle green," said Harold, suddenly revealing what might prove to be a fancier postwar style. "We all felt it. Everyone who was with him out there knew he was something special."

"Clay? *Special?*" Peter could not disguise astonishment. It was one thing deliberately and cold-bloodedly to turn a man into a legend but it was quite another to mistake one's own artifice for the real thing.

"You never liked him, did you?" Harold was tolerant.

"Of course I did. *You* were the one who made fun of him. Thought he was stupid. Said so."

Harold shut his eyes and shook his head with a small

smile. "No. No. No. Now you're projecting onto me your own feelings." He opened his eyes. "I *always* found him interesting. But I admit I never thought there was anything larger than life about him until we met again in the Philippines and I saw how he had changed."

"And he saw how you had changed."

No sharpness could penetrate the armor of Harold's new self-love. "Men do in war," he said quietly and Peter wondered what would happen if he were to shove his one-time friend off the cliff and into the swift river below. If nothing else, the world would be spared '*Dateline Washington*.' But the fit passed, and Peter listened politely as Harold once again started to evoke the day when Clay committed his act of heroism. But just as Clay was due to run from the flaming hangar with the dying man in his arms, Peter said, "I must go. Business."

"That magazine?"

"Yes. I'm sorry you don't like it. I thought you would."

"Maybe once. But the world's not as simple as the Aeneas Duncans suspect."

"Maybe once," said Peter, unable to contain his sense of the ridiculous. "But actually the world's quite simple now. The tyrants are dead. Virtue reigns in the West. And the survivors must all be good. *We* try to be very good. Do you?"

"I have faith in the final purpose of history," said Harold, raising high the Hegelian standard.

Peter laughed. "Are you *still* a Marxist? After those things you write for Father?"

"No matter what you and your friends may think of my politics, I've always been opposed to the exploitation of man by man."

"Yes, I remember." In the days before the war everyone had talked like that. But now new phrases gave a different tone to the old sentiments. Harold was out of date. "Today," said Peter, reveling in cant, "there are other necessities."

"You haven't joined the party, have you?" Out of date or not, Harold recognized the Stalinist "necessities."

"No," said Peter. "I'm still a Republican."

"Dilettante!" Harold had the popular writer's unerring ability to select the one word which vulgarizes even as it characterizes, sacrificing accuracy to mere vividness.

Peter responded with a serenity he did not entirely feel. "But where would artists be without dilettantes? You must have us to appreciate you, to define you, to delight in you. The word delight comes from the Latin, you know." Peter smiled grimly. *Delectare*, to delight. Or in Italian, *dilettare*. You delight us all, Harold."

"You have changed."

"Not enough." Beyond the bank of laurel that separated their rocky meeting place from the terrace, a familiar voice sounded. "Peter, who are you with?" Between branches of laurel appeared the white face of Irene Bloch, hunting lions.

"Harold Griffiths. You must meet him," said Peter. "History requires you to be friends."

5

Against the façade of the house, two special night lamps attracted insects in order deliberately to incinerate them in a yellow glow. On the terrace, beneath the lamps, Blaise and Clay sat in straight iron chairs and listened to the soft Southern voice of Dr. Paulus.

"She is deeply disturbed, as any layman can plainly see, and her pattern of behavior is in many ways highly abnormal. But there is a certain disagreement among my colleagues as to the precise nature of her problem."

"I should have thought that the problem was perfectly apparent, even to your colleagues." Blaise took the lead as Clay intended he should. Completely at peace, Clay smoked one of Blaise's cigars and stared at the exact spot where, a few hours earlier, Burden had told him that he was certain to win the primary because the incumbent would soon be appointed to the judiciary. "It was not easy to arrange," said the older man with that curious dying fall to his voice which Clay had often tried to imitate and sometimes unexpectedly achieved, ceasing, whenever he did so, to be himself, becoming wiser and gentler in manner, which meant infinitely more dangerous in action.

"The President . . . how strange it is to call *that* man the President . . . and I are not intimate, to say the least. But . . ." Light as a feather, Burden's hand had rested on Clay's arm. Sitting in the dark, Clay saw himself as he had been that afternoon, listening eagerly to the details of the elaborate plot which Burden had spun in order to trap incumbent Congressman and naïve President. He had apparently succeeded. "The announcement will be made to coincide with the ceremonies at the State Capitol."

"I can't thank you enough."

"Possibly not." There was mischief in Burden's smile, noted by Clay, who had also been observing how much the Senator had aged in his absence. The mouth had settled permanently into tragedy while the eyes were dull.

"You'll enjoy Congress. I did when I was your age."

"Meaning that you don't now?"

"I don't *enjoy* anything any more. But I will say that without the Senate I would be lost. After a time, nothing seems real except one's work, and of course the morbid study of whoever happens to be at the other end of the Avenue. The President . . . any President . . . is our natural enemy, which is the way it should be. Don't be one of those fellows who depends on Presidential favor. In the long run, it's a mistake. Of course in the long run it's not wise always to be in opposition like me. But that was . . . that is the way I am."

Clay caught the change of tense. He wondered if the old man was ill; the valetudinarian tone was unlike him.

"I don't think," said Clay, "that a new member of the House is apt to be noticed, no matter what he does."

"There are ways of being noticed." A long blue-veined hand pushed hair from tired eyes. "But *inside* the House. By the leaders. Never go outside for glory. If you do, they'll see to it you won't be able to do a thing. And that's all that matters finally, doing what needs to be done." Obviously aware that he might have gone too far in praise of virtue, Burden smiled. "There is nothing more satisfying, or rare, than doing something for oneself which also benefits others, if only by accident."

Clay laughed, as he thought he was meant to. But the old man gave him a sudden sidelong glance, hard to interpret. When he spoke again, the tone was no longer ironic. "I must say that the people as people have never exactly filled me with love, but sometimes one does feel a certain compassion for them. Particularly back home when I drive through that endless flat country, from one small town to the next . . ." With excitement, Clay thought of his own future in that same country.

"And I look about me at the things I've done and I think, well, this highway was my doing, even though nobody remembers now, or cares."

"But they do!" Clay said what the old man wanted to hear. "There's Day Township, population 1868 and growing. Day Mountain, 2400 feet high. The James Burden Day National Park. And a Day Street in every electric light town in the state."

"But who, they'll ask, was Day?"

"Presidents are forgotten, too. Anyway, the roads are there and you put them there."

Sitting in semi-darkness, staring at the spot where earlier Burden had stood, Clay saw the old man as plainly as if it were still afternoon and they were standing side by side, surveying Blaise's guests upon the lawn.

Dr. Paulus spoke, "Of course, Mr. Sanford, your daughter has a problem and we'll do all we can to help her."

"I know she has a problem and I know you mean to help but *how* can you help if she refuses to stay in your institution?"

"We'd hoped she would stay of her own free will so that her problem could be . . ."

"But she won't stay of her own free will! She is an alcoholic. She is not responsible."

"But, Mr. Sanford, our problem is that she is not certifiable. She is, according to the best available opin-

258

ions, responsible for her actions in the usual legal sense."

Clay intervened at last. "It seems to me that the real problem . . ." He frowned at using the word "problem" again. ". . . is to find some way of legally forcing her to take treatment."

"I wish there were a way, Mr. Overbury, honestly I do and I have racked my brains trying to find some way of helping your wife who is seriously disturbed . . ."

Yet "seriously disturbed" hardly described Enid's appearance that evening at Laurel House. She had arrived just as the last of the guests were leaving. She looked splendid and she was sober. She had an overnight bag with her. "I want to have a long talk with you, Father. You too, Clay." Her voice had been hard. "But first I need a good night's sleep. I haven't slept in a week because I wasn't allowed to have sleeping pills at that charming place you sent me to. So we'll talk in the morning when I'm bright-eyed and bushy-tailed." On that ominous note she and Frederika had gone upstairs together.

At dinner when Blaise asked Frederika what Enid had said, mother would not allow wife to say anything beyond, "She seems perfectly sane to me. And she hasn't had a drink in weeks, and doesn't intend to start ever again."

"But what does she want?" Blaise was persistent.

"To be let alone." Frederika was sharp. "To be allowed to divorce Clay and live in peace. You can hardly blame her for that."

"No, you can't." Clay was pleased that his voice, husky from a long silence, sounded sincere and emotion-laden.

Meanwhile, Blaise had summoned the hapless Dr. Paulus who was now on his feet, his soft round face sickly in the yellow light of the insect burners. "I will certainly ask to have this problem reviewed again, of course I will, sir. You can count on that."

"I do count on it." Blaise took the Doctor's arm, as though placing him under arrest, and maneuvered him through the French window. The screen door banged after them.

After a moment, Clay went inside. In the main hall

he paused. Blaise was still at the front door, bullying the Doctor. Suddenly thirsty, Clay went into the library and switched on the lights.

Enid sat in her father's leather chair, bare feet on the brass fire-fender. She wore a dressing gown but no nightdress. In the sudden light, she blinked.

"How'd you like Dr. Paulus? Isn't he something?" She mimicked the Doctor's thick plaintive accent. "He sure does understand my problem. Or . . ." She resumed her usual voice. "*Your* problem, as it's turned out."

With the cold eye of a diagnostician, Clay searched for suspected symptoms and found them: on the floor beside her chair was a tumbler which might have been full of water except that the bright dazedness of her eyes meant that the glass contained vodka. Tentative diagnosis confirmed. "You've been drinking," he observed neutrally.

"Wouldn't you?" She responded with her usual passionate irrelevance, "after what you and Father have put me through?"

"He wanted to help you, that's all." Carefully Clay separated himself from his accomplice.

"Sure. Sure. Well, you know what you are, don't you? What you both are." She sat up straight, and pulled the robe tight about her.

"Don't you think you better go to bed?" From the driveway, gravel groaned as Dr. Paulus's car drove away.

"Well, you're not going to get away with it. No. No. You're not going to get away with it." She shook her head several times until she made herself dizzy. Clay watched her so intently that he was not aware that Blaise had entered until the sudden scowl of his wife's face revealed that the principal author of her pain, as well as being, had joined them.

"You're drunk!" Blaise's scowl matched hers.

"What if I am? Better than being the way you are."

"Dr. Paulus says that you're mentally disturbed. You need help."

"He said a mouthful!" Clay often wondered upon what subculture Enid in her moment of drunkenness relied for vocabulary. Sober she spoke plain English but when she drank she became a real guy, a straight shooter who, let's face it, went all the way to the well to help a pal. Perhaps she read Western novels in secret.

"Sure I need help, and I've already got it, a tough lawyer, the best in town. I talked to him this morning and I gave him an earful."

"What do you need a lawyer for?" Blaise kept his voice low and reasonable. But his hands were clenched fists.

"First to keep me away from the funny farm . . ."

"The what?" Clay had not intended to interrupt but the unfamiliar phrase struck him oddly.

"That nuthouse you two are so eager to lock me up in."

"We wanted to help. That's all." Blaise sounded sincere.

"Help who? You and Clay, or me?" Enid did not wait for an answer. "Then my new lawyer is going to get me a divorce with all the trimmings."

"What trimmings?" Clay felt his hands go cold. "You have the child. You have everything."

"There's still the money . . ."

"Clay has no money. You do." Blaise was irritable. Then, interpreting her vagueness as weakness, he started to browbeat her.

But Enid rallied; eyes came back into focus. "It's not Clay's money I want, it's yours."

"You can have anything you want. You always could."

Clay felt alarm. Something strange was about to happen. Enid had never shown the slightest interest in money; at worst in the old days, she fretted at its lack but now that she had the income from her trust, she was indifferent to possessions.

"That's what you say now," she said with a certain unease, as though trying to recall why it was she had mentioned money. She took a long drink; the vodka refreshed her memory. "*He* says . . . Hartshorne the lawyer says . . . it's the least you can do for me after what you've tried to do, and considering what I know."

"What do you know?" asked Blaise softly.

261

"That you want me put away because a divorce would be bad for Clay's career."

"I was always willing to let you get a divorce. I am still willing." Clay was careful.

"That's what you said but I know different." Her voice was becoming shrill. "I know what's what and so does the lawyer, and don't think we haven't got both of you just where we want you. Let's face it, I've got all the cards."

"What cards do you think you have?" Though Blaise's words were menacing, he took a step backward, away from her, as though to protect himself.

Unsteadily, Enid got to her feet, hands in the pockets of her robe. "And don't think that when I'm through everybody won't know, because they will." She took a step toward Blaise, restoring the old distance between them. "You're in love with him."

The words meant nothing to Clay. She might have been speaking of the weather. He played the sentence back to himself and found he could not make sense of it. But though the actual words refused to give up their meaning, at another level of consciousness he had indeed received the full impact of Enid's malice and throughout his system the alarm was sounded.

Blaise said nothing. He stood with clenched fists in front of him, mouth ajar, breathing heavily. Enid looked from one to the other with casual amusement, the drunken manner discarded as though it had been a mask she could put on or take off at will.

"You didn't think I knew, did you?" She turned to her father. "You hated him when I married him because you really wanted him for yourself and then you hated me because I was the one who got him, though God knows I would've been willing to share him. There's enough to go around, isn't there, Clay?" She looked at Clay, who did not move or speak.

Disappointed at his silence, Enid turned again to Blaise. "After all, Clay will do anything to help his career. That's why he let you fall in love with him, even though he really thinks you're a disgusting, filthy old . . ."

With a harsh cry, Blaise charged: fists held before him like battering rams. Enid was ready for him. Like a matador she leapt out of his way, arms thrown wide for balance. The dressing gown fell open. But in that instant it was not her body that Clay noticed; it was the pistol she held in her right hand. He started to shout a warning; but then did not. There was no longer a part for him to play.

Blaise rounded on her again, arm raised high to strike, unaware of the pistol which Enid fired straight at him. There was the sound of a balloon bursting. A tiny puff of white smoke blossomed between them.

For a long moment the three stood in a circle, Blaise with his arms still extended before him. Enid with the pistol held far from her side. Clay with one hand outstretched, as though to restrain in flight the bullet which had rent the air. Thus they remained in frozen attitude until the door to the library was flung open and Frederika, her night face old and unadorned, stood in the doorway and regarded them as if they were a display of living statues. When at last she spoke, her voice was surprisingly unagitated and sad. "What have you done, Enid?"

Enid turned to her mother and, in turning, let fall the pistol on the hearthrug. "Nothing, Mother," she said. "Nothing at all."

Seven

1

"BUT NOT HAPPY?"

"Happy is a relative term, Mr. Sanford. We all have our days. And just look at this one, will you now!" A soft small hand indicated the window against whose panes wind-driven rain struck the glass like thongs of water.

"No one of course is *absolutely* happy," answered Peter, eyes on the gray-black November sky, all that he could see of the Maryland countryside, for the window was set high, no doubt to make escape difficult. "But does she seem to be . . ." he chose a word he knew Dr. Paulus would like ". . . *adjusted* to her situation?"

"Oh, I think so. Yes, indeed, I do." The Doctor gave him a roguish look, as though to say, "We're all in this together," not realizing to what extent Peter was the enemy. "We have the therapy for her. She's taken to picture paintin', and very talented she is. In fact, Mrs. Paulus asked her for one of her pictures only the other day . . ." A slight frown revealed the possibility of a maladjustment. "She said she would let her have it just as soon as she put the final touches on it!" He finished smoothly.

Peter smiled, imagining the dialogue. "But then with so much improvement, she'll be ready to leave one of these days."

The white smooth forehead contracted, revealing vertical and oblique creases of unusual depth. "Well, now . . ." the Doctor began. "Well, now," he repeated. "Let's not go too fast. Her condition is good . . . considerin', but that's not saying much. You see, she is a schizoid personality . . ."

"We are all schizoid, Doctor. But is she a schizophrenic?" Peter realized his tone was too sharp, and that he had revealed too much, Like all priests, mental therapists did not enjoy it when their parishioners betrayed too intimate a knowledge of holy offices.

"Yes, Mr. Sanford, she is. A board of examiners confirmed my diagnosis two years ago."

"And there can be no review?"

The creases vanished, a soft rounded smile produced two dimples. "I don't think you quite understand our procedures." Dr. Paulus was tender. "To suffer from schizophrenia is like suffering from leukemia. The disease is incurable and progressive."

"There have been remissions of leukemia."

"There have been none as far as schizophrenia goes."

The Doctor was becoming irritated but Peter pressed on. "What about the new drugs? What about Freud's theory that some day schizophrenia would be found to be the result of a chemical imbalance, to be corrected with the hypodermic needle?"

"That day has not arrived, and until it does we prefer to keep our schizophrenics sequestered, for society's sake, as well as their own. Some of them, after all, are homicidal." With that final word, significantly uttered, Dr. Paulus turned Peter over to a male nurse, who escorted him through a corridor of the McKinley Gothic mansion to a large corner room where Enid sat facing an easel on which was set a canvas, empty except for a single slash of scarlet paint down the center.

Without a word, the male nurse switched on the overhead light. Then he departed. Through the window, the day was now black as night.

Brother and sister regarded one another. Enid was unchanged. If anything three years of enforced sobriety made her look even younger than she was. "Welcome," she said at last, "to Belsen."

"At least they haven't made you into a lampshade yet." He kissed her cheek.

"I wish they would. Turn that damned light off, will you?"

Peter switched off the light. The black window became gray. In the dim light, Enid's features appeared abstracted, like a face glimpsed beneath water, newly drowned.

"I'm told you've become a painter."

265

"He's mad as a hatter, Dr. Paulus. And God knows I know *all* the symptoms by now! Washes his hands twenty times a day, keeps looking into the mirror to make sure he's still there. And then there's Mrs. Paulus, a night-blooming swamp flower if ever there was one. *Her* neurosis is thinking she's a lady, tacky bitch. Give me a cigarette. I've used up my quota." She took a cigarette; there was an arc of matchfire in the gloom; then she said, on exhalation: "Oh, what I'd give for just one dry martini."

"You haven't got religion yet?"

"Never! They may be right, you know. I don't think I could ever give it up, on my own."

"What's it like when you're not drinking?" Peter wanted very much to know. When he dieted, he felt uncommonly virtuous and assumed Enid must react in the same way.

But she did not. "It's absolute hell, except for the phenobarbital they give me. That helps, but not enough. I'm ready to jump out of my skin. Anyway, what's wrong with being a drunk? It's *my* body, my funeral."

"The others . . ."

"Yes, I know all about the others." The voice was hard. "And how are they?"

"Well, Clay was re-elected . . ."

"I know. I read the papers."

"Then you know as much about him as I do. I've hardly seen him since . . . well, since . . ."

"My attempted murder?" Suddenly Enid laughed; her old self momentarily restored, taking delight in her own folly. "Oh, it was worth it, to see their faces! As far as I can recall," she added thoughtfully, "I was pretty crocked. Otherwise I would have blown Daddy's head off instead of putting a bullet through the left eye of our great-granddaddy Aaron Burr."

"Do you think it would have been much help, killing Father?" Peter smiled at her in the gray twilight but he knew she could not see his face any more than he could make out her expression beneath the gray sea.

"It would have made me very happy, for a while anyway." She sighed. "He is such a monster! I've tried to

266

explain this to Dr. Paulus but I'm afraid his duty to Father makes him unsympathetic. After all, he's being paid to act as if I were really crazy. Am I?"

"No."

"Sometimes I think I must be. I mean, you tend to become what people say you are."

"Well, *I* don't say you are."

"You are a friend! And I never trusted you. I wonder why?"

Peter experienced pain. Having known for most of his life precisely what it was he felt for Enid and having been denied the one thing in life he most wanted, he had settled for a friendship, which now, in a word, she proved had never existed.

"I suppose I thought you were sneaky. Then of course Father preferred you to me and I was jealous." This was so extraordinarily false that Peter chose not to contradict her, wondering as he occasionally did, if she might not indeed be mad. "Anyway that's all academic. I'm here and they're together. What else matters?"

"Clay's not living at the house any more. He's got his own place, on Woodland Drive."

"With Alice?" She said her child's name in a studiously flat way.

"No. Alice is with Mother. She's turning out very well, they say."

Peter tried to think of a neutral topic. She had mentioned the painting of Aaron Burr. Lately, Peter had been reading the papers of Charles Schermerhorn Schuyler, the illegitimate son of Aaron Burr and himself the father of Emma, Grandfather Sanford's second wife. "Aaron Burr isn't our great-grandfather," he said.

Enid was not much interested. "Oh. Father always says he is. Wasn't somebody a bastard?"

"Yes. Charles Schuyler. The father of Emma, the princess."

"I met a Prince d'Agrigente years ago. In Paris." Enid was talking about something other than herself. Progress. She described Emma's son by her first husband. "A tall weedy old thing. With a monocle. He took me to lunch at the Jockey Club. I ate snails for the first time. He called me *cousine*."

"Emma must have been fascinating. I've been reading about her in Schuyler's journals. I think she may have killed our grandmother."

"I'm quite sure that murder runs in our family." Enid was grim again.

Peter chattered. Anything to distract her. "I've got Schuyler's journal. I've also got some pieces of an autobiography that Aaron Burr was working on. For Schuyler, I suppose. He was Burr's law clerk, as well as son. Only Schuyler didn't know of the relationship until the old man was dead. I think maybe I'll try to put it all together. There's a lot of valuable primary material. Old Burr is self-serving. But always interesting. And Schuyler has his charm, too. I've never been able to read any of his books but they were much admired in their day. When he died, William Cullen Bryant wrote the obituary for the *Post*." But Enid was not listening. He had lost her attention.

Enid stubbed out her cigarette: bright sparks sprayed the darkness. "I read that Clay went to the races last Sunday with Elizabeth Watress, the socialite daughter of Mrs. Lawrence Shattuck and Schuyler Watress of Oyster Bay."

"They see each other from time to time." Peter was neutral. "But then I hardly see either of them any more." Since Elizabeth had taken up with Clay she had made it clear to Peter that new circumstances demanded new friends. He was not offended. At the most she had been a pleasant companion, an occasional alternative to Diana, who still cared for him rather less than he did for her, just as "Clay likes Elizabeth but not as much as she likes him."

"He'll use her, one way or another. Just the way he did me. Just the way he's using Father. Do *you* think they are having an affair, Clay and Father?"

Peter laughed. "You're the one who thinks so, not me."

"Clay would, you know, to get what he wants."

"But Father wouldn't." Peter was certain that this was true, if only because, sexual preference to one side, neither man would allow himself to appear absurd or vulnerable in the eyes of the other.

"I'm not so certain." Enid was stubborn. "I'm sure

they're up to something. For God's sake," the voice suddenly broke. "Get me out of here!"

"I'm trying." He told her rapidly of his latest legal maneuvers but even to his own ear they sounded unconvincing.

"I don't think I can take much more of this." In the dark she now resembled a statue of a woman seated. "I've thought about running away. It can be done. But you'll have to help." In a low voice she told him of her plan. She would steal Dr. Paulus's car ("he always leaves the keys in the car"). Peter would then meet her in Silver Springs with another car and a false passport, and she would drive straight to the Mexican border. Once on the other side, she had a friend in Mexico City who would help her. As she spoke, she sounded as excited and eager as a child describing a holiday. Peter agreed with her that the plan, in theory, had merit but they should wait first to see if the board would review her case; meanwhile, she would have to be patient.

"And face another Christmas here? No thanks." She was grim. "They serve turkey, dry as a blotter, and then we all sit around a Christmas tree that's covered with tufts of cotton and colored paper, made by a pair of old loons who've been here thirty years and live only for decorating that tree once a year, and all the while Mrs. Paulus plays the piano and the nuts all sing together and I tell you . . . I cannot . . . bear it . . . one more minute!" She was close to tears, which did not come. Instead, she leaped to her feet, switched on a lamp, and reached for one of the canvases against the wall.

"Now," she said briskly, "let me show you some pictures. Here's my latest. Father burning in hell. It's a good likeness, don't you think? And that's me there, with the pitchfork."

2

Gray diagonals of rain upon a dead lawn turned to mud. Burden groaned at the sight, and said, "Naturally I'll run again. I'm in good health." His heart fluttered; a rain of dark specks fell between him and Sam Biermann; hysteria, he decided coldly, and the rain stopped. He had learned how to cope with most of the tricks his mind saw fit to play upon the susceptible flesh of an aging body which more and more reminded him of a time bomb, set to explode at a certain moment, and no way to pull the fuse. Each second brought him closer to the end which would be, he both feared and hoped, nothing. Hoped because nothing is no thing and not bad. Feared because nothing is not good. And so, wanting an alternative, wanting at heart something human and finite, his once desultory search for reassurance had become obsessive. Yet none of the culture's familiar anodynes would do. Christianity had been ruined for him by Baptist preachers and Jesuit politicians. Attempts to contemplate "Om" had failed; he was no Brahman. He studied his beloved Plato, but found little consolation. Socrates' argument on the nature and continuance of the soul struck him as peculiarly tinny. He himself could have argued the case better, for a fee. He much preferred the bleakness of Aeschylus. "Take heart, suffering when it climbs highest lasts but a little time." That was acceptable. Since happiness lasts such a notoriously short time, its shadow, pain, must be as brief. But once the suffering was done, what then? "Men search out God and searching find him." Here the cold vision of Aeschylus had faltered. Having glimpsed the pit, the poet drew back, arguing that the journey itself was the answer. If it is, I am nearly done, and have found the answer without knowing it, which is useless. He turned from a contemplation of the rain and nothing, to life and politics, to Sam Biermann, his ancient sounding board.

"You've got no competition, I can see. And nationally it ought to be a good year for you Democrats, particularly now the President's been re-elected. Of course you'll probably have a primary fight."

"I always do nowadays." Actually, until the previous election, no member of Burden's party had ever dared challenge him for he had been the state's most famous son. But now there were a thousand young men ready to take his place. Eventually one would. Meanwhile he held what was his, won fairly in battle.

"Do you think Clay will enter the primary against you?"

Burden was amused. "Never!"

"How can you be so certain?" Sam's mournful eyes studied him closely.

"I'm *certain* of nothing in politics." Burden felt himself grow irritated. To relieve the familiar tension, he took a deep breath, exhaled slowly. "But off the record, Clay's after Momberger's seat, not mine. It makes better sense, doesn't it? Jesse comes up for re-election in '52. By that time Clay will have spent six years in the House. He'll have a political identity by then, which he doesn't have now and which he needs. You just don't come from nowhere and go to the Senate. You must mean something." But as Burden spoke he wondered in all conscience just what it was that *he* had meant when he first proposed himself to the voters, an obscure young lawyer who wanted to be President. The answer was, not much; but as the years passed he had so created himself that, finally, he did become what he seemed to be (despite one lapse), and that was the most any man could hope to achieve in a political system where the one unforgivable sin was to tell the dangerous truth. "Hypocrisy our shield, inaction our sword," he once had observed in the cloakroom, to the laughter of his peers, who knew exactly what he meant. He had learned very early that to do any good thing in the Senate, one must first present it as an act of self-interest since to do good for its own sake aroused suspicion. Mrs. Roosevelt had been genuinely hated for what seemed to many to be a genuine lack of self-interest. Ultimately she had been effective only because certain Senators, disliking her, decided that she was at heart a superb Machiavelli, using the public money to

271

attract the unwashed to the Roosevelt banner. Self-interest acknowledged, even she could occasionally work a miracle in the Congress.

"Anyway, nobody's mad at you, like last time. Those California Niseis." Sam shook his head sadly at the memory. "That was a mistake."

"But I was right." Burden broke his own rule and sounded virtuous in private.

"Being right never got a man a vote."

"That's true enough. Do you think I should take a swing around the state in the spring, show the flag?"

"I do. You've been Senator so long a lot of new voters don't even know who you are. And a lot of the old ones think you're dead."

Burden did not show his distress. "I'm not surprised. I haven't been too active lately. I need better . . ." He took a deep breath, hating the new phrase, ". . . public relations."

Sam nodded. "It's true. Things aren't what they used to be. Now along with your radio and your newsreels, there's this television, and even in the backwoods they read *magazines!* It's not like when they just read the one paper, *our* paper. Oh, it does hurt! No doubt of that. Why, at this moment Clay is the most popular man in the state all because of the magazines and the newsreels, and now they say they're going to make a movie about him, in Hollywood! Like he was Sergeant York. It's amazing!"

"A lot of money is being spent," observed Burden neutrally, glad that he would never have to face Clay in a primary. Clay had made that clear during the election of 1946 when Burden had introduced him around the district, particularly in the farm towns where Burden was strong and Clay was viewed with suspicion. Is he a churchgoer? does he drink? is his wife really crazy? Burden had discreetly allayed all fears. In fact, his confidential talks with church groups about the tragedy of Enid's madness had created considerable sympathy for the young hero who seemed to have so much and yet, in fact, was doomed to remain married but wifeless for the rest of the madwoman's days.

Waiting for the first returns that night in the Sunflower Hotel at the county seat, Burden had said, "You're going to win big."

Clay had agreed. "But one thing I'll never forget. I owe it to you." And he had looked at Burden gravely, with a son's eyes.

Burden had been embarrassed; sincerity tended to demoralize him. "You owe more to Blaise. To yourself. To what you did in the war." But Clay had shaken his head. "It's all those years I spent working for you that made it possible. Watching you, learning the ropes. That's what did it." Then he had indicated to Burden that if all went well, he would move for higher things in 1952. On that one issue Clay was absolutely plain: "I'll support you any time for anything, the way you've supported me." That night, Clay defeated his Republican opponent by the largest plurality in the history of the district.

So the alliance was made and after four years in the House, the young Representative and the old Senator still maintained their cordial alliance and though it was no longer that of son and father, the new arrangement of grateful pupil and revered teacher was perfectly agreeable. Burden had even been able to show his disciple a number of shortcuts to power within the tightly disciplined hierarchy of the House, so unlike the leisurely even anarchic Senate where Burden's colleague Jesse Momberger watched with a cold eye the rise of a new power in their state, and sought ways of containing it. But there were none for the source of that power was Laurel House from which flowed endless money and publicity. Even Burden, at times, grew weary of being forever asked, "And what was your impression of Clay Overbury when you first met him?" Had not Sam (*his* Sam) spent most of their afternoon together discussing Clay? But that was inevitable since "the little bastard's better known in New York City than he is back home," the senior Senator had recently observed to the junior Senator, who had said, "It does the state no harm to have a celebrity in Congress." To which the senior Senator had snarled, "It's not the Goddamned state I'm worried about."

Kitty's voice ended the interview. "She's here! She's here!" Indeed she was. Diana came out on the porch, attended by her mother and Peter Sanford, who "met me at the station." She kissed her father happily and shook hands with Sam, who promptly shook hands again and made his departure, leaving the family to themselves and Peter.

"Doesn't she look well!" Kitty hugged her daughter with innocent pleasure and Burden agreed. Even in the dull November light Diana was unexpectedly glowing, face tanned from the desert sun. "She looks just like an Indian. She gets that from Burden. He has Indian blood, but he's ashamed to admit it."

This canard was ignored. One of Burden's uncles had married an Osage Indian, which was the closest Burden came to being Indian. But in recent years Kitty's inner voice had begun to reflect a mind which had grown not only lax but melodramatic. At times she alarmed Burden, with her abrupt revelations that murder was afoot, incest common and no one legitimate.

In the draughty living room they sat about a new fire which improved considerably Burden's mood. Diana told them about Nevada, where "We lived in cabins, ate nothing but tough fresh beef, and tried to avoid rattlesnakes and lustful cowboys."

"Diana!" Kitty's eyes gleamed with pleasure.

"Don't worry, Mother. I avoided both. But many of the ladies succumbed to the cowboys. Poor things. When they weren't weeping about the past, they were weeping about the future. The cowboys gave them something to do in the present. Anyway, I learned to play bridge and read all of *l'Education Sentimentale,* in French, slowly."

"Now you're free." Though Burden had always found Diana's coolness refreshing, he did wonder at times whether or not that coolness might be simply coldness. Not since her grief at Clay's abandonment had anything much moved her, as far as he knew, which was not well since for some years they had exchanged no confidences. He was aware that she had come to hate Billy Thorne but by never once admitting this to her father, she had deprived him of a normal pleasure in being able to remind her (but *not* doing so) that from the beginning he had been right. But right or wrong, the marriage was now over. "Where is Billy?" asked Kitty. "I haven't seen him in a coon's age."

"I don't know." Diana turned to Peter. "Where is my ex-husband?"

"No one knows. He left us last month, after accusing Aeneas Duncan of being a tool of the bourgeoisie, which I suppose meant me. He left the office without his coat or hat. We still have them, if you'd like a souvenir."

"No thanks." Diana stretched like a cat. "Freedom is nice, isn't it?"

Burden told her how pleased he was to see her happy. Yet as he spoke he found himself looking at Peter, who sat like the youthful Buddha, smiling at the fire. If Peter had been having an affair with Diana, would Billy Thorne have continued to work with him? He assumed not but then the arrangements of the young were baffling to him. Apparently, adultery was acceptable if those involved were sufficiently "adult." At the margin of Burden's consciousness a social revolution was taking place and though his first instinct was to disapprove, in actual fact he was profoundly indifferent to what others did, except for Diana. Married to Peter, Diana would be rich, with a great name. Of minor importance, Peter would make a good son-in-law for a garrulous politician. More than once Burden had been aware that he was telling Peter things which he would never have confided to a contemporary. Something in the young man's manner made him want to tell him what he really felt. Not that he for a moment confused the other's politeness with true interest. Yet Peter Sanford was the sort of person he wished instinctively to persuade; and so, spurred on by that smiling neutrality, he offered confidences which were no doubt betrayed or, worse, forgotten. It made no difference.

"I read with interest your piece on Hiroshima. Most eloquent, I thought."

"Did you really read it?" Peter looked at him with what seemed genuine surprise.

"I always read your magazine."

"In a state of apoplexy," said Diana, inspiring her mother to say, "I don't like Burden's color at all. He's too red in the face. And not a good red, which means he'll have a stroke and then I'll starve to death because there's nothing in the bank and the insurance is piddling."

Feeling the final stroke begin, Burden raised his voice in order to bridge if not to dam Kitty's boiling stream of consciousness. "I always read Aeneas Duncan with rising blood pressure, that's true."

Kitty stopped speaking, and smiled happily at her reunited family. Diana looked at her mother with such hate that Kitty mistook it for love. She took her daughter's hand in hers and held it tight.

Peter did his best to help out. "Aeneas is living in New York now and I don't think he'll be writing too much about politics. At the moment he prefers to butcher poets."

"He shall be missed," said Burden lightly. "But now *you* are beginning to write. That was your first piece, wasn't it?"

Peter appeared embarrassed. He is shy, thought Burden, pursuing his quarry. "Are you going to do others?"

"If there is any demand." Peter looked to Diana as though expecting a negative.

"Oh, there'll be a demand. He's very good, don't you think, Father?"

"Impressive, yes, and not shrill, unlike Mr. Duncan, whose habitual tone is one of moral outrage."

"This is an outrageous time," said Peter mildly.

"All times outrage." Burden was flat. "But do you really feel we were wrong to use the atomic bomb on Japan?"

"I'm not sure that I 'feel' it. But I do think it, yes. We should have merely demonstrated the bomb, blown the top off Fujiyama, something dramatic, and they would have surrendered. There was no reason to destroy two cities."

"I wonder." Burden did wonder. Like everyone else, he had been bemused by the breaking of the atom. It was plain that the world would never be the same again, but whether or not this was a good thing depended on one's temperament. Since his was pessimistic, he could imagine all too easily the mushroom clouds, the firewind, the radioactive ash, and, at the end, an empty planet glittering like a blind eye in the sun. Yet he asked, "What is the difference, morally, between one bomb doing the work of the thousand bombs which would have been dropped anyway?"

"The difference is that with the invention and demonstration of that one bomb we had the means to end the war, which we did, but to please the military we destroyed two hundred thousand civilians, and that was wrong."

Burden knew all the arguments. What interested him was Peter's unexpected passion. Gone was that air of detachment which had charmed as well as puzzled Burden. It was good to know that the young man could be serious about something but, on the other hand, it was distressing to think that his next son-in-law might be as given to furious partisanship as the first. "You obviously have a good deal to say," Burden murmured.

Peter laughed, to his relief. "I'm afraid I have very little to say, but a good deal to add."

"He added," said Diana. "Oh, Peter will be formidable once he gets the proper range. He must write about politics in every issue."

"No one can stop him either," observed the young Voltaire. "He is the publisher."

"And we're a success. We break even. No deficit. Irene is so pleased."

Peter then described for Diana's benefit the recent funeral of Samuel I. Bloch, who had died unexpectedly in Jersey City during a board meeting. "We should build him a monument," said Peter, "and dedicate it to the Unknown Husband."

Burden recalled for them Irene's behavior at the funeral. According to Irene, Mr. Bloch had always been an Episcopalian; horrified, his family had refused to attend the funeral, just as she had intended. Standing alone in black in a Gothic chapel of the National Cathedral, she had received condolences with a regal air. But when she saw Burden, she threw her arms around him and pressed her cheek to his. "What will become of me?" she had sobbed in his ear. Aware that all eyes were upon them, he had extricated himself as best he could with a promise to see her soon.

"I suppose now you'll marry Peter," said Kitty, suddenly letting go Diana's hand. "He's got awfully fat, but then he's rich and you'll have security."

Diana fled the room, and Peter pulled in his stomach. Kitty turned to him. "I made a cake this morning, knowing you were coming. It's the fudge pecan you like so much. Would you like some now?"

"I am *not* hungry," said Peter, voice trembling with irritation.

"But he's *always* hungry," said Kitty for the inner record. "He must be sick, probably ate too much for lunch. I'd put him on a diet, if I were Diana. After the wedding, that is."

"No wedding is planned, Mrs. Day." Peter broke the house rule of never commenting upon Kitty's announcements.

"Wedding?" She looked at him with surprise. "What wedding?"

Burden did his best to soothe Peter and to silence Kitty. As he went about his diplomatic task, he knew that Peter was precisely the right husband for Diana who would indeed be penniless once he was gone, not that he had any plan for an immediate departure from the world, certainly not before he had got her settled and himself re-elected.

3

Harold opened the door. "Come in!" His voice was loud, commanding, as though he wanted to intimidate Clay, or impress others not seen. Inside the small foyer, Harold shut the door and bolted it. He whispered rapidly: "They're inside. Both of them. I'm sorry I got you into this. I couldn't think of anybody else to call."

"It's all right." Clay was soothing. "I'll handle them." Clay was careful to betray no nervousness as he followed Harold into the glass and steel living room with its view of Rock Creek Park; the building was new, one of the first to be put up after the war when the old city of red brick and New England marble was slowly engulfed by glass and concrete, a victory of fused sand over hewn rock. Even Clay, who usually liked the new, experienced a certain nostalgia for what had been.

The two men got to their feet as he entered. One was short and stocky with a round face and button nose. The other was tall and thin except for a large stomach, obviously designed for a fat man and attached by mistake to a lean one.

"This is Congressman Overbury," said Harold. The men looked at one another; they seemed not to know what to do when Clay held out his hand, the politician's usual reflex. Swiftly Clay withdrew the hand.

"I understand there's been some trouble." Clay stood at the center of the room, ready to begin whatever offensive was necessary.

"That's right, sir." It was the short one who answered, his manner deceptively gentle. Clay knew the type and prepared for the worst. "Your friend Mr. Griffiths here has committed a serious offense which is known under the District Code as a Section 22-1112A."

"Identification." Clay was abrupt. He must keep them on the defensive.

"Identification?" The lean-fat man repeated the word as though it were somehow an insult.

Clay snapped his fingers at the short man who was closest to him. "Identification," he repeated coldly.

"Yes, sir." The short one was polite and not in the least flustered. He withdrew his wallet, and showed Clay his identification; the other one did the same. Clay took a notebook from his own pocket and slowly wrote down the names and serial numbers of the two members of the District vice squad.

"I suppose you'd like to see my identification," he began but the small one said, "No, I recognize you, Congressman, from your pictures."

"Yes." Clay was flat. He looked at Harold who hovered nervously behind a sofa, as though ready to take cover at an instant's notice should the enemy open fire. On one side of his face a scarlet discoloration of the skin was beginning to turn blue. "Was it necessary," asked Clay, "to beat him up?"

"He tried to resist arrest, sir." The tall one spoke tonelessly for the record.

"Put up a fight, did he? Well, Harold has a lot of guts. He's just the type to take on two policemen twice his size in a . . . it was a public place, wasn't it?"

"The men's room of the Capitol Theatre, yes, sir. At 1:47 P.M."

"Witnesses?"

"Just us, Congressman." The short one permitted himself a small smile.

"So after the offense was committed . . ."

"A 22-1112."

"Exactly. You beat him up."

"When he tried to resist arrest we was . . . we were forced to restrain him." The lean-fat man was official historian as well as principal witness to the offense against his companion's decency.

"Then instead of booking him, you came here. Is that right?"

"We felt," said the short man in his gentle slightly effeminate voice, "that since Mr. Griffiths was such a well-known writer for the papers that we probably ought to be able to straighten this out some way or another, which is why we let him call you."

"Harold, did you approach this man, or did he approach you?"

"He spoke to me first. He followed me into . . . the place where it happened."

"Are you trying to tell me that *he* made the advances?"

"Yes." Harold cleared his throat repeatedly. "Yes, he did."

"That is not what happened, sir, as my colleague will testify. Mr. Griffiths made the advance to me, asking first if I had a light for his cigarette which I gave him of course and then when I went into the rest room in question, he followed me and committed a 22-1112, as was duly witnessed."

"What were *you* doing loitering in the Capitol Theatre?"

"We do not loiter, sir. We were on duty. We had been asked to look in by the management of the theatre who were worried about that certain element. You see, small schoolchildren go there, on the weekend especially."

"Mr. Griffiths has just said that you made the advance. If so, that is entrapment, which is against the law."

"It is his word against ours, sir." The short man was quietly pleased; they were safe.

"In the last year how many times have you been propositioned?"

"About seventy times, sir."

"And you never made the first advance?"

"No, sir."

"Seventy times strange men wanted to have sex with you. Would you say this was due to your handsome appearance?"

The short man scowled inadvertently. "It's all due to the fact that I am ordered to keep an eye on places where that sort of thing might happen, that's all."

"And it always does, particularly to you."

"I have my job, sir."

"Now, Mr. Onslow," Clay had carefully filed the other's name for future use. "The fact that you did not book Mr. Griffiths but chose to bring him home and allow him to telephone a friend suggests to me that neither of you wants any trouble with the newspapers, not to mention Mr. Sanford, and so you have decided that this whole business might, under the proper circumstances, be forgotten."

The two men exchanged a look. It was the lean-fat man who answered. "Naturally nothing can be forgotten that happened between him and us . . . between him and we . . . which was against the law. The law is what we must uphold and obey all of us, as you'll agree, Congressman. But it did seem that a man of Mr. Griffiths's prominence . . . and connections," a gesture at Clay, "ought not to have a thing like this on his record, a permanent black mark, you might say, which could prove embarrassing to his employer . . . and to his friends, especially they . . . those . . . who are in the public eye."

"The price?" Clay was blunt. Behind the sofa, Harold, who had been kneading his face, dropped both hands and came to military attention.

"Two thousand dollars," said the short man.

Clay picked up the receiver of the telephone and

dialed for the operator. When she answered, he said, "Police."

The lean-fat man moved toward him, ready for violence. "What do you think you're doing?"

"Reporting blackmail, extortion, shakedown."

From Harold a cry: "Clay, *don't!*"

"It's your word against ours," said the short man but the menace he intended was undone by the sudden dropping of his voice on the word "ours."

"You will find that between your word and mine, you will not be believed, Mr. Onslow. Nor will you, Mr. Gover." A voice in the receiver said, "Police Department," and Clay said, "Vice squad, please."

"You may think you're a big shot, Mr. Congressman," began the lean-fat man.

"I am a big shot, Mr. Gover, as you're about to find out." A voice said, "Vice squad," and Clay said, "This is Congressman . . ." With a swift gesture Gover broke the connection. He stood so close to Clay that he could smell stale talcum powder on the man's face and beer upon his breath.

Acknowledging their physical closeness, Clay chose a quiet small voice. "Do you want to be killed?"

"You're the one who's off base, Mac, not me."

Clay took the man suddenly by the shoulders, and with one swift movement swung him from right to left, as if he were a door. Then he got past him into the center of the room where the short man stood, arms ready to grapple.

Behind Clay's back the lean-fat man said, "There's nothing to stop us saying *you* was picked up, too, Mr. Big Shot." As the harsh voice continued to threaten, Clay turned to the weaker of the two.

"Mr. Onslow, you're an intelligent man. You saw a chance to make some money out of Mr. Griffiths's error and I don't blame you. I don't grudge you the money. I'm sure Mr. Griffiths doesn't either but unfortunately there is no guarantee that once he starts to pay, you will ever stop asking for more. Oh, I know you may not think you'll ever put the squeeze on again but when Christmas rolls around and you're a bit short of cash, you'll say to yourself: well, why not pay a visit to Mr. Griffiths?" Clay spoke rapidly but clearly, aware that the bright-eyed detective was totally absorbed in what he was saying. "Now for Harold's sake I can't permit that. For yours, too. After all, blackmail is a dangerous business, particularly if somebody other than those involved knows about it. And somebody does know. I know. And that means you're in as much trouble as Harold because one word from me to the police department and you two gentlemen will be permanently unemployable in this city, and don't think I won't say the word just because Harold might get some bad publicity in the process. He can survive it. But you can't. Now I suggest, Mr. Onslow . . . Mr. Gover, that we forget that any of this ever happened."

"But suppose we don't. Suppose we . . ."

With a gesture Clay silenced the lean-fat man. "If you don't get out of here right now, I will telephone . . ." Clay had saved to the last his ultimate weapon. Before arriving at Harold's he had found out not only the name of the head of the vice squad but he had also learned the man's nickname, and several other relevant details. He used them now, pretending intimacy. As he did, he moved back to the telephone, eyes on the short man, the weak link which snapped. "Well," he said, in a thin voice. "Well . . ." He stopped.

Politely, Clay waited, hand on the telephone receiver, delighting in battle. But the war was over. The lean-fat man picked up his coat and hat and without a word left the room, followed by the *agent provocateur,* who smiled meaninglessly as he hurried to join his colleague.

With the shutting of the front door, Harold sank onto the sofa, close to tears.

"You damned idiot!" Clay's distaste for the whole affair erupted. He denounced Harold who received the abuse with head bowed.

When Clay had finally stopped, he said, "I should never have got you mixed up in this. I'm sorry. But when I couldn't find Blaise, you were the only person I could think of, who was tough enough . . ."

"You might have called a lawyer."

"How could I tell a lawyer I hardly know, something like this?"

283

"Yet you could tell *me?*" Clay's anger began again.

"I didn't think you . . . well, of course you'd mind but . . ."

"But you felt that maybe I suspected all along?"

"Something like that. But anyway I did do you a good turn out there. I mean writing what I did . . ."

"I don't need instruction. I know my loyalties." Clay was sharp. Politics was largely a matter of keeping track of debts, and Clay was an excellent bookkeeper. As of today, Harold was forever in his debt. Thinking of this, he allowed good humor to replace righteous anger.

"Anyway, I don't want to know anything about your private life, ever. So forget about it. Only," Clay could not resist adding, "don't forget you're living in one of the dirtiest towns in the country, where everybody, officially and unofficially, is watching everybody else, building a case, for future use."

"I was stupid," said Harold.

"Yes, you were." Clay was not unkind.

Harold reverted suddenly to his usual manner. "*You* never get caught, with those damned girls of yours."

"They're over twenty-one and I draw the shades and lock the door and practice birth control."

"While their husbands . . ."

"I know only widows."

"And Elizabeth Watress."

* * *

She was waiting for him in the lobby of the Shoreham Hotel, among placards and banners rejoicing in the election of the thirty-third American President. As Clay crossed the lobby, Elizabeth got quickly to her feet and he noticed, as he always did when he had not seen her for some time, the brilliant concentration of the smiling face in which the eyes, curiously enough, reflected nothing, despite their splendid darkness. He kissed her cheek rapidly and chastely. He was, after all, a married man, and the lobby was filled with people who knew him.

"*He's* here!" Elizabeth was ecstatic. "The President just came in! It was so exciting, the way everybody cheered. I didn't know whether to curtsey or not. I felt like it. He's in the ballroom. Why were you late?"

"Business. What else?" He took her arm and together they moved toward the ballroom where a Midwestern governor was entertaining with Democratic exuberance yet Republican extravagance the soon-to-be-inaugurated President.

At the door to the ballroom, Clay paused and waited until the hovering photographers had recognized him. This was usually a swift process but with a President in the ballroom the interest of the press in any one of the half thousand members of Congress was apt to be slight, no matter how striking the Representative's appearance, how glorious his war, how superb his companion. But finally they rallied round.

Clay knew the ones from the news services by name; the others he pretended to recognize. Elizabeth clung to his arm, simulating fear and delight in equal portions. She had once confided to him that the one thing she would most like to be was a movie star, on the practical ground that if one liked the world's attention (and candidly she had admitted that she very much wanted to be recognized as a beautiful woman, attractive to men), the movie star alone commanded universal interest. Not even the President could compete with the fame and sexuality of a star adroitly publicized.

Clay had disagreed. He saw no reason why a politician, even such a traditionally dull figure as the President, could not be presented in the same way as a movie star to the public. "But," she had observed, "how many politicians look like you! and are young! and a hero!" Clay had laughed. "You put things in their proper order anyway." He had not told her that this same order was the very one exploited by Blaise and the public relations firm which had been engaged to maintain Clay's celebrity in the shadowy precincts of the House of Representatives. Youth was exploited (promise of future greatness) as well as war record (a film of his wartime adventures was now being made) and physical appearance (whenever he appeared in public, girls would clamor at the photographers' prompting). Yet, as Clay knew, that which begins falsely becomes with constant repetition true. The girls now mobbed him without urging; aware that since others were said to react in this way, they must, too. As a result he had received the ultimate accolade: a dry insult from the Speaker of the House: "I always enjoy *seeing* that young man speak."

Blaise had determined that for the next few years, Clay must be presented not only as a youthful idealist but also as an alternative to the usual politician. Clay had agreed, confident that he was indeed unlike the usual politician, although he realized that in actual performance he had been somewhat less than vigorous. For the most part he favored increased military spending while viewing with ritual alarm the predatory Soviet empire as it threatened to dominate Europe and turn to hot what everyone now referred to as "the cold war." In the House itself he had made as many friends as he could considering his enviable status. It was taken for granted that he would soon move on. But when and to what no one was certain, including Clay, who could be his state's governor, if he chose; but he did not choose this thankless office which involved, for the most part, haggling over building contracts with state legislators, usually bought.

The Senate was the obvious place to go. But he had vowed not to run against Burden in 1950. On the other hand, 1952 seemed a century away, and the prospect of four more years in the House was dispiriting. Despite his legendary youth, he did not regard himself as young. More to the point, in four years he would be forty-two and if his career was to be, literally, prodigious he must by then have made a significant political mark, an impossibility for any member of the House who did not possess seniority and its prize, a committee chairmanship. Meanwhile, he circulated, and waited, and tried to win the President's confidence.

"Good to see you, Clay!" The President was pink with excitement; in the bright light of the newsreel cameras his thin gray hair glistened as though made of metal while thick spectacles magnified enormously small shrewd eyes.

"Good to see *you*, Mr. President!" Clay pumped the

hand of his party leader warmly. "Did you get the letter I wrote you, sir . . ."

But the grinning President had been removed by his host the governor. That was exactly right for a two-term Congressman, thought Clay irritably: one minute with the sovereign, and a photograph to be sent as quickly as possible back to the state.

"He looks so . . . sexy!" exclaimed Elizabeth, delighted to have shaken the Presidential hand.

"Sexy? Good God, you *are* crazy. That's the President."

"And that's what I meant," said Elizabeth evenly, and Clay laughed. Not many girls were so honest. He enjoyed Elizabeth much of the time. Their affair had begun, ludicrously, in the stalled elevator of a new apartment house. Since that time, they had seen one another often and if she found his promiscuity distressing (he had been reasonably candid with her), she was careful never to betray jealousy. Meanwhile, she made herself useful to him, for through numerous Shattucks and Watresses, she seemed to know everyone in the outside world, that is to say New York City.

One Labor Day weekend they had motored to Southampton, where for three days in an old house belonging to her Uncle Ogden Watress, Clay drank gin and tonic (not bourbon and water), played tennis on a grass court (not clay) and lunched daily at a beach club overlooking an oval pool in which the noise of interchangeable towheaded children drowned out all talk of the stock market (not politics). Elizabeth was an excellent guide, financial ("Oh, he has to have money, because she does and she's a Democrat") as well as social ("Gladys was his second wife which means that Tony is Gene's half brother and Gladys Junior is their stepsister").

Like an anthropologist in search of a link between himself and another race, Clay studied the New Yorkers, tried to analyze in what way they were different from the Washingtonians. For one thing, they made less noise. They were low-keyed in their responses; they seldom boomed good-fellowship, feigned or true. Most striking of all, they did not believe or even pretend to believe that deep in the common man

287

resided wisdom; and not to believe in the people was heresy in Washington. After all, had it not been *they* who had sent father, grandfather, uncle to the capital? Despite Millicent Smith Carhart's aristocratic bluntness, she liked nothing better than to relate how some vulgarian had expressed in his quaint way a truth, entirely obscure to those who had been expensively educated and led fancy lives. But at the Racquet Club the common man was not admired; at the Knickerbocker Club he was seldom mentioned; at the Brook he was unknown.

But though Clay found the New Yorkers' disdain of the people somewhat alarming (after all, his own career depended entirely upon the franchise of the simple), he did enjoy listening to Uncle Ogden (a banking genius, according to Elizabeth) dismiss with scorn that electorate which had inflicted the demonic Roosevelt and now the mediocre Truman upon a republic which "don't you see, was never intended to be a democracy." Yet for all their complaining, Clay was uncomfortably aware that at heart the New Yorkers did not take politicians seriously. Between elections they even regarded their man Dewey with contempt, their quadrennial support of him the result more of a horror of the people than a display of enthusiasm for a candidate who was bound, sooner or later, to betray the sacred money to the few for the profane votes of the many. They had been stung before. Fortunately, Clay's publicity made him appealing even to those who would ordinarily have fled at the approach of a Western Congressman. Then of course he was genuinely helpful to anyone who wished to thread the Congressional labyrinth in pursuit of gold. Finally, all men are attracted to someone on the rise. And he was rising. Had not the President in his progress deliberately paused, so that photographers might record his approval of Congressman Overbury?

"Old Harry certainly didn't give you much of his time, did he?" A familiar abrasive voice sounded in Clay's ear. It belonged to Billy Thorne. Full of sweet Manhattans, he chewed the stem of a cherry.

"Hello, Billy." Clay tried to push past him.

"Miss Watress, I don't suppose you remember me but we met . . ."

"I don't think I do," murmured Elizabeth, flute beneath brass. She clutched Clay's arm and gave him a helpful shove which, unfortunately, propelled them into a long table.

But though they were trapped, Clay refused to show impatience. In politics everyone must be pleased. "What're you doing now?" he asked, as though he wanted very much to know the answer. Elizabeth clutched his arm for what seemed moral support but when he looked at her out of the corner of his eye, he saw that she was entirely absorbed in the stumpy figure of the grinning President, grabbing at hands in his circle of light.

"I expect to work for him." Billy indicated the President.

"How can you?" This was abrupt, but not unnatural.

"Why not?"

"Your . . . well, your radical past might make it difficult."

"Those days are over." Billy was blithe with anticipated power. Resting his weight on the false leg, he swayed from side to side, like a demented metronome. "I expect to be at the White House after the first of the year."

"Well, let's hope your job doesn't require Senate confirmation." Unintended malice is the most wounding. Clay regretted having spoken so brusquely.

The metronome came to a clicking stop. "Luckily I don't have to depend on *my* ex-father-in-law. How about you?"

"Blaise is a most useful man." Clay remembered to smile. "Our relations are friendly."

"Yes, we all know about *that*."

Billy's overemphasis had its effect. Clay wondered as he often did what people really said of him and Blaise. Before the war, Washington gossip was concerned almost entirely with adultery. The subject was endlessly diverting and as long as those involved maintained appearances, no man was ever much censured. But though appearances were still maintained with prewar care, particularly by those whose lives were public, private gossip had become singularly brutal. The war, Freudian analysis, and popular novels had revealed all sorts of recondite and undreamed-of vice. No one was spared, not even Millicent Smith Carhart, whose long friendship with Lucy Shattuck was now highly suspect, and there was much discussion as to did they or did they not and if they did what did they do? In any case, it was taken for granted that whatever one seemed to be, one was really the opposite.

"Oh, Clay! Clay!"

Irene Bloch seized him with long-fingered hands. "How simply dreadful!"

Irene turned to Elizabeth who took a step back, startled: was *she* dreadful!

Then Irene's gaze took in and promptly let go the image of Billy Thorne. He did not matter. With one hand she clung to Clay while with the other she pulled Elizabeth toward her. "I heard it on the radio, in my car. Just now, on the way here. What really happened? You know how they are on the radio, just an announcement, no details. *Mais quel désastre!*"

"*What* did you hear on the radio?" asked Clay carefully. Irene's eyes went wide as she heard the question; then she drew Elizabeth even closer to her. In times of trouble thus do the women of the tribe share the common grief.

"You don't know?" Each word was pronounced with wonder and delight. "You really have *not* heard?" She looked first at one, then at the other, ravished to be fate's messenger. "Then that explains why you're here at a party. I wondered, of course."

Clay's face went warm. He was suddenly dizzy. Now he would be told.

"She's dead," said Irene Bloch. Tears suddenly streaked her ash-white cheeks. "Enid's dead!"

4

"I know the error was mine and I will not shirk the responsibility." Three times in the course of an hour Dr. Paulus had said this phrase, and each time the word "shirk" became "shuck," to Peter's annoyance. By attending to such details he was able not to comprehend "this highly tragic affair," again in Dr. Paulus's phrase.

They were gathered in the library. Though the day was cold, the fireplace was empty. Against the dark paneling the portrait of Aaron Burr, its left eye recently restored, represented Enid at the conference.

Since it was Dr. Paulus who brought the news, he sat in Blaise's chair. Frederika was enigmatic in a bright tweed suit, antithesis of black. Blaise sat on the bench before the fire, chin upon clenched hands. Clay stared out the window at a row of fir trees arranged like pawns at the start of a game of chess. Peter observed them all from a leather chair beside the door.

Dr. Paulus told his story. From time to time he touched handkerchief to his lips, which was perverse since they were dry while his cheeks glistened with sweat. "I don't know how I forgot. I never do forget. At least never before, not once in all my years at the Home. But this one time I did. I left those keys in the car. I don't suppose it's any excuse to say that I was under considerable tension myself, of an administrative nature, I should say, not psychological," he added, his old unctuous authority returning briefly, a reminder to himself of who he had been that morning and would be soon again once he had escaped from Laurel House and its savage lord.

"This was at noon, just thirty minutes . . . a mere half hour before our luncheon is served." Peter writhed at the word as well as the thought of what that "luncheon" must have been.

"She had been with my wife up until shortly before eleven, discussing art which is . . . which was their favorite subject when together, my wife majored in art, at Louisiana State, and she so much enjoyed the pictures Mrs. Overbury painted. They were very close, the two girls. Anyway, they were together in the atelier . . ." It took them all a moment to work out ah-tell-eer. ". . . until just about eleven, when Mrs. Overbury said she thought she'd like to lie down before lunch and Mrs. Paulus said, 'Of course, honey,' and left her in the atelier. Well, as we can piece together the story, Mrs. Overbury then went to her room where she gathered a few belongings and wrapped them in a piece of canvas, the kind she painted on. We don't allow valises in the rooms, for obvious reasons. Then at about noon she came outside and went over to my car . . ."

"You don't have guards? There's nobody to keep an eye on who goes where?" Blaise's voice sounded querulous though from his expression Peter realized that he meant to bluster.

"As you well know, Mr. Sanford, we do *not* have guards in the prison sense or in the sense that our patients are violent or wish to escape . . . which they aren't and don't, and are screened in advance for just that. Disturbed they are, of course, and capable even of little . . . eruptions but not violent. So we are not a prison, even though some might like it better if we were."

Good for Paulus. Peter turned to look at his father who stiffened, started to answer, then abruptly covered chin and mouth with two fists. As for Clay, he was now watching the doctor, his expression pleasant. Peter could not begin to guess what Clay felt. He had arrived last, saying that he had been at a meeeing when he heard the news. For the first few minutes he had been nervous. But the mood of the others was contagious; now, he was passive and apparently serene. Grief not begun; shock not yet ended, they were all like gods, surveying a hero's death upon some windy height, below heaven.

"But we do have nurses and others who are in constant attendance and, in a way, our patients are always under what you might call surveillance. But this particular noon," he frowned and blotted his mouth. Peter thought he heard a rasping sound as two abrasive textures met. "It so happened that Mrs. Paulus was in the other wing of the new house while I was involved in an administrative matter of some complexity, and so it was then that Mrs. Overbury got into my car and drove away."

Clay was suddenly alert. "If you never left your keys in the car before, how did she know that this time you would, and pack her things in advance?"

"Well, now, Congressman . . ." As Dr. Paulus intoned the title richly, the Southern cadence of his voice conjured up a vision of the old Congresses, his people's traditional shield against the hostile North. "I have given that matter some thought and I have discussed the matter at length with my wife and others, and I have learned that Mrs. Overbury had lately taken to strolling each forenoon in front of the main house where I park my car and so, in retrospect, it seems clear that she was indeed waiting for that one occasion when I might inadvertently leave those keys in that car."

"But what about *today?*" Clay's voice, suddenly hard, erased all memory of old Congresses. He was the new order, impatient and precise. His voice, Peter had often noticed, became markedly Western whenever he spoke of his state or discussed the business of the House, as if by a shift in accent he meant to remind himself and others that he was in fact what he was in title, representative.

Clay put Dr. Paulus through his paces. He was relentless inquisitor as well as grieving husband. But of course there was no grief in him, thought Peter bitterly. In the dull autumnal light Clay's hair seemed gray not blond, and Peter suddenly saw him as he would be in twenty years' time, strong-faced and plausible, the President. It was not impossible. But for now: might not Enid have seen the keys *before* she went to her room to pack her belongings? Well, yes, sir. Maybe, sir. That was the best the committee chairman could wrest from the evasive witness, but it was sufficient to justify the inquisitor's display of weapons. The rest of the testimony followed simply enough.

"She reached the main highway shortly before one o'clock. She must've made very good time because she was quite a ways south of Richmond when it happened."

When it happened. Peter saw the highway; saw the sharp bend it made among tall pine trees. The sun shone bright and cold; he could smell the pines. Just beyond the bend in the highway was an intersection, invisible to travelers from the north and of no interest at all to this traveler from the north who wanted only to reach the Mexican border as soon as possible. Peter watched, helpless, as an old truck containing two cows pulled slowly onto the highway from a rutted side road. There was no one in sight when the farmer started to make his turn into the right lane. Then Enid rounded the bend, doing eighty miles an hour.

Now stop the story, Peter told himself. Start to revise. Enid pulls sharply into the left lane, is safe, does not with a hideous hollow sound crash into the rear of the truck, smashing truck and herself to pieces.

"The driver . . . a farmer . . . suffered concussion but is now conscious and will be all right. The two cows were killed and the injured party will have to be paid for the loss of what was the sum total of his working capital. Naturally I instructed the lawyers to examine with a fine-tooth comb the liability clause which . . ."

For the first time Frederika interrupted. "Had she been drinking?"

Dr. Paulus took a moment to answer. A drop of sweat clung like a tear to his chin. Then he nodded. "The alcoholic level of her urine was eighteen per cent. She must've stopped somewhere on the way and . . ."

Nothing matters now, thought Peter. He shut his eyes; the lids as dry as Dr. Paulus's lips. Over and over he repeated to himself the phrase "it's just as well" which he knew would be constantly sounded in the weeks to come. But it was not just as well, he thought fiercely, opening his eyes. They had murdered her, just as they had intended. He turned to Clay to find that Clay was watching him; the blue eyes wide and clear and knowing. Each knew the other's thought. It *was* just as well.

* * *

The Sanfords and Clay sat in the first row of the crowded church. In the street outside people had gathered, strangers attracted if not by the tragedy at least by potential scandal. Inside the church, though all the magnates were on hand to comfort Blaise, there were not many of Enid's old friends, those bright girls and boys of before the war who had danced at Chevy Chase, hunted near Warrenton, swum at Rehobeth Beach, got drunk at Middleburg; a golden company whose every movement was, in Peter's memory at least, underscored by popular music. Resplendent youths in white duck made love to bright girls in flowery dresses and for what had seemed forever it was summer; then the deep purple did indeed fall and the war killed some while those who survived changed, married, grew older and the music which had gone round and round stopped, and for Enid had come out here.

They rose and sang, "A Mighty Fortress Is Our God!" Peter joined in the singing, anything to distract himself from looking at the coffin and imagining what it contained. Better to contemplate the quick as they brooded upon the dead. Elizabeth Watress sat between Millicent Smith Carhart and her mother. The three ladies, all in black, resembled the Norns as they sat in the front row across from the Sanfords. Once Elizabeth glanced at Clay but he did not respond; he sat, eyes lowered, like a good boy told not to squirm in public. Beside him sat his daughter, fascinated by the display. From time to time she looked up curiously at her grandmother who wept without a sound, behind a black veil. Blaise, vague and disassociated, twice dropped his hymnal and each time Clay retrieved it for him.

Then the minister said Enid's name and Peter suddenly found himself staring at the coffin. But the lid is really a door, he told himself; slowly, like an idiot, he repeated the thought over and over to himself. A door. A door. Now open the door, the heavy metal door. *I found you, Enid, come on out. Why? They'll never find us here. But what about the game? To hell with the game. There's no air. We'll suffocate. You are yellow, aren't you? Anyway, it's empty, thank God. Remember all those wild turkeys they brought back from Aiken? And every time you took a bite there'd be a mouthful of shot! Come on, you want to, don't you?* The door slammed, with a heavy sound of air being both compressed and expelled. The car crashed into the truck.

"Lord, let me know mine end, and the number of my days; that I may be certified how long I have to live. Behold thou hast made my days as it were a span long, and mine age is even as nothing in respect of thee; and verily every man living is altogether vanity."

Outside the church, black limousines lined Lafayette Square. The coffin was already in the hearse when Peter stepped out into daylight and saw Diana, who said, "It's awful, isn't it?" To which there was no answer but "Yes, it is."

Sky sunless; grass brown; trees bare of leaves and empty of birds. A cold wind circulated among the mourners. But Peter was beyond any notice of the day or of the company for at the back of his eyes he had begun to feel pain while in his chest something harsh and loud demanded utterance. Then as the coffin was lowered into the freshly dug trench, the world was veiled; his eyes burned with salt. Fortunately, the minister's office of the dead was spoken in a voice so deliberately beautiful that Peter was able to stifle easily the animal cry within.

"He cometh up, and is cut down, like a flower; he fleeth as it were a shadow, and never continueth in one stay."

When it was all done, not wanting to speak to anyone or be looked at, Peter broke away from the mourners and hurried back to the car, where a man he had never seen before stood waiting.

"I'm Al Hartshorne." Peter allowed his hand to be shaken. The man was small, easy to overlook. A lawyer, he told Peter; a friend of Enid's. "In fact, I was going to handle the divorce for her."

"Yes, I remember her saying something about it . . .

about you." Peter wished the others would hurry up and rescue him from a conversation he did not want. But the funeral party was some distance away, moving slowly among stone crosses and marble angels, a dark straggling company.

"Poor kid. She had the lousiest luck. When they put her away like that, she told me you were the only one who stood up for her, the only one."

"Well, it's over." Peter wanted to sound harsh, and succeeded.

The lawyer looked at him with some surprise. "But I don't think it is. That husband of hers is still alive."

Peter was jolted into consciousness by the unexpected ferocity of a man he had assumed would say no more than what was expected and decently go away. "Of course he's still alive." In the middle distance, Clay seemed to be supporting Frederika, who needed no support, but they made a touching picture for the photographers, who were as usual present to record each station of Clay's ascent. "Do you suggest we kill him, for Enid's sake?" Peter rounded on the lawyer, as though he were the enemy.

"Well, you admit he killed her, locking her up."

"He wasn't the only one." Peter looked at Blaise, who seemed to be giving the minister detailed instructions, no doubt making suitable arrangements for Enid in the Episcopal paradise.

"*She* thought it was Clay's idea and that Mr. Sanford just went along."

"She must have told you a good deal about us." Ironic understatement: there was no one Enid would not discuss her most intimate affairs with. She must have been entirely candid with her lawyer and possible savior. Apparently mere death would not end her mischief.

"I guess I do feel like one of the family." What had she told him? *All right. I'll shut the door. There's plenty of air.*"

"Anyway I've prepared quite a dossier on the Congressman there."

Beneath a tall monument, Clay dried his daughter's eyes. Ecstatic, the photographers pushed to one side minister, Blaise, Frederika. This was what they had come for. Peter looked away, unable to bear the sight. Also, from where he stood, the child had suddenly, unexpectedly resembled Enid, a miniature Enid who blew her nose beneath a monument to William Kay Rollins . . . whose replica no doubt existed somewhere at this very moment, full of life and blowing its nose, too. The seed continues. Do we? Yes or no? If yes, what monotony. If no, no.

"We had collected a lot of evidence proving adultery. Different girls, the usual sort of thing, but quite a lot of it. He likes to go to bed with two girls at a time. While one waits and watches in one bed, he has the other in the other bed. Then when he's finished . . ."

"Lechery never lost a man a vote."

"I'm sure it has." The lawyer was mild. "But there was something really interesting I found out."

"Not the business about my father and Clay." Peter was irritable at the thought.

"No, nothing like that. I always told Enid I thought she was a bit overboard on that one."

"Enid was a damned fool." Peter astonished himself.

"In some ways." The tone was agreeable. "But we loved her, didn't we?" The question required an answer.

Peter avoided the small bright eyes, so like those of a stuffed bear he had slept with for most of his childhood until one day Enid, to spite him, had thrown it into the river. "Yes, we loved her. What about Clay?"

"I have been in touch with a man who was with Clay in the Philippines. In fact, he was there when all the hero business happened."

Peter anticipated what was next. "And your friend says that Clay was not a hero?"

The lawyer nodded.

"I don't believe it. There must've been a hundred witnesses when Clay carried that man out of the burning hangar."

"The man was dead by the time the medics got to him."

"Clay could still have done what he did. Anyway, you can't prove he didn't."

"But I can. You see, Clay wasn't at the airfield when all this happened."

Holding his daughter's hand, Clay approached the car. Looking at his enemy, Peter refused to believe that he was not a hero. To give meaning to their struggle, Clay must be great and therefore dangerous to the Republic.

Peter demanded proof. According to all the dispatches, Clay had commanded the attack on the airfield.

"He led the attack in the sense that he was commanding officer, yes, but actually he wasn't involved in any of the action because that morning he had cut his foot . . ."

"Cut his foot? For Christ's sake, do better than that!"

"I'm only telling you what I was told by a friend of mine who knows the doctor who was looking after the foot while the attack was going on."

"Then how could he have been decorated, if he wasn't there?"

"He *was* there just at the end. And of course it was his unit that did the fighting."

"Then if he was there at the end he could have carried that man out of the burning hangar." Peter was impatient. "After all, if he was decorated there must've been at least one witness."

"Yes, there was one witness. But only one." The lawyer smiled. "Harold Griffiths."

Mystery solved. He should have guessed the truth from the beginning. "How did they get away with it? Everybody must've known the story was phony."

"Nobody knew for certain except the doctor. In all the confusion, Clay *could* have done what Mr. Griffiths said he did. Besides, Clay was a popular officer. Nobody grudged him the medal."

"Except the doctor in question."

"He doesn't grudge anybody anything. In fact, he'd forgotten about the whole thing until he took his two boys to a drive-in to see that movie they made about Clay and of course he remembered it all and thought it quite a joke, and told his friend of mine who told me."

Clay was now within earshot. His voice carried on

the cold wind. "We'll go straight home, dear. Don't cry. That's a good girl." Then he was beside them.

The lawyer was jaunty. "I'm Al Hartshorne, Congressman. Come to pay my last respects."

"Thank you." Clay helped the child into the car. "I remember you very well," he said in a voice that was perhaps too neutral. He turned to Peter. "You better help your mother."

Peter obeyed him. It seemed the thing to do.

Eight

1

"I HAVE A statement to make."

"Could you start again, Congressman. And step back . . . that's right. There was a shadow across your face. More to the left. That's fine."

The Caucus Room of the Old House Office Building was filled with what looked to be most of the Washington press corps. They were in a friendly mood. There had even been some applause when Clay entered, an uncommon tribute from journalists largely indifferent to minor politicians-on-the-make. But Clay was a favorite. For one thing, writers in need of money could be reasonably certain that Blaise's team of publicists would find a market for almost any article that featured the young congressman. Best of all, the interview itself would be conducted at Laurel House, in the company of handsome girls as well as famous men, off duty and complaisant, like bears in a national park. The golden ambience of Laurel House was particularly attractive to Washington journalists accustomed to the somewhat depressing domestic arrangements of the usual legislator. Even those members of the Congress who were wealthy did not live on the Sanford scale, with yachts and private planes and all the conveniences of large money. The journalists were overwhelmed, as they were meant to be.

Blaise once confided to Clay that though there were men in Washington who could not be bought for a million dollars in cash, there was not one who could resist a week's trip on a yacht in the company of film stars. The winning was seldom permanent, since treason is the essential business of even the most frivolous clerk. But with certain predictable exceptions, the press supported Clay because he was an attractive figure in a profession not noted currently for the charm of its practitioners, witness the First Magistrate, whose folksiness did not appeal even to the mythical folk who had elected him largely because they liked the charmless man with the moustache even less than they liked him. Clay, however, was young, celebrated, with access to the sort of fortune without which no politician can take the prize; or so certain grim commentators maintained, looking upon Truman as an accident in a society where soon only the very rich or those in thrall to the rich could afford to play the exciting game of king-of-the-castle.

Clay knew that his remarkable situation automatically made him Presidential and he was pleased if somewhat surprised to note that the thought of his eventual success caused no resentment, doubtless because it was too far in the future; others would come first. Meanwhile the press favored him, tactfully ignoring the fact that, to date, his political performance was not inspiring. But then the old hands knew that to rise, the ambitious politician must be careful not to do anything that might in any way cause distress or alarm. So far none realized that Clay's dim record was the result not so much of an unzealous temperament as of a conviction that at this moment in the Republic's history the people wanted only to be let alone to watch television and forget the exhausting trials of the recent war. To offer them adventure in their current mood would be disastrous. Later, if required, thunder might roll, lightning flash; and Clay had perfect confidence that when the time came he could make whatever weather the bright days of his primacy required.

Clay stared straight into the blinding television lights, like a sun worshiper certain of the ultimate beneficence of his god. He was pleased to note that on the most important day of his political life he was not in the least nervous. He even enjoyed the lights which obliterated the room, giving him the sense of being entirely alone, except for the recording camera and the impersonal millions.

"All right, Congressman. Let's go."

Clay turned in to the camera's lens and began to speak. He knew the words by heart. The text was

302

careful and sincere, with nothing in it to alarm or inspire. Yet it would set him in motion. "After much deliberation . . . response of friends . . . desire for further service . . . problems that need fresh approach . . . action . . . future . . . I announce my candidacy for the United States Senate."

That was it. No one was surprised. Everyone knew that sooner or later Clay would run for the Senate. Last winter he had made a tour of the state without once setting foot in his own district. That was all the clue the press needed. They predicted that this was Clay's year to move, and he did not disappoint them.

The lights contracted to darkness. He blinked his eyes, saw hands raised to attract his attention.

"Congressman . . . Clay . . . Mr. Overbury . . . I have a question . . . Sir . . ."

The voices mingled, one into the other. He pointed to an arm at the back of the room. He was rewarded with an unfamiliar voice. "Sir, assuming that you're elected to the Senate . . ."

"*I'm* not assuming anything." Amiable laughter. The room was slowly coming into focus. The arm belonged to a stranger. That was bad luck. He had wanted to begin with a planted question.

"Of course, sir. Anyway, *should* you be in the Senate, I would like to know just what your attitude will be to the hearings which are now going on in reference to the charges made by Senator McCarthy as to the exact number of Communists currently employed by the State Department."

Clay had several answers ready, depending upon the way the question was phrased. He began cautiously. "Well, for one thing, I assume that by next November those hearings will have been concluded . . ."

"Even so, sir, what is your position *now?*"

Clay's baritone topped the other's tenor; he knew all the tricks of drowning out other voices without seeming to raise one's own. ". . . concluded and once they are I'm sure the Tydings committee, with all the help it is getting from the FBI, will be able to pinpoint just who is a Communist and who is not and then the Executive will act accordingly." Clay started to recognize a woman in a large hat, but the relentless tenor was again raised.

"That's all very well, Congressman, but I think as candidate for the Senate, you should make your own position crystal clear as to what you think of Senator McCarthy's crusade to rid the Executive Branch of the many Communists who have taken root there during the last twenty years . . ." There were rude murmurings from the liberal journalists, but Clay refused to play up to them. One slip of the tongue and he would be smeared up and down his state as soft on Communism or worse. The issue was hot.

"I'm afraid I don't personally know how many Communists there are in the Executive Branch of the government. But if there are any, I have every confidence that they will be rooted out."

"But how can anybody get at them, unless Democratic Senators like you stand up to the President and those other fellow travelers and *demand* that White House files containing the names of thousands of Communists be released to Senator McCarthy . . ." The tenor suddenly went falsetto. There was mocking laughter from the back of the room.

Clay smiled, off the hook. He was mild. "I honestly can't see the President as a Communist fellow traveler." Nervous laughter. "But if old Harry is traveling anywhere in my direction, why, as Democrat, I'm perfectly willing to give him a lift." There was applause at this necessary piety.

Quickly Clay recognized the nearest arm, realizing too late that it belonged to Sam Biermann, Burden's friend and ally.

"Now, Congressman." The voice was slow and folksy. Clay prepared himself for battle. "You're on record as having said that you didn't intend to run for the Senate at least until 1952, wanting to get, you said . . . I have the exact quote right here . . . 'a maximum of experience in the House of Representatives first . . .' "

"That's right, Sam, I did say that. But how was I to know that I'd get the maximum experience two years ahead of schedule?" Everyone laughed while Clay maintained the poker face of the frontier wit.

Sam did not acknowledge the pleasantry. "You also went on to say, it's right here in the interview . . . that you would never (and now I quote) 'under any circumstances consider challenging Senator Day in a primary because I look upon him not only as my closest political friend but also as what you might call a father, the man who brought me to Washington in the first place.'" Suddenly a man sneezed. The effect was comic but it went unnoticed in the eager silence. Everyone was interested in what the response to this would be.

Clay took his time answering. When he finally spoke, he was careful to give the impression of a man troubled but in the right. "Whatever I said then I will say now. I regard Senator Day as one of the finest men I have ever known and if it hadn't been for him, I might never have got here. All that's true. It's also true that I would never oppose him for anything."

Clay paused; then he took the plunge. "Now I'm not going to speak for him. I haven't the right. But I will say this, though the Senator has not *personally* told me his plans, I have been assured by others that after thirty-six great years in the United States Senate, Burden Day will *not* run again this year."

An explosion of excited talk forced Clay to raise his voice in order to be heard. "Let me repeat. I have entered this race in the firm conviction that James Burden Day will *not* be a candidate for re-election!"

Arms waved. Clay's name was shouted. He pointed to Harold Griffiths.

"Congressman!" Harold Griffiths's voice was clear and proud. The room grew still. Though Harold was the butt of many Washington jokes, none could deny the popularity of his column, in which the West's decline was daily noted and duly mourned. Hardly a day passed that freedom was not about to be irrevocably lost to the Antichrist. For Harold, Armageddon was always imminent and the United States never ready to do battle for the Lord; the once superb American armies long since dispersed by politicians who had been duped by canting liberals, lulled by Eleanor Roosevelt, misled by Chiefs of Staff who systematically betrayed the American fighting man, exchanging that marvelous creation of smooth flesh and hot blood for complex and sophisticated weaponry, as though a mere machine could ever take the place of a well-muscled arm. Harold was happiest at the brink; the vision of a smashed earth informed with agony a syntax of such confident confusion that Peter Sanford had created a new word to define Harold's richly clotted prose, "barococo."

"I think that most of us are agreed that you'd be a fine addition to the Upper House. We need young blood in positions of power. But, sir, assuming you are nominated next month and elected next fall, what will your posture be concerning military appropriations in the light of your own military experience, as holder of the Distinguished Service Cross, while taking into account the current Soviet menace in Europe, particularly to Berlin . . ." Harold filibustered until the first shock of Clay's statement had been somewhat absorbed.

Clay's answer to Harold was nearly as long and ceremonious as the question. More questions followed. The worst seemed over, until a sharp voice said, "Tell us, Congressman, why are you so certain that Senator Day will *not* be a candidate for re-election?"

At the back of the room stood Peter Sanford, large bellied but firm-fleshed, a huge and to Clay entirely mysterious presence. They were enemies, of course. Enid's dying had accomplished that. Yet whenever they met socially, Peter was pleasant and Clay had yet to be the victim of one of those spiky sentences for which his brother-in-law was becoming known, the abrupt and savage saying of the unsayable. Even *The American Idea* had so far treated Clay gently, to the extent that he was noticed at all. But despite all outward signs of amity, it was plain that Peter hated him; a matter of some consolation to Clay, since the man who hates is invariably at a disadvantage, in politics if not in life. Over the years, Clay had disciplined himself to hate no one, with some success.

"Hello, Peter." Clay was casual. "My brother-in-law." Uneasy laughter from those who knew that the two were not friends. Startled, Harold Griffiths stepped back against the wall, as though to protect himself from possible ricochet.

"I asked," said Peter, "what makes you so certain that Senator . . ."

"Now, Peter, you know I can't divulge sources any more than you can or any other journalist. Didn't I say that it wasn't for me to speak for Burden Day? Yet isn't the fact that I'm running proof that he is not a candidate?" That was an error. One must never phrase the weakest argument as a question.

Clay tried to continue but Peter was too quick for him. "No, it doesn't. The only thing it proves is that *you* are running . . ."

"But I would never oppose him."

"But suppose," Peter's voice rose, and Clay allowed it to drown out his own. There was nothing left for him to do but play victim and gain sympathy. "Suppose your information was wrong? Suppose Senator Day *is* a candidate? What will you do then?"

The room was quiet. The risk was great. Clay took it. "Senator Day will not be a candidate for re-election. But," Clay paused. He flung the dice. "If he is a candidate, I shall of course withdraw from the race. Ladies and gentlemen, thank you."

Swiftly Clay crossed to the door. Win or lose, he had made every front page. The press corps was leaving the room as quickly as he.

* * *

"But how do we get out of this?" Blaise was distraught. "Burden *is* running again. You know that. Everybody knows that."

Clay ignored him; he spoke into the receiver. "Look, this is important. You must find the Senator. Yes, I know you have your orders. All right. Ring me back. I'm in Mr. Sanford's office."

Clay put down the receiver, and answered Blaise. "I'll handle him. Don't worry."

"How can you handle him?"

But Clay turned his back on Blaise's wrath and looked out the window at Ninth Avenue, sordid by daylight.

Blaise's voice continued. "It was good strategy to say he *probably* wouldn't run, implying he's sick and old but then to say that you're willing to step aside if he does run when you know perfectly well . . ."

"Peter was there." As Clay spoke, a brightly painted girl stopped two sailors outside the Old Dominion Bar and Grill. "He did the needling. He asked the question which I had to answer. He's trying to make it tough for us, isn't he?" Clay watched Blaise's reflection in the window. Blaise gripped the arms of his chair, like a man anticipating the dentist's drill or a crash landing. "I don't suppose there's anything you can do." Statement, not question.

"No." Blaise was curt. "He does what he likes."

"I see." Clay did not press the point. It was sufficient that he had made it. Meanwhile, the girl went off with one of the sailors while the other sailor went into the bar where Clay had once picked up a girl from Raleigh. They had made love on the sofa in his office. She wore no stockings and wanted no money. Thinking of her, he wished he were the sailor across the street in the bar, free to pick up a girl and make love and not have to listen to Karl, his administrative asistant, who had just entered the room, full of alarm.

"Here's the latest poll."

Clay seized the document. He did not share the old-fashioned politician's aversion to the new science of polling. They feared it because if they were not delicate human instruments uniquely able to forecast the weather of their constituencies, they were nothing, their curious art made irrelevant by statisticians using slide rules. But Clay wanted only to know which issues were hot and which were cold, preferably before anyone else knew. And so, at regular intervals, Blaise's firm of consultants reported on the mood of his constituents; and he was able to respond accordingly. As a result, he was the most popular of the state's delegation to Congress, until now.

"What's wrong?" Blaise turned to the aide. "Is he down?"

"Three points," said Karl. "But that's not the problem . . ."

"Burden's gone up five." Clay slammed the paper onto Blaise's desk. "What happened?" He turned to

308

Karl as though he were responsible. "What's the analysis?"

"We don't know yet. Might've been that speech he gave Monday at the State Historical Society. It was broadcast. Had a lot of impact. I've got a recording if you want to . . ."

"One lousy speech doesn't account for a jump like this. What's the old bastard doing? Where's he been? Who's he been talking to?"

"I don't know exactly . . ."

"But you ought to know exactly. I mean *we* should know exactly." Clay seldom lost his temper with those who worked for him. At worst he tended to take them for granted; a treatment which he knew did not distress the dedicated.

"I guess it's sentimental, what's happening." Karl retrieved the crumpled poll. "He's been Senator since before most of us were born and now he's going around the state, reminding everybody of the good old days."

"No mileage in that," muttered Clay. Over half the electorate did not know that there had been a Depression in the '30s, while a third could not identify either Senator. Most, however, had heard of Clay. Although his film had failed in the country, Blaise had seen to its promotion in the state.

"Judge Hooey just called to say that Burden's definitely going to announce his candidacy over the weekend. If he does . . ."

"I withdraw. Have you got a job for me, Blaise?"

"I'm not sure we want you, after this." Blaise was bewildered; he was also angry that Clay chose not to confide in him. But Clay had no intention of confiding in anyone. At moments of crisis, he preferred to act on his own.

Then Senator Day's office was on the line. When Clay asked, "Where is he?" a hostile voice (was it Dolly Perrine?) said, "The Senator's not coming back to the office. But he will be home for dinner . . ."

"But where is he *now*? This minute?"

"He's at Mrs. Carhart's house but . . ."

2

Could they speak of no one else? Burden readjusted his aching shoulder against the side of the armchair. A very clean break, according to the doctor who had peered down at Burden as he lay on his back in the X-ray room of the hospital to which he had been taken in an ambulance from the scene of the accident, a flight of steps on the Senate side of the Capitol. He had fallen from top stair to bottom and as he did, a bone in his shoulder broke with a crack he could hear through the flesh. In his pain he had a sudden vision of man as vegetable: were not bones twigs? sap blood? and what in nature more resembled a hand than a leaf? Satisfied with this beautiful perception, he had fainted at the foot of the stairs.

* * *

Now five months after the very clean break, he was still in pain. But there was nothing to be done. Once the age of brittle bones splintering began, it would not end until, bedridden from a fall, he would succumb to that swift pneumonia which fills the lungs with water, completing with a drowning the famous cycle that began the day the waters of the womb broke. Better, he decided, to take a gun to one's head and go in flame, though between fire and water he preferred the cooler elements.

Millicent Smith Carhart was undecided about Senator Joseph McCarthy. On the one hand she was convinced that at every level of American life, crypto-Communists were at work (look at the behavior of the Negroes since the war), and yet, "He is such a distasteful man. That dreadful face, those jowls, that voice."

"Don't worry. He won't last." Burden was soothing.

"But one does worry. And he can do such a lot of damage before he's finished." She poured tea. Vapor from the pot briefly obscured her face. Burden thought of oracles. What was it Cicero had said? But he could not recall. Lately whenever he started to quote from memory, the words often failed to come in proper sequence, leaving him with a frustrated sense that a door in his mind was part shut.

"Senator Tydings will finish him off. Remember when Joe said that he would let his case rest or fall on whether or not Owen Lattimore was a Communist? Well, his case fell, thanks to Senator Tydings."

"Oh, I think Lattimore *must* be a Communist, don't you?"

"There is no evidence that he is."

"Yes, but there is none that he is not."

"Now *you* sound like Joe McCarthy."

Millicent frowned. "I know of course that he's probably hurt a good many innocent people, which is terrible, but after all there *are* Communists in the government and they are changing this country and if he can tell us who they are, well, then maybe it's worth a bit of confusion."

"The President," Burden indicated the portrait of her uncle, "would not have agreed with you."

"I'm not so sure. Anyway those were different times. But tell me, what's he really like? I don't dare ask him to the house."

"I hardly know him. Thank God." Burden's aversion to the demagogue was not only political, it was physical. He could not bear the sight of the man. Only once had he actually talked to him. When a journalist wrote that Burden might head the subcommittee which would investigate the Senator's charges that the State Department was full of Communists, McCarthy had come to his office and in front of the bust of Cicero he had thrown a heavy arm about Burden's shoulders and declared, with a tiger's grin, that although they were on opposite sides politically, they were both anti-Communist. "At least I *assume* you are," he added with cheerful menace. Anyway, he was certain that the facts would speak for themselves and, by the way, "Have you seen your ex-son-in-law lately?"

Burden removed himself entirely from the subcommittee. As it was, he would have sufficient trouble in the coming election without being denounced as a Communist. In ordinary times such charges would have been laughed at. But the times had ceased to be ordinary when the Soviet developed an atomic bomb. The fact that such a primitive society could with apparent ease achieve military parity with God's country meant only one thing: the recipe for the bomb had been stolen from Los Alamos and given to the enemy by high-ranking traitors. It was then, quite by accident, that an obscure senator wanting to be re-elected found that to accuse others of treason was the easiest way of becoming a hero to many, a villain to some, a source of interest to all.

Since the first of the year, Burden had received an alarming number of letters from constituents insisting that he openly side with McCarthy in his attack on the State Department. Burden's responses were patriotic but evasive. After all, it was only a matter of time before McCarthy hanged himself; his lunatic performance before the Tydings committee was proof of that. At first the Senator had said that there were two hundred and five Communists in the State Department; then he said there were fifty-seven; as of Friday there were eighty-one. And on he rambled, making charges so wild that it was hardly possible to sort them out, much less refute them. Had it not been for the coming primary, Burden was certain that at some point he would have spoken out against the demagogue. But for the moment it was not possible. Once re-elected, however, there would be plenty of time to do in the mucker, a turn-of-the-century word to which Burden was partial.

"But if what he says is all untrue, why don't some of you Senators try to stop him?"

The door in Burden's mind suddenly swung open. He quoted: " 'He would learn that to accuse and prove are very different; and that reproaches unsupported by evidence affect only the character of him that observes them.' "

"Who said that?" But even as she spoke, the door shut again upon a lifetime's treasure. He was saved by one of the gray maids who announced that Congressman Overbury was on his way to Dupont Circle to speak to the Senator, if it was all right with Mrs. Carhart. Permission granted, the maid departed.

"What is happening?" asked Millicent.

Burden shrugged. The pain in his shoulder came and went. "Clay has just announced that he'll enter the primary next month, *if* I don't run again."

"But you will run, won't you?" Millicent was alarmed. The saddest aspect of being "permanent" in Washington was the abrupt way friends had of disappearing, turned out by voters. She had once told Burden that in her youth she had enjoyed the constant comings and goings, particularly as viewed from the White House. But now that she was old she wanted no change of any kind, including death, which she regarded as the ultimate electorate, withdrawing one by one and in capricious order its favorite sons.

"Of course I will run. And win." But Burden was by no means certain that he could beat Clay, despite the excellent response to his speech before the Historical Society. In a curious way, as his power in Washington diminished, his constituents' affection for him increased. It was as if they had come to realize that he was the last surviving link with their crude yet hopeful origins. He represented, if not them, their past, and when he went they would be marooned entirely in a present that puzzled them in a way that the past, as viewed with sentiment, did not. Oh, the old warrior still had a string or two to his bow, he thought grandly, but the effort of bending the bow was great and his vision was not what it had been.

"But why would Clay say such a thing?"

"We shall soon find out." At first Burden had not believed Mrs. Blaine when she told him what Clay had said. He had asked her to repeat the exact text. He then told her to summon his administrative assistant from what was to have been a quiet weekend in the country.

"Lucy despises him, you know." Millicent stared thoughtfully into her cup, reminding him of . . . what was her name who read cards, tea leaves? "All hail Burden Day, king-to-be!" He had finally given her up when it was plain to everyone except the cards that he would not be President. Mrs. Foskett. A smell of cabbage in the hall. The garden party for the King and

Queen. The heat. "Because of Elizabeth. You know Lucy's daughter, don't you, by Schuyler Watress?"

Burden nodded, recalling white skin, long dark eyes: to be young like Clay, to have women; nothing else mattered.

"Well, while Enid was still alive but put away, he saw Elizabeth constantly, but then the moment Enid was dead, he dropped her."

"A bad conscience perhaps." That of course was what people used to say. Now of course hardly anyone even pretended to worry about right and wrong. Today's man knew no motive but interest, acknowledged no criterion but success, worshiped no god but ambition. Clay was most suitable for the times.

"I don't know what *he* felt, but Elizabeth was heartbroken. She's engaged now, you know, to a boy from New York. So all's well, though Lucy says . . ."

Comfortably they talked of Clay and Elizabeth, of marriage and divorce, of the old Washington and the new. They even spoke of Diana and Peter. Tactfully, Millicent did not mention marriage. Burden said that he liked Peter very much. Millicent thought him sharp-tongued and arrogant. Burden said that was merely the fashion. Nowadays journalists dismissed those who actually governed as freaks, entertainers, fools. What Mencken had begun, they gaily continued. There was no one they did not patronize. Only the week before, Harold Griffiths had dismissed the President as a man of no intelligence, entirely dominated by his Secretary of State, a dilettante lawyer with a bad tailor. This sort of attack was infinitely more deadly than the thundering partisan insults of earlier times. Fortunately, few columnists were quite as pompous as Harold Griffiths or as politely savage as Peter's magazine, which, paradoxically, was read almost exclusively by its numerous victims. Yet Burden was more pleased than not with the success of *The American Idea* because it gave Diana something to do. Her relations with Peter were mysterious to him. Recently, when he had suggested that some day she might want to settle down and have children, she had said, "But Father, I don't like children." Overwhelmed by her candor, he had almost con-

fessed that he disliked them, too. But of course he had
not disliked her, or very seldom.

Then arm in arm, Mr. Carhart and Clay entered the
dusty drawing room. "Look," said Mr. Carhart, "at this
young fellow I found lurking in the hall."

"Not just any young fellow. I'm your cousin, remember?" Not without charm, Clay recalled a genealogical
connection which so delighted Mr. Carhart that he was
all for taking Clay into the study for a look at what
he referred to as "The Tree" but what Millicent called
"The Forest of Disastrous Connection." For each sovereign or celebrity discovered amongst those myriad
branches, a thousand thieves and murderers, Jews and
Moslems blossomed thickly in the far reaches of a
dynasty which, traced back far enough, would necessarily include the entire human race, making Mr. Carhart, mad with pedigree, a reluctant saint to whom all
men were, demonstrably, cousins.

"Now don't bore Mr. Overbury, dear. He's come to
talk to Burden, not us."

Clay was diffident. "It's awfully rude, my coming
here like this, uninvited . . ."

"Our Cousin Clay . . . or rather *my* Cousin Clay . . .
is always welcome." Mr. Carhart looked at Clay fondly,
as though he were already hung from a branch, a box
drawn around him like a mandala. Millicent maneuvered her husband to the door. "Let us know when we
can come back."

Burden's shoulder hurt. He twisted against the cushions until the pain lessened. Clay remained standing
beneath the President's portrait. He looked unusually
vigorous and self-confident, thought Burden, recalling
his own early self and wondering what would have
happened if the two young men had met. Which would
have conquered?

"I suppose you've heard what I said at the press
conference?"

Burden nodded. For the moment he chose to listen.

"The question was asked, incidentally, by Peter Sanford."

Burden nodded, amused at the thought of son and
son-in-law in fierce combat, with Blaise as battlefield.
Between those two it was difficult to say which would

win. Clay of course had already seized Blaise, but then Peter probably did not consider that a loss. Frowning thoughtfully, Clay sat on a bench and began to play with the teakwood handle of the teapot. He explained himself at length, saying nothing at all. He ended with, "You see, I really thought that with your health the way it is you wouldn't want to run."

Burden sat up straight. Pain shot through his shoulder but he bore it stoically. He was not ill, not old. "My health?" he exclaimed, as though the phrase were strange. "But I'm in excellent health."

"Well, there was the stroke you had that day with Mrs. Bloch."

Well played, thought Burden coldly: *with Mrs. Bloch*. He would remember that. "I fainted. I recovered. I am well."

"Of course you are. For a man your age, you're remarkably . . ."

"I am not yet a hundred!" Burden growled and Clay let go the teapot's handle, as though it had burned him. "I am perfectly capable of serving one more term in the United States Senate, and I intend to, as you know."

"Honestly, I did not know." Clay looked at him, eyes wide. "Anyway, let's say I was misinformed."

"You were misinformed. I had planned to file next Thursday, but since your . . . astonishing announcement, I will announce my candidacy tomorrow, too late for the weekend edition but . . ." He smiled as though to say the incumbent does not need the Sunday papers. "After that I suppose it's all academic. I mean you'll have to withdraw, won't you?"

Just as the blow fell, Burden recalled: I am willing to know the whole truth; to know the worst, and to provide for it. Who in the name of heaven said that? For a moment Burden wrestled with the door to memory; pried it open sufficiently to see another passage, written in letters of fire: He was accused of taking bribes, a charge to which he pleaded guilty. His disgrace followed, and he passed the last years of his life in retirement. So it befell the brilliant Sir Francis Bacon.

Now Burden's own trial was at hand. He looked at

his prosecutor and felt affection. At this moment Clay seemed entirely young and vulnerable, not to mention boyishly eager, for if Burden were to say the right word, Clay's rise would be effortless; the wrong word and, like a torrent, mud would engulf them both and Clay might lose forever that lovely momentum which had brought him to the point where one could declare without witchly exaggeration that he was indeed king-to-be.

Burden smiled, meaning to disarm. "You want this very much, don't you?"

His challenge was quick. "Didn't you?"

Burden nodded. "But not at any price."

Clay looked at him with what seemed genuine surprise. "Is *this* such a high price to pay?"

Burden winced involuntarily. The truth was as unbearable as it was unalterable. He had accepted a bribe. He had been found out. He deserved to be punished. But not by Clay, unless hell was a fact. "It is a bad beginning for you."

"And a bad end for you. That's why it ought to be avoided." The pause was stagy but the intent was no doubt sincere.

"You waited for such a long time." Burden chose to marvel at Clay's farsightedness. And it was marvelous to be able to arm secretly in such a way that when war came, one's unsuspecting victim was rapidly blitzed, undone, in this case, by a weapon of his own making.

"I never intended to make any use of . . ." Again a sentence unfinished, out of delicacy no doubt. After the brutal hammering, lay the corpse gently in its grave.

"But you have. Or mean to."

"I must. You understand that."

"Is it really possible that for ten years you've had all this prepared, just in case?" It was the long smiling deception which most astonished.

Clay did not lie, a bad sign. "Yes, just in case."

"Still waters . . ."

"Don't run at all." Clay laughed. It was an old joke between them. Burden smiled at his assassin. He had

317

treated Clay as a son who would, as was proper in legend, strike him down and take his high place.

"Did you talk to Ed Nillson about this at the time?" Burden was surprised to find himself so curious about details.

"Yes. He paid off the Congressman who gave me the recording, and told me not to bother you."

"I wish you had." Burden was wry.

"You know, I was pretty innocent in those days." Clay was suddenly confiding. Even *in extremis* their old manner with one another was maintained. "I couldn't believe that you'd ever do such a thing."

Burden shut his eyes, looked for death beneath the lids; saw instead his father's face. Victory at last! The envied son broken and dishonored. The Confederate corporal had triumphed, as each had known he would from the day the boy had said to the man, "I will succeed," and the man had said, "You're crooked enough, that's true, with your weasel words and bending ways. Why not be President? It would serve the country right. All thieves, all liars, the lot of them! Oh, you'll go far." To which the boy had answered, "I will go far because I'm not weak like you. I don't complain. I'll win, in my own way." Derisive laughter: "A whore's way. Well, take it. Why not? Me, I prefer to be my own man, with my own wounds . . ." "Damn your wounds!" "Duly damned, Mr. President. Now you go to hell!"

To hell he went and the devil sat opposite him, forcing him to recall how he had done what he had said he would never do. Worse, the whoring had been in vain.

Clay continued to confide. "I thought it was absolutely impossible. There you were, the most incorruptible man in the Senate, or so I thought. That's why at first I just couldn't believe it. But then I saw how it made sense. That year was your year to go for the top. And we had to have money. And where else could you get so much so fast?"

Deliberately Burden jammed his bad shoulder against the arm of the chair. Pain came and went in long exquisite waves but, unaffected and undiminished, the true agony continued.

"After that, I must say I really admired you. The way you were always able to maintain your image of being some sort of political saint, too good to be true, while there you were . . ."

It must stop. "I'm glad you really admired me." Burden intended irony, achieved pathos. Started again. "Well, all that's in the past, isn't it?"

"At the moment it's in the past." For the first time Clay threatened.

"Millicent!" Burden's voice sounded harsh to his own ears, a Promethean cry; the vulture's beak was at his heart.

Millicent entered. "Can we come in?"

"Yes," said Burden. Painfully he started to get to his feet. Clay ran to help him, took his arm. It was like old times.

3

"Now I should like to say a word to this committee, composed as it is of highly . . . perhaps even *alarmingly* representative Americans. It has been my observation that your interest in maintaining political conformity, though no doubt sincere, is subordinate to your collective . . . if you will forgive the word . . . passion for publicity. After all, politics is the only profession in which mediocrities can gain the world's attention through slander."

The committee chairman beckoned to the sergeant-at-arms. "Get him out of here." Another committee member shouted, "He's in contempt of Congress!"

But Peter would not budge. Coolly he continued: "Gentlemen, you invited me here to discuss Communism and that is what I mean to do. As we all know, Communists have infiltrated the White House, the Pentagon, the schools, the press, the churches, the movies. They are everywhere, secretly dismantling the Republic. Now what is to be done? How can we stop this dread rot at the core of our society? I have a solution. Every citizen must swear a *daily* oath of allegiance to the flag. In this way we can soon discover who is a good American and who is not, for, as we all know, agents of the Soviet prefer death to swearing allegiance to our somewhat busy flag. Once identified, the enemy can then be deported to Russia, allowing the FBI to return to its proper task, which is giving the niggers a hard time.

"Now, let us ponder the struggle for men's minds outside the land of the free. The Communists offer a Utopian vision which is particularly attractive to two types: the ignorant and the degenerate. In fact, since for statistical purposes all ignorant dupes and sexual degenerates are *ipso facto* Communists we may then assume that *any* sexual degenerate is by definition not only an ignorant dupe but a Communist or at the very least a fellow traveler. Since the Senate has established that all State Department personnel are homosexual, it can hardly surprise us that they are simultaneously ignorant dupes as well as Communists in need of rooting out. The fact that the Senator himself has a penchant for young men . . . the word 'penchant' comes from the French and means . . ."

"Here's his testimony. What the hell are you doing?" Aeneas entered the room just as Peter was playfully wagging his finger under the chairman's nose.

"I was," said Peter, "talking to myself."

"About what?"

"The subject varies. Just now, I was making a speech to the House Un-American Activities Committee."

"That's as close as you'll ever come to giving it. You'll take the Fifth, like everyone else, except our friend Billy Thorne. He sang like a bird. Here." Aeneas tossed the testimony into the bed where Peter lay, propped up by pillows, the proofs of a dozen articles strewn about him. He spent half the day in bed, working, telephoning, receiving the staff of *The American Idea,* whose offices were on the first floor of the large house he had bought for himself and the magazine in a Negro slum.

To date Peter's neighbors had shown not the slightest interest in the magazine's attempts to call attention to their sad lot. If anything, Peter and his friends were suspected of holding orgies. Why else would white folks want to hide out in a respectable Negro community? Most of his white contemporaries tended to agree with their dark brothers. At best they thought Peter eccentric in having, as they regarded it, declassed himself. Yet despite the ambivalence of his social position, Peter found his native city more than ever diverting. The politics enraged and delighted him. He also enjoyed observing the way time so shaped acquaintances that each resembled a vast novel-in-progress with numerous chapters one had to skim or guess at, since only a few pages at a time could ever be carefully studied; yet it was upon such slight evidence (most dangerous for the critic!) that the quality of the whole was judged.

Aeneas fortunately was a book he could read at leisure. Interest in politics revived by McCarthy, Aeneas now divided his time between Washington, where he helped put out the magazine, and New York, where he lived with a child psychologist who lisped. He never stopped writing. Recently he had created a stir by declaring that since the liberal community is, by definition, masochist, there must at all times be a sadist to wield the scourge. This meant that McCarthy was entirely necessary, even admirable, since interacting liberals and McCarthyites could re-create society, something to be desired. Though Peter profoundly disliked this sort of emotional writing, he realized that it had great appeal in an age that worshiped passion, and he suspected that as time passed the division was bound to widen between the many who felt and the few who thought—or was it, he sometimes wondered, simply between those who thought they were feeling and those who felt they were thinking? Pondering the radical, he examined Billy Thorne's testimony.

At the committee's invitation, Mr. Thorne had agreed to testify. He had also agreed to waive the Fifth Amendment because, in the words of the committee's counsel, he wanted "to make a clean breast of it." And he did. In the course of twenty pages of testimony, he had named everyone he had known in the government who was or might have been a Communist.

Peter let the testimony drop upon the sheeted swelling of his stomach.

"Why?" He turned to Aeneas, who had folded himself neatly into the chair beside the bed and was reading the nearest galley proof. The true literary man will read anything rather than read nothing.

"He wants a job."

"Who would hire him? The government won't. Certainly not after this."

"They might. Anyway, other people will. All you have to do nowadays is say you're sorry and accuse others. Confess and prosper. Did you see what he says about us?"

Peter nodded. His eye had gone first to his own name. "I'm a dupe. You are a fellow traveler. But we are not Commies, as far as he knows. I would never have thought it of him." Absently Peter patted his large stomach, as though it were a good dog. "If ever there was a martyr it was Billy Thorne."

This of course was precisely the sort of statement that Aeneas could turn to advantage. "But don't you see? He *will* be a martyr. Hated by his own kind. Traitor, Judas Iscariot, stool pigeon. If you want to suffer, and he does . . ."

". . . a true liberal," said Peter helpfully.

". . . what better way to achieve total pain than . . ."

From the street there was the sound of a shot. "Now they're firing at us!" Peter pulled the sheet to his chin.

Aeneas crossed to the window and looked out. "I see no guns. Must have been a car's exhaust."

"Is the man still there?"

Aeneas nodded.

"What's he wearing today?"

"A top hat and a red, white, and blue vest like Uncle Sam."

"Nice. What does the sign say?"

" 'Commies live here.' That's the first line. Then right under that, 'Go home to Russia, if you don't like the U.S.A.' "

"I don't think he's as nice as he looks," said Peter thoughtfully. "You'd think he'd have something better to do than picket us."

"Sometimes I think the mad will win." Aeneas

turned back into the room. "You should see the mail this morning. One letter was written on toilet paper. It had been used."

"Eloquent."

"By and large, anal erotics tend to be crypto-fascists, with the possible exception . . ."

Diana came into the room. "Peter, I've got to talk to you. I'm sorry, Aeneas."

When Aeneas had gone, Diana sat on the edge of Peter's bed. It was as if they had been married twenty years.

"What's wrong?"

"Everything!" She picked up Billy's testimony.

"Is it Billy?"

"Good Lord no! It's Father. I didn't know about Clay's press conference until this morning when I read the paper. Naturally, I went straight to the house and there was Mother with the press, babbling away because Father wouldn't see them."

Diana folded Billy Thorne's testimony in half and then in quarters; an attempt to fold it into eighths failed. "I found him sitting on a bench in the garden. When I spoke to him he didn't even hear me, didn't see me."

"He looked suddenly very old," Peter said to himself, getting what he thought was the range. But apparently the Senator was simply distracted. "Actually he seemed quite cheerful. Then when I asked if it was true, what Clay had said, he . . . he . . ."

"He said it was?"

Diana nodded and Peter realized that what at first he took to be grief was healthy rage. "He said he'd thought it over and decided that there was really no point in serving another term which could lead nowhere since he was out of the running for President. He said he was tired of the Senate and he wanted to make some money before it was too late, since I was . . ."

"Clearly never going to marry again."

"Thanks." Diana flicked his stomach with her forefinger. "But he wouldn't tell me why he was giving up."

"Perhaps he did. It's quite possible to be tired of the Senate. I am."

323

"It's the only thing he cares about." She frowned. "Clay's done something to him."

"What could he do?"

"I don't know. A threat . . . something. I thought for a moment it might be the . . . the Ed Nillson business."

"But all that was quite innocent, wasn't it? Nillson didn't even go to jail."

"But innocence doesn't mean a thing if you *seem* to be guilty."

"Appearance is all, substance nothing." Peter's favorite theme: he ticked it off mechanically. Then: "Will he change his mind?"

"No. He'll announce his retirement on Monday. And that will be that." Then she wept and Peter comforted her, thinking hard.

At last Diana wiped her eyes on the sheet. "You really ought to get up. It's demoralizing the way you lie in bed half the day."

"But I get bored just standing around. In bed, I can think, scheme, plot, and I am doing that even as I dry your tears with Kleenex."

"How I hate Clay!" The passion was unexpected.

Peter studied her thoughtfully, wondering what she really felt. Then he put her to the test. "I can keep him from being elected."

Diana looked at him with red eyes.

"Do you think I ought to?"

"Yes." The flatness of her response was reassuring.

"So do I." Peter was thoughtful. "It will crush my father."

Even in her pain, Diana smiled. "Isn't that what you want?"

Peter laughed. "Yes, I suppose that is what I want. Denied a father's love, I have also been denied a father's hate. Now I can achieve it. Poor man."

"You will. He loves Clay." She got to her feet and crossed to the mirror.

"How do you mean that?" Peter studied her suspiciously.

"It's plain that he does." She rearranged her hair, with swift gestures.

"So Enid thought."

324

"I don't mean physically, at least I don't think I do. I never know about those things. But it is not natural for one man to involve himself so completely in another's career that he sacrifices his own daughter, not to mention . . ." Diana was prepared to continue at some length on the subject of Blaise. But Peter was not. He flung back the sheet and sat up slowly, pleasantly aware of the huge body that gave the appearance of unusual physical strength. A false impression for which he was grateful, since he was a physical coward: he would go to any length to avoid pain, to outwit death. As a result of this natural cowardice, he had redressed the balance of his own temperament by the constant exercise of a moral courage that made it altogether too easy for him to be unpopular in a good cause.

"Let us behave ethically, as well as historically." He pulled off his pajama top.

"What does *that* mean?" She put down her comb.

He pushed a book at her, open to the page where he had checked the sentence "History has to do with results; motives and intentions are the business of ethics." "Kirkegaard. It's always nice when a writer in fashion has something useful to say."

He picked up the telephone and buzzed for his secretary in the office below, and told her to ring Al Hartshorne.

"Who is Al Hartshorne, and what are you doing?"

"He is a lawyer, and I am behaving historically."

"You're certain that what you're going to do will defeat Clay?"

Peter nodded, and let the trousers of his pajamas fall to the floor.

"You look," said Diana, "like a Japanese wrestler."

"Tell Aeneas that the search for identity has ended."

In the shower, beneath hard-driving water, he began to compose sentences in his head.

4

Blaise adjusted the knob of the television set. A hollow voice filled the room: ". . . beyond the Han River. Meanwhile, Communist units have already crossed the thirty-eighth parallel and the army of the Republic of Korea is reported to be in full retreat. This afternoon President Truman will meet with the National Security Council and it is expected that he will . . ."

"He'll back down. The American people won't fight!" Bitterly Harold Griffiths addressed the television commentator, as though he were somehow responsible for the decadence of a nation.

"It is known that General MacArthur favors direct American intervention in Korea . . ."

"Thank God for Mac!" Harold was cheered by this bright counterpoint to the announcer's solemn theme.

"In the light of Tuesday's U.N. Security Council resolution, the free world is now committed to render such assistance to the Republic of Korea as may be necessary to repel armed attack. However, not until the President's press conference this evening will we know to what extent American forces will be used . . ."

"Turn it down, Blaise." Clay was peremptory. Other things came before a mere Asiatic war. Blaise obediently turned off the sound, just as General MacArthur appeared on the screen; a long dyed lock of hair was carefully plastered across the bald high curve of his head, giving the general the look of an aging roué attempting to recreate with cosmetics the appearance of a loving youth.

Clay motioned to Karl, who stood beside Blaise. "Show them the press reaction from back home."

Karl gave Blaise a thick manila folder. Without a glance, Blaise passed it on to Harold, who studied the press clippings, intently searching for his own name.

"I suppose," said Clay, "that it could be worse."

Harold looked up, stricken. "I'm being called a liar, do you realize that? Right here it says . . ."

"Yes, Harold." Clay was patient. "I am also thought to be a liar, as well as a fraud."

"I could sue for libel. I'll *have* to sue for libel." Harold stopped suddenly, no doubt aware that the object of his suit would be his employer's son. For a moment Clay found himself enjoying the situation. But Harold was not without ingenuity. "You know who's really behind this, Burden Day."

Blaise looked at him blankly. Harold continued, "He and that daughter of his persuaded Peter to write all this. It's just the sort of thing that that old crook . . ."

Clay stopped Harold with a gesture. "Relax," he murmured. He suspected that Harold knew not only about Nillson and Burden but also about his own dealings with Burden. Fortunately Harold was, like it or not, his permanent ally. "Actually the press back home," Clay observed judiciously, "isn't as bad as I thought it would be. Those papers that support Democrats say this is just a smear . . ."

"Which it is!" Harold's voice was loud. "Unfortunately, most of the papers in that God-forsaken state of yours are Republican and they . . ."

"They'll never let the voters forget that I am a fraud. That's quite true." Clay was pleased that he could say the worst about himself without distress or shyness.

"Which you are not!" Harold struck the press clippings with the flat of his hand; much too vehement, thought Clay, who observed mildly, "That is our story anyway."

Clay saw Karl smile; and he wondered what Karl really thought. When Peter's story had first appeared, the reaction of the staff was one of shock and indignation. But then, as the days passed, Clay detected a change. It was plain that questions were being asked, and the fact that they were meant that he was in serious trouble.

Peter's attack had been shrewd. Ostensibly he was writing not about Clay but about the uses of money and publicity in politics. He cited a number of national legends which were, he maintained, the cold-blooded

327

creation of men whose usual work was the selling of commodities on television. Then, almost casually, he discussed the buildup of Clay. He paid tribute to Clay's natural charm and political dexterity. He did point out that Clay had accomplished nothing in the House of Representatives, but he added fairly that this might be more the fault of the system than of the man. Nevertheless, though Clay had done nothing for which he could be admired, he was universally regarded as one of the most important young politicians in the United States. Peter asked why and then answered his own question. Money was being spent in large sums to sell a product, and so far the sales campaign had been a success. Through the press, which could always be bought in subtle ways, and through television, where time is literally for sale, a man as personable as Clay could be entirely recreated to fit whatever image of leadership the electorate at the moment desired. Peter then revealed what the researchers had decided was the 1950 ideal in politicians and he demonstrated how Clay had been made to seem youthful but not callow, conservative but not reactionary, religious, but not zealous, and though a widower (a bit of tragedy always enhances a legend) a loving father, as witness the countless pictures of Clay with his daughter at Laurel House, playing games, riding horseback, walking hand in hand through the poison ivy of the Potomac Heights. Then, almost as an afterthought, Peter revealed what had really happened at the Lingayen Airfield.

". . . called me a liar. It's plain slander . . ."

Clay cut Harold short. "You'll survive. Don't worry. No one expects the truth from the press. The problem is how I get off the hook."

"Because politicians are expected to be honest?" Harold took his revenge.

Blaise glared at him. "We're all involved in this. You wrote the story. I published it and Clay . . . well, he's the one who has to fight a tough election."

"It would help," said Clay to the television set which now showed the Secretary of State getting out of a long limousine, "if we could sue *The American Idea*." For a long moment no one answered. Harold and Karl

328

were embarrassed. Blaise stared wretchedly at the floor. Clay waited patiently. When he saw Blaise had nothing to say, he continued. "I know it's difficult to sue your own son. But then, if you agreed, I would be the one to bring suit."

"Could you win it?" Blaise looked at him as if he were asking quite a different question.

"I can certainly prove damages if I lost the election. But by then, of course, it would all be academic. We'd never actually go to court."

It was Karl who came to the point. "Everything depends on this doctor who says you weren't at the airfield during the action . . ."

"*Clay was there.*" Harold set his jaw until he resembled General MacArthur, who once again had flashed onto the television screen; hawk's profile against a stormy sky.

Now that Peter was no longer the issue, Blaise was himself again. "I don't think we'll have much trouble throwing a scare into the doctor."

"Could we get a denial?" asked Karl.

"Why not?" Blaise was brisk. "I know one of the trustees of the doctor's clinic. He's promised to bring pressure to bear. Don't worry."

"But the damage is done." Harold was gloomy. "One way or the other, we all look cheap as hell."

Unfortunate phrase, thought Clay, as a secretary brought him the latest poll. As of today, he would lose to the Republican candidate by eight per cent.

"What's the bad news?" asked Blaise. Not wanting to answer, Clay switched on the television's sound. For a moment he listened to the voice: ". . . yesterday's resolution by the House of Representatives that the draft be extended for another year was passed unanimously by the Senate. Senator Taft, however, complained that the President was usurping the powers of Congress by committing the United States to what, in effect, is war . . ."

Decision made, Clay turned to Blaise, and for the first time that day, he smiled.

The false-hearty voices and over-affectionate gestures of embarrassed men made painful Burden's now infrequent visits to the Senate cloakroom. To his colleagues as well as to himself, he was already on the outside, his place in the world usurped by a younger man.

For thirty-six years Burden had watched men come to the Senate and go, and if the going was involuntary, it was always unbearably sad. As he had been to others, they were now to him: affectionate but clumsy and altogether inadequate in the presence of the common nightmare, a career's end. Once he had given up all hope of the Presidency, he had taken it for granted that he would remain in the Senate until his death, a touching tableau which would take place on a leather sofa in the cloakroom, surrounded by friends to whom he would address a few final remarks, for the *Record*. But unless he were to die before January, this dream was ended, too. He was finished; he would never return, and everyone knew it. They also knew that he had somehow been forced out of the race by Clay. Fortunately, none suspected the truth, and he could at least depart with honor intact.

The cloakroom was crowded, and for the first time in weeks, Burden was no longer the sole object of pity. The day before had been the first Tuesday after the first Monday in November, and during that day the sovereign people had voted.

"It's hair-raising," said one Senator. "Never seen anything like it." He pulled Burden into the group. "You're lucky, getting out, still undefeated champion."

With awe, they spoke of Senator McCarthy. Until now, The Club had not taken him seriously, regarding his publicity as a kind of theatre. Now they realized to what extent they had underestimated him. He had campaigned against his Senate enemies, and he had been victorious. Even the majority leader of the Senate had gone down in defeat.

"The dirtiest campaign in the history of politics," declaimed an elderly Senator, famed for the savagery of his tongue.

"The people are nuts on this Communism thing. Calling Tydings a Communist!" Heads shook at the thought.

"Perhaps," said Burden, "the time has come to take a stand." But the time, apparently, was not yet at hand. If Tydings could be defeated, no Senator was safe. The people were in an irresponsible mood and the wise man did his best to soothe and humor them by seeming to agree that the war in Korea was going badly because of traitors at home. It was a somber time in the country's history, and Burden was delighted. If he must fall, why not the Republic, too? Broken marble where the Capitol was, scorched skulls among the tangled grass of uncut lawns. Glorious vision!

Momberger entered the cloakroom from the Senate floor. He signaled Burden.

"Lousy news." That was the apparent consensus. With some passion the two colleagues denounced the electorate. Neither really blamed McCarthy. When the people went mad, there would always be someone to incite them to greater follies. McCarthy could not be held responsible; the beast was simply true to itself, and could not be otherwise.

"But it was a near thing for Clay." Momberger gave Burden a sheet of figures. "Final figures, county by county."

Burden studied the list of counties, *his* counties; he knew each one as if it was his own child, knew how it had voted for forty years, knew why, could judge with some accuracy how it would vote. The numbers on the page represented not just an abstract electorate but friends and allies, enemies and detractors. He took some satisfaction in the narrowness of Clay's victory: a plurality of twenty-two hundred and four votes out of more than a million cast.

"We damned near lost the state." Momberger looked grim; in two years' time he himself would have to face the same voters.

Burden was soothing. "There's nothing here to worry you. In two years McCarthy will be gone."

"I'm not so sure. And just look what he did to Tydings and Benton and Lucas. Why, he chewed 'em blood raw." Momberger's frontier phrases had been acquired, Burden knew, not on the frontier but from a thousand Western novels read during a Pawtucket, Rhode Island, childhood. Now of course Jesse was so venerable that people assumed that he had indeed traveled with Davy Crockett, known Pat Garrett, and dealt as an equal with the brothers James. Of the Senators, Burden alone knew Momberger's secret.

"You would have made a better race, you old fool! Why in hell didn't you run?" Momberger looked at him narrowly, head slightly cocked, eyes half shut against the desert's glare.

"Oh, Jesse . . ." Burden sighed. He had given out so many stories now that he had forgotten which one he had confided to Momberger. Officially, of course, he was leaving the Senate because he felt that the time had come for him to cease to be an actor and join the audience. Unfortunately, the suspicious probings of others had encouraged him to elaborate. There were, he intimated, books to be written, universities to be taught at, a Federal judgeship to be filled, and of course money to be made for the first time in his life. In the last few months he had hinted at everything from a fatal illness to a lifelong desire to be Ambassador to Ireland (this madness he had confided to an intimate of the Secretary of State, and he writhed at the thought of what that worthy must think of his pretensions, for he was not loved by the Administration).

"Thirty-six years is long enough in this place," he said to Momberger, who replied, "Like hell it is!"

A page approached Burden. "Your office just called, Senator. They said Mr. Sanford's arrived."

Momberger looked at Burden, somewhat puzzled. "Now what are you up to with Blaise Sanford? You're not fixin' to be one of those lousy columnists, are you?"

"Not Blaise, his son."

"That rich little Commie . . ."

"A friend of Diana, remember?"

"You don't have much luck with sons-in-law, do you?"

In the corridor outside the Senate Chamber, Irene Bloch embraced him. *"Cher ami!"* The voice rang out. Tourists paused to stare.

"What an election!" She held him by his wrists, as though he might, like St. Theresa, levitate.

"Cicero said that life is like a place in the theatre . . ." But Burden was not allowed to finish.

"So many dear friends defeated! Poor Senator Lucas, a saint, gone!"

"We all must go, Irene. I'm late for an appointment."

"But *you* will never go. I mean you'll stay on in Washington, won't you?"

"What else? Where else can I earn a living?" But the attempt at pathos failed, too. She was not listening.

"To know that you are still here makes it all so much better. Now where is Senator Taft?"

Burden said that he had not the slightest idea.

"According to his office, he is on the floor. You've seen the poll of course?" She stared past him, searching for Taft.

Burden shook his head. Stealthily he got one wrist free of her.

"Taft is the practically unanimous choice of the Republican leaders, which means he's absolutely certain to be nominated."

She frowned as Senator McCarthy, squat and smiling, crossed the hall, attended by Irish.

"What about General Eisenhower?"

"Not a chance." Irene was flat. "They don't like him and neither do I. Did you see what Harold Griffiths wrote about him yesterday? Even *he* has given up on Eisenhower, and you know his passion for the military."

"Peter Sanford is waiting for me." Burden got the other wrist free.

"Comme il est méchant!" But she said it gaily. "You must come and have tea with me soon, *à deux*." She smiled significantly and tapped his face with an elegant claw. "After January, anyway; I'm booked until then."

* * *

Peter sat alone in the outer office, reading a paper-back book which he thrust guiltily in his pocket but not before Burden had seen that it was *The Federalist Papers*. Burden had noticed that since the war interest in the American past had waned, at least outside the academic world. For the majority, history began with the New Deal, and any contemplation of the old Republic was downright antipathetic to those who wanted reform in the present and perfection in the future, a category to which Peter so notoriously belonged.

"Where's Mrs. Blaine?"

"Gone out for lunch, she said."

"I am deserted. You see me among the ruins of Carthage. Ponder my fate and count no day happy unless it be your last."

"You are in melancholy form!" Peter laughed appreciatively and followed Burden into the inner office. In the center of the room stood a large packing case, half filled with books.

"But you are still here for another three months . . ."

"Even so . . ." Burden stretched out on the leather sofa. "I want to depart stealthily, a bit at a time, unobserved. So that by the time my term ends, I shall have vanished without anyone noticing it."

"You fear pity?"

"Who does not?"

"Women do not. Some men." Peter showed Burden a newspaper folded open to an inside page. "There he is, being told about the election."

Burden gazed at the photograph without emotion. In the uniform of a colonel, Clay shook the hand of General MacArthur, who was gravely "congratulating the Senator-elect. Since his nomination in June, Colonel Overbury has been on active duty in Korea. As a front line officer with the U.S. First Cavalry Division, Colonel Overbury refused to campaign for public office, saying, 'The people of my state know by now what I stand for. As a fighting soldier, I am not at liberty to say anything except that this dirty business has got to be done, and I am doing what I can, in my small way.' "

Burden let the paper drop. "He's won!" That seemed the least as well as the most that could be said.

Peter nodded; his wide body barely fitted into the rocking chair. "It was genius, going back in the Army."

"It would be ironic if now he were to become a true hero just to disprove your story." Burden found himself, perversely, wanting to attack Peter, to support Clay.

"Luckily he hasn't gone that far. He's been at headquarters most of the time, but who will ever know that? Particularly after all those photographs of him in action. Apparently he plans to stay in Korea until January. Then he'll return in glory to take his seat in the Senate."

"He'll make a good Senator." Burden almost meant what he said.

"Good?" Peter's expression of disbelief annoyed Burden.

"Yes, good. He is ambitious, therefore he must be good."

"Or at least not be notoriously bad."

"He will certainly be diligent . . ."

"Or give the impression."

"*That* takes diligence." Burden chuckled, despite his own agony. "You must be compassionate. There's nothing more difficult for the modern politician with his eye on the White House than to seem to be busy without actually doing anything for which he might later be held accountable. He'll work hard, don't worry."

"For himself."

"He would be unnatural if he did not."

"Then I want unnatural men to govern us."

"To *govern?* No one governs in this house!" Burden exploded. Truth at last. "The thing's too big. When I came here, a Senator who wanted to do something could often accomplish it, if he cared sufficiently. But now? We say 'Yea' or 'Nay' and our yesses and noes are usually perfectly calculable in advance. Yet, believe it or not, there was actually a time when legislation originated in the Congress. I myself, in early days, once wrote a law which became the law of the land. Now of course we receive our legislation already prepared for us, the work of a thousand lawyers in a hundred bureaus, and nobody here bothers to read a fraction of those bills we approve or disapprove."

"It is too big."

"It is too big."

But Peter would not accept Burden's dark view. "Individual Senators still have power in some things. Clay will have power."

Burden shook his head. "Not in the Senate, he won't. He'll be just another yes or no and the whips will know in advance just how he'll vote."

"Perhaps one should abandon the whole system."

"We have abandoned it," said Burden. "We now live under a Presidential dictatorship, with periodic referendums which allow us to change the dictator but not the dictatorship."

"Perhaps that is the only way this sort of society can be governed."

"It would be a shame to think so. But then I am reactionary, a normal state at my age."

"We all react to the hateful present, even though there was nothing better in the past." Peter was bleak. "I'm confident of that."

"Of course there were better times." Burden rose to the challenge, thought of Shiloh, tried to speak of Lee and Lincoln, but Peter would have none of it.

He drowned out Burden. "The apes have always governed us, and our complaints are simply monkey chatter . . ."

"No!" Burden surprised himself by his own passion. "We had our golden age." He indicated the portrait of Jefferson above the mantelpiece. "I admit it was brief and that like all things human it went wrong, which was no one's fault. Things do with us, and neither your monkeys nor the apes can be held responsible. The good is rare, that's all, and not easy for most of us to live with."

Peter was stubborn. "There was never a golden age. There will never be a golden age and it is sheer romance to think we can ever be other than what we are now." He was radiant in his despair.

Burden sighed, knowing the mood too well. "Well, if that is so, then let us say that there was a time in our history when a few men of influence wanted things to be better than they are, unlike today when all that matters is money . . ." He stopped, and smiled. "But no matter how things are or were or will be, *you* go on as I do—or used to—trying to make things better. After all, if you were really so pessimistic you wouldn't publish *The American Idea* or be concerned with anything but pleasure in the moment."

"Pleasure in the moment varies from person to person." Peter was cryptic. For a long moment both men were silent while Peter rocked back and forth and Burden contemplated the painting of Jefferson. Then Peter said, "Why do you think that what I wrote about Clay had so little effect? It was the truth, and it was devastating."

"Apparently not. In any case the public is impressed only by winners."

"But winners have become losers. They've even gone to jail."

"But to say that Clay was a false hero . . ."

"And I *proved* that he was . . ."

". . . only confuses people who have already accepted him as what they think he is, a genuine hero, the subject of an extraordinary amount of publicity. That's all that matters, the large first impression. You cannot change it, short of a public trial."

Peter gave a sigh which became a groan. The rocking chair creaked beneath his weight. "I suppose I am naïve."

"Optimistic is a better word. You think to be right is enough. It never is. Though I must say if it hadn't been for the war in Korea, I think you would have defeated Clay. Why do you hate him?" Burden was curious to hear the answer.

"Why do you?"

"But I don't." Burden told the truth.

"But he forced you out. You should hate him."

Burden sat back in the chair, suddenly alert, aware of danger. "How do you know that?"

But Peter seemed not to have heard him. "Diana thinks it's because my father prefers Clay to me. But that's too simple. I've never much liked my father, which means I should be glad he's got himself involved with Clay because it will end badly."

337

"All things do. You say he forced me out . . .?"

"It's really Enid." Peter stopped his rocking and clutched his huge knees; he seemed carved from stone. "Clay killed her, you know."

"Ah . . ." Burden gestured to show how impossible it was for him to comment upon the private affairs of a family not his own.

"Oh, I know she might not have survived anyway, but they did edge her out."

"Now you would like to edge out Clay."

"It would be satisfying."

"The way you think he edged me out?" Burden put the question directly.

"Yes." Peter looked Burden full in the face. "It was that old business about the Indian land sale. Rather than be exposed by Clay, you quit the race."

On Burden's desk a brass ruler lay diagonally across a copy of the *Congressional Record*. Not liking the angle, he readjusted the ruler so that it neatly bisected the document at the center. "How," he asked, "do you happen to know this?"

"I have a friend at the *Tribune* who occasionally lets me see things in advance. Harold Griffiths has written a column describing the whole business. It's already set in type."

"Why is Harold Griffiths writing this now, when I am no longer in politics?"

"He thinks you had something to do with what I wrote. Since he can't attack me because of Father . . ."

Unable to contain himself, Burden asked the question that ought not to be asked. "Do *you* believe I took a bribe?"

"Why shouldn't you?" Peter got to his feet, his voice suddenly loud. "Considering what the others are, why should you be different?"

"One must be." But Burden's voice was inaudible.

Peter spoke through him. "There is no virtue in any of us, Senator. We are savages and don't say it was better when he was alive." Peter struck the painted face of Jefferson. "He lied and cheated and wrote lovely prose and collected recipes and wanted to lord it over this foolish land and did and died and that was the end of him. And don't say that it matters what opinion

338

the future holds of you, for the human race will stop one day, not a moment too soon, and then it will not have mattered one single damn who was an ape and who was a monkey in this filthy cage."

Peter was at the door; he paused in his tirade and stared briefly at the framed text from Plato. Then he turned back to Burden, his voice normal. "If I were you, I'd appeal to Blaise. He likes you, as much as he can like anyone outside of Clay, and that's not really liking but what the Greeks called the 'unfortunate passion,' and speaking of Greek your Plato's wrong." He pointed to the text on the wall: " 'Each of us is not born for himself alone.' It's a forgery. Plato never wrote that letter. Perhaps he should have written it but he didn't. What can I do to help you?"

* * *

They crossed Chain Bridge and turned left on the road toward Great Falls. It had been years since Burden had made this journey, and he found the countryside sadly altered. Wooden frameworks of new houses stood, their pale wood raw against dark trees while billboards advertised entire new communities where life could be lived on easy terms with every modern appliance, a mere twenty minutes from downtown Washington. Burden liked nothing that he saw. But he refused to be distressed by anything today. He would think of nothing but the cool woods that smelled of mushrooms and decay.

"That's the turnoff there, at the gas station."

"O.K.," said the chauffeur, a young Negro found for him by Henry who had gone to work for the government with Burden's reluctant blessing. To lose the somber Henry was like losing a brother but he could not refuse him the chance to become available for a government pension. Solemnly Henry had departed that summer, promising to reappear every Sunday to tend the roses, and in fact he did make an occasional appearance at the house to discuss politics with the Senator and spray a rose or two. He also spoke privately and at length with his replacement but so far he had yet to convince the young man that his employer should be addressed as "Sir." Passively, Burden disliked the new driver but the effort to find another was beyond him.

Nor was Kitty any help. She had no interests now except the birds, for whom she was currently building an elaborate sanctuary. In their twittering company her days were spent. Wearing a bathrobe and slippers, hair all undone, she seldom spoke to anyone, which was just as well, for with age her mind had filled with fantasies and instead of blurting out embarrassing truths she now revealed eccentric dreams that astonished and repelled even those who knew her best. But she was happy among her birds, and Burden envied her for having so completely escaped the human. There would be no pain for Kitty ever again, other than brief sorrow at a bird's fall, made instantly pleasurable by a burial service witnessed by trees. Now that he needed her, she was gone, which was fair enough, for in the days when she had needed him he had taken her for granted, had left her behind while he pursued the Presidency, year after year, back and forth across the continent. Now there would be no more journeys; he was home again but the girl he had married half a century before had ceased to exist and in her place an old woman with thin hair crumbled stale bread to feed birds.

"Where do I go now?" The voice combined hostility and petulance. Burden looked out the window. They were on an unfamiliar road with new houses to left and right, each with its high television antenna drawing from the air crude pictures and lying words. Oh, detestable age! he thought, hating all.

"It's straight ahead. Just keep on." He had recognized the patch of woods where Henry usually parked. At least the pine trees were unchanged, unspoiled.

"But what do you want me to do?" The black face looked at him, stupid in its self-absorption.

"I want you to wait," said Burden coldly; then he turned and walked toward the woods where North and South had met in deadly battle and, that day at least, the South, his South, had won.

Burrs stuck to his trousers as he made his way slowly through tall grass, but he did not pause to pick them

340

off. He was intent on finding his hill. Everything depended on that now. Once he had achieved it, all would be well. He would be safe from attack, protected by that Southern victory, redolent of virtue, courage, honor. Like burrs the words stuck to his mind. And though he reminded himself that words meant only what one wanted them to mean, he also knew that, once invested with meaning, words became magic, and could destroy as well as sustain.

The field was the same. But upon the hill where he used to sit, trees had been cleared, a cellar dug, and in orderly piles cement block was stacked. The bullet would long since have been dug up by the bulldozer which had scooped out the cellar of the house-to-be.

"What're you doing here?" The voice belonged to a sad-faced man in blue jeans and windbreaker.

"I'm sorry." Burden was gracious. "I am Senator Day."

"I didn't ask who you were. I asked what are you doing here. This is private property."

Stung, Burden stepped back, away from the profaned hill. "I'm sorry. I didn't know anyone lived here. I used to visit . . ."

"I've got signs posted. I'm sure you can read."

"Yes. Very well. Thank you." In a rage, Burden turned his back on the man. He had said who he was and yet the man had persisted in his rudeness. So a world of honor ends.

Burden made his way back through the woods to the car, aware that the man in the field continued to watch him as if he might suddenly set the woods afire or in some other way diminish the value of the property.

Burden's driver had turned on the radio full volume. He was listening raptly, thick lips ajar, to the thunder of a lover's lament.

"Turn that damned thing off!" A long slow look as the young man absorbed the command. Then he switched off the radio and, slowly, opened the car door for Burden.

"Take the river road. I'll tell you when to stop." As the car started, Burden realized that he was shivering. He held his hands together and with all his strength forced each hand to steady the other. But tremors still went through his body. Obviously a delayed reaction to what Peter had told him. By deliberately refusing to address his mind to his own ruin, the body had been forced to absorb the shock the mind disowned.

He tried to imagine what the next few days would be like. The story would break on Thursday. He could anticipate the sneering tone. Lately Harold had taken to writing exposés of small (never great) corruptions in the Congress. Padded payrolls and illegal campaign contributions were the usual crimes, momentarily embarrassing to the legislator involved but seldom causing much damage. Americans had always believed that their representatives were corrupt since, given the same opportunity, they would be, too. As it was, the common folk daily cheated one another, misrepresenting the goods they sold and otherwise conducting themselves like their governors. If Clay Overbury was able to present himself as a war hero and be elected, why, then, they reckoned, more power to him. After all, he was no different from the used-car dealer who makes a profit on a car he knows will not run properly. Of course, "If you can't be good, be careful" was the national wisdom, and it was hardly wise to be caught. Yet Burden was by no means convinced that Clay, for one, would have been defeated even if he had not had a war to hide in. The people seemed genuinely uninterested in moral matters. What mattered was winning, and Clay had won. For that matter if he himself had become President in 1940, the taking of Nillson's money would have been regarded in retrospect as a brilliant necessity which in a sense it had been. Even now he regretted not so much the selling of his vote as the abandoning of his responsibility to the Indians.

Sweat clouded his face while cold arms and legs twitched as though they were on strings, manipulated by someone not himself. He must regain control. He recalled a visit recently made by him by one of the Indians whose land was sold to Nillson. "Best thing ever happened to us, selling off that land. No damn oil in it anyway, and if we had stayed there we'd gone right on the way we was, ignorant as all hell. Now I

342

got my own business and . . ." Success story: a bad action with good results.

But Burden refused himself this easy comfort. He had all his life believed that one should behave in a certain way despite the example of others, and for most of his life he had been honest. Even as he sounded most royally all the depths and shoals of honor, he had made few compromises with his own sense of virtue. That others did not share his scrupulous niceness merely made him all the more pleased with himself. Now all that was at an end and he would be revealed as what he was, worse than the others because they at least never for a moment believed that it was better to be honest than dishonest, noble than ignoble, good than bad; no sophistry as to what was *truly* good could save him from himself, not to mention from the world's contempt once Harold's column had been printed. And to be truthful, it was the thought of what others would say that gave him the most pain. To know that they would laugh at him for being found out, take delight in the end of his career and then, easily, forget that he had ever existed, since what, after all, was he, but just another crooked politician who had had his day?"

"Stop here."

The driver put on the brakes too quickly. Burden's bad shoulder struck against the side of the car. He cursed softly. Then before the fool could ask what he was supposed to do next, Burden told him that he was to wait. "I'm going to take a walk. You can play the radio if you like."

Trees without leaves descended a steep slope to the Potomac, whose brown waters swirled about sharp rocks that broke the river's flow, like so many stepping-stones set out for a giant's use.

A narrow path zigzagged among trees to which he clung as he hurried, like a boy, toward the river, nothing in his mind but a desire to escape entirely the present and the human.

Abruptly the path turned to reveal a ruined cabin with roof half gone, door sprung and windows broken in. He stopped and looked inside. The floor was strewn with yellow newspapers and ashes from old fires. He thought of the soul's dark cottage which, battered and decayed, let in new light, but only to reveal, on closer inspection, empty beer bottles, used contraceptives, and a man's shoe. He continued his descent through the cool woods, the roar of water upon rocks growing louder with each step.

The path ended at a narrow rocky beach. Between tall boulders worn smooth by the last glacier, his father stood, wearing a torn Confederate uniform and holding a rifle, just as he had that day in the field at Manassas when his son had failed to recognize him. But there was no mistaking him now. The blazing eyes of the furious boy he had never known were those of the man who had been his life's tormentor.

Burden spoke first. "You were right," he said. "It has all gone wrong. You should be pleased." He took a tentative step toward the Confederate corporal, who took a step back, revealing as he did the torn cloth of his tunic, bright with a new wound's blood.

"You're bleeding still!" The triumphant shout caused the boy to hold his rifle in such a way as to bar Burden's approach to him. But in his passion Burden was not to be put off by mere death. All life was now concentrated in that single gaping wound and all that needed doing in the world was the staunching of the blood.

With stiff fingers Burden removed a handkerchief from his pocket. Then he walked toward the wounded soldier, half expecting him to run away. But this was no ordinary youth; it was his father honorably struck by an enemy's bullet in the field of battle. The Confederate corporal did not flinch even when at last they were face to face.

For a long moment Burden stared into the blue eyes that perfectly reflected empty sky. Then slowly he extended the hand which held the handkerchief. Now only the rifle barred his way. He waited patiently until at last, marvelously, the rifle was lowered. With a cry he flung himself upon the youth who was his father, plunged the handkerchief into the wound, lost his balance, fell against the beloved, was taken into those long-dead arms, and like impatient lovers, they embraced and together fell.

Nine

1

LIKE A STRANGER not certain of how he would be received, Peter entered the crowded drawing room to find the chandelier of the Prince Regent replaced by a fantastic affair of colored Venetian glass. But then everything in the house had been changed except the people: Regency crystal might give way to Venetian glass but Lucy Shattuck endured, only a certain leatheriness of face betraying the possibility that in time she, too, would stop.

"Peter, dear!" As she embraced him ritually, she muttered in his ear, "I've never seen anything like what she's done to the house!"

"It's not exactly austere." Vivid colors, exotic glass, modern furniture of extravagant design had been combined to create an impression of bold opulence which he did not altogether dislike once he had got used to the idea that Laurel House was simply a building like any other, a piece of real estate which, having changed hands, must necessarily change character, and so, blithely, the setting of his youth had been swept away by an interior decorator, fulfilling a client's dream.

"If Frederika could see this, I think she'd die!" Lucy seemed delighted at the thought of her old friend's apoplectic death.

"Well, she'll never see it. She's sworn never to set foot in the house again." Though Frederika had been the one most eager to sell ("too many memories"), she had complained bitterly when the house was finally bought by Mrs. Ogden Watress. Fortunately, the distraction of recreating Laurel House in a pre-Depression Renaissance palace on Massachusetts Avenue kept her from brooding; Blaise, on the other hand, was delighted to be living in town, closer to his headquarters on Ninth Street.

"Your father's here, believe it or not."

"I do believe it. Why not?" Across the room, Mrs. Watress, seeing Peter for the first time, gave a glad cry and abandoned her two companions (members of the Administration, each wearing identical rimless spectacles) in order to welcome Peter to his old home.

"Well, what do you think? Haven't I done wonders?" Irene indicated primitive sculpture, Venetian glass, a Monet above the fireplace.

"I would never have recognized the house," said Peter accurately. "Only the outside is the same."

"Not for long. I am adding a Palladian wing, because of Ogden and all those animals he's shot. We're going to have a gallery in which there will be nothing but stuffed heads!"

"Yoū must charge admission," said Lucy Shattuck. "I'll pay, gladly."

Peter refused to catch her eye. "How does Mr. Watress like living in Washington?"

"He'll get used to it." Irene was more than ever superb in her confidence. "And of course he knows so many of the Eisenhower people, like Foster Dulles. In fact, *cher* Foster was the Watress trustee."

"Yes, I know," said Lucy drily. "I too was a Watress bride. But even *cher* Foster couldn't keep Ogden and Schuyler from going broke." Lucy's malice was exuberant and impartial. She always had the absolute lowdown on everyone; in the case of the Watresses, however, there was not much that even she could reveal for that beleaguered family had become public property when Senator Clay Overbury married Elizabeth Watress in a splendid ceremony marred only by the unexpected appearance of Schuyler Watress, who had insisted upon giving away his daughter, to Elizabeth's horror since Schuyler was not the most anonymous of alcoholics. Yet he had behaved reasonably well in the church, and once the ceremony was over he had the grace to vanish altogether; not to be heard of again until the autumn, when he sent the newlyweds a press clipping describing a polo match in which he had scored three goals at Santa Barbara. There was no accompanying letter. Happily, his place at the wedding reception was more than filled by his former wife, Lucy, and his recently bankrupt brother Ogden, not to mention the best man, Blaise, who had acted, Peter duly noted, like the father of the groom.

The wedding reception had been held at Laurel House and though no one was ever quite certain whether or not Irene Bloch had been invited, she was there and made history. Within minutes of having met Ogden Watress, she decided that the time had come to put off her widow's weeds, and though she later confided to Peter that she was at first reluctant to give up her name, she had finally made even that sacrifice for love. She became Mrs. Ogden Watress in a ceremony performed aboard a ship of the Cunard Line, en route to Le Havre. For plain interest and delighted gossip, Irene's marriage created almost as much interest in the city as the more glorious wedding of Clay and Elizabeth, and it was agreed by all the ladies that one had to take off one's hat to Irene. She had triumphed. No one could ever again overlook or patronize her. With the purchase of Laurel House, her victory was total. All came to Irene, except Peter's mother, who was not missed.

"Ogden has the most extraordinary business acumen!" Irene gazed benignly at her tall, hulking, red-faced husband, who was showing several puzzled guests a piece of modern sculpture so large that it nearly barred the way to what had been in Peter's day the cardroom but was now, as far as he could make out from where he stood, an art gallery ingeniously lighted.

"Then he must've changed since I was married to Schuyler. In my day it was a competition between the two boys as to who could lose the most money."

"Peter and I detest business, don't we?" Irene beamed at Peter who agreed that business was not his forte. "We are *au fond spirituel,* which is why it's so amusing that together we make money."

Lucy was curious. "Is that Communist manifesto of yours really profitable?"

"Oh yes." Peter was mild; no criticism of *The American Idea* ever distressed him. "As a matter of fact, we're almost mass-circulation now, thanks to Senator McCarthy." During the Congressional hearings in which the demagogue had found significant and sinister the promotion of an obscure Army dentist thought to be sympathetic to the Left, *The American Idea* had launched a series of attacks on the Senator, who subsequently began to fail, and Peter liked to think that this decline was due at least in part to the work he and Aeneas had done. In any event, the investigator himself was under current investigation by a Senate subcommittee and after four years of national distress, the United States Senate in its ponderous way was now upon the verge of censuring McCarthy for having behaved discourteously in their house.

"Elizabeth!" Irene greeted Lucy's daughter, who looked even more beautiful, Peter decided, than she had before her marriage.

Irene thought so, too. "It's being a mother that's done it! Look at her, Lucy! Look at how lovely *our* girl is!"

"She certainly looks better than she did when she was pregnant and covered with hives. Hello, dear." Lucy gave her daughter an offhand kiss. Then, wanting excitement, she turned to Peter. "Are you two friendly this year or not?"

"I'm always friendly," said Peter, not offering his hand to Elizabeth, who did not for an instant let her broad smile fade.

"So am I!" Her eyes glowed. "At least I try to be because Clay says never let politics become personal. But I can't always help it. There are times when I get absolutely furious when some little twerp attacks Clay, and then of course I say something simply awful and then Clay's furious with me!"

"Implying that only a little twerp would attack our Clay?" When not in her element, Lucy could be counted on to create it.

Quickly Irene tried to keep what peace there was. "We must all be friends! Besides, aren't we all related? I'm Elizabeth's *tante* while Clay and Peter . . ."

"You are my aunt, aren't you? And I'm so glad!" Peter found Elizabeth altogether impressive. In the old days, she had particularly disdained "gruesome" Irene but now she was downright loving, unlike her mother who continued to torture Irene just as though she were still the Mrs. Samuel I. Bloch who crashed parties and not the savior of the brothers Watress as well as co-sponsor of Senator Overbury's career.

". . . while Clay is Peter's brother-in-law . . ."

"He *was* my brother-in-law," Peter sounded more sharp than he intended.

Elizabeth's large jaw set, though the smile never faded. "But family loyalty continues, no matter what."

"Oh, mine does." Peter wondered if he had ever really liked her. "But to *my* family, not him. To Enid, in fact."

"But there's Senator Watkins!" Irene abandoned her relatives.

"Enid was a wonderful girl." Elizabeth spoke as though in defense of the dead. "And a tremendously *loyal* person, and I think that's the most important thing in the world."

"Do you really?" Her mother was amused.

"Loyalty may be the most important thing in the world," said Peter, "but that was the one quality Enid lacked."

"*How* can you say that about her?" Elizabeth's fury, never far from the surface, erupted at last to her mother's obvious delight. "Why do you always have to attack everybody? Particularly poor Enid, who's dead."

"I wasn't attacking her, I simply said that loyalty was not Enid's strong point."

"Elizabeth is quite mad on the subject of loyalty," said her mother. "I think she gets it from Clay. In the old days we never even used the word, did we, dear?"

"Oh, yes, we did—at least I did." On familiar ground with her mother, Elizabeth regained her poise. "I've always felt one should know exactly who one's friends are, and what to expect from them." She turned to Peter. "I'm keeping a little black book."

"To list your friends or your enemies?" Peter was amused.

"Oh, enemies! After all, revenge can be as sweet as love."

"Good heavens, what a child I've produced!" Lucy

was almost respectful. She changed the subject, as though suspecting that her own name might head the list. "Is Clay with you? Did he come?"

"Yes. He's in the library with Mr. Sanford. They're watching Clay on television, on tape, being interviewed."

"You should join them," said Lucy to Peter, who said that he would rather not. "Anyway, don't miss what Irene's done to the room. She has hung the walls with burlap. I wonder how Blaise feels, coming back to Laurel House and finding it so changed."

Though Lucy had challenged Peter, it was Elizabeth who responded. "Mr. Sanford adores Irene and he thinks she's done wonders with the house." Elizabeth looked at Peter, daring him to contradict her.

"Of course," said Peter placidly. "Irene has always been one of Father's favorites. In fact, you were here the first time she ever came to dinner."

But Elizabeth did not recall the occasion. With a smile, she whispered that she wanted champagne. Peter and Lucy watched as she made her way across the room, all eyes upon her.

"She is marvelous to look at," said Peter.

"But not in Enid's class." The mother was unexpected.

"No," Peter agreed. "But let's hope she has a better time of it."

"She will, if she doesn't take to drink like her father. Anyway they are a perfect couple."

Peter nodded. "She's always been keen on Clay."

"I don't know about Clay but she's certainly keen on glory. She would do anything to be noticed." Lucy's usual ironic tone was suddenly missing.

Peter looked at her with some surprise. Then he said noncommittally, "Most people would."

"Most people would do something but not *any-thing*."

"Well, if there were not people like Elizabeth and Clay, there would be no history. The great things go to the voracious."

"Must we have history?" Lucy suddenly grinned; in the hot lighting of Irene's drawing room, she resembled a desiccated lizard.

"It passes the time."

"Oh, that passes anyway. Actually, I'm filled with admiration for my child. She's got exactly what she wanted, and I can't think of any woman I've ever known who has except . . ."

"Irene!" Both spoke the name at the same time.

"*Tante Irène,*" Lucy repeated happily. "Poor Ogden! He was always such a snob and now look at him! But then the Watresses were born to be humiliated by women. I certainly gave his brother a hard time of it."

The entrance of Millicent Smith Carhart put an end to their intimacy. Lucy joined her old friend and as the two ladies made their progress through the crowded room, Peter meditated on the nature of the game all played, which was, simply war. A conquers B who conquers C who conquers A. Each in his own way was struggling for precedence and to deny this essential predatoriness was sentimental; to accommodate it wrong; to change it impossible. Yet Peter was not prepared to accept the fact that, even for him, there might exist no alternative to being fierce carnivore in a jungle war plainly destined to continue, with or without him, until man's end.

Not happy, Peter went into the dining room, where, as he had hoped, a buffet had been set out beneath an elaborately ugly mobile of bronze which appeared to revolve of its own accord, in perpetual motion. Though the table was dominated by the inevitable smoked ham and smoked turkey, a row of silver chafing dishes looked promising. His mood improved as he lifted a cover to reveal a combination of what appeared to be chicken livers and water chestnuts. He ate one, burning the roof of his mouth. Despite the pain, he ate another, marveling at whatever genius had first thought to combine two such complementary textures.

As Peter helped himself from a second dish, Harold Griffiths said, "Irene's cook is Armenian. But he's rather good at bogus Canton dishes."

"Not so bogus," said Peter, his mouth now filled with snow peas and black mushrooms.

"Wait until you've tried the real thing on Formosa.

351

Chiang Kai-shek's chef is perhaps the best Cantonese cook in the world."

"Waiting to be unleashed, no doubt."

But Harold was now far too serious a figure to acknowledge this sort of pleasantry. The most war-minded of the columnists, he favored an immediate invasion of the Chinese mainland, as he always did after his annual pilgrimage to the deposed warlord on Formosa. Only that morning in his column he had extolled the wisdom and vigor of the Generalissimo, the beauty and subtlety of his wife, the fine masculinity of their golden troops, ever on the elert to reconquer the land they had lost to darkness.

Harold asked, politely, if Diana was coming and, as politely, Peter said that she was. But despite their apparent ease with one another, Harold had not forgiven Peter for having revealed what had happened in the Philippines, nor had Peter forgiven Harold for having taken revenge not upon himself but upon Burden Day, whose death was announced in the same edition as Harold's column revealing the Senator's corruption. Promptly, sympathy had gone to Burden, who was thought to have killed himself in despair, although Diana maintained that he had drowned accidentally, since he would most certainly have sued Harold Griffiths for libel, as in her grief she had wanted to do, until she was told that one cannot libel the dead.

Now though Harold Griffiths invariably asked him about Diana (in Washington Peter knew that he and Diana were regarded as an old married couple who had somewhat eccentrically avoided the conventional ceremony), she still did not speak to Harold, which made him sad, since what he had done was no more than his job in which chips must fall, as he liked to observe, as chips will, where they may. Peter himself had never discussed the matter with Harold or with Blaise if only because in a sense he thought himself to be as guilty as they. Had he not written *his* piece, Harold would not have struck at the Senator.

While Peter devoured butterfly shrimp and Harold ate turkey, they discussed McCarthy, the one subject on which they could agree. Each hoped that the Senate would vote for censure. "In fact," said Harold, "Clay's discussing it right now on television."

"Does he favor censure?" Peter could not resist adding. "At last?"

Harold's response was predictable. "You don't understand what pressure Clay's been under."

"But that's the one thing I do understand. If he wants to be nominated for Vice President, he must pick up support in the Northern cities, particularly among the Irish, who regard McCarthy as chosen by God to shield them from civilization."

"Clay will vote against McCarthy tomorrow." Harold was stolid.

"Then that means it's the safe thing to do, which is good to know." He ate a shell of pastry containing crab; the sauce was too bland; it needed mustard. "Tell me, do you think Adlai Stevenson will want Clay to run with him in '56?"

"Why not? He'll certainly have to take someone like Clay to balance the ticket, someone who is, well . . ."

"Reactionary?"

"He's not that and you know it."

"Then just how would you describe Clay's politics? I'm really serious. I want to know." Although he had found the pastry shell somewhat too heavy for the crab, Peter ate a second one; and this time he detected in the sauce a delicate trace of curry.

"He's a pragmatist. He has to put this thing together with what he has to deal with." The answer was prompt.

Peter speared a chicken liver with a silver toothpick. "Pragmatist really means opportunist, doesn't it?"

"If you are not an opportunist, how can you possibly become President?" Harold sounded brisk and tough. Peter had noted in his years as a publisher that a great many of those who wrote about politics were, like Harold, drawn to the ruthless, the brutal and the autocratic. Since clerks deal so much in ink, Peter had once rather fancily written, they yearn for blood.

"Perhaps one can't!" Peter was distressed to find grit in the chicken liver. "Actually it's Clay's hypocrisy I mind the most. Those righteous little sermons he gives while he is forever wheeling and dealing . . ."

"Come off it!" Harold was sharp. "That's the way it's done."

"But I don't like the way it's done."

"That's too bad of course." With his fingers, Harold trimmed the fat off a slice of smoked ham. "Because the world's not apt to change."

"That's good to know." Although in recent years Harold had become nearly as gluttonous as himself, Peter found this likeness not at all endearing; if anything, it made Harold less sympathetic to him. "I suppose, all in all, you do like the world the way it is. Clay is rising. The West's declining. What more could you want?" But Harold did not answer; instead he helped himself to turkey, while Peter devoured ham. Then they were joined by two pretty girls, who were hungry. Harold, courtly and flirtatious, embarked upon an elaborate discourse on Chinese cooking, punctuated by a loud barking laugh which caused the girls, fed, to flee.

Harold pretended to find them attractive. "Cousins of Ogden Watress. Damned good-looking girls, don't you think?"

"Oh, yes," said Peter, amused as always by Harold's strenuous display of heterosexuality. "But I prefer food, you know. I must say we're both a bit like Eugene Pallette, remember? In that film where he died of overeating . . ."

"It was Guy Kibbee." For an instant, the old Harold surfaced, to be promptly recalled by the new. "Odd thing happened the other night," said Harold, mouth full of shrimp. "Clay and I were at the Sulgrave and he was looking out over the dance floor at all the girls when suddenly he said, 'How many have you gone to bed with?' and I said 'Oh, one or two' and he said, 'I've been to bed with the whole damned lot!' "

"Where was Elizabeth when he said this?"

Harold looked suspiciously at a dish of saffron rice. "He was speaking of the past."

"The present, from what I hear. How does she put up with it?" But Peter's question was rhetorical, since Elizabeth's acceptance of Clay's promiscuity was already a part of Washington's folklore. She had even been known, on occasion, to place good-looking girls

354

next to her husband at dinner as though by deliberately thrusting a girl in his way, she might share indirectly in a sexual life from which she was so notoriously excluded. Washington was about evenly divided between those who thought her a woman of stone and those who thought her uniquely clever and, in the best sense, un-American. Peter tended to admire the way she handled a difficult situation. But then she and Clay were more allies than lovers, her ambition every bit the equal of his.

The dining room began to fill with people who, unlike the girls, were eager to listen to Harold. He obliged them. As Harold discussed the news of the day, Peter suddenly realized that he existed only as a performer responding to occasions. With equal facility Harold could be failed poet and friend of the press lord's son or the G.I.'s chronicler or wise counselor to a nation which must soon prepare itself for the final war between the atoms of light and those of darkness. Aware at last of the other's nature, Peter was relieved that what he had regarded with some distress as a lost friendship was merely an old performance dropped from repertory.

Peter left Harold to his audience and went into the hallway just as a group of guests arrived. But once he saw that Diana was not among them, he started to go into the drawing room. At that moment Blaise emerged from the library. Simultaneously, father and son each decided to avoid physical contact; they did not shake hands. Instead Peter indicated a huge vivid splotch of a painting on the opposite wall. "Things are not what they were!"

"It's horrible!" Though Blaise was now politically allied with Mrs. Ogden Watress, he was not about to embrace all her works. "Thank God Frederika isn't here to see it."

"How is Clay? He is in there, isn't he?" Peter pointed to the library door.

"Yes." His father seemed uneasy. "We've been watching him on television. Have you seen what Irene's done to the cardroom? Looks like a horror museum."

Aware that his father did not want him to go into

the library, Peter said, "I haven't seen Clay in months. I suppose I ought to say hello." And he left Blaise to the usual clients who had begun to gather.

Clay sat in front of the television set. Beside him was Aeneas Duncan, who said, "I just got to town this morning. I was going to call you later."

Peter said that it was quite all right, wondering, as he spoke, what Aeneas was doing in the enemy's camp.

Peter greeted Clay, who gave him a boyish smile in sharp contrast to the grave face of Senator Overbury which looked out at them from the television set. The program was ending and the participants were being identified. In the gray unsteady light of the cathode tube, Clay looked mature and responsible, quite unlike his present self, which was unexpectedly youthful, as though he did not have a care in the world. "I had a couple of close calls there," he said, indicating the television set. "They were really out to get me. You'd've enjoyed it." It was part of Clay's new charm that he treated avowed enemies with the same confiding ease that he treated allies.

"Did they smoke you out on McCarthy?" Peter was equally light. "Will you vote for censure?"

"There's nothing to smoke out. I said I favored condemning him. No, where they tried to trip me up was . . ."

Peter caught the change of verb. "You favor condemning but not censuring him?"

"It's all the same thing." The distinction seemed not to interest Clay.

"But it is *not* the same. Is it, Aeneas?" Peter turned to his editor and friend.

"Well, no, it's not." Aeneas might be tortuous in his reasoning and perverse in his responses, but he could not be anything but accurate when facts were involved. "In the Senate, to condemn is much milder than to censure. In this case, it's a device to get everyone off the hook."

"And Clay wants to get off the hook."

But Clay seemed not to have heard. He was staring thoughtfully at himself on the television set. "Those lights are murder," he said at last. "And look at the

356

way they keep shooting me from below. It looks like I have a jowl!"

"Obviously a liberal cameraman." Peter noticed that where the portrait of Aaron Burr had hung, an elaborate collage of old newspapers had been arranged.

"No," said Clay suddenly, switching off the set. "I'm not on any hook. McCarthy's finished." He tapped the television set. "And that's what did him in. He had a bad television image, poor bastard. I feel sorry for him."

"But you do condemn him, in the Senate at least."

"Oh, yes. Yes. I'll dance on his grave like everyone else." Clay had lost interest in the subject. It was not in his character to waste time on theory or in analyzing what had ceased to be relevant. "I'm writing a book," he said just as Peter sat down on what looked to be a bench but was actually a Chinese lacquered tea table; it crashed beneath his weight.

Clay laughed. Aeneas smiled worriedly. Peter remained where he was on the floor, the fragments of the table all about him. With dignity, he crossed his legs and asked what the subject of the book was.

"The American idea, what else? But with a small 'i.' Why don't you throw the pieces in the fire? Nobody will miss it." Clay was amused by the accident, which Peter chose to ignore.

"And what is *your* idea of the American idea?" From his position on the floor, Peter was judicious.

"I hope the book will make it plain."

"But make *what* plain?"

"What I believe to be the way we are and the way we ought to be."

"What are we?"

"For one thing, the best alternative to Communism." Clay was brisk.

"Well, Aeneas can set you straight on that one. And what *ought* we to be?"

"Good," said Clay.

"Oh, *that!*" Peter snorted. "That's easy, isn't it? At least to say."

"Not easy at all," said Aeneas worriedly. "Actually, it's the hardest thing there is to define. Even Wittgenstein . . ."

"Hard for us, yes, but for Clay to be good means to contain Communism, balance the budget . . ."

"I think he's more ambitious than that."

At last aware of what was happening, Peter did not try to disguise his astonishment. "Aeneas! You're going to write the book for him!"

"I said I'd help. You know, an idea here, an idea there." Aeneas was uneasy but not apologetic.

"But *which* of your ideas? The necessity of abandoning the two-party system, the similarity between the orgasm and the Bomb, the fact that television advertising is the principal cause of cancer?" Peter found Aeneas's defection not only astonishing but curiously exhilarating. He turned to Clay. "Aeneas is filled with ideas. You must pick and choose carefully."

"I plan to." Clay was very much at ease. "I don't expect to be too far out . . ."

"Naturally." Peter looked at the nervous Aeneas and asked, quite gently, "But why, Aeneas, do you want to be so far in?"

"That's not the way I look at it. After all, I'm just helping out." But Peter could see that Aeneas was suffering; his inner dialogue furious, to say the least.

"He's first-rate, too," said Clay. "And philosophically we're not as far apart as you might think."

"A philosopher king!" Peter got slowly to his feet. "Well, you are stunning. Both of you."

"Thank you." Clay rose, too. He smiled. He was most winning. "Don't look so worried, Peter. It will all come right in the end."

"For you, or for the country?"

"Oh, it's the same thing. Didn't I ever tell you that?" But though Clay's manner was teasing, Peter knew that he meant exactly what he said.

"No, it is not the same thing." Peter held his ground like some unwieldy obstacle fallen by accident in the other's path.

"Well, who's to say?" Clay tried to step around Peter, who deliberately blocked the approach to the door, not yet willing for his quarry to escape.

"I am to say, among others."

"Then say it! Explain to the world just what is so

wrong with me. What is, by the way?" Clay continued to smile attractively.

"I wrote it once," said Peter. "I said it all, I thought."

"But no one believed you."

"But that makes it no less true. To be blunt, you are not what you seem. Of course most people aren't either, but between what you are and what you appear to be there is a million dollars' worth of publicity, trying to make us believe that you are a war hero, which you're not, a serious and thoughtful Senator, which you're not, a man inspired by the best motives, which . . ."

"How can you possibly begin to know what and who I am?" The voice was hard while the face was now as gray as the one which a moment before had looked out at them from the television screen.

"I know what you've done and what you've not done. Politically you play chess. If the polls indicate a move to the left you move to the left. A computer could anticipate your position on any subject." Peter turned to Aeneas. "You were right about him all along. He practices politics in a vacuum. There is nothing to him but a desire to be first."

Clay stepped away from Peter and moved toward Aeneas, as though seeking an ally. But then suddenly he stopped, aware that he might seem to be retreating. He turned to Peter and said, "You envy me because your father is interested in my career and not in yours . . ."

The unexpectedness of the attack made Peter laugh. "No! Try again. Never having had a father, you exaggerate their importance to those of us so equipped. I am not jealous of you for anything except perhaps your extraordinary luck; it's awe-inspiring, but then it has nothing to do with you . . ."

"You are jealous of me." Clay was dogged. "Because of Enid."

Peter wondered if he had perhaps underestimated Clay. He knew that the enemy was bold but he thought him constitutionally incapable of truth. "I'm not sure," he said, "that jealous is the word. But I will say that I can never forgive you or Father for murdering her."

With a clinical eye, Peter noticed that Clay's face had become blank, as if cast in metal.

When Clay spoke, his voice was without expression. "I did what I thought was best for her. She was an alcoholic and they told me that she was incurable. Perhaps we were wrong to put her away. I don't know. But I did care for her, though perhaps not as much as you did."

Peter braced himself for the blow which he knew was about to fall.

Clay was now prepared to go the full distance and bring down the house. "She told me what happened. She told me everything. That's why she was always frightened of you. Because of what the two of you did that day in this house, in the basement, in the storage room, together."

In the room's stillness, a clock struck the half hour. Clay picked up the remains of the lacquer table and put them on the desk. "I'll tell Irene someone broke the table. I suppose she can have it fixed." He crossed to the door. He paused. "Enid had no secrets. She was also a liar so perhaps . . ." But Clay did not finish. Instead, he left the room.

"Well," said Peter to Aeneas after a long silence, "the hero has found his author."

"It's not that at all." Aeneas was even more shaken than Peter by what he had heard. Between the middle class to which he belonged and the class whose existence he often denied, there was plainly a division more significant than any he had suspected: the guilty dreams of the one were suddenly revealed to be the essential acts of the other.

"Good luck," said Peter, starting to go, but Aeneas took his arm, as though for support.

"Really it's not what you think, my helping him."

"I haven't told you what I think." Peter was bland. "But tell me, why are you helping him?"

"For one thing, I think he will be President." Aeneas was uncharacteristically straightforward.

"That is certainly possible, which is why we must see . . . *I* must see that he fails."

"You don't think people change or grow?" Aeneas echoed the latest publicity. According to magazine writers, Clay had in recent years both "grown" and "deepened," until now it was admitted by all but the hopelessly partisan that he possessed a "new maturity."

"Of course people change: they change their tactics. Clay's got the conservatives. Now he needs you. It's perfectly simple."

"Assuming you're right, then just to be practical, isn't it a good idea to join forces with him, to try to influence him?"

The case Aeneas was constructing was altogether too predictable and Peter cut him short. "Don't be naïve." He left his old teacher behind. "He will use you. You will never use him."

"You're unfair." Aeneas was dogged. "I think there is more to him than that."

"Well, write his book for him and then we'll see." Peter went to the door, not even bothering to inquire when and how and at whose initiative this remarkable alliance had been wrought.

But Aeneas would not let him go. He wanted comfort. "If Clay were able to accomplish all the things that you think ought to be done, would you still oppose him?"

"But he won't. He'll go on just the way he always has, making the obvious moves. But even if he were suddenly to be miraculously useful, I would still oppose him."

"Why? Because of . . . because of . . ." But ten years of Freudian analysis had prepared Aeneas only for symbolic behavior.

"You know the reasons. After all, you taught me half of them. Nothing concerns Clay but himself, and that self is not good enough, particularly if things should go badly for us."

"Is there anyone else who's any better? Aren't they all the same?"

Aeneas's sudden gloom made Peter laugh. "You sound like I used to. I'm the one who was brought up to believe that all of this was just a game and no matter who takes the prize, life goes on—while *you* possessed the moral sense, saw purpose in history, wanted radical change . . ."

"But I still do. I haven't changed. I only . . ."

"You have changed if you think that Clay is what you want."

"I think he is educable." Aeneas was obstinate. "The fact that he's come to me is proof . . ."

"Proof that he's not a fool." It was now plain to Peter that despite Aeneas's obvious unease the process of rationalization, already begun, would presently resolve itself in Clay's favor. Power was irresistible even to this once incorruptible clerk. As last testament to an old friendship, Peter made a confession. "You know, in a dreadful way, I'm much closer in character to Clay than I am to you. I was brought up to respect deeds, not theories; victories, not virtues. I see politics as men inprovising. You see it as a series of stately position papers, reflecting some vast historic process. In the long run, you may be right. But the prizes in the moment go to the busy empty men like Clay, and though I may be unfair to the breed I do have his range, something you will never get."

"But he's not so empty. And he's certainly far more liberal than you give him credit for, and with the help of people like us . . ."

"Oh, Christ, Aeneas, you are a fool!" Peter had not meant to roar but he was very much his father's son, filled with that magnate's passion to impose his will upon others. But where his father had chosen a conventional path to familiar heights, Peter had tried to go down to the roots, hoping to find the source of his own discontent with a world altogether too eager to take him in and give him whatever he might in the usual way want. Yet he knew that what he really wanted was simply to know what was good, and since he could accept no absolutes he could do little more than resist what appeared to him to be altogether bad, aware that the moment he ceased to say 'no,' he would sink like Aeneas to Clay's level, which was: does it work or not, does one rise or fall? Now, dazzled by the prospect of actual power, Aeneas had been absorbed by Clay, to Peter's sorrow if not surprise, for to be human is to be predictable. There was nothing left to do but apologize. "I'm sorry," he said. "I didn't mean to shout at you."

362

"I understand." Aeneas was trembling. "You're under stress of course, after what was said . . ."

"I'm always under stress." Peter smiled. "Well, good luck."

"I'll be moving to Washington." Aeneas looked singularly wretched at his own fine prospects. "He wants me here, full time."

"Then we shall see more of you," said Peter, their friendship at an end. He opened the door to the hall. "Anyway you'll enjoy the *real* thing," he said, "no matter how it ends."

2

Clay had not meant to say everything, but for a moment he had lost control. Goaded by Peter he had used his ultimate weapon, a rash thing to do for which, he knew, he would doubtless have to pay. But any defeat of Peter was irresistible, he told himself, in extenuation, as he entered the drawing room, becoming immediately the center of attention. During the last few months Clay's publicity had become so intense that where people had once regarded him with interest because he was a young man on the rise he was now regarded with wonder as *the* young man on the rise. There was no one like him in the country, a fact which he had come to take for granted. It was all working out just as Blaise had predicted it would.

Across the room, beneath a modern tapestry, stood a girl he had not seen before. She was tall, slender, with blond bright hair and freckles. Exactly what he needed at the moment, but he despaired at ever getting to her for between them was a room filled with people eager to talk to him, to see and to touch him; the space between him and the girl was like some desperate obstacle course in which buried land mines and twisted clumps of barbed wire had been ingeniously set. Nevertheless, he would attempt the dangerous passage for the girl was definitely worth it. Not once had she looked in his direction.

"Blaise says you were superb on television!" Clay knew that Irene's enthusiasms were impartial. She was equally enamored of Senator Taft, Governor Stevenson, General MacArthur, and of course the President, whom she had recently cornered at a reception and insisted that he speak French to her since had he not, single-handed, liberated that *doux vert pays,* France? But now that Irene was Mrs. Watress her enthusiasm for anyone celebrated was somewhat breached by the fact of her new relations, and as she had already made a significant contribution to Clay's central fund, she tended to save her best hyperbole for the husband of her niece, the First Lady-to-be.

Clay said that he thought he had not done too badly on television.

"But of course you did well. You always do well because you are a *complete* person. That's really the secret, you know, to everything!" Irene looked about the room she had created and at the people she had summoned to fill it. "One must be bold. But then one must be *dans le vrai* at the same time."

Millicent Smith Carhart joined them, with Lucy Shattuck in tow. Of all the old Washington ladies, Millicent was the one who most bored Clay but because of Elizabeth he went out of his way to charm her, not an easy task since he knew that she thought him responsible for Burden's suicide.

"They say that you are going to vote to condemn that awful man!" Mrs. Carhart clung to Lucy for support.

"That's my intention." Clay gave her the most winning of all his smiles but her pebbly eyes, clouded with cataracts, did not see it.

"I'm so glad! He went altogether too far, and we mustn't allow that." Millicent looked somber. "Things," she said darkly, "are fragile enough as it is nowadays."

"Really," said Lucy Shattuck, "you make us sound like one of your Meissen teapots, full of cracks."

"If only we were so distinguished," said Millicent. "You know the last time I spoke to dear Burden Day, he wanted to censure Senator McCarthy and it was *I* who said no. I've never been so wrong."

"It might have been premature then," said Clay, watching the girl who was talking now to a young man he did not recognize. He must somehow get to her before she was forever lost to the stranger. But though Millicent persisted in her talk of Burden Day, Clay refused to be distressed. What was past was past; he never looked back. At the time, however, not only had he been upset by Burden's death but furious at Harold for having caused it. After all, Harold had known of his arrangement with Burden and simple loyalty—not to mention good sense—ought to have kept him silent. But Harold was vicious, as Blaise pointed out, and one must accept him the way he was or not at all. In any case, Burden's death had come as a shock to Clay who had truly loved the man in whose company he had spent most of his youth. Even at the end, Clay had continued to like and admire the Senator, and he was confident that the old man felt the same way toward him; after all, Burden Day had survived a good many political wars and he knew that when the time comes for one to go, when the last battle is lost, there is nothing to be done but give way as gracefully as possible. Had he not proven, by taking Nillson's money, that he was eminently practical, and understood the world he was living in?

Clay tried to extricate himself from the ladies. He said that he must have a word with Harold Griffiths. But Millicent would not let him go. "Tell us first about the President. What does *he* feel about McCarthy?"

"The President is a Republican," said Clay. "He doesn't confide in me. In fact, I hardly know the man."

"But that's impossible!" Millicent sounded shocked. "Anyway the President must be delighted at what's happening. He's so much like my uncle, a friendly *good* man!"

"I'm sure he is," said Clay, who was quite sure that Eisenhower was neither friendly nor good. At their last meeting, the President had addressed him as "Overbury," as if he were a junior staff officer and not a member of the august Senate whose constitutional weight was every bit equal to that of the First Magistrate.

Clay finally escaped the ladies and made his way to

Harold at the room's center; en route he exchanged pleasantries with half a dozen strangers who, knowing him from television, assumed that he knew them. Just as he got to Harold, the girl and her young man, arm in arm, went into the cardroom.

"Who is she?" asked Clay in a low voice, indicating the door through which the girl had just passed. "The tall one, freckles."

"A cousin of Ogden Watress . . . of your wife," added Harold mischievously. "She's here for the weekend. Engaged to someone in New York. Whether or not she will, as your Hollywood friends say, put out, I don't know."

"Thanks for the résumé." Clay was dry. The fact that the girl was related to Elizabeth might make things complicated—for the girl, rather than for himself since he regarded sex as an appetite, nothing more. But that, he knew, was not entirely true. As he grew older, he found that he needed more and more women; and not simply for pleasure. What delighted him was the victory not only over the woman who had consented but, indirectly, over all the other men who had ever wanted her. He was already excited at the thought of the girl's engagement to "someone in New York"; through her, he would be able to conquer that mysterious "someone in New York," not to mention the young man who had just escorted her into the cardroom.

Clay wanted simply to overwhelm. And though there was always danger of scandal, he had no intention of changing, despite Blaise's veiled warnings. Veiled because Enid's accusation had made each man profoundly wary with the other. Neither confided in the other, outside politics. Yet Clay was reasonably certain that Blaise's interest in him was not sexual. Rather, it was a living out of old ambitions. As Clay achieved power over men through the conquest of their women, so Blaise achieved a sense of power in the world through the manipulating of Clay's career.

Not unnaturally, Blaise was apprehensive. Recently he had indicated that perhaps Clay should not be quite so—as he put it euphemistically—"social." But Clay was fatalistic. What would happen would happen; it was much too late, in any case, to change his nature, as Elizabeth had discovered.

From the beginning Clay had made it a condition of their marriage that he would continue as he was and she had agreed, pretending to herself and to him that since her position as his wife could never be endangered, there was no rational reason for objecting to his brief pleasures. But of course she did object, though never directly. He was sorry to give her pain, but he was not about to be other than what he was. Besides, she had never not known just who and what she was marrying and though he liked her and took pride in her worldly success, she did not interest him as Enid had. In fact, unconsciously dramatizing the difference between the two, he had made it plain to Elizabeth (without ever directly saying so) that if she wanted discreetly to take a lover she could, and he rather suspected that she had for lately she had been unusually relaxed and easy with him, even in private; proving that their marital happiness would eventually depend upon the offices of others.

"How did your meeting with Aeneas Duncan go?" asked Harold.

"He's with us." The young man who had accompanied the Watress cousin into the cardroom returned alone, a hopeful sign.

"Incredible!" Harold sounded truly amazed, and Clay wondered if he might not be jealous of Aeneas as a potential rival. "If you can con Aeneas Duncan, you can do anything!"

"Con? I don't know what the word means." Clay was delighted that the girl was alone.

"Peter will be furious."

Clay frowned; pleasure in the girl ceased. "He came into the library when I was with Aeneas. He knows everything, except that it was Aeneas who came to us."

"Well, he is being isolated bit by bit." Grimly Harold predicted the end of *The American Idea,* but as he spoke, all that Clay could think of was Peter and Enid together, making love. He had not believed Enid when, drunk one night, she babbled the whole story. It was the sort of extravagant lie that appealed to her, like

367

accusing him and Blaise of being lovers. He had quite forgotten the story until, confronted with Peter's hostility, he had recalled it and, on impulse, struck, discovering as he did from the expression on Peter's face, that for once Enid had—terribly—told the truth. But he refused to ponder the implications; refused to acknowledge what was, in effect, a victory for Peter, a victory too painful to contemplate, for to have been second with Enid was to have been nothing. He dismissed the past, plunged into the moment.

Harold spoke of a meeting he had had with Adlai Stevenson who was, apparently, receptive to the idea of Clay as a running mate; the Governor, however, had made no promises since, as he pointed out, there was no assurance that he himself would be nominated for a second time. Both men reflected on their party's titular leader. Harold found Stevenson's style appealing but Clay did not. It was too impassioned. Clay particularly disliked the constant moralizing which sounded as if the politician might really mean what he was saying, and that was impossible. But, hypocrite or not, there was no denying Stevenson's appeal to the young. They flocked to him. While Eisenhower's banality reassured the middle-aged majority, Stevenson's rhetoric thrilled those who, rightfully, ought to be Clay's admirers. But time was on Clay's side. He could afford to wait in all things—except for the girl in the cardroom.

Clay left Harold and crossed quickly to the door to the cardroom, where he stopped, astonished: the room was so filled with painting and sculpture that it resembled an art gallery in which guests moved self-consciously from exhibit to exhibit, as though not certain whether or not the objects were on sale.

In front of a squat stone figure with pendulous ear lobes, she stood, quite alone, apparently absorbed by the sculpture. After first making sure that no one was watching either of them, Clay walked up to the girl (was there a man alive who did not want her?) and said, "Hello!"

3

Blaise stood alone at the end of the hall, looking out a frosted window at what had been his realm.

"I suppose she'll build a Chinese pagoda or perhaps a Japanese teahouse," said Peter as he joined his father at the window. For a moment they were in harmony. Blaise denounced Irene's works until he reminded himself that, "when something's sold, forget about it."

"Very sensible." Peter drew a cross on the icy window pane. "I just talked to Aeneas."

"Yes, he's agreed to help out. *I* thought it was a good idea." Blaise was blunt.

"It certainly is, for you and Clay." Peter was serene. "Sad for me, of course."

"Yes." Blaise put an end to that. "Irene's a bit on the spot, too."

"Because she's involved with both Clay and me?" Blaise nodded.

"You aren't by any chance going to suggest that she get off the spot?" Peter was curious to see just how far his father would go in Clay's behalf.

"No. I never advise, unless asked. She hasn't asked."

"But if she does?"

"Clay must be President." Blaise was surprisingly and for him, uniquely, still.

"He has taken you over entirely, hasn't he?" Peter matched his father's calm. "Enid was right."

With one hand, Blaise swept the cross from the window pane, as though erasing his son's last words. "Enid . . ." he began.

"I don't know *how* right she was and I don't want to know. But you have gone too far with Clay."

With a certain pleasure, Peter saw the familiar rage begin but before Blaise could speak, Peter cut him short. "All I've said is what everybody thinks only they are too afraid to speak out."

"Then I suggest you learn fear, too." The color had risen in his father's face.

"Too late for that." Peter was cold.

"You are so . . . *vain!*" Blaise gave the word the full force of his voice, causing newcomers in the hall to whisper among themselves.

"There is always a price to be paid for survival." Peter was delighted at his father's emotion. "Anyway, vanity is natural to us both."

But Blaise was still capable of surprise. He continued his own thought. "Because you think you understand everything, you took Enid's side, without ever knowing what *she* had done." Peter was startled. Used to having his simple statements of liking and disliking accepted as law, Blaise did not have the habit of explanation.

"What had she done that I should take into account?" Peter regarded his father curiously.

"That she was the one who broke up the marriage. She had the affair, not Clay. He caught her, not the other way around and then, for her sake, for the family's sake, he took the blame."

"I don't believe it!" Peter was surprised not at what Enid had done for she had been capable of anything as he knew best but at Clay's taking upon himself the blame. It was out of character unless he had altogether misjudged the enemy, which was unthinkable. Even so, he experienced a moment of panic.

"Ask your mother. Enid told her everything, just before she . . . before the end. So you see, none of it was Clay's fault."

Peter caught a glimpse of what he took to be the truth. "Perhaps not. Perhaps he did protect her . . . not a stupid thing to do since that was the best way of winning you, the sort of gesture you would approve of; and did. But even if that is what happened, he is still the man who had her put away and because of that she is dead."

"I put her away. The responsibility is mine." Blaise gave full weight to the proud pronoun.

Peter respected his father's inability to misrepresent himself and so, for telling the truth, he gave Blaise

370

precisely what he deserved. "Then Enid was right. You do love Clay. And you are mad." Before Blaise could respond Peter flung open the door to the terrace. A cold wind chilled them both. "Not that there's anything to be ashamed of. Quite the contrary. You're to be envied. I don't love anyone except Diana, and that's not really in your grand style at all. I just wish it had not been Clay. He is not worthy. But then it's no business of mine. Anyway," he smiled, recalling something Aeneas had once said, "it is the quality of the passion that matters, not the object." Peter stepped outside, and shut the door after him.

Peter stood on the terrace and took deep breaths, as though wanting to clear his lungs of all the air he had ever breathed in Laurel House. Then light-headed from too much oxygen and not feeling the cold at all, he crossed the lawn. Beneath his heavy tread, frozen grass made a crackling sound as he proceeded past the marble Venus and the plaster Pan, last relics of Frederika's time.

To his surprise, Peter found himself thinking of Billy Thorne whom he had met by accident a few weeks before at the house of a conservative banker whom Peter saw from time to time, partly because he had always known him but mostly because he could, in a matter of minutes, determine by his host's conversation the spiritual weather not only of the conservative establishment but of their President, a confused and confusing figure who had, by agreeing to a truce with the North Koreans (while seeming to prosecute with vigor the holy war against Communism) delighted Peter both in the deed, which he thought admirable, and in the word which he found perfectly American in its unconscious hypocrisy. He was not surprised to find Billy in the banker's house for though Billy was not yet a convert to Catholicism (the usual last harbor for disillusioned absolutists of the Left), he did talk a good deal on television about the Communist conspiracy. Yet for all his activity, Billy seemed oddly subdued when Peter greeted him. They spoke of McCarthy and Billy said that crude as the man was, he had done good work in bringing to light the extent of the Communist conspiracy. To which Peter responded by saying that, personally, he had been shocked at how small and poorly organized the Communist conspiracy was, assuming that Mc-Carthy had revealed any of it. Then he asked Billy what it was that had convinced him finally that Marx was wrong and Eisenhower right. Wanting to appear consistent, Billy twisted and turned his arguments in such a way that Marx and Eisenhower became briefly the Castor and Pollux of a new order. But then he was candid. "I realized that you cannot change anybody except at the point of a gun and I didn't want to hold that gun." But Peter's suggestion that perhaps change might be accomplished less dramatically, was not acceptable to Billy's extremist nature. When one god failed it was necessary to choose another, and Peter, godless, thought it tactless and cruel to censure a temperament so unlike his own.

Now he stood at the edge of the pool in which a log of wood had been placed to keep expanding ice from cracking the cement. For an instant the sun shone, and the pale rays warmed him; then clouds hid sun and sky; soon snow would fall. He crossed to the poolhouse and tried the door to the men's changing room but it was locked. At the far end of the terrace, he paused and looked down at the half-frozen river and thought of James Burden Day.

It had been a desperate time for them all, particularly when Diana had tried to persuade Ed Nillson to bring suit against Harold Griffiths and Nillson had told her bluntly that the story of the land sale was true. Diana had not mentioned her father again to Peter except once when they were trying to determine exactly how much money Blaise had spent on Clay's election to the Senate. The figure they arrived at was close to two million dollars. Deploring not only his father's extravagance but the system that made it necessary, Peter denounced both until Diana said, "They all do it. So why shouldn't Clay and your father?"

"For one thing it is—not that I suppose anybody cares—illegal."

"What on earth does *that* mean?" She was contemptuous. "Law does not apply to them. And no one is in the least distressed except you and me, and poor Father who felt that he had to play the game their way and, when he did, was promptly caught. That's what killed him."

"Being caught?"

"No, trying to be like them. He really believed that there were some things one ought not to do while Clay realizes that the only thing one ought never to do is lose the game. That's why he'll win. He's exactly what the times require."

To which Peter had responded, inevitably, "Then we must see to it his winning is not easy."

She had agreed to that. The longer they knew one another, the closer they became, and Peter was now certain that the moment was almost at hand when he could make the gesture that at last she required and he had always wanted but was not about to make until he was certain that her distaste for Clay was not simply one of the usual masks for love. Now he was as certain of her as he could be of anything and though he had begun by caring more for her than she had cared for him, by withholding a part of himself, not to mention the fact of marriage, her feelings had shifted into balance with his own. Finally, not only was she what he wanted, she was what he needed for she alone understood the sudden storms of revulsion against his own kind which periodically caused him to despair, and though she shared with him his disgust, she never even briefly ceased to think it worth the effort to continue to say and do what ought to be said and done. Loving her for this constancy, he was often able in her company to forget for long moments what he knew to be the human case: that the generations of man come and go and are in eternity no more than bacteria upon a luminous slide, and the fall of a republic or the rise of an empire—so significant to those involved—are not detectable upon the slide even were there an interested eye to behold that steadily proliferating species which would either end in time

373

or, with luck, become something else, since change is the nature of life, and its hope.

8 May 1962, Barrytown, New York—15 September 1966, Rome

Afterword

Between 1965 and 1975 I wrote, out of sequence, an American Trilogy. Although *Washington, D.C.* was the first to be published, it is actually the last volume in my narrative of life in the United States, as experienced by one family, from the Revolution (*Burr*) to the gilded age (*1876*) to the high noon of the American Empire, *Washington, D.C.*

These books?
Fiction.
Keep telling
yourself that
as you read.

Here are the facts.

The conclusions are up to you.